Discover more at millsandboon.co.uk

SECOND CHANCE VOWS

JULES BENNETT

BLACK SHEEP BARGAIN

NAIMA SIMONE

MIX
Paper from
responsible sources

FSC
FSC® C007454

This book is produced from independently certified FSC™
paper to ensure responsible forest management.

For more information visit www.harpercollins.co.uk/green

Printed and Bound in Spain using 100% Renewable electricity at
CPI Black Print

MILLS & BOON

First Published in Great Britain 2022
by Mills & Boon, an imprint of HarperCollins*Publishers* Ltd
1 London Bridge Street, London, SE1 9GF

www.harpercollins.co.uk

HarperCollins*Publishers*
1st Floor, Watermarque Building,
Ringsend Road, Dublin 4, Ireland

Second Chance Vows © 2022 Jules Bennett
Black Sheep Bargain © 2022 Naima Simone

ISBN: 978-0-263-30386-5

0822

SECOND CHANCE VOWS

JULES BENNETT

To all my loyal readers—thank you for making my dreams come true.

One

This corset was much too tight, but seeing as how she was already at the party, there was no going back.

Unfortunately, the ill-fitting costume was the least of Delilah Preston's worries tonight. Why had she agreed to meet a guy blindly? Her divorce wasn't final, but Alisha Martin had been so persuasive and wouldn't take no for an answer.

Which is how Delilah found herself dressed all in black from her eye mask, to her corset and leather pants, and stilettos. She'd even donned black nail polish for the event. She hadn't wanted to invest in a new costume she'd likely never wear again, so going as a shadow seemed fun—or at least the most fun she was ready to have at this stage in her life. Maybe she could simply sneak out when she was ready to leave. She hadn't exactly been in a partying mood over the past several months.

Having a marriage crumble into a pile of unrecognizable pieces would do that.

But, this was her first outing in a month and she had to do something about her lack of social life or she'd drive herself insane. Staying home binge-watching one series after another only grew more depressing by the day.

Alisha Martin was a new client to Angel's Share, the bourbon distillery Delilah owned with her sisters. Elise, Sara and Dee had started their distillery journey over a decade ago when they'd purchased the old castle in the heart of bourbon country. The impressive stone structure had been a teen hangout back in the day, but when the sisters decided to get serious about opening a distillery, they knew they needed something unique to set them apart in this man's world. What better place than an abandoned castle?

And the name had been easy for them. When bourbon went into a barrel to age, some of the liquid evaporated and the old saying was that the portion missing was sent to the angels.

Delilah loved everything about this world they'd created. Not to mention they'd met so many amazing people through the years. They'd secured a solid client base and they'd also made some great friendships through their connections.

Alisha had been to the distillery several times over the past month to get a variety of bourbons and gin supplied for her charity event, Home Sweeter Home. She was such a giving, caring person that when Alisha insisted Delilah show up for this costume party for the children's orphanage, Dee couldn't say no.

Then Alisha had texted last minute to say there was a really nice guy Delilah should meet who would also be at the party. In that instant, Dee wasn't so afraid of saying no, but her reply had gone unanswered.

Okay. All she had to do was go in, see Alisha, make her donation and slink out. The all-black shadow costume would be perfect for this stealth mission. She really should have sent Sara or Elise in her place, but her sisters were busy leading their own lives. Good for them. At least two-thirds of her tight circle had something to look forward to.

Delilah pulled in a deep breath and headed up the concrete steps that led to the double glass doors of The Grandeur, a historic mansion turned event space. The greeters opened the doors to let her in and she offered them each a smile.

As soon as she stepped inside, the music, laughter and chatter hit her all at once. This wasn't something she was cut out for. She liked things nice and quiet in her office where she could focus on the business and her new clients. She enjoyed a relaxed atmosphere and serenity. She thrived on peace, which was ironic considering her life lately was anything but peaceful.

What she did not enjoy was the boning on this corset. The damn thing had fit last year. Must have shrunk in her drawer.

Resisting the urge to adjust her costume, Delilah made her way into the ballroom and glanced around at the sea of people. She should have asked what Alisha was going to be dressed as. It could take a while to find her considering nearly everyone wore a mask.

Having a good portion of her face covered was a good thing, though, because there wasn't a doubt in her mind that her pretentious in-laws would be here.

Correction—soon-to-be former in-laws. If there was a way for them to shove their name and money in front of people, they were first through the door...which was why they certainly did not like it when their only child married a girl who had been adopted and came from humble beginnings.

Delilah tucked her black clutch beneath her arm and wove her way through the crowds of people milling about. She assumed if she headed toward the stage at the front of the ballroom, maybe Alisha would be there and Dee could slip her the donation quick and easy. Then she could escape as stealthily as she'd come in and there would be no run-ins with Camden's parents, no introduction to this mystery man that Alisha had set up for her.

"Delilah?"

She spun around at the familiar voice and forced a smile. "Alisha."

Her client and new friend was stunning in her white-and-gold goddess costume. With her flowing blond hair and striking green eyes, she looked absolutely flawless, like an actress from a movie set.

"I thought that was you," Alisha stated as she moved closer. "I don't know what your costume is, but I'm jealous of how gorgeous and fit you are."

Delilah laughed. "I'm a shadow and believe me, this costume is holding in all the rolls. I'm not actually this curvy."

More like frumpy. Some people lost weight during a breakup, but Delilah seemed to be finding the pounds. She couldn't help that angel food cake with extra whip had been bringing her comfort over the past several months.

"Well, regardless, I'm so glad you could come," Alisha went on. "I just spoke with the guy I was telling you about. He arrived right before you did, so this is perfect timing."

Delilah cringed. "I appreciate you wanting to play Cupid, but I'm not really in a position to meet anyone new. I'm actually not even divorced yet."

Alisha placed a hand on Dee's shoulder. "That's ironic you say that because he just told me the same thing. Listen, he's super nice, so maybe he'd be a good friend to have since you're both going through the same ordeal. Sometimes talking to a stranger is therapeutic."

Maybe so. The only people who really knew her situation were her sisters. Delilah didn't like failure, never wanted to believe that her marriage was over, but she and Camden weren't on the same page anymore and attraction and chemistry would only carry them so far.

Alisha smoothed her hair away from her face and Delilah caught a glimpse of an impressive rock on her very important finger.

"Is that new?" Delilah asked, reached for her hand. "It's gorgeous."

Alisha beamed. "It is. I just got back from a little impromptu vacation that took quite a different turn than I was expecting."

"Sounds intriguing." Delilah released her hand and smiled. "I look forward to hearing about it when you're free."

"It's quite a story." Alisha smiled. "We'll do lunch soon and I'll tell you all about it."

Love literally seemed to be surrounding Delilah. No matter where she went. She was truly happy for all of these people in her life. She just wished her own marriage hadn't turned into such a heartbreaking mess.

"Oh, here he comes now." Alisha's eyes landed over Delilah's shoulder as she smiled and waved at someone. "He's the one dressed as a pirate with the eye patch."

Delilah glanced around and spotted the stranger Alisha described. The sexy man with tight black pants and a billowy white shirt, dark scruff along his square jawline, one deep brown eye staring back at her was no stranger at all.

This was her husband.

Camden was coming to tell Alisha that he was going to skip out and to thank her for the invite. He definitely wasn't up for meeting anyone new although he'd thought he was ready to socialize, but the instant he'd gotten here, that proved to be wrong. His parents were thankfully out of town so at least he hadn't had to deal with that face-to-face encounter. Dodging their phone calls was more than enough of a workout without adding a social event to the mix.

He shifted his focus to the event host across the room and made his way toward her. Alisha stood next to a woman dressed in all black with a black mask over her eyes. Oh, hell…

She might be trying to disguise herself so nobody would know who she was, but he knew. Camden knew every dip and curve of that body as he'd lain beside it for the past five years.

"Delilah, this is Camden, the guy I was telling you about."

Cam waited for Alisha to finish the introduction before he reached out his hand. "It's a pleasure."

Dee's mouth opened wide and he couldn't help but smile as she placed her hand in his. That spark of chemistry and awareness never got old, never fizzled out. Their attraction had always been high and hot. If sex alone could keep a marriage together, they wouldn't be in the situation they were now.

But their jobs, his family and lack of communication

were leading them down a path he never thought he'd be taking.

Camden wanted his wife back. He'd made no secret about that, but Delilah claimed she had put up with enough and she didn't see them moving forward in a direction she needed to go. They couldn't get their futures on the same page and for that reason alone, she'd asked him to file the divorce papers, which he did reluctantly.

The irony that he did this for a living didn't escape him. He was a divorce attorney who never thought his firm would be working on his own case.

"Oh, excuse me," Alisha added. "The caterer is motioning for me."

As soon as she stepped away, Delilah separated their bond and clasped her hands together. He didn't know if she was trying to rub away his touch or secretly hold on to it. Either way, he had an effect on her and she sure as hell had a hold over him. All of this damn baggage that they'd carried for years had finally broken both of them. Failure had never been an option for him and he certainly didn't like that feeling now.

Being a divorce lawyer and having his own marriage fail seemed like such a slap in the face. This was not the life he'd envisioned or worked so hard to achieve.

"What are you doing here?" she whispered as she leaned in closer.

"Alisha is the sister of the newest guy at our firm," he told her. "How do you know her?"

Delilah pointed at a server walking around with a tray of tumblers and cocktails. "She's using Angel's Share spirits tonight."

"Where are Sara and Elise?" he asked.

"My sisters were both busy tonight so I had to make an appearance."

And he was sure that pissed her off. His Delilah was quiet and much preferred staying behind the scenes. She kept her head down and her drive high. The woman was passionate about every aspect of her life from her work to their marriage…and he hadn't appreciated her when he'd had her.

The music switched from upbeat to something more soothing and slow with a sultry beat…but of course. Just one more thing mocking him and this entire situation.

Camden took in her body-hugging outfit and the half mask that left her red lips exposed…and way too damn tempting. He'd always loved the contrast of her dark skin with red lipstick. She knew it, too. Any time they'd gone out, she'd always put on his favorite shade—the exact one she was wearing now.

That made him wonder how many other times she'd worn it since they separated and she moved out of their home.

Her moving out and leaving the house to him had been yet another bone of contention between them.

Camden reached for her and settled his hand right in the dip at her waist. She stilled beneath him and he cursed himself for ever allowing their relationship to get to the point his own wife questioned his touch.

"Dance with me."

Those dark eyes stared back at him. He wanted to rip her mask off and see her entire face, but part of him liked this allure. And maybe she liked it, too. She hadn't walked away and she hadn't said no, so that was at least a step up from their last encounter when he'd kissed her in a back room during another very public event. He hadn't seen her since the gala at Angel's Share celebrating the launch of their ten-year bourbon, so they hadn't talked about the private moment.

"Cam."

He took her clutch from beneath her arm and escorted her toward the dance floor, stopping long enough at his table to set her purse down. She didn't hesitate, but he knew her mind and she was running through all the reasons this was a bad decision. Well, he was going through all the reasons this was the best decision.

With an expert move, Camden spun her around and gave a slight tug until she fell against his chest. Her hands clamped around his shoulders, and her delicate touch nearly singed through his thin shirt.

"We shouldn't do this," she murmured, but made no motion to pull away.

Camden started swaying with her body moving perfectly against his. She wouldn't cause a scene, not here. She might want to run like she did at the Angel's Share gala last month, but that had been a little easier for her to escape from.

"Why is that?" he whispered as he leaned in closer. "Because you're afraid?"

"I'm not afraid of anything."

"No? Then why haven't you returned my texts since the kiss?"

Her eyes darted down and they both knew he'd just made a solid point. Which was pretty much his job, but he never once wanted to use his career skills on his own wife. He wanted them to be a team; he'd wanted her to be his forever.

But she'd started wanting more than he thought he could give. A high-profile career demanded most of his time and she fell further and further back in his life. Added to that, his parents had always been an invisible wedge between them. Whenever they could, they made a special point to leave veiled hints that Delilah's social background didn't match theirs. He shrugged it off, but Cam didn't realize Dee took it to heart.

For years all of those differences festered and grew, until one day Dee had simply had enough. If they were together too long, those differences between them would rise back up into an argument and the cycle would start all over again.

He wanted to break that series of unpleasant patterns they found themselves locked in. He had no idea how, but he had to make her see that they belonged together. He never lost anything in his life and he sure as hell wasn't about to start with his wife.

"That kiss was a mistake," she told him between gritted teeth.

"Didn't feel like a mistake." Camden slid his hand to the small of her back and held her closer. "It felt like you wanted more."

Her eyes snapped to his. "What I want and what I can have are two very different realities."

So she did want him. He knew that part of their relationship would never die no matter what. Now if he could figure out how to bridge her wants and her needs and stay true to his own needs, they'd be back on a level playing field.

Maybe that's all they needed—to get back to the basics. Maybe they should start over and lay a solid foundation first. Every moment of their lives together had been hectic and rushed, what with his schedule and traveling all over to his high-profile clientele as he started his own firm to her building up Angel's Share with her best friends who were also her adopted sisters. He was damn proud of her and all she'd accomplished. Maybe he hadn't shown her or taken the extra time to tell her.

How the hell could he turn this marriage from a loss to a win?

"There's nothing wrong with giving into your desires." He shifted back to the moment and the woman in his arms...exactly where she should be. "We're both adults who want each other."

"It's not right," she declared.

Camden spun her around, slowly maneuvering her closer to one of the tables his firm had sponsored. Having her admit out loud she wanted him seemed like a victory he should celebrate and hone in on. There could be no room for negativity, not if he wanted to move forward with her.

"What's wrong is ignoring each other because when we get too close, we want to tear our clothes off."

Delilah went still beneath him and he stopped, too. Her eyes continued to hold his gaze and he knew what she was thinking. They'd been married for five years and there was no way she could lie to him...or to herself.

Camden knew she had so many thoughts rolling through her mind. There wasn't a doubt that right now she was contemplating what it would be like to sleep with him again. Would it be worth the risk? Would they fall back into old habits and still have a broken marriage?

At this point, he just wanted tonight. He just wanted his wife back in his bed. He'd worry about the rest tomorrow. He'd been without her for too damn long and that kiss last month, coupled with the leather pants, tight corset that did amazing things to her breasts, and her soft red lips, had pushed him way too far.

That was the crux of the problem. There was never *enough* Delilah and that's what scared him the most. Even after the years they'd spent together, there was always more of a need that he simply could not control.

"You're still the sexiest woman I've ever known," he added. "One night. We don't have to think about or even discuss the divorce or anything else."

She closed her eyes and pulled in a deep breath. "That's how we got into this mess, Cam. When we only give in to our desires and don't care about the consequences or the reality surrounding us and working against us."

"What consequences? And the reality is, we already filed for divorce. Neither of us has expectations. It's one night, Dee. Your place or mine. Wherever you want."

When her lids fluttered open, there was that familiar passion staring back at him.

He had her. They'd never been able to deny each other. Their physical intimacy was unlike anything he'd ever had before and he knew if he lost her for good, he'd never find this again.

Camden's body stirred and they were going to have to leave before he made a scene by giving his wife a proper kiss and figuring out how the hell this corset thing worked. He'd seen this piece in their closet a few times and always wondered when she'd wear it…he'd always hoped for a private showing.

"My place," she told him. "I can't go back…"

Home. The word hovered between them just the same as if she'd said it. When she decided they had to separate, he'd told her he would go, but she said she needed a new start without the memories.

That was another revealing sign that she still loved him. Staying in the house he'd purchased before they got married would only remind her of all the things they'd shared within those walls. Hell, he lived through it every single day, but he tried to keep busy and stay out of the home as much as possible for that very reason.

As much as Delilah wanted to erase him in her attempt

to move on, he wasn't about to let that happen. They'd started off so hot for each other, skipped a good bit of the get-to-know-you phase and headed down the aisle. Sure, they'd rushed things, but did that make their relationship wrong or a failure? He refused to believe any of that.

Had he filed the divorce papers? Yes. Did he have regrets? Hell, yes.

His parents had accused her of looking for easy money and help with her business venture, but they didn't know Delilah. She never took a dollar from him to help with the progress and growth of Angel's Share. She was too proud and too headstrong to take handouts and he admired her for that…even if her determination could be frustrating at times.

He'd played the middleman for years between his family and his wife. Delilah had apologized, thinking she'd been the catalyst that had driven them apart, but all she did was open his eyes to the controlling, shallow people who had raised him.

Now that they were split up, Camden was even more protective. Delilah was still in such a vulnerable position with their marriage crumbling and Milly passing away. The woman had raised Dee and her sisters and she'd been the only mother they'd known. Suffering such a devastating loss after separating from Cam hadn't put Delilah in a position to put too much into fighting for their marriage. She was emotionally drained and exhausted from the hurt and pain she lived with daily.

The divorce wasn't official, but the clock was ticking. The final papers would be in any day and then he'd have to face the reality that she could be lost forever… which also meant he'd be losing. He'd been lucky that the first time the papers had been filed, there had been some things that weren't right, so they'd had to refile. Thankfully he'd caught the mistake before signing.

But Camden hadn't been lying. He wasn't going to think of anything but tonight.

He gripped her hand, grabbed her clutch off the table and found the nearest exit.

Two

What did she think she was doing?

Avoiding her soon-to-be ex was the only way Delilah was ever going to get over him. So how did she find herself cozied up in the front seat of his SUV?

Letting him lead her from that overly crowded party had seemed like a good idea, but now red flags started waving around in her head and she really should start paying attention to them.

Being reckless is what got her caught up in a marriage built on a crumbling foundation.

"Don't start thinking," he commanded as he maneuvered through town. "I can practically hear your thoughts."

She had no doubt. Camden Preston knew her better than anyone, including her sisters or Milly.

Her *sisters*. That was a whole other area that weighed so heavy on her mind. Finding out her best friends—

adoptive sisters—were actually her biological sisters…
that life-altering news hit only a few weeks ago and everything was still so fresh.

She hadn't told anyone about what happened. Her first
thought had been to run to Camden for support, but those
days were over. Seeking a divorce meant severing all ties
and starting over.

Yet here she was in his car heading back to her place
because the memories of their house would be too much.
They'd created a life there. They'd loved, they'd laughed
and ultimately, they'd grown apart in the very place she'd
thought of as her haven. There were simply too many
emotions wrapped into each and every room.

She wanted Cam. Of course she did. Not a day went by
since she'd walked out that she hadn't craved his touch or
wished she could settle in beside him in their bed. Seeing
him at her gala last month had been like another slap to
the face, as if she needed the reminder of all she'd lost.

When Cam had asked to speak to her privately, they'd
slipped into the back room and he'd kissed her. No words,
no touching. He'd backed her against the wall and covered her mouth with his as his body, so perfectly aligned
with her own, pressed against her…and she'd thought of
little else since.

The man had always been potent. He'd always been
able to turn her on with just a look, but kissing her without touching her anywhere else had nearly had her begging right there in a back room, mere steps away from
two hundred guests at the black-tie affair she and her
sisters hosted.

"Relax."

Camden reached for her hand just like he had count-
less times before…but this night was different. This night
they weren't together, they were still on opposite sides

of that invisible line that had been drawn between them. They were each too stubborn and driven to cross over and compromise.

But some things, like careers and family, couldn't be compromised. No matter their feelings for each other, there were still very real issues at hand. Camden had mentioned children about a year ago and that was definitely something they should have discussed before marriage because he wanted them and she hadn't thought much about it. That was the least of their issues, though. His horrid parents and that damn schedule of his kept them torn apart without bringing children into the mix.

"Wanting each other doesn't have to mean more than just that."

Camden stroked the back of her hand with his thumb, pulling her from their differences and problems and back to the fact her body was heating up just like it always did with this man. His strength and warmth had always been major turn-ons and now, after being without him for seven months, she was barely holding on to her self-control.

Delilah couldn't even concentrate on what he was saying, not when every part of her was revved up. Her desire and need trumped all of those glaring warnings she should be paying attention to.

"Don't talk," she told him. "Just…drive."

If he kept talking, she'd keep thinking, and if she kept thinking, she'd talk herself out of going back to her new place with him…because the unspoken intentions were extremely clear. Sex was all that could be on the table tonight. Not their differences, not their divorce and not all of the very real emotions that still lived so deeply within them.

But Camden was right. They were both adults. They

were still married and just because they'd filed for divorce didn't mean they couldn't be intimate. At least now she knew there were no expectations. She was heading into this night with eyes wide open and knew full well everything this was...and wasn't.

They'd both be temporarily satisfied and right now, that's all she wanted. She'd been without Cam's touch for too long and if she could have a sliver of a distraction, she was going to take it. Maybe this was the closure they both needed.

When Delilah had left their shared home, she knew starting over would be difficult, but she hadn't thought about how she would handle the physical side of losing her husband. And that was just her marriage—the other part of her personal life was falling apart as well. The only thing that seemed to be going right for Delilah was her career.

Angel's Share was a success and its sales were skyrocketing. They were not only the only female-run distillery in the country, they were surpassing most others, and with their ten-year bourbon now on the market, sales were increasing faster than projected. People came from all over the country, and even outside the US, to see their castle-turned-distillery. They'd tapped into a gold mine and she couldn't be more proud of all she, Elise and Sara had created.

But that's everything she'd wanted, right? She'd wanted to prove she and her sisters could do something no woman had ever done before. She wanted to prove to everyone, and herself, that she was meant to be in this position and she could not only compete in a man's world but also dominate.

She wondered if the cost had been too high, though.

"There is nothing more than this night," she informed him. "There can't be. I can't work backward, Cam."

Her intentions had to be crystal clear. If she'd sacrificed for her career, she couldn't start reliving the past or she'd just keep going in circles and not moving forward like she planned. Everything was planned...except this damn divorce. That had never been part of her life goals.

The distillery had given her that sense of belonging, of acceptance. She'd never fully felt either of those things with Camden and his family. There had always been that invisible wedge between them and there was no erasing that...not as long as his parents were so disapproving.

Camden squeezed her hand and released it. Then he curled his fingers around her inner thigh, setting off all sorts of other bells than just moments ago. When he touched her, all the heavy barriers between them seemed to vanish and everything in her wanted to just take everything she truly desired.

"What costume is this, anyway?" he asked. "Besides sexy as hell."

His hand massaged way too close to that juncture where she ached most. Instinctively, she slid down in her seat. Why did she have to want the one man who didn't have the same vision for the future as she did? How could they be so perfect on so many levels, yet so wrong on others?

"Um... I'm a...a shadow. I wanted to disappear in the crowd. I actually thought your parents would be there."

His hand shifted just enough and cupped her heat, nearly causing her eyes to roll back in her head. He'd always been such a selfless lover, always putting her needs first.

"They're out of town. And disappear?" he asked with a subtle laugh. "Not possible, babe."

Babe. The word slid out as he continued to massage her. His endearments had always been laced with a heavy seductive tone. Her weakness had always been his touch, whether it be simple or a stepping-stone to something more. He'd had a hold over her physically and emotionally that she'd fought to break free from...and clearly she hadn't fought hard enough.

"You're tensing up again," he murmured as he turned into her driveway. "We can't have that."

He stopped the vehicle halfway up the drive beneath a canopy of trees and put it in Park. Moonlight filtered through the minuscule openings between the leaves, casting the gentlest glow into the vehicle.

"What are you doing?" she asked.

Camden didn't answer. Another career skill she knew he carried over into his daily life had always been less talking and more action. It was those nonverbal communications she needed to be worried about. The man was a master at getting his way without using a single word. Then again, she wasn't exactly arguing. How could she when she'd missed this very thing?

He reached over, grasped her face in his hands and pulled her mouth to his, as if he couldn't take another second of being this close and not tasting her.

It had been too damn long. An entire month without his lips, and even longer without his body. Delilah wondered if he fully intended to strip her in the front seat of his car or if they'd actually make it up to the house before she combusted.

Delilah came to life in his arms...just like he'd expected. She might put up a verbal fight, but she wanted the same things he did—physically, anyway. Emotionally, they weren't on the same level. Yet.

But Camden wasn't here for the emotional aspect. He wanted his wife and he knew full well she wanted him, too. This separation between them had gone on too long.

Delilah shifted in her seat, then brought one hand up to the side of his face. His beard scraped against her hand, a sound he always loved. She freely opened for him and moaned the moment his tongue swept against hers. His entire body stirred, aching even more than before. There were too many barriers, too many gadgets in the way. He'd been unable to stop himself like he was some damn teenager without self-control.

Just when he was about to put an end to this madness and take her up to the house and into a bed like she deserved, Delilah pushed him back. For a half second he thought she was putting the brakes on, but then he saw her eyes. There was a hunger staring back that he recognized.

Camden fell back against his seat and Dee started stripping out of her heels and peeled the leather pants down her lean legs. Watching her bare legs work the leather the rest of the way down and finally off nearly had him embarrassing himself.

With the corset still in place, accentuating the fullness of her breasts, Delilah climbed over the center console and straddled his lap. She bumped the horn and jumped, then started laughing.

"I'll scoot my seat back," he muttered as he watched her going to work on the zipper of his dress pants. "Or we could just go on up to the house."

"You started this too early and I can't wait," she panted.

The moment she released him and covered him with her hand, Camden dropped his head back against the seat and groaned. As much as he wanted her in the house where he could fully explore that body he'd missed, he also had gone way too long without his wife's touch.

And knowing she was this on fire wasn't surprising. Delilah had always been a passionate woman. He could read more into this moment, having her wrapped all around him, but he was still realistic. He knew tonight was all about being physical. Delilah wasn't thinking beyond right now...which was just fine with him. He was having a difficult time thinking, too.

Camden filled his hands with bare backside and guided her so her core would replace her hand. His silent gesture had her reaching to grip his shoulders a second before she joined their bodies.

The cry she let out had him gritting his teeth to remain somewhat in control. With Delilah's sweet body working against his and those familiar pants and moans, he was seriously struggling to let her have her way—but he was willing to give her any physical thing she needed.

Cam wanted to touch her more, wanted the rest of their clothes off and not to be in the front seat of his damn car...but right now, he was going to take what he could get because he needed this. They both needed this. And if she needed to keep hold of those reins in this rollercoaster marriage, he wasn't going to argue.

Cutting off their relationship so completely hadn't been right. He didn't want to be that man who couldn't hold his own marriage together and watched it crumble in his hands. The fact that he looked incompetent as a husband would never sit well with him.

But the weight of this heavy failure wasn't something he could focus on right now. He wanted to take in every single euphoric moment with his wife, even if this wasn't exactly how he'd imagined things. He'd rather have her in their home, in their bed…not in the driveway of some rental home she'd found.

Delilah threw her head back as her hips jerked faster. Her body clenched all around him as she ultimately stilled and bit down on her bottom lip, a sure sign she was struggling to maintain her composure. No need to hold back on his account. He wanted her to let go. He needed to see her come undone, to know he was the one who made her feel this way. And he wanted her to know it, too. Camden gripped her hips tighter and held her in place, triggering her release as he let his own climax take over.

Her warm breath tickled the side of his face as she leaned farther into him. Her body trembled, or maybe that was his. Either way, he wasn't ready for this moment to end, despite the fact they were in his car like teenagers. This was his *wife*, damn it. He wanted to ride this high and carry her with him and forget everything else and all the reasons they couldn't make this marriage work.

Carefully, Camden shifted her body slightly and rested her head on his shoulder. He reached around her and put the car in Drive.

"You're not seriously driving," she murmured against his neck.

"I want you in the bedroom, Dee. Or at least outside of this car. I'm not nearly done."

Her lips grazed his skin and he nearly ran the damn car into the landscaping as he pulled up near the front porch. He couldn't get the car in Park fast enough before he killed the engine and threw open his door.

"I'm glad this place is shielded from your neighbors," he told her as he maneuvered out of the SUV, cupping her backside to keep her against him as he looked over her shoulder.

"Privacy is always important," she muttered. "Go to the garage and use the keypad."

She gave him the code and he was in the garage and had the door going down within seconds. He hadn't been inside her new house and honestly he'd never wanted to be. He'd wanted her to rethink their future together and come back home where she belonged.

Their living arrangements were definitely a conversation for another time.

"I never thought you'd be here."

"That makes two of us." Cam headed toward the door leading into the house. "Where's your bedroom?"

"There's a guest bedroom down here." She pointed without glancing up from the crook of his neck. "First door on the right down that hallway."

A pang of anger hit him as he realized she didn't want him in her bedroom, but he was here and he had to take his own advice. This night wasn't about any attempt to reconcile—he didn't even know if such a thing was possible.

Everything tonight was purely physical. No emotions could or should be involved. Letting all of their feelings intermingle with sex was how they'd fallen so fast and hard with each other and ended up walking into the courthouse for a spur-of-the-moment wedding not long after meeting.

Had they set themselves up for failure from the start?

Maybe so, but he had every intention of changing the outcome and not signing those damn papers.

Camden followed her directions and stepped inside the bedroom. Slowly, he eased her down his body until she came to stand before him. The only light was from the hallway, but it was more than enough for him to take in the sight of his breathtaking wife as she stood before him wearing only a corset. Her hair had come undone and spread all around her shoulders. Her red lipstick had worn off, but those eyes were still heavily made-up, which gave her even more of that vixen aura.

That was his Delilah. She could be anything from sexy siren to sweet seductress. He'd loved both, but apparently that hadn't been enough. Sex and love didn't hold a marriage together. Her goals hadn't aligned with his and they'd both been shocked to find out how the other saw their future together because nothing was remotely the same.

He'd mentioned family and she hadn't really thought much past her career. He'd thought maybe she'd slow down with that, but she was just getting started. Not that he didn't value her job. He just hadn't wanted her to feel like she had to have such a demanding career.

Throw into the mix his disapproving family and the entire situation went all to hell.

Damn it. Why couldn't he turn off these strong feelings? Why couldn't he have worked with the relationship they'd had and seen where things were going wrong? He wanted to fix things, but what if he was too late? What if he'd lost it all forever and once that stamp of failure had been placed on their union, there would be no resolving the situation?

The intimacy, the passion…his wife had been everything. But she thought she was making the right move for both of them—so why were they both utterly shattered now?

"Now who's the one thinking?" she asked, tipping her head and raising her brows.

Her hands came up to the little tie right between the swell of her breasts as she gave a tug, her eyes never wavering from his. Camden couldn't look away, but he sure as hell could help speed up this process. He made quick work of shedding his own clothes and a moment later, the corset peeled back and fell to the floor behind her, leaving her entire body completely bare and beautifully exposed.

"You're still so damn perfect."

He reached for her once again, lifting her up with his hands on her round backside until she wrapped her legs around his waist. Camden crossed the room to the bed and pressed her back against the thick post.

Her hands were all over him, her core hovering just above where he still ached for her. She'd always done that to him. He'd never been able to deny her anything…at least in the bedroom.

"Slow down," he whispered against her shoulder as he trailed his lips over her heated skin. "No need to rush when we have all night."

She trembled again.

No, that wasn't a tremble. That was a cringe. She'd flat-out recoiled against him and in that instant, Camden had the realization that they had very different plans for the night…much like their different views for their marriage.

Slowly, he eased her back down and took a step away. How could he have made such a mistake? To think he could slide right back into her life like they didn't have a mound of problems driving a wedge between them.

Raking his hand through his hair, Cam turned and headed across the room toward his clothes. There was nothing left here for him, for them. He could want the hell out of her, he could have her many times over, but that wouldn't change the fact she had already checked out. He'd hoped, even put a little faith in thinking they would be intimate after months apart and she'd see just how good they were together. That she would be reminded of when and how they fell in love to begin with.

As Camden dressed, Delilah said nothing. He couldn't help but risk a glance her way. She stood there, hands at her sides, completely bare. Her hair was still tossed about her shoulders, her lips swollen, her eyes now filled with unshed tears.

This entire scene summed up their lives. Hot and passionate fighting against angst and brokenness.

His heart ached, but at the same time, he couldn't back down on how much he wanted this marriage to work and apparently she couldn't forgo the idea that they weren't meant to be. And maybe they were simply two different people who hadn't gotten beyond the heat before they said "I do," but he didn't think so. If there wasn't something tangible between them, then this split wouldn't hurt so damn bad.

"I can't do all night." She blinked and glanced away, wrapping her arms around her midsection. "Not anymore. It's just... I can't."

He'd pushed too far. He'd wanted to spend hours with his wife, wake up to her lying against him and make love to her all over again. She wanted fast, frantic sex in the front seat of a car, and to sleep alone.

Who the hell had he become? He'd never been a man like this. Before he met Dee, Camden had been all about the flings and the one-night stands. Now he balked at the idea of anything temporary. He'd seen too much damage between couples in his line of work and had vowed never to marry, but then Delilah came into his life and nothing had been the same.

Who the hell had a one-night stand with their spouse?

Soon-to-be ex.

He still wasn't ready to let that thought turn into a reality and he wasn't going to let her give up. He could fight hard enough for both of them because Delilah never just quit on anything…except him.

Camden had nothing to say. What else could there be? She wanted one thing, he wanted another, nobody was compromising, but they both wanted sex. Their relationship was as simple and complex as that.

"Things didn't have to be this way," she told him, turning her focus away.

Cam pulled in a deep breath and sighed, still unsure what he could say to defend himself that hadn't already been put out there.

"No, they didn't," he agreed. "I only wanted—"

"I know what you wanted, but that just isn't possible."

Her voice cracked and so did his heart. This wasn't going to go anywhere productive tonight. Their emotions were too raw and coming off of sex certainly wasn't the time to figure anything out. Not only that, she was still recovering from Milly's death. He should have known her heart was too vulnerable, too exposed to handle anything else.

Despite everything happening around her and to her, Delilah would never admit vulnerability. But there was only so much someone could take and he wanted to make sure he was there for her when she broke. He would never walk away from the one good and solid person in his life.

Maybe his actions made him selfish or a masochist, he didn't know. But he did know he had to take things day by day and maybe even hour by hour.

Silence settled heavy between them, driving the wedge deeper. Camden didn't want to wait any longer. He had to get out of here. She needed her space right now and, quite honestly, so did he.

He turned, letting himself out the way he'd come in.

Getting his wife back had been his main goal since she moved out, but after tonight, he didn't even know if that was possible anymore and he came to the damning realization that this might end in defeat.

Three

"Why are we in the boardroom?"

Sara and Elise both glanced up from the obscenely long table as Delilah stood in the doorway with her bag and phone in one hand and her Angel's Share insulated coffee mug in the other. There was not enough caffeine for this day. Not only had she overslept and forgotten all about the meeting *she* had scheduled, she'd barely gotten any sleep last night after Camden had left.

Her body still hummed from the all-too-brief encounter, but they'd still managed to screw up the night. Or rather, she had. But she was done holding in her thoughts for fear of hurt feelings. They were both already hurt and they deserved honesty on every level. Not clearing things up was how they'd gotten into this mess to begin with. She'd gone along with everything believing a picture-perfect life could be theirs simply because love and physical attraction should have been enough, right? She'd believed everything would work itself out.

Another life lesson learned the hard way.

"We're in the boardroom because we're having a meeting," Sara stated, then glanced at her watch. "That started twenty minutes ago."

"I had a bad morning."

That was the only excuse Delilah was ready to give right now. Between the soon-to-be ex who'd blown her mind in the front seat of his car last night and the fact she and her sisters had just had their lives torn upside down and inside out with the loss of their beloved Milly, it was a miracle there was only coffee in her mug this morning.

"You look like hell."

Delilah pulled out a chair and glanced at Elise. "You look lovely today, too. Thank you."

"You know what I mean," Elise amended with an eye roll. "Stay out too late dancing the night away at the charity event?"

Taking a sip of her coffee seemed like the logical step here in lieu of answering. She set her mug back down and dug into her bag for the folder she'd grabbed off her desk before coming into the boardroom.

"So I know we all have mentioned moving Angel's Share into a venue for weddings and other events," she started, still dodging any question regarding last night. "Well, I was contacted by the governor's wife and they want to have their daughter's wedding here next year. So, that does give us some time to hone in on costs and setup options. Then there's the drink side we need to consider—"

"Hold up."

Delilah stopped as Sara held up her hand.

"Can we get back to why you were late and why you

look like you haven't slept in days?" her sister asked. "Because this definitely isn't like our usual Delilah. After that, we'll get to the topic of weddings because Elise and Antonio will be wed on this property first."

Delilah glanced from Sara to Elise and noted both ladies were staring at her fixedly. Clearly they were not going any further until she answered some questions. She should have known they'd see right through her and that she'd not get away with dodging them so easily. Had the roles been reversed, she'd also demand to know what was up.

Unfortunately, Delilah didn't have the answers. Oh, she certainly had the facts of everything that happened, but anything beyond that was a hard no. The why and the how were still muddled in her mind and she didn't know if she'd ever fully comprehend the unbreakable bond to Cam. Would she ever be able to make a break from the one relationship that was toxic?

"I know you were worried about running into Cam's parents," Sara added. "Is that what happened?"

That might have been less dramatic and heartbreaking than the way things ultimately ended. At least she could have walked away from them. There was no ignoring that invisible pull toward her husband.

"They weren't there and the charity event was fine," Delilah admitted. "I didn't actually stay too long, but I did get the Angel's Share donation in."

She might have forgotten last night and only done so this morning via a few clicks on her computer, but she still managed to get it in, which was all that mattered. She had left too early and missed the silent auction, so she added a little extra to her online support.

"Please tell me you didn't go as that ridiculous shadow idea," Elise groaned.

"I'll have you know that costume was a brilliant idea for someone who wanted to go unnoticed," she defended with a slight lift of her chin.

"Hard to go unnoticed when the hostess was trying to fix you up with someone," Sara murmured with a snicker. "Did you actually see this guy?"

Saw him, danced with him, had sex in the front seat of his car.

"It was Camden."

The gasp from both sisters echoed in the boardroom. But, in true Sara fashion, her shock turned to delight.

"That's wonderful," she squealed with a clasp of her hands. "You two are meant to be. You'll realize it yourself. I just hope it's before you guys sign those papers."

Sara always had hearts dancing around her head. The woman believed in all the fairy tales they'd watched as children. And true love had worked out and triumphed for Elise and Antonio, but things just weren't meant to be for Delilah.

This conversation would lead to absolutely nowhere. Delilah had explained to both of her sisters when the marriage started falling apart that just because there's chemistry doesn't mean there's a solid foundation. And just because she wanted and wished—none of that could make miracles happen.

"Sara, you are going to have to get this reunion out of your head. Cam and I are getting divorced. There's too much between us that only we know, but trust me. It's over."

Sara's eyes widened and her lips thinned. Delilah didn't mean to be rude, but she also couldn't let her sisters believe any untruth. Keeping that sliver of hope among her small circle would only cause more heartache down the road.

"The modified papers should be in anytime," Delilah went on. "And once they're signed, I can move on."

Silence settled in the spacious room as her sisters continued to stare at her with concerned expressions. No matter what they thought about her situation, Delilah was ultimately the one who would have to live with these decisions.

"Do you want to talk about the root of the problem?" Elise asked after a moment. "I mean, we've tried to give you your space, but it's been months and we've all been through so much since then. We simply want to help."

Delilah nodded, knowing her sisters only wanted what was best for her. But no matter how much they were there for each other, there wasn't a thing they could do to fix this mess.

"I don't want any of this to bring down the high that Angel's Share is on or your engagement," she told Elise. "Let me handle things my way and you all go on about your lives."

Elise rolled her eyes. "You honestly think we're just going to ignore the issue simply because it's tough? And you aren't bringing anything down. This is life. It can be chaotic, sad, happy, a mess—you just never know. We're here for all of it."

Delilah pulled in a shaky breath and really tried not to bust out into the emotional breakdown she was barely holding back.

"Can we just shift our focus to your wedding so I can get back to the governor about his daughter?" Delilah asked, hoping they went with her lead.

When both sisters nodded, so much weight lifted from Delilah's shoulders. Finally, she could focus on something she could control…work. This was where she could shine, where she had the most confidence and could really be herself.

Since the gala, overseeing new VIP clients was now her territory instead of Elise's, who was bogged down in sales. But as they ventured into becoming a rental venue for parties and weddings, Dee was champing at the bit to really spread her wings, adding Event Coordinator to her résumé. The more work, the better.

"Have you all set a date?" Delilah asked.

Elise nodded. "Finally. We're looking at something soon and small. I wanted spring, but that weather is so unpredictable and I'm in a hurry to marry the man of my dreams."

Delilah forced her smile in place, trying to be happy for her sister and not compare the two relationships. Elise and Antonio were absolutely perfect for each other. They'd met when he'd come from Spain to do a tour of vineyards and distilleries in the States and they'd immediately fallen in love.

No way would Delilah let her own personal life put some dark cloud over her sister's happily-ever-after. Because no matter how her own marriage had started and ended, Delilah did believe love was for some people. Elise and Antonio were living proof.

"Any other details you want to share?" Sara asked. "Colors, dress ideas, food."

Elise pursed her lips and shrugged. "I was thinking I should probably hire a wedding planner, but I don't know if anyone is even available for something so soon with barely any notice. Most brides take over a year to plan these things."

"A wedding planner?" Sara gasped. "Why would you do that when you have two sisters?"

Elise glanced from Sara to Delilah. "You two want

to help? I just assumed we were all too busy to take on something like this."

"A wedding?" Sara laughed. "I've been preparing for this my entire life."

Sara tapped on her computer, then on the control panel in the middle of the table, and within moments, a spreadsheet popped up on the drop screen behind Elise's head. Sara reached across the table once more to dim the lights.

"The plan really should go in this exact order for a flawless, magical day," Sara began.

Delilah stared, completely stunned at this extremely detailed list. Though she shouldn't be surprised. Of the three sisters with their vastly different personalities, Sara had always been the hopeless romantic and she was just waiting for her knight to ride into town.

Delilah, on the other hand, wasn't waiting for anyone to save her or make her future complete. She was making her own way and didn't want someone else slaying her proverbial dragons.

"I'm not sure I need quite this much of a presentation," Elise told her sister. "It's all a bit overwhelming and we aren't wanting anything so grand."

Sara's brows drew in; her lips turned into a slight frown. "Nothing grand? Are you going to elope all alone with just a plain old dress and no flowers, too?"

Elise's eyes darted to Delilah.

"Oh, sorry," Sara murmured. "I didn't think."

Delilah smacked her hands on the glossy tabletop, causing both sisters to jump.

"Stop tiptoeing around me," she exclaimed. "Yes, I eloped. No, I didn't have flowers, but my dress was new. Yes, I'm getting divorced. And, yes, I slept with Cam last night—"

"What?"

"Well, damn."

Elise and Sara both spoke at the same time and Dee realized she'd let her secret slip. She sank back in her chair and let out a deep breath as she tried to collect her thoughts and figure out a way to backpedal.

But the words were already out and there was no taking them back.

Delilah closed her eyes. "Can we pretend I didn't say that?"

"Not likely," Elise replied. "But if you don't want to talk about it, we can table that discussion for now."

Well, that was something because she wasn't ready to face her feelings on the night, let alone talk about it and be asked questions she had no answers for.

She risked looking back at her sisters and instead of seeing judgment, all she saw was compassion. She'd almost prefer the judgment. Knowing they felt sorry for her really grated on her last nerve, but she knew they cared. They weren't the enemy and she had no reason to put her frustration on them. She had nobody to blame but herself...and Cam. It took two to make or break a marriage.

"Let's recap." Elise ticked off on her fingers. "We have a high-society wedding to plan, after my big day of course, and we need to get started on that with a calmer checklist than what Sara has, Dee slept with Cam even though they're divorcing, and we're going to only discuss business until Delilah says otherwise. Did that sum up our meeting?"

Dee knew Elise was only trying to make light of everything, so she couldn't help but add her own bit.

"Should we go ahead and throw in searching for our biological fathers or is that too much for a morning meeting?"

"That's definitely too much," Sara agreed, nodding her

head. "I mean, we do need to talk about what all is going on now that we know the truth, or part of it anyway."

Losing Milly and finding out they all three had different fathers on top of everything else going on was enough to have them leaning on each other a little more than usual.

"Listen," Delilah started. "I know that I'm cranky, I know I look like hell this morning—"

"Sorry about that," Elise chimed in.

"No worries. It's the truth. I'm just in a pretty bumpy spot in my life, but I'll get back on track."

Her cell buzzed on the table and she glanced at the screen. Her heart immediately leaped up into her throat.

I don't regret last night

When her eyes focused back on Sara, her sister smiled. "Are you ready to talk yet?"

Delilah wanted to, but not here and not when they had so much else to do. Angel's Share was such a big part of their lives and required one hundred percent from each of them if they were going to continue to grow and dominate this industry. They didn't come this far to start slowing down or get too relaxed.

She wanted nothing more than to confide in her sisters because they would support her and offer sound advice. But she just wasn't ready. Her head was too cloudy to try to process anything they'd say and she had a terrible feeling once she started talking, she'd start breaking down, and she'd never been a pretty crier.

Her eyes slid over her screen once more and those nerves in her belly swirled again at Camden's words.

Because, if she was being honest with herself, she didn't regret last night, either.

Four

Delilah had just pulled some leftover takeout from the microwave when her cell rang. She sat the unopened box on the kitchen island and tapped her cell, putting the call on speaker.

"Hello."

"Dee, it's Alisha. Is this a bad time?"

"No, of course not. How can I help you?"

"I'm so sorry to bother you after hours, but I had to call and apologize."

Delilah eased the box open and eyed the two-day-old fried rice. She really needed to hit the grocery store.

"Why are you apologizing?" Delilah asked. "I had to slip out early, so if anyone is apologizing, it should be me."

"Oh, I was so busy I didn't know when you left," she admitted. "But, I just found out that Camden is your husband. Well, almost ex. I'm mortified I was trying to set you guys up."

Yeah, well, it worked. Moments after the meetup, they were having sex in his car.

"Don't be sorry or embarrassed," Delilah soothed. "You had no idea and I appreciate the gesture that you were trying to make my evening a little nicer, so thank you."

Alisha laughed. "Well, I didn't expect a thanks, but I'll take it. I felt so bad when my brother told me. I honestly had no idea and we're both still new to the area, so I'm finding my footing. Your donation was extremely generous and so appreciated, by the way."

"My sisters and I are happy to support our community and worthy causes. From what I saw, you had a rather successful night."

"We did. The children will certainly benefit from all the kindness poured out from this community."

Another call popped up on her screen and Delilah recognized the name of the real estate agent she'd used to secure this rental.

"Alisha, I'm sorry, but I have to take this other call," Dee told her.

"Oh, no worries. Thanks again and I'm still sorry for my mistake."

"You're welcome and I'll text you about lunch. I still need to hear about that engagement."

"I can't wait."

Dee tapped her screen and answered the other call.

"Hey, Kayla."

"Delilah. Is this a good time?"

She stared at the less than appealing leftovers and finally closed the box and put it back in the fridge. Now that she was alone, cooking for one just seemed a waste of her energy.

"Perfect time," Delilah replied. "Is everything okay?"

"As a matter of fact, yes," Kayla told her. "I have a proposition that came my way and I need to pass it along to you. Now, don't immediately give me your answer. This is something you'll need to think about."

Delilah stood in front of her fridge, staring at the bag of bagels and the carton of eggs, wondering if either were in date. When was the last time she'd even gone to the grocery? She wondered how quick something could be delivered.

"What is it?" Dee asked.

"I have a client who is moving to the Benton Springs area in the next month and she wants to buy your house."

Delilah spun around and eyed her cell on the counter. "My house? As in, the one I'm renting?"

"Um…no. As in the one you and Camden still own together."

Delilah gripped the edge of the countertop and pulled in a deep breath. Someone wanted her house? No, it wasn't hers. Well, legally she was part owner, but she wouldn't be going back and she didn't know how Cam would feel about selling. She actually assumed he'd stay there while she found her footing elsewhere.

That was one of the modifications needed in their divorce papers. She'd wanted the house put back in his name since he'd bought the place before they were married. There was no need for her to have any part of his past since she wouldn't be part of his future.

Yet, she'd loved that house. When Cam had first shown her his place, she'd fallen in love with the views down into the valley. Living up on a hill and being secluded had been absolutely perfect for them.

As memories started to hit her hard, the lump of regret and sadness threatened to overtake her. She had to stay positive, she had to keep looking to her future, because if she fell back into life with Camden, she knew in the end she'd be a letdown to not only him, but his family. Something he would never admit, but she wasn't stupid or naive and she didn't want to be the driving force that eventually tore him and his parents apart.

"I honestly have no clue about selling," Delilah finally answered. "I can talk to Camden and let you know or have him call you directly since the home will legally be his soon."

"That would be great. I'm definitely not pressuring either of you, but the opportunity is here now if you think selling is a possibility. I promised my client I would present their offer."

Delilah nodded, though no one could see her. Words were becoming difficult to get past that growing lump in her throat. If he sold, that would be another portion of their life together that was lost forever.

"Try to get back to me when you can," Kayla went on. "I'll be showing my client other properties as well, but I just remembered your home checked off all their boxes."

Yeah, that home had checked off all of her and Cam's boxes, too. They'd christened every room, and as much as she'd loved their physical relationship, she'd also craved the simple things that never happened. Sitting on the front porch swing with a glass of wine at the end of the day or enjoying the hot tub on the back deck while under the stars. But he traveled so much, meeting with his elite clients, and she had been busy here working on the distillery.

Delilah ended the call and sent a text to Cam. Her

hands shook, which was absurd. This was part of the moving-on process she wanted…she *needed*.

We have to talk

She gripped her cell as she headed down the hallway toward her bedroom. Dinner was the farthest thing from her mind. Suddenly all she wanted to do was curl into a ball and cry at the thought of their home going to someone else. Yes, she'd left, but that had been because she couldn't handle staying and living with all of those memories. But, selling, if that's what Cam was interested in, would be another final step of closure in this new journey.

She knew she couldn't have her life both ways. She was either in or out and she'd chosen to leave. There was too much between them and ultimately, she knew if she stayed, Cam would end up resenting her and she'd start wondering if she'd ever come ahead of his job.

A nice bath and a glass of wine was what she needed. She'd been trying to focus on self-care lately when time allowed and if there was ever a day she needed to unwind, it was today. Everything seemed to be closing in all around her and she just wanted to take a step back from reality.

While she loved her work, she threw herself even harder into it when she and Cam first split. Her sisters finally made her realize that working to exhaustion wasn't the way to deal with a broken heart. The distraction might work for a short time, but ultimately did more harm than good.

Delilah checked her cell as she placed it on her bathroom vanity. No reply from Cam. She shouldn't be surprised. That part had always been an issue. Communication…or lack thereof. He'd been married to his job before they came together, but she thought she might actually get bumped up in the ranks of his priority list.

Clearly that never happened.

She drew her bath, poured in a generous dose of her favorite lavender bubble bath and headed back to the kitchen for the wine. No doubt when she and Cam finally talked, he would want to discuss the other night, but she had to bank that experience as another memory. Never again would she be intimate with her soon-to-be ex. Their time was over and she was officially moving on—broken heart and all.

The entire day had been one headache after another. Demanding clients seeking the impossible and refusing to budge only left him with more frustration than usual. Of course, it could also be his own personal life spiraling out of control that contributed to his migraines as of late. But he'd already had to plan yet another trip to Texas to meet with one client who really should star in her own *Housewives* show. Nothing was ever good enough and if she laid out one more demand, Camden wasn't above dropping her or giving her an ultimatum.

He'd stayed at the office much too long, longer than usual. The sun had set hours ago and he headed through the dark, winding roads that led to his home on top of a hill on the edge of town. He'd been working himself too hard, not taking breaks, throwing himself into everything his clients needed or wanted, and booking extra trips. Anything to exorcise Delilah from his mind...but clearly nothing was working.

What he needed was a damn break.

No. What he needed was his wife back.

Delilah had called and texted a few times and he hadn't gotten a chance to call her. Each time he picked up his phone to contact her, something else would pop up that needed his immediate attention. Then his father had called and that conversation had been the proverbial cherry on top.

Camden's lights slashed through the darkness, landing on the two-story home he'd shared with Delilah for five years. The place had been so perfect for them, but with her gone, it seemed so damn empty and depressing. He'd never noticed when he'd lived here alone before they got together, but now, the void was all too obvious.

He tried to only come home to sleep and shower. Other than that, he kept himself busy and out of the home that held way too much history.

As he approached, Camden recognized the black car in the drive and his gut tightened. He didn't know whether to be excited or worried. The woman had his emotions all over the place these last several months.

Delilah parked in her old spot just in front of her garage door where she had for all the years they'd been married. That sight shoved him right back to all the times he took for granted she'd always be there.

Camden pulled up beside her, confused that she'd shown up without warning, but she had called so maybe that's what she was trying to tell him. Definitely something she could have just texted, so something else must be going on.

Delilah did still have a few boxes in one of the spare bedrooms, but other than that, she'd cleared out most everything she wanted. That was something he wasn't going to fight over. He couldn't care less about a sofa or dishes. He could buy anything he wanted, including another house. He just wanted Delilah. Couldn't she see that? Didn't she understand that this giving up wasn't what either of them stood for? They were both fighters.

They wouldn't have made it this far being so successful in their careers if they were passive people.

They also wouldn't have made it in five years of marriage if they just threw in the proverbial towel when things got tough.

A quick glance told Camden that his wife wasn't in her car, but then he spotted her on the front porch in the swing. He was so damn tired and had planned on coming home, showering and crawling into bed. A new burst of energy suddenly spiraled through him at the opportunity that presented itself.

While he didn't know what brought her here, they needed to discuss how they'd left things. The last thing they needed was another issue coming between them… and he wouldn't mind another round of the other night.

Camden headed up the curved stone path leading to the steps. Delilah glanced up from her phone as he ascended to the porch. Her eyes immediately went to his, drawing him in. She pointed her bare toes on the concrete porch and stopped the swing. Without a word, he closed the distance and took a seat beside her. Once he was settled, she set the swing back into motion.

Moments ticked by in silence, with only the occasional squeak from the hinges of the swing.

"I always wanted this," she said after several minutes. "A starry evening, you on this swing with me as we discussed our day, maybe a glass of wine in hand. Not a care in the world. Impossible, I know, but it was a dream I had."

This was the first time they'd sat together on this swing…ever. They'd been out back on their patio a couple of times, but never right in this spot. He'd had no clue this was something she'd always wanted. Had he ever asked? Or worse, had she told him and he didn't pay attention?

Why was she letting him inside her thoughts now? Did she want to drive that wedge deeper or make him feel like a complete jerk? Or maybe she just needed him to know before she walked away for good.

Maybe had he been more attentive to her and less to his job, they would have shared nights like she wanted. Camden had worked his ass off to get where he was. Then when they married, he worked just as diligently to keep her happy. He wanted to be her provider and assumed that was his role when they married. But Delilah needed no one to care for her. She could do anything on her own, and maybe that hurt his pride and ego a bit, but it was also another reason he'd fallen deeper for her. She was such an amazing woman, one that he'd been damn lucky to have.

But he hadn't let her go quite yet. They were still married, which meant there was still a chance to pull this marriage back to life.

"I can go get that glass of wine," he offered.

"It's a little late."

She didn't mean the time of night and they both knew it. Delilah kept the swing moving gently and he wished like hell he could rewind time and sit just like she'd described.

"Sorry I didn't get back to you earlier," he told her. "I got so busy and… I know that's not a good excuse, but it's the truth."

She remained silent as the swing kept moving. He waited for her to reply or tell him that was the problem with their marriage, but what came out of her mouth was certainly unexpected.

"Kayla called and has a buyer for this house."

Cam planted his feet flat and stopped the swaying swing. His focus immediately went to Dee, who was star-

ing straight ahead as if she hadn't just dropped a monumental statement between them that would continue to
take them further apart.

"Are we selling this house?" he asked, shocked she'd
even mention such a thing.

She shrugged, but still didn't look his way. What was
she thinking? Is this why she had come? Did she want
him to get rid of this aspect of their lives together?

"What did you tell Kayla?"

Now Delilah shifted her attention to him, lifting her
knee between them and stretching her arm along the
back of the swing. She blew out a sigh and seemed as
frustrated and lost as he was…all the confirmation he
needed to see that she was having doubts or at least she
wasn't happy with their current arrangement.

"I told her I'd have to talk to you and that in the end
the house would go back to your name and you'd have
the final say."

Camden could hardly tolerate sitting here talking
about the end of everything like this was the new normal. Which it was, but still. This wasn't right and neither of them were happy, so why the hell was he letting
this go on?

They both had been through so much, at the expense
of their pride, their happiness—his parents' behavior,
the death of Milly. Everything had come crashing down
around them and they were buried beneath the rubble.

Something had to change because this entire situation couldn't keep going on. He needed a break and he
wanted time with Delilah without all this outside noise
around them. They had so much negativity knocking
them from all sides.

Was it any wonder they'd fallen apart? Other than their
honeymoon, they hadn't done anything for just them-

selves or to help this marriage be successful. Oh, she'd accompanied him a few times on a business trip here and there, but that wasn't the same. That was still work and one of the main issues she had with him.

"Come away with me."

Delilah's eyes widened as she jerked back at his demand. He was a little shocked that his thoughts had been spoken aloud, too, but he wasn't sorry. Now he had to hurry and justify his outburst so he didn't look like a selfish bastard who just wanted to carry on what they'd been doing the other night. There was more to their relationship than sex…there had to be.

"We need this, Dee," he told her. "I know we're separated—"

"We filed for divorce. Twice, actually, since the first papers were wrong."

"But we still want each other," he retorted. "Just come away with me for a long weekend. Our work can wait. Hell, everything can wait."

Delilah rubbed her forehead and laughed. "You're not making any sense. We can't just run away, Cam. We're not going to be married as soon as we sign those papers. And even if we went away for a few days, everything will be waiting on us when we get back."

"Name the last time we put us first," he demanded. "Never. We never have. Just give me the next four days away from this place to show you that this marriage isn't a loss. We don't have to call it quits because things are hard. After four days, if you still want to sign those papers, I won't fight against it."

Though he had zero intention of losing this final battle because watching her walk away one last time would destroy him. He never wanted to face a reality where losing was part of his story. And he didn't want to face a reality without Delilah.

Just because she moved out and they filed those damn papers didn't mean he could turn off his feelings so quickly or as easily. All he wanted was one more chance to prove to her that they could build on what they started, and there had to be some way they could come to terms.

They needed to get back to the basics they'd skipped years ago. Maybe then she would see how serious he was about her and their future and about making this marriage the most successful part of both of their lives.

"I'm asking for four days." He stopped resisting and finally placed a hand on her thigh. "If you're afraid to be alone with me, then that should tell you that we still have reason to be together. That pull hasn't gone away, Dee. And if you go and feel nothing, then we'll go our separate ways."

But he knew that would be impossible. The way they combusted in the front seat of his car the other night was all the proof he needed that they had so much more time together. He couldn't just erase that hope.

"You expect me to believe you're going to put your work on hold for four days?" she asked with a disbelieving snicker.

He needed her to see just how serious he was and that he wasn't playing games. If that meant putting his entire life on hold for a while, then so be it.

"You can hold on to my phone for those days." Camden held her gaze, making sure she knew just how invested he truly was. "I won't work even one minute."

She blinked as if she couldn't believe what he was saying. The quiet night surrounded them and the fact that she hadn't flat out said no really spoke volumes. He couldn't give her the chance to turn him down. This getaway might be exactly what they both needed…what they should have done at the first sign of trouble.

But that was the problem with broken hearts and couples splitting. He'd seen it all for years. Everything was a slow progression. People didn't decide to split up in the blink of an eye. Something seemingly harmless would wedge its way into a couple's life and that wedge would only expand because it had gone unnoticed.

Never in his life did he think this would happen to Delilah and him. Of course he was used to seeing marriages fall apart, but he never would have put himself in that same bracket. Maybe that was just his pride, but right now, Camden didn't feel as if he had much left to cling to.

In his vast experience and the high-society clientele he'd worked with, there was usually a healthy level of greed associated with the divorce. One partner found someone they felt was better or they wanted money and freedom. There was always something they were moving on to and they always thought it was better than what they already had.

But that wasn't the case with Delilah and him. They had no one else and he never wanted anyone else. She was it for him and he'd damn well prove that to her until she understood how much she mattered.

"What about your parents?" she whispered.

"I'm not inviting them."

A hint of a smile danced over her lips, which was exactly what he wanted. He needed to see her genuinely smile, to know he put that emotion back in her. He didn't want her to associate only her negative or sad feelings with him. There was once a time when she was either laughing or loving. He hadn't seen those emotions from her in far too long.

Damn it. How had he let this aspect of his life become

so faded into the background? Anything worth having and worth succeeding at should be first and foremost.

"You know what I mean," she corrected, the grin gone.

Camden nodded. "There's no reason they need to know what we're doing in our lives."

"But they do. They always know and they never wanted this marriage from the start."

Cam squeezed her leg. "I didn't grow up waiting to be married to who my parents approved of. I wanted to marry you, so I did."

There was too much history to get into tonight and all he wanted was a confirmed yes for this trip. But if he gave her too much time, she'd back out and let her fears and doubts cloud her judgment.

"Say yes and I'll have the pilot ready tomorrow morning," he told her. "Just... Damn it, Dee. Give in to what you want."

She closed her eyes and tipped her head back. He knew the thoughts that were swirling around in her head. The pros and cons were slamming together and Camden wasn't going to give her an opportunity to turn him down. He wanted time alone with his wife, the woman he still couldn't get enough of after five years of marriage.

"Stop trying to rationalize everything," he ordered. "Go with what you want, not with what you think is right."

She pulled in a deep breath and faced him once again. "I just don't want to prolong this pain."

Damn it. He understood exactly what she meant, but what if this ended in something far better than either of them intended? If there was even an inkling of a chance, he was going to wade through this mess they'd created and grab hold of that sliver of hope.

"We've already said we're ending the marriage," he

told her. "So if you need to think of this as one last fling, that's fine. But I'm taking this trip as an attempt to show you that we shouldn't give up when there is still something there worth fighting for."

Her unshed tears glistened in the soft glow of the porch lights. Knowing he'd caused any amount of hurt was hands down the absolute worst part of this entire ordeal. All he'd wanted to do was be her support and her rock, financially and emotionally, yet somehow in his warped way of thinking, he'd screwed everything up.

Camden came to his feet and stared down at her. "I'll be at the airport at ten in the morning. That will give us both time to let anyone know that we are unavailable for the next few days. My plane will be ready and all you have to do is show up with a packed suitcase. Destination is a surprise if you decide to come."

Delilah stood as well and chewed on her bottom lip, a sure sign she was thinking this proposal through.

He waited for her to reply, but she merely stepped around him and off the porch. Cam turned and watched as she got into her car and drove away into the night. He stood there for quite a while after those taillights disappeared, wondering if he'd see her tomorrow, but also wondering if he'd pushed her too far.

Five

"This is the most ridiculous thing I've ever done," Delilah muttered to herself as she turned into the airport lot for the private planes.

One last time. This would be the last thing she did as a married woman with her husband. A getaway was exactly what she'd wanted while they'd been married and she deserved this, damn it. Not only had she thrust herself even deeper into her work since the split, she couldn't deny that the idea of having him alone for a few days had stirred her desires all over again.

So what if she was only thinking of herself right now? When she and Camden weren't discussing heavy topics or having guilt trips laid on them, they enjoyed each other's company...both in bed and out. She'd take these final four days and be completely and utterly selfish.

After all, she was sacrificing her own happiness so that he could find his.

In the long run, he would thank her. He wouldn't want to live in the middle of her and his family forever. That wasn't fair to any of them and sure as hell not the way a marriage should go.

Delilah pulled into the spot closest to his private hangar and cursed herself again for being so damn easy. He'd dangled sex and a mystery trip in front of her and she'd just packed so fast and sent out texts to her sisters, ready to go last night.

So what? She was human and she had needs. A trip with a man she knew could make her wildest fantasies come true…what woman would turn that down? Besides, he'd already given her the out she wanted. At the end of the four days, he wouldn't argue anymore about signing those papers. This trip was a win-win all the way around.

After messaging her sisters last night, they'd both been understandably nosy and concerned. Delilah only told them she was taking a few days off and getting out of town. She didn't tell them with whom because she had been too tired for the phone calls or late-night visits that would have very likely ensued.

As Delilah pulled her suitcase from her trunk, Camden stepped up beside her.

"You're late."

She couldn't help but bite back a grin. "Only ten minutes."

When she turned to face him, she noted he wasn't smiling as he lifted her luggage from the car. His brows were drawn in and he'd obviously been legitimately worried she wouldn't show.

Interesting. Maybe he wasn't only in this for the physical getaway, but that's exactly how she had to go into these next few days. Her heart had no place here…she wouldn't be that naive again. If she opened up that wound once more, she feared she may never heal and properly move on.

He sat the suitcase down and reached into his pocket. "As promised."

Camden handed over his cell and she was positively stunned. The man lived on that device, but he wasn't one to scroll on social media. He was all work, all the time. The lifeline between his clients and him was always open, no matter the time of day or night. Owning his own firm meant more responsibility. He took so much pride in being the best in his field and making a name for himself.

Which is just one way they complemented each other so well. They'd been drawn by that work ethic at first.

No, actually they'd been drawn in by lust, but the get-to-know-you phase came later and they quickly realized how much they had in common.

Delilah took the phone and slid it into her purse. "I can't believe you are relinquishing this for the entire trip."

Cam released the luggage handle and closed the distance between them. Before she realized his intentions, he had her face framed between his strong hands, but with a delicate touch as he stared into her eyes.

"There are more important things right now and the only thing I'm doing on this trip is my wife."

Desire curled low in her belly and she wondered if they'd even make it to their destination before they tore each other's clothes off. Their encounter the other night had only reminded her of how amazing they were together—physically, anyway. And every moment since then, she'd wanted him all over again.

But something even more concerning than desire hit her. Delilah's heart flipped. Damn it. Hadn't she just told herself her heart couldn't get involved? She'd very carefully removed herself from his world and tried to delicately unweave each thread of their former life together.

She'd wanted to come before his career for the past five years, but it seemed he always just assumed she'd be around. There were times he'd figured if he bought her a piece of jewelry or had a designer come to the house to create any new seasonal pieces she wanted, that would make up for the void in his absence. Being bribed with materialistic things wasn't how she was raised and that wasn't the marriage she wanted.

Although, he'd just said she was important for right now, so maybe he was fine temporarily putting work aside. Long term, though…that was another story. The five years they'd been married had been truly a feat and she was shocked they'd made it that far.

"Where are we going?" she asked.

His eyes dropped to her mouth, then back up to her eyes as he smiled. "It's a surprise."

When he released her and took a step back, Delilah pulled in a breath and willed her desires and bundle of nerves to relax. It wasn't like she hadn't been alone with her husband before.

But this is the last time.

Just the idea of something being final had that familiar lump of sorrow forming in her throat. Leaving had been the most difficult decision she'd made, but she'd gotten stuck in this rut of working and coming home to an empty house because Cam always stayed so late at the office. The cycle had to be broken and she was the one who had made the decision to step aside and make a better way.

This break would be good for them. They'd come into this relationship hot for each other so it was only fitting they…what? Have an exit fling?

Good heavens. This sounded even more ridiculous

than she'd first thought. Who went on a final romantic trip with their spouse? Most people getting a divorce were thrilled to be rid of them and threw divorce parties. Not Delilah. She'd packed lingerie for the occasion.

"There you go thinking again," he scolded. "I can see it. You get this look on your face like you're having some mental conversation trying to decide if what you're doing is right or wrong."

He knew her so well—of course he'd recognize her uncertainty. Even though she'd voiced her concerns for quite some time now, Cam knew her thoughts, but he'd never called her out before. Living with someone for five years would make you pretty in tune to their emotions. She just never thought he was paying that much attention… Perhaps he was. Or, at least he was now.

"This just feels…odd."

He took her hand like he had many times over the years and led her to his awaiting plane. The pilot stood at the base of the steps and nodded his greeting with a tip of his hat.

"I've seen it all when it comes to divorces," he assured her. "Taking a trip before ending things is about the least crazy thing I've heard."

She recalled a few of the outlandish stories he'd tell her about some of the firm's clients. Of course he never told names for privacy reasons, but a few of the divorce stories were enough to make her feel better about herself and this trip she'd agreed to. At least she hadn't asked for an exorbitant clothing and shoe allowance on top of alimony like one of his clients.

"I hope I packed the right things," she said as he handed over the luggage to the pilot.

Cam gestured for her to go ahead of him onto the

steps. "You didn't have to pack anything as far as I'm concerned."

Delilah rolled her eyes. "Of course you'd say that. I actually packed a little of everything to cover all my bases since you didn't tell me where we were going."

She mounted the steps and ducked her head as she stepped into the aircraft. They hadn't used this plane much considering one or both were always too busy with work to take vacations. When she'd mention taking time off to spend together or to just get away from their hectic schedules, he would always say the timing wasn't right for him...ultimately, she finally just quit asking.

On two rare occasions, he took a trip to meet high-profile clients when she'd tagged along, but still every aspect was all about work. He had stayed busy with meetings and she'd found random things to do around the town. Lonely and boring—two other adjectives she didn't want to describe her marriage. No relationship should be that way and she deserved better. So did Cam, which was why they shouldn't be together. If she left, maybe he'd realize that there was more and that he should want something beyond work and being the most sought-out lawyer in his field.

Delilah looked around trying to decide where to sit. No matter where, she assumed Cam would cozy next to her and very likely get this romantic trip underway. Nerves danced in her belly at the anticipation. She had to keep reminding herself these next few days were only part of their final goodbye...this wasn't the time to rekindle anything because the end result would be the same.

Delilah opted for a seat on the leather couch and sank into the buttery-soft material. The two sofas on either side of the aisle were much cozier than the plush chairs in the back. She crossed her legs and waited for Cam to board. She assumed he was talking to the pilot.

Moments later, Camden came on board and headed toward the back of the plane where the bedroom and the kitchen were located. In all the times she'd wanted to escape, part had been because they needed to, but part had been because she'd never had such luxuries growing up. Not that she ever needed all the bling and high-society living. She loved her humble childhood where the main component was Milly teaching them all the ways to be independent and strong. Those were the life lessons instilled in her and now she was making a life she could be proud of.

Being married to Cam had spoiled her, though. She loved being on a team with a determined, successful man. A man who worked just as hard as she did and had an ethic that matched her own. She'd always figured if she married someone who didn't have that drive that there would be an imbalance. Perhaps she should have married someone completely opposite.

She truly wished she had the answers, and she wished turning off feelings could be a simple process without all the mess of confusion and pain. She didn't want anyone hurt by her actions of making that final decision, but she also couldn't let this marriage drag on any longer. She deserved more. They both did.

Camden reappeared with a bottle of wine in one hand and a full glass in the other. He took a seat next to her and handed over the stemless glass.

"I know you like to finish the bottle once it's open," he joked.

Delilah shrugged. "Cork stoppers are for quitters."

She swirled the contents and gave an obligatory sniff. Light and fruity, her favorite. While she loved the rich, earthy notes of a bourbon, she occasionally wanted something lighter.

"It's from a new vineyard in Georgia," he told her. "I have a client whose family owns it and he sent me a box of each of their varieties."

"You must have really done right by him to get that many boxes of wine."

"I'm good at what I do."

Delilah took a sip of the wine as worry spiraled through her. She'd trusted his firm to file the papers in accordance with what they had discussed. She didn't think he'd screw her over and she truly believed he cared for her in his own way…just not the way she needed him to care or to love.

"How is it?" he asked.

"Delicious."

She licked her lips to savor the taste and realized her mistake the moment her focus shifted to him. Those expressive eyes remained fixated on her mouth and that familiar stirring of desire slid through her. She had to set some ground rules or at least figure some things out before they went any further on this impromptu getaway.

Delilah gripped her glass as the plane taxied down the runway. If this trip had happened seven months ago, she would have been in heaven. Knowing that he was putting forth more effort into their marriage before she walked out would have definitely been a turning point in the right direction. She didn't always like to relinquish control, but she wouldn't have minded being whisked away on a spontaneous surprise trip. Unfortunately, that never happened and part of her felt like he was in a panic trying to save something that had already failed.

"I need to know what your expectations are here," she told him.

Camden nodded and settled back, his instant lawyer mode seeming to take over right before her eyes. He relaxed against the couch and extended his arm along the back. His fingers started toying with the ends of her hair as she fastened her belt. Another familiar moment she couldn't escape. Everything was familiar, comfortable... except for the part where this relationship and romantic trip had an expiration date.

"I have no expectations," he informed her. "Whatever happens will be up to you. Of course I want my wife in my bed. I've made no secret about the fact I never wanted this marriage to end. I can admit I haven't been the best husband. I thought I was doing what you needed, but..."

The plane lifted just as Delilah's stomach knotted up. She took another sip of the wine and then set it in the cup holder on the table at her side before shifting in her seat.

"Talking about the actual marriage is probably not a good idea." She tucked her hair behind her ear and chose her words carefully. "This trip isn't a reunion, Cam. This is our final goodbye. We're putting a lid on this box that holds our memories and our time together."

He edged closer, so close she could feel the warmth of his breath and breathe in that signature clean, woodsy scent of his cologne. She'd bought him that cologne last Christmas. She'd been out shopping and immediately knew he would love the scent. Just another reminder of something that was coming to an end. No more shopping for her husband for a holiday or birthday or any other special occasion.

"I'm not pressuring you for anything, but I'm also not ready to say goodbye," he murmured. "And no more talk of endings or marriages or anything outside of this trip. I just want to get back to who we were years ago when we didn't care about anything else but each other."

Those broken pieces of her heart shattered just a little more. She often thought back to when they first met. She traveled down their journey in her mind, wondering where things had started going wrong. But she could see now that they were doomed from the start.

If he wanted to only focus on them, she could work with that. At least she knew how everything was going to end and she could take these final days and have her fill of Camden. She'd use these memories to last her because there would be no more made after this.

"No marriage talk," she agreed, then sighed and steered the conversation to something else. "So, when are you going to tell me where we're going?"

"You'll see when we get there."

"Okay, then can you at least tell me how far it is?"

He shrugged. "Not far."

Delilah rolled her eyes and groaned. "You are such a lawyer with those vague answers."

"And you are terrible at waiting to see what your surprises are because you want everything planned in a nice, orderly fashion that you have total control of."

She picked up her drink again and swirled the last bit around. She should be offended, but he was dead-on. She did like to plan things and wanted her life just the way she mapped it out...which was why this whole divorce nearly destroyed her. Closing such an important chapter of her life, one that was supposed to be the happiest, was certainly never one of her life goals.

"You know I hate surprises," she muttered against the rim of her glass.

Camden laughed. "You love surprises, you just hate when someone else is doing the planning and you don't know all the details."

True. She did pride herself on control and having everything planned out. Her sisters always teased her for all of her planners growing up, but look at her now. Part owner of the country's only distillery run by women. That's why she was in charge of all new client accounts, too. She could get everything set up in a nice, uniform manner to make sure there were no bumps in the road.

"I didn't like that time you surprised me with lilies," she joked.

"I had no clue you were allergic," Cam defended.

That had been the first and last time he'd ever gotten her flowers because he'd been terrified of sending her to the emergency room again. He had surprised her in other ways, though. He'd randomly bring home her favorite takeout or have some gift delivered to their house. Then there were the clothes. So many clothes from designers he'd pay to come to their house. Most women would love such things, but she could shop just fine on her own.

Everything had boiled down to monetary things, which she appreciated, but then she started just wanting simplicity and his time instead of a gift. He had never been willing to give where it actually counted. Sacrificing his time from work or sacrificing a portion of his family to put her in that place would have made all the difference. She wished he would have stood up for her against his family before things spiraled out of control.

She didn't want to be his number one all day, every day. She completely understood he had a family and a career before her, but he'd never attempted to mesh all of those things. Didn't he understand that marriage took a lot of work? Had he believed that once they married the hard part of winning her was over?

She circled back to the fact they weren't going to discuss the marriage, which meant if she wanted to enjoy her trip, she needed to not think about all the ways they'd failed. She still cared for him, still enjoyed her time with him. So that is what she'd focus on.

"Can you just tell me if we're leaving the country?" she asked.

Camden reached over and topped off her wineglass. "We're staying in the US."

Her mind went all over the place. Were they headed to the coast? The mountains? They'd taken a honeymoon to Hawaii so maybe he was trying to recreate their memories by jetting off to their favorite resort.

"You'll never guess," he added with that sexy, crooked smile. "I can see your mind working, but we'll be there before you could ever think of what the destination is."

As the plane leveled out, Delilah unfastened her belt and came to her feet with her glass. She needed to move, because even though their banter had been light, he was still right there. So close, so tempting. She wasn't naive. She knew this trip would bring about a repeat of the other night…which was still something they hadn't talked about.

"Have I been there before?" She turned back to face him as she crossed her arms and stared down at him. "Or is it some place we've been together?"

Camden laughed and shook his head. "We're not going to Hawaii and I'm not telling you anything else."

Delilah pursed her lips and tried like hell to think of where they'd be going. They both loved the beach, so she had a pretty good idea they would be heading to a coast, but which? And they'd only decided this last night, so who had openings? Maybe a client of his had a rental?

"How did you find something on such short notice?" she asked.

He simply stared up at her and winked. That simple gesture was another punch of lust to her gut. He'd done that so many times over the years. When he held a secret that he wasn't about to let her in on, she merely got that wink. The combo with that naughty smile never failed to get another tug of arousal from her.

In his defense, her question had been ridiculous. If Camden wanted something, he got it. While he might have been raised with money and means, he didn't rely on his family name or his parents to obtain his goals. He'd become the best attorney to elite clients and had made a name for himself and his firm.

That determination and tenacity were just two of the qualities she'd fallen for when they'd met. They paralleled each other in so many ways, yet in the end, she knew if she stayed, they'd end up resenting each other. There were just too many negatives working against them.

Why did love and relationships have to be so damn difficult?

Camden patted the seat next to him. "Have a seat. You've got a little while before we land."

Delilah eyed him another moment before she crossed the narrow space and settled in once again. She fastened her belt back into place and took another sip of her wine. She might not know where they were going, but one thing was certain. This trip would most definitely be locked in her memory bank, and very likely her heart, for the rest of her life.

Six

The moment their driver pulled away from the home where he dropped them off, Camden turned his attention to Delilah. Her reaction coming over the bridge to the private island and up the tree-lined drive had been exactly what he'd thought. But now that they were standing in front of the pale blue two-story beach house, he wanted to see her delight.

When he'd first mentioned a getaway, he knew exactly where he'd take her if she agreed. Honestly, he'd started to give up hope that he'd ever get her here, but now his vision had become a reality.

Would she understand the meaning of this place? Should he even say anything? Maybe she wouldn't notice the special touches, but he hoped she did. He hoped she realized everything the place embodied.

"This house is beautiful," she exclaimed as her eyes seemed to travel over the second-story porch, then back down to the immaculate grounds. "Are we the only ones staying here?"

"We are."

She turned her attention to him and that megawatt smile that he'd missed so much now spread across her face. Damn, but she was gorgeous. She had such a natural beauty that he'd initially been drawn to. When he'd first met her at a mutual friend's wedding several years ago, there had been instant chemistry. One slow dance and a few glasses of wine later had been the start to their dynamic relationship and they'd been inseparable since.

Well, until several months ago when she insisted on moving out and demanding he file for divorce. He hadn't seen that coming and he would never forget that initial blow...or the lingering pain.

"Does this place belong to a client?" she asked.

Camden offered her a smile. "Something like that."

He reached for the handle of her bag and his, then nodded toward the entrance.

"Lead the way," he told her. "There's a code for the door."

She made her way up the decorative concrete path and his eyes were immediately drawn to her sexy, curvy frame. Following the sway of his wife's hips had been his favorite hobby for the past five years.

Cam gave her the code to enter and once again watched her face as the door swung open. The entire home had been remodeled and, per his orders, the kitchen had been well stocked for their visit...plus a few other little surprises.

He'd left strict orders for everyone to be gone before their arrival and for complete privacy during their stay. Camden wanted absolutely no distractions or outside interruptions coming between him and his wife...because she was still his wife and he'd fight for her to hold on to that title up until the very end.

"The inside is even more breathtaking than the outside," she gasped as she moved into the spacious open floor plan, placing her purse on the coffee table.

The wall of windows provided a stunning view of the calm ocean. The sun shone high in the sky, giving a sparkling effect on the crystal blue water. The bright light beaming through seemed to frame her in a beauty he hadn't considered before. He knew he'd wanted her here, he knew she'd love it if he could just get her to agree to come, but he hadn't taken into account how reality would impact him even more than the fantasy.

She belonged here. *They* belonged here.

"How on earth did you get this place on such short notice?" She spun around and faced him, but remained at the windows. "I mean, the view is gorgeous and the house is like something out of a magazine. If I lived here, I'd never leave. I'd have to find a way to change careers and work from home."

The pang in his chest only stemmed from regret. He had nobody to blame but himself for putting her in a position that made her feel like her only option was to leave. Marriages definitely took two people on the same page working just as hard as the other, but Camden was man enough to admit the majority of the blame for all the missteps along the way.

"You're in luck," he told her, ignoring the luggage and making his way across the room toward her. "You don't have to leave this house or the private beach, or even the island for the next four days. You can be as free as you want. We're the only ones around and I've made sure everything you could ever need is already here."

Delilah's eyes widened. "I have no clue how you did all of this in such a short time, but I'm impressed."

Camden stepped in front of her and barely resisted

reaching out. He had to be patient. He had high hopes for these four days, but time was not on his side.

"There are definitely moments worth the sacrifice and extra work."

Her tongue darted out and swept across her bottom lip, stirring his desire even more. As if he needed any help in wanting his wife. Desire and passion were two of the main areas they excelled at.

"You really went all out for just four days," she murmured.

Camden shrugged. "Maybe there will be more than four days."

"You shouldn't get your hopes up," she told him. "This isn't a stepping-stone to some glossy future. This is our final trip together. We're making our last memories, Cam."

She might think that now, but he had plans to make her think differently. Some men might take that remark and just give up. Giving up wasn't even in Cam's vocabulary and he knew it wasn't in Dee's, either. They had something special and yes, they might be fighting outside forces, but that didn't mean it was time to call it quits or let anyone or anything else decide their future.

He wasn't going to argue with her, though. His actions would speak louder than any words ever could. And it was those actions, or lack of, over the past five years that had started crumbling their marriage—among other things. But, Camden could and would do his part. Maybe this was too little, too late, but he wanted his wife and he was damn well going to enjoy her during their time together.

"Are you hungry?"

Delilah stared at him, clearly taken aback by his change of topic.

"Um…not really. I wouldn't mind walking along the beach."

"Then let's get changed. I'll take your suitcase to your room."

"Aren't we sharing a room?"

That hope she'd told him not to get up suddenly rose even more. How could it not at her question? She'd assumed they'd be together sharing a bed like they always had…which is exactly what he wanted, but he would never force her or purposely make her uncomfortable.

Cam's heart kicked up as her dark eyes stared back at him. She always had the most expressive gaze, one any man could get lost in. He'd been a victim many times to that strong hold she had over him.

"I want nothing more than you in my room, but I also want you to feel like you're in control here."

"We're on a trip away together and we're still married…for now," she quickly amended. "Put my luggage in the same room as yours."

Before he could turn or even reply, his cell chimed from the pocket of her purse. She stared at him and had the audacity to grin. She might be enjoying this aspect a little too much, but he didn't mind. Whatever it took to show her he was serious, and he loved seeing her smile.

"Is that going to go off all the time while we're here?" she asked with a quirk of her brow.

Camden nodded. "Most likely. Feel free to silence it or just turn it off."

"Has this thing ever been turned off?" she asked, walking to the coffee table before pulling the ringing device from her purse.

She glanced at the screen and stilled, then blew out a sigh and turned the phone for him to see the screen.

His father.

"Answer it," she told him.

No way in hell was he answering. If there was a legitimate issue, his father would leave a message and he could call him back. Camden had always felt smothered as an only child, but he hadn't realized just how much his parents wanted, and tried, to control his life until he married Delilah. If he answered that phone, he would be putting Dee second once again and he had to make her feel certain that she was first in his life now.

But he had obligations and commitments. Taking an hour off was one thing, but four days was an entirely different situation. There were clients who would need him, though he'd told his assistant to take over while he was away. Not having access to the world he'd built did give him pause…but he had to do this. He promised Delilah he would. If he ever wanted a chance, now was the time to make that sacrifice.

Camden took the phone from her hand and declined the call before shutting the whole thing down. As he handed it back to her, he didn't miss the way her eyes widened in surprise or the way her mouth dropped as if she couldn't believe he'd just done that. Yeah, part of him couldn't believe it, either. Oddly enough, the move felt right.

"I meant it when I said these next few days were just for us," he informed her. "Now let's change and take that walk. I have some surprises for you later."

He hoped she was starting to see that he was changing, that he had actually changed and realized what was important. And he hoped like hell he didn't stumble along the way and screw everything up again.

Camden had told Delilah to change and meet him down on the beach. She had no idea what he was doing, but she'd thrown on her bikini and a lace cover-up, tossed a few things in her bag and headed that way. She followed the natural stone steps leading from the house to the sand and still had no idea how he managed to get a house on a private island all to themselves with virtually zero notice.

The man did have powerful friends and high contacts, so no doubt he just asked, but still…

"Perfect day to spend outside."

Delilah spun around as Camden crossed the path with a basket in hand. He'd also gotten more casual and showed up in a pair of navy board shorts and no shirt, leaving that well-defined chest on display. Of course she'd seen and touched every square inch of his body, but she never tired of taking in such beauty.

"What do you have there?" she asked, pointing to the basket.

"Just one of the many surprises I have in store for you." He started heading down the beach. "Follow me."

Intrigued, she fell in step beside him. Camden reached for her hand, something he hadn't typically done when they were together.

"What are you doing?" she asked.

"Romancing my wife."

Part of her wanted to scream that he should have done this for years, but the other part of her opened her heart just slightly, wanting to let him back in. He'd gone to so much trouble and did everything for her…for them. He was trying. He legit wanted her back, she had no doubt about that. His desire to hold on to her as his wife was never in question, but the reality of what they could and couldn't do was.

And just because he went to all this trouble and she was going to force herself to set aside all negative thoughts didn't mean things would work out in the end.

Sweet romance and heated nights wouldn't make their foundation strong and they both knew it.

"I thought you brought me here just to have sex the whole time."

Camden's rich laugh had her smiling. "As much as I love the idea of you being naked for four days, even I need a break. Besides, we never just relax. We're both married to our jobs and never made time for anything else."

"One of us would have made the time," she corrected.

"That's a fair statement," he agreed. "My schedule and clients are demanding, but I am working on that. It won't be an overnight fix, but I'll get there."

She'd never even heard him discuss wanting to fix the problem. Up until she left, Camden never even admitted there was a problem. For him to be so open and willing to change...another part of her heart opened a little more.

"Through there." Camden pointed toward a little opening in a grove of cypress trees. "That's our spot."

Delilah ducked beneath a thick branch and followed the sandy path toward the opening that revealed a stunning cabana. The large thatched roof shaded a white bed and two fat ottomans on either side of a small table. One side of the cabana faced the water just at the curve of the island.

"This is incredible," she exclaimed. "I know we're in Georgia from the license plates we passed on the highway getting here, but this reminds me so much of Hawaii with the tropical vibes."

"The whole island is pretty remarkable," he agreed as he sat the basket on the table. "We could have had a little picnic on the beach, but I figured you'd like this more."

She glanced up at the palm-style ceiling fan. Clearly there had to be some solar power out here, which made the secluded spot all the more amazing. The soft breeze slid through the open sides and the subtle lull of the water relaxed her more than she thought possible.

Delilah stared out at the ocean and wondered when was the last time she'd had such a beautiful day.

"This view is breathtaking. I could stay here all day."

"I agree."

She glanced at Camden, whose eyes were fixed solely on her. There went that flip of her heart once again…and Delilah had that tug of something that went beyond physical. He'd always called her beautiful or pretty and oftentimes sexy, but the way he could look at her and make her actually feel those things was a talent he possessed.

But this vulnerable gaze of his drew her to face him fully. Something about Cam seemed softer, and maybe it was the relaxed atmosphere, but perhaps it was more. She'd never quite seen this side of him and she wondered how long it would last.

A sliver of hope pushed through the fear inside her and she found herself taking one step, then another, until she stood before him. Cam reached up and tucked her hair behind her ears, never taking that intense gaze from her.

A lock of his dark hair blew across his forehead, but he never wavered. His fingertips trailed down her jawline, then her neck, then down the V of her cover-up. Delilah trembled, instinctively arching into his touch.

"You've always been so responsive," he murmured. "Just one touch sets you off."

Only his touch had that effect. She'd never come close to having anything like this with anyone else.

With his eyes still holding hers, he reached for the hem of her cover-up and eased it up. Slowly, the lacy garment swept over her head a second before he flung the unwanted article off to the side.

Delilah stood before him wearing only her two-piece blue bikini. She'd never been comfortable with her body and the extra pounds and dimples in her thighs, but she'd never felt anything but sexy when she was around Camden. He always had a way of making her feel like she was flawless, erasing any ugly thoughts she had about herself. Camden was definitely good for the self-esteem.

"Did you pack this skimpy suit for me?"

He outlined the triangles of her top with just one fingertip along her bare skin. Delilah's stomach knotted with arousal and anticipation. The man could draw out foreplay in the most delicious ways and make her nearly beg before he satisfied her.

"I packed it for myself," she corrected. "But if you want to enjoy the view, go right ahead."

A smile danced around his lips and she couldn't help but stare at that mouth that had pleasured her so many times over the years.

"Oh, I'm enjoying," he told her. "But it's served its purpose."

With an expert tug, he had the ties around her neck and behind her back undone, sending the scrap of strings to the floor. Cam then did the same with the ties on her hips. Delilah shifted to let the bottoms fall as well.

When she started to reach for Camden's shorts, he took a step back.

"No," he commanded. "Let me look at you. I need to see you in this light. So bare and beautiful. So amazingly perfect for me."

How could words be just as much of a turn-on as his touch? Her body burned for him—she ached in a way that only Camden could elicit.

Delilah turned from him and slowly made her way over to the large bed in the middle of the cabana. The breeze whispered over her bare skin as she lay on her back, lifting up on her elbows to stare at him. But Camden was already in motion and the hunger in his eyes was unmistakable.

Her husband was about to have his way with her and she couldn't wait.

Seven

There was nothing Camden wanted more than for Delilah to remove his shorts, but he hadn't wanted to rush things. He meant it when he said he wanted to look at her, to take in all her beauty.

But the little minx had sashayed across the cabana and now lay on the bed tempting him with that sweet, curvy body. How the hell could he take things slow now?

An idea hit him and he turned to grab something from the basket on the table. If she wanted to play seductive games, she had met her match.

With a small container in hand, Camden crossed to the bed where she lay looking up at him with a soft smile on her face. He came to stand beside her and placed the container on the edge of the bed. After popping the lid, he reached inside for one fresh berry.

"Don't move," he ordered. "Watch."

He took one single berry and placed it between her

breasts. Then he grabbed another, placing it just below the first. He continued this until he had a trail down her abdomen stopping just above her heat.

He glanced up to her face and her eyes met his. She continued to stare at him as he leaned down and plucked one berry between his teeth. One by one, he followed the trail with his mouth. He took his time, growing more aroused by the second. Delilah started squirming beneath him and he knew she was struggling just as much as he was.

Good. He wanted her aching and needy. He wanted her to crave his touch and her release. He needed her to want nobody else but him for anything.

He swallowed the last bite as he settled between her legs. Camden stared up her torso to find her looking down at him, her breathing heavy. He lifted both of her legs over his shoulders and smiled a second before he covered her core with his mouth.

Delilah cried out and that sound was the most beautiful he'd heard in a long time. He cupped her backside, lifting her even more so he could pleasure her. A second later, Delilah's hands were in his hair and her hips were jerking. He knew she was close. So close that he slid one finger into her and sent her over the edge.

She came undone around him and Camden relished her passion. This is exactly what he'd wanted from her. He'd wanted her to forget everything but them and just let go.

Once her trembling ceased, he came up on his knees and glanced down at her flushed body. Heavy-lidded eyes stared back up at him and she reached out.

"Now, Cam. I need you."

Physically, yes. But what about emotionally or long-term? When would she admit that?

Definitely a conversation for another time. Right now, he wanted nothing else to even enter his mind other than how to please his wife…and she'd clearly stated she needed him.

Camden joined their bodies and braced himself with his hands on either side of her face. Her ankles locked behind his back as her heels dug into him, urging him on. He needed more. There was never enough.

Leaning down, he captured her mouth with his. She threaded her fingers through his hair and returned the kiss. There was nothing like having his wife wrapped all around him and taking in all her desire.

But after satisfying her and watching her passion explode, Camden was barely hanging on here. He jerked faster and reached down to grip her hips, tipping her higher.

And that did it. She tore free of his kiss and cried out as her body bowed into his. Camden let himself go, gritting his teeth and straining to remain as close as possible to her. He didn't want this magical moment to end. He didn't want to leave this cabana or face anything that would be waiting for them after this getaway.

Camden eased to the side, cradling Delilah in his arms and pulling her with him. He came to lie on his back with her draped all over him. Her hair tickled the side of his face, but he didn't care. That used to annoy him, but now…he wasn't about to move.

"Do you have other tricks in that basket?" she asked after several moments of silence.

Camden laughed, trailing his fingers up and down her bare back. "All of that is food for us, but we're all out of the berries. Sorry about that."

She eased up and glanced down with a wide smile on

her face. "Oh, you can eat all the food if that's what your plans are for it."

He loved seeing her this playful and relaxed. This is exactly what he'd had in mind when he brought her here.

She moved up even farther and straddled his lap as she stared around the cabana.

"Does this place remind you of Hawaii?" she asked. "I know I've said that, but there are just so many touches in the house and here that take me back."

That was the idea.

"There are several similarities," he agreed. "Do you like it here?"

Her attention jerked back to him. "Like it? I'm ready to live here, but I have a distillery I can't exactly pick up and move."

"You could always escape here on weekends or once a month for a reset," he suggested.

"That would get rather costly." She eased off his lap and off the bed. "Though I do think a recharge once a month isn't a bad idea. Even if it's just for a day. Elise, Sara and I have been going nonstop these past few years gearing up for this ten-year launch."

Camden sat up and watched as she grabbed her bikini and retied everything back into place. Such a shame to cover up the perfection, but having her strut around in that little two-piece sure as hell wasn't a bad view.

"You guys have done a remarkable job," he told her. "Even if I didn't know the owners and sleep with one of them, I'd still love the taste of the bourbon."

She faced him now with a wide smile. "We love hearing people praise our spirits. We worked hard on all of it from the taste to the packaging. I'm just glad the ten-year is out and we can breathe a little sigh of relief. I'm hoping that leads to more anticipation when we reveal our fifteen and twenty in the future."

The bourbon process was rather lengthy, but Delilah wasn't one to give up on anything. When she wanted something, she worked too hard to keep it.

Which was why having her move out had hurt so damn bad. He knew she left in part for his sake. He knew she left in some attempt to set him free so he'd be happy in the long run and to keep the relationship between him and his parents secure.

To hell with all of that. He was the one who should be the protector, but how the hell could he protect Delilah from herself?

Camden slid off the bed and went to grab his shorts. He didn't want to bring up any topic that would remind her of what they were fighting against.

"Do you want to have a picnic in here or take it out to the beach?" he asked.

She pursed her lips and glanced out toward the ocean then back to him. "Definitely outside. I love the mountain views where we live, but I want to be on the beach as much as I possibly can while we're here."

"I figured you'd say that." He picked up the basket and gestured for her to lead the way. "You've always loved the water. That's something we'll make a point to add into our schedules."

When she opened her mouth, no doubt to argue, Camden held a hand up. "Don't say it. Let's just enjoy the day."

She closed her mouth and nodded. Relief spread through him that she didn't have a comeback about this being their final trip. Maybe they were making progress or maybe she was just appeasing him. Either way, this was a victory and he was going to ride this high for the next few days.

After that, well…only time would tell what their future held.

"Maybe sunscreen should be packed next time."

Delilah stared at Cam's broad, bare shoulders in the reflection of the mirror. The en suite bath was something from a magazine. The spacious room could have been plucked straight from her mind. Every single thing in here was exactly her taste from the freestanding bathtub inside the monstrous shower to the chandelier over the makeup vanity area to the white chaise in front of the massive walk-in closet.

"I'd take a little sunburn if it meant spending the day with you like we did." His eyes met hers in the mirror. "I wouldn't change a thing."

Yeah, she wouldn't, either. The lovemaking, the picnic, playing in the water…there was so much that had happened. So many memories had been made in just this first day. She'd certainly seen a different side of Camden, and he hadn't mentioned his cell or his work one time. He truly seemed at peace and completely comfortable decompressing.

While she on the other hand had a mountain of anxiety coursing through her. All of the what-ifs kept bumping into one another inside her head.

What if she tried to go back and things worked out? What if they didn't? What if today was a glimpse into the future they could have? But what if it was just a temporary thing?

No matter what question popped into her head, another one came right on the coattails to counteract it.

Why couldn't he have done all of this before? Because

doing it all now almost made her wonder if he was just afraid of failing or if he actually loved her.

Before she could say anything, her cell chimed from the bedroom. She hesitated, but Camden smiled.

"We never said you couldn't answer your phone," he joked.

Delilah laughed as she went through to the bedroom. She'd left her cell charging on one of the nightstands and spotted Sara's name on the screen. She waited, wondering if she should answer or just let it go to voice mail. After losing Milly, she usually answered everything, but now, well, she didn't want to get into a conversation about where she was or who she was with.

"Aren't you going to answer that?"

Delilah glanced over her shoulder at Camden, who stood in the wide doorway wearing nothing but a towel. Her eyes raked down his bare chest and to the knot securing the towel he held at his side.

"I'm thinking," she replied. "Are you getting in the shower?"

"If you keep looking at me like that, I won't make it to the shower."

Her eyes darted back up to his and the ringing finally stopped. The silence surrounded them, the sexual tension enveloped them.

"Who are you dodging?" he asked.

"Sara."

He nodded and, without a word, he released the towel. The white terry pooled around his feet as he simply continued to stare and smirk her way. That man knew what he was doing. He knew she'd never been able to turn down his advances. That's precisely why she'd fled the back room at the Angel's Share gala when he'd kissed her. If he'd even attempted to touch her in any other way, she would have jerked him into her office, locked the door and said to hell with her duties.

"Are you calling her back or joining me?"

Her cell chimed again, indicating a voice mail. If Sara left a message, there must be something important. She pulled her attention from temptation and tapped on her phone, putting the message on speaker.

"Hey, sis." Sara's chipper voice came through the cell. "I know you're on sabbatical, but I wanted to let you know I talked to the PI I hired and she might have some leads on my father, and I wanted to know if you wanted—"

Dee paused the message and regretted putting it on speaker. She would listen to the rest later in private, but clearly there wasn't an emergency. She risked turning back around and seeing the look on Cam's face.

He looked exactly how she thought he would…confused. With those dark brows drawn in and arms crossed over his chiseled chest, the man looked like he wanted some answers.

"How about that shower?" she suggested as she started back across the room.

When she stood before him, he took hold of her shoulders and gently squeezed.

"Want to tell me what that was about?" he asked.

Part of her did want to tell him, but the other part was afraid of opening up that aspect of her life if Cam wasn't going to be part of her future. Her thoughts were so damn muddled, she figured she should err on the side of caution rather than blurting out the truth followed by all her fears.

"Not now," she replied.

A sliver of hurt flashed through his eyes, but it was gone in an instant. She knew he wanted her to share her life, but if they did indeed divorce, she couldn't keep him in all her loops. Once that divorce was final, all ties would be severed and tying up another one would only keep them bound even longer. There had to be an actual end for both of them to move on.

"We agreed not to discuss anything outside of us and here, right?" she asked.

Delilah didn't wait for a reply as she reached for the hem of her sundress and pulled it up and over her head. She didn't have a stitch of clothing beneath and her nakedness quickly distracted Camden.

His lips thinned, his eyes traveled over her and his arousal was impossible to ignore.

"You're trying to change the subject," he murmured.

She reached for him and started backing him into the en suite and toward the tile-and-glass shower built for a party.

"It's working." She smiled. "You don't care about that phone call when you have other, more important things on your mind."

"There's only one important part of my life and she's always on my mind."

That bold statement warmed her, and her heart started healing…she only hoped it didn't break again. How could he shatter her and then attempt to rebuild? She couldn't let this happen. Anything outside of physical could damage her once again, and the fear that curled through her was very real and very scary.

Before she could travel down that maudlin path, Camden gripped her waist and lifted her off the ground. She squealed from the shock, but laughed as he carried her into the shower and immediately turned on all the sprays. The two rain heads and side jets pelted her as she wrapped her arms and legs around Camden's body. He adjusted the temperature, thankfully making the chilled water warmer.

Then Delilah found her back against the tile at the same time his body joined hers. Everything happened so fast, yet so perfectly. Delilah used the wall as leverage to move her body against his. Water sluiced all around them and her hair clung to her shoulders and onto his arms.

When Delilah's eyes met his, her breath caught in her throat. Cam's dark stare held hers with an intensity she hadn't seen too often. The way he moved combined with that passionate glare had her body climbing.

This was how they were, though. Intimacy could be fast and powerful or calm and gentle. No matter how he made love to her, Delilah always felt cherished.

Didn't that count for something? He showed her in so many ways how he felt and maybe she'd misunderstood the way he showed his love.

But being cherished didn't mean the man had completely changed. It only meant he didn't want to lose and he was fulfilling that promise to make these the most relaxing four days.

But four days wouldn't erase all the neglect and hurt from their past.

"Stay with me, Dee," he murmured as he leaned in closer. "Stop thinking, stay right here where we both need to be."

He was right. She had to get out of her head, at least for the moment.

Delilah framed his face with her hands and captured his lips. She loved kissing him, she loved having his hands all over her as she grew closer to her release. There were times she simply couldn't get enough and being without him for seven months only heightened her need.

The other night in the car and earlier at the beach had only whet her appetite for her husband.

Cam slid his hands between their bodies and touched her where they joined…sending her body soaring. She closed her eyes and moaned as her climax slammed into her. Her knees tightened against his sides and his hips jerked even faster, drawing out her pleasure.

Within seconds, Camden stilled and tensed as he let himself go. She clung to him, wanting to feel every bit of his release. He dropped his head to her shoulder and pressed her a little harder against the tile.

Moments later, he eased back and brought his head up. "Did I hurt you?"

Delilah smoothed that dark, damp hair from his forehead. "Not at all."

"Damn. I should have taken my time, but…"

"Yeah, but…"

Their desire was stronger now than ever. Those words didn't need to be said aloud they were both so aware. She could think of little else.

"Do you want to talk?" he asked, helping her to stand on her own feet.

"About what?"

He spun her so the spray wasn't right in her face and slid his thumb across her bottom lip. "That phone call earlier."

Delilah chewed on the inside of her cheek and glanced away.

"Hey." He cupped her face and turned her attention back to him. "No matter what happens or the outcome with us, I still care. I always will. You can trust me with whatever is going on."

"You haven't always stood up for me or made it clear I can trust that you'll be there."

The muscle in his jaw clenched and he waited a beat before he answered. Dee wondered if she went too far, but those words needed to be said. Hiding her feelings for years certainly hadn't helped this relationship.

"I never want my trust to be in question." He stroked her bottom lip as he continued to hold her gaze. "I mean it when I say I've changed and that you are the main priority in my life. No matter what, I need you to know that and the only way for you to realize is for my actions to back up my words."

Those actions hadn't been backed up before, so only time would tell if they would now. She knew in his heart he was sincere, but she also knew that outside this little getaway bubble they were in, real life would likely consume him once again. Not to mention, if they went their separate ways, she couldn't keep depending on him as her sounding board. She had to stand on her own two feet and work through her own issues without Camden.

For the first time in months, she wondered if she should stay and try to make this all work…but she also shouldn't be making any postcoital decisions regarding her marriage and her future.

Eight

Delilah padded her way from the bedroom and down the hall. She hadn't explored the house since arriving yesterday. She'd been a little busy enjoying herself, but her stomach growled and Camden was still sleeping so she figured she'd find the kitchen and get breakfast started.

She passed by the living room, pausing for just a moment to appreciate the breathtaking view once again. She figured the kitchen had to be off the living room and she was right. This room might just be the showstopper. The rest of the house was incredible, but this oversize eat-in kitchen would sell the house. Whoever owned this property was one lucky guy.

There was a wall of glass doors that would open to allow the space to be one big entertainment area. The covered patio had cushy sofas and hanging chairs with lush plants all around. And the infinity pool that overlooked the ocean was another upscale added bonus.

Delilah made her way toward the large center island. There were stools around three sides to accommodate plenty of guests. Who needed a home this large? Whoever it was clearly had a big family or they just loved living the high life with lavish things.

When she turned to find where the coffee was located, she spotted a gorgeous bundle of flowers in the window above the sink.

Hibiscus and they were fresh. Another added touch from the people who rented out this place.

The flowers with the ocean in the background had her once again thinking of her honeymoon. Camden had given her a pink hibiscus each evening for her to put in her hair before they went to dinner. She couldn't help the smile that spread across her face as she stared at the blooms.

This trip was exactly what she needed and she was so glad she decided to meet Cam at the airport. There was still that fear inside, though, that all of this was temporary. She'd come on this trip dead set on having a fling with him and making this their final goodbye, but she was so torn. If their life could be like this all the time, maybe there was hope. Maybe they stood a chance. Granted this was a mini-vacation and things couldn't always be sunshine and rainbows in any relationship, but now that they both saw how good things could be…could there be a future?

There was still that issue of his parents' disapproval, and Camden wanted a family. She had her own family drama going on right now with discovering her adoptive sisters were actually biological half sisters and that their adoptive mom, Milly, was in fact their aunt. Her own family had solidified even more and even though the revelation had caught her off guard, she felt even closer to her sisters. She wanted that personal, intimate connection with Cam and she'd always assumed whomever she married, she would also have that tight bond with her in-laws. Unfortunately, the opposite had been true.

Delilah rubbed her head as she searched for coffee in the pantry. According to documents they'd uncovered in Milly's house after her passing, Delilah, Elise and Sara's birth mother had been an addict and ultimately passed while in prison. Milly had shielded them from the hurt and sought them out as toddlers to adopt all three. Milly had been a saint to be a single mother of three young girls, but she'd made everything look so easy.

And now Delilah had the choice whether to look for her biological father or let it go. Originally she didn't want more disruptions in her life, but now she wanted to know where she came from. She wanted to know her heritage. Her mother had been white, so Dee clearly got her darker skin and hair from her father. Did she look like him? Did she have other siblings she didn't know about?

Elise had decided not to search for her father, but Delilah and Sara were both interested enough to want to do some digging. Delilah wasn't sure what she would do with the information if and when she found the man.

It was all still too much to take in. Every change in her life seemed to explode all at once lately and she could only deal with one crisis at a time. Which was the exact reason this trip and the serene setting did wonders for her frazzled nerves and battered heart.

"Are you going to stand in front of the pantry until breakfast appears?"

Startled, Delilah spun around, her hand to her heart. "I thought you were sleeping."

Camden rubbed his bare chest as he walked into the

kitchen and glanced around. "I was, but I typically don't sleep in so this was a change."

"I remember," she told him. "You were always up and out the door before I even had my first cup of coffee."

He came to stand in front of her and leaned in for a quick kiss. "I should have stuck around and had a cup with you."

Considering they could do nothing to change the past, she didn't want to get into the "could have" or "would have" scenarios.

"You can have that cup now," she offered. "Do you know where things are? I assume you've been here before?"

"I've been here a few times," he admitted. "Go sit out on the patio and I'll whip up something for us."

Delilah laughed. "You're going to cook breakfast?"

Clearly offended, Cam crossed his arms over his chest and raised a dark brow. "How hard can it be?"

"Well, don't let me stop you." She patted his cheek and offered a smile. "I'll take my coffee first, if you don't mind."

As she started to skirt around him, Cam snaked an arm out and around her waist, pulling her back against his side. His eyes held her in place and that desire started brewing once again.

"I don't take orders very well," he murmured. "But, considering you're standing here wearing my shirt and looking sexy as hell, I'll allow it."

She'd tossed on his shirt and nothing else before she'd left the bedroom. She wasn't trying to be sexy, more like trying to be quiet so she didn't wake him, and his simple white tee was the closest thing she'd reached for. But if this would get her added perks, she'd be wearing nothing else the rest of this trip.

Delilah opened the sliding glass doors all the way to let the morning breeze in. Everywhere she went on this property, whether inside the house, the cabana or on the private beach, kept her wishing she could stay here. But, this wasn't her home—it was just an amazing vacation. She wondered how much this went for and if she could get it for her and her sisters to have a girls' trip some-time. They could all use a break if leaving the distillery at the same time would even be a possibility.

She settled into the corner of one of the sectional sofas and propped her feet up. She'd have to take advantage of that pool tonight. Swimming beneath the stars, or better yet, skinny-dipping, had quite the appeal.

Something crashed in the kitchen, quickly followed by a string of cursing. Delilah merely smiled and decided to let Cam figure it all out. She kind of liked him taking charge and looking after things. She'd never been one to relinquish control, but if he wanted to do this for her, she wasn't about to argue.

Him wanting to care for her was sweet. Oh, he'd said that's what he wanted to do all along, but that version of caring and this were totally different. She didn't need to be cared for financially—she needed care for her soul. She needed that emotional support more than she needed anything else.

Could Camden really be that guy now? Did her leav-ing and filing for divorce give him some sort of wake-up call? She hadn't even thought that possible. She truly didn't know what to expect or think when she'd left. All she knew was that she couldn't stay any longer. The longer she stayed, the more that tension and re-sentment would grow. She loved him too much to have him resent her down the road. There was also an un-healthy amount of resentment from her side. The times when Cam could have stood up for her, been there for her, he hadn't. Now he wanted to rectify all of that and she truly believed that's what he thought he could do, but only time would tell and she didn't know if she had more to give.

Delilah still didn't see how everything could work between them. A few days in paradise on a secluded island wouldn't solve their problems, but this did make her see that she still loved him. She enjoyed their time together if their time could always be like this…with a caring, thoughtful husband who put their marriage above all else. Oh, she knew any relationship had bumps and dips, but she had grown tired of going up against the only people in his life. His parents had gone so far as labeling her a "gold digger" when she and Cam married and they'd stuck by that even though she'd proved that she could stand on her own.

Milly had instilled independence and strength in each of the girls. Having her gone was definitely a void, but her spirit and legacy lived on and Delilah wanted to make her proud. Milly had always loved Camden and believed Dee and Cam belonged together. When they separated Milly assured her that she and Cam would work it out. Delilah could sure use some advice right now from the sweetest lady she'd ever known.

Two monumental moments in her life had collided— Milly's death and the impending divorce—and Delilah wasn't sure how to grieve, quite honestly. Her emotions seemed to be torn in all directions and the fear that she was doing everything wrong was a real threat.

"Fresh coffee, a splash of unsweetened almond milk, and sugar-free vanilla syrup."

Delilah shifted her attention to Camden, who stood before her presenting her with her favorite coffee. She reached for the steaming mug and inhaled the robust aroma.

"I'm impressed you had my coffee order items delivered here," she told him as she took a sip.

"Impressing you is my new mission," he stated. "It should have been my mission all along, but I took you for granted and assumed you'd always be around."

Delilah gripped the warm mug with both hands and blinked up at him. "It's just coffee, Cam. It's okay."

"It's not okay," he countered. "It's these little things that you needed, that I recognize now."

He raked a hand down his jawline; the coarse hair of his beard bristled against his palm. He struggled, that much was evident, but she hadn't realized just how much so. All this time she'd been thinking about her pain, her problems, but Camden had been experiencing his own anguish.

Cam moved and sank onto the edge of the sofa next to her hip. He stared out at the water and she waited for him to grapple with his thoughts. She didn't know if he was going to share anything or if he just needed a moment. Either way, she was here.

And maybe that's what he needed. She'd been wanting him to be there for her emotionally, but had she been there for him?

Damn. Had she been selfish this entire time?

"It's so ridiculous," he muttered with a soft laugh. "The day after you left, I went into our bathroom to get ready for work and it hit me. I stared at that stupid bath mat and cursed everything because I missed seeing your tiny footprints on there."

Delilah nearly upended her coffee at his vulnerable statement. She'd never heard him admit anything so sweet, so from the heart. Did all of this stem from him wanting to win or did he legitimately want to expose his true self and emotions?

She placed her hand on his thigh. "Cam—"

A buzzer from the kitchen went off and Camden came to his feet. The moment passed, but it would forever live inside of her. His admission healed something in her own heart, a piece that had been shattered. But the fact he'd been so open with her was another layer of balm that soothed her pain.

How could they just move on to breakfast and a normal day after this? He'd exposed a piece of himself. He'd never been that open before in all their years of marriage. She didn't want to gloss over this or not recognize how important this was for him…for them.

Trust had to be a key player in any relationship from here on out. If she'd discovered anything recently, that was certainly it. Milly had lied, though her reasoning was justified on her part, but still, the sting of that betrayal continued to linger. She had to trust that Cam was doing all of this for her for the right reasons and not just because he hated failing. There was more to a marriage than just winning.

Delilah sat her mug on the accent table and came to her feet. As she made her way into the kitchen, she couldn't help but laugh as Cam waved a kitchen towel through the smoke over the stove and turned on the exhaust fan.

Another string of curses had her laughing even harder. Camden glanced over his shoulder and sighed.

"I hope you like your bacon well-done."

"It's my favorite."

Who knows. Maybe vulnerable admissions and burnt breakfasts were their new beginning. Maybe this was a chance at something new and they could work on seeing

how they could maneuver this life together, because the
only way to do that would be to start over.

This vacation wasn't just a respite for her mind and
spirit but a fresh start for their entire future...if she could
trust everything happening here.

Nine

"So tell me about this guy Elise is engaged to."

Camden sat on the second-story porch just off the main bedroom. He'd tucked himself in the corner of the sofa and Delilah had sat at the other end with her legs extended along the cushions, her bare feet propped in his lap.

"Antonio is amazing and they are so perfect together," she told him, her voice dreamier than usual. "He's so supportive of her and she's the same for him. He'd come from his small town in Spain to do some tours of vineyards and distilleries for his family's restaurants. He and Elise got locked in the cellar of the castle and apparently fell in love."

Camden laughed as he slid his thumb up the arch of her foot and back down. They'd been out here since the sun went down and their wineglasses had been emptied, but neither was ready to get up. He was fine with that.

The longer he had her relaxed and talking, the more hopeful he felt that she was coming around.

"That's quite a meet story," he replied. "I take it he's moving here?"

"He's going to be doing a great deal of traveling, but they will mostly be in Kentucky. They're getting married at the castle. It will be our first major event and we're planning to open it up for more after that."

Camden nodded in agreement at the idea. "That sounds like a brilliant business plan. Turning an old historic castle into a distillery was your first excellent move. You guys have really tapped into something magical."

"We have, but if the product isn't good, then nothing we do will matter," she explained. "I'm just glad we have that great gin that we were able to slide into the industry while we waited on the bourbon to age in the barrels."

"You're so damn sexy when you talk business."

Delilah laughed and leaned forward to swat at his shoulder. "You always say that."

"It's true," he defended, moving to stroke her other foot. "That intelligent mind of yours is just one of the reasons I fell so hard for you. You and your sisters were already in the process of perfecting your bourbon, you had the castle and had just finished renovating and then opened it to the public for tours. You were talking about the process of how to bottle and the goals you all had. It was amazing to watch you check each one off your list."

Delilah tipped her head and rested it against the cushion. The stars shone bright tonight with the full moon. The subtle sound of the waves relaxed him even more. What if he'd taken her away on a trip like this from the start of their marriage? What if, instead of working his ass off to prove to her he could care for her, he actually showed her?

"I know your parents think I was struggling with An-gel's Share, but—"

"No."

There was no way in hell he was going to let any neg-ativity ruin their peaceful evening.

"No matter what they believe, then or now, I know the truth. I never once thought you were using me."

"I've discovered how important family truly is," she went on. "Especially lately. And the idea of continuing to be that barrier between you guys really guts me. Mil-ly's death just drove home that our separation was the right thing to do. At the end of the day family is really all you have and can fulfill a piece of you that no career could do."

He released her foot and shifted until he faced her. He eased in closer and rested his hand on her thigh.

"Listen," he urged. "Everything going on between my parents and me started long before you. I didn't re-alize it until we married. They've been controlling all of my life and I didn't know any better but to let them. So when I defied everything they wanted from me, they didn't know what to do and you took the brunt of their anger. But I had dealt with them for so long that I never took what they said to heart. I now realize that you did."

He paused, then replayed her comment in his mind. Something niggled at him, something that he wanted her to open up about. He wanted, needed her to trust him with everything if this was going to work. How else could they move on? Because he knew she was thinking about it. Delilah wanted this just as much as he did...but she was afraid and it was his job to make her feel secure.

He suddenly had new goals for this marriage, and he took his jobs very seriously. Now he just had to figure out how the hell to juggle it all because failure in any aspect of his life was not acceptable.

"You said you realized the importance of family, especially lately," he reminded her. "The loss of Milly is a big part of that, but is there more? Maybe something that has to do with Sara's phone call last night?"

Delilah stared at him for a moment before turning her attention out toward the ocean. Camden waited. While he wanted to know, he also didn't want to push her to where she wasn't comfortable.

"Sara found some letters," Dee stated, still staring out into the starry night. "Old letters and documents in Milly's house last month. We found out that we are actually biological sisters."

"What?"

She faced him once again. "Well, half sisters."

"Dee, that's amazing."

He stroked her leg and inched even closer at this shocking news. The three of them had always been so close, like best friends raised as sisters, but to know they had some of the same genes—that was such a shock.

"That's what Sara called about," Delilah went on. "She wants to find her biological father. Elise said she's happy the way her life is and she's not interested in looking."

"What about you?"

"At first I didn't want to because life was chaotic enough, but after thinking about it, I want to know where I came from," she told him. "I want to know if I look like my father or if I have other siblings. But then I think like Elise and I'm happy with the family I have, and do I want to disrupt someone else's life? He might not want to know he has a child somewhere, or on the other hand, maybe he knew about me and didn't want me."

Camden's heart clenched. He couldn't imagine all the

thoughts and doubts swirling through her mind. Add all she'd been dealing with regarding their marriage and Milly's death…

"Do you know anything about your biological mother?" he asked.

Delilah nodded and sat up straighter, pulling her legs in and crossing them. Clearly the topic had her on edge and unnerved. He didn't blame her. He had no idea what was going on in her head right now. This was a bomb of information that she likely was still trying to process.

"She was Milly's sister, actually," Dee finally stated. "Our mom was an addict and went to prison so we were placed in foster care. Long story short, Milly tracked us down and adopted us. Our mother ended up dying in prison so I never knew her, never even saw a picture of her."

Even with the constant friction with his own parents, Camden couldn't imagine never knowing either of them or having one taken away. There was no common ground here or any possible way he could fathom what she was going through. Having someone listen who wasn't one of her sisters would be the best thing for Dee right now.

"My thoughts are all over the place," she went on. "Some days I want to know who my father is and other days I think it's best I don't. I know Milly was protecting us, but was that because this was so much to handle, or maybe our fathers were not good people. I just don't know. I do think that if I had the information, I'd have a little relief, you know? Like, everything is there and if I decide I need to reach out, then I can."

"That makes sense," he assured her. "You would have the control that way and some of your life will be back in your hands."

She offered a soft smile and tipped her head. "You get

it. I wasn't sure what you'd say or even if I was going to tell you."

He reached out and took her hand, giving a gentle squeeze. "I'm glad you did. Have you talked to Sara since she left that message?"

Delilah shook her head. "The girls don't know about this trip. I just told them I was off the grid for a while and would see them in the office when I get back."

Camden didn't like the lump of fear that settled in him. He knew why Elise and Sara didn't know about Dee's plans. She wasn't ready to tell them anything was going on. She'd told him coming in that this was a final trip, their last goodbye and their final memories together.

But he'd thought for sure she'd started coming around. He knew Delilah so well and there wasn't a doubt in his mind that she was thoroughly enjoying herself and finally releasing some of her stress. Of course, he'd had no idea just how much she'd been holding in.

"Whatever you decide, I want you to know you can count on me," he told her. "I'll support you or give you advice. Anything you need."

She blinked and the moonlight caught the shimmer of unshed tears in her eyes.

"This," she murmured. "This is what I need. Just for you to be present in the moment, to listen to me. You don't know how many times I wanted that. I *needed* it."

The guilt of all those years of not opening his eyes and paying attention weighed heavy on him. He couldn't change the past, but he could sure as hell change the present and future. He had to prove to Delilah that she was just as important as his career and family. But trying to put everything in that first place slot was going to be damn difficult.

Without a word, Camden eased her legs aside and

came to his feet. He bent down and scooped her up into his arms, cradling her against his chest as he carried her back into the house. She rested her head against his shoulder and sniffed. The only time he'd seen her cry in all their years together was at Milly's graveside. Even though they'd split, he still had to be there to offer his support. Not to mention he'd loved Milly, too.

But even when Delilah had told him she was leaving, she hadn't shed a tear. She'd been stony and strong and determined. That was his Delilah. She'd always been so resilient, but there was only so much any person could take. He never wanted to see her break, and he knew she'd never admit she needed help or might be falling apart, but he was glad he was the one here.

Cam moved over to the bed and gently lay Delilah down before crawling in beside her and pulling her into his arms. She nestled against him, her hands clutching his T-shirt as if holding on for a lifeline.

"I'm not going anywhere," he murmured against her forehead. "I'm always here. No matter what."

He just hoped like hell she would always be there, too.

"What now?" Delilah asked, following Cam's lead down to the beach toward the cabana area. "You don't even have the basket. Did you forget the fruit?"

He smiled as he reached back for her hand.

"I didn't forget anything," he assured her. "Everything is down here."

They had one more day left and she was not ready to see their time here come to an end. The way Camden had comforted her last night, held her and soothed her pain...that was so much more than she'd ever thought she'd receive from him.

Her heart had flipped. Camden had turned over something within her he'd never done before and the connection had absolutely nothing to do with intimacy or sex. He'd been the rock she didn't know she'd been needing. She knew she'd wanted him mentally present, but she didn't realize that she'd started to crumble until he'd picked her up and carried her to bed. They hadn't made love, he'd simply held her.

Who knew absolutely no words would be the key to starting that healing process?

"Stop here."

Delilah came to a stop at his command and glanced around.

"What am I supposed to be doing?" she asked.

"Close your eyes."

She jerked back and shook her head. "Oh, no. I'm not closing my eyes. You know I don't like surprises."

He shielded her eyes with his hand. "You love them. We've already been over this. Now just let me do this for you."

She sighed and obeyed, but that didn't mean she had to like it. That whole fear of the unknown always sucked the fun out of the actual surprise, but she was learning to relax…or at least she was trying. So far everything Cam had done for her had been absolutely spectacular. He'd spoiled her in every single way.

Was this really the new Camden? Was her husband turning into the person she'd needed? If he was, was there even a possibility they could forge a deeper bond and overcome the issue that his parents caused? Trust was something that had to build over time and much more than four days allowed for. But she was seeing a change, she was seeing his efforts, and that had to count for something…right?

"I'll cooperate, but only because you've done so well with the surprises," she joked.

Camden's laughter had her smiling. One large hand covered her eyes and the other took her hand and led her through the soft sand.

"There's nothing in front of you but me," he assured her. "Just keep coming. We're going inside the cabana, so I'll tell you where the steps are."

He led her carefully and she trusted him completely. How could she not? Camden really did have her best interest at heart and he seemed to be thriving in growing their bond even though she'd told him this wasn't a stepping-stone into their future. The man wasn't giving up and everything about that attitude was sexy as hell.

Camden guided her into the cabana with ease and then he released her.

"Open your eyes."

Delilah blinked and took in the sights. Two ladies stood beside large white tables. Soft music filled the open space and there were fresh pink hibiscus all around the place. In vases, lining the floor to the tables, across the bed.

She turned her attention to Cam, who merely smiled at her.

"You can't relax without having a nice massage," he told her. "I remember how much you loved them."

From their honeymoon. They'd gotten a massage every single day.

But this...this was all so amazing. He'd managed to get people onto the island and all set up and she'd had no clue.

"You went to a great deal of trouble for this," she murmured.

Cam merely shrugged and gestured toward the tables and smiled. "No trouble at all and you need this."

That she could definitely agree with. She had no idea if Cam finagled this all this morning after her mini-meltdown last night or if he had this day planned all along. Regardless, he knew exactly what she needed. This wasn't just a getaway; this entire trip was an awakening.

"Hello, my name is Ann and this is Carey," one of the masseuses said. "We'll step out while you two undress and get under the sheets. Then we'll get started on your deep tissue massages."

As they stepped out, Delilah turned to Camden and threw her arms around his neck. She smacked a kiss on his lips and eased back.

"You're going to make this very difficult to leave here," she told him.

His hands went to her backside and he gripped the material of her sundress and started pulling it up. She shifted so he could pull the garment over her head.

She'd put her swimsuit on beneath because she'd had no clue what they were going to be doing.

"New suit?" he asked, his eyes raking over her.

"I've had it a year or so, just never had a reason to wear it. There's not exactly been opportunities, working fourteen hours a day and gearing up for the bourbon launch."

He reached behind her neck and untied the red halter top, then went to her back and did the same.

"You look amazing in red," he muttered as his fingertips trailed over her bare breasts. "Maybe I should send the ladies away and work on you myself."

"Let's let them do their thing and then you can do what you want later," she proposed. "I'll even wear the red if you want."

He dropped to his knees and started sliding the bottoms down her legs. "Oh, I want," he stated, staring up at her.

Once she was completely undressed, she had to move toward one of the tables before she forgot about the women and let her husband have his way.

"They're going to come back in soon and you're not going to be ready." Delilah climbed onto the table and covered her bottom half with the sheet. "Better hurry so we can get to our own private plans later."

He kept his dark eyes on hers and reached behind his neck to grab his T-shirt. He jerked it over his head and then eased his shorts down. He took them and all of her clothes and placed them on an accent table before coming back to the tables.

Once he lay on the one next to hers, he reached across and took her hand.

"You belong here," he told her. "Just like this. Beauty surrounded by beauty. I'm glad you came with me."

Yeah, she was, too. The ladies came back in before she could answer. Delilah simply squeezed his hand in response and couldn't wait until they could be alone again.

Ten

"Just let me retire here and tell my sisters to visit."

Camden laughed and stared at Delilah's back. She stood at the edge of the balcony off their bedroom, staring out at the sunset, with the wind blowing through her hair. She wore some little pair of shorts that barely covered her backside and a tank that didn't quite cover her midsection. She was breathtaking and now more than ever, he wanted her to fight for this, for them, because he wasn't about to give up.

"There's no reason we can't come back," he told her.

He remained in the open doorway from the bedroom, leaning against the jamb. He could stand here all evening and watch her as she enjoyed the private island and all its beauty. This was exactly how he'd imagined her and everything she'd needed to start to heal. They both had healing to do, but his sole purpose right now was succeeding with this marriage.

Her hair whipped in the wind as she glanced at him over her shoulder.

"Will there be a chance for us to come back?" she asked.

This was tricky. Every moment with her could make or break their future. But he had to be honest and he had to lay everything on the line.

"We can come here any time you want, Dee. I own the island and the house."

Her eyes widened as she turned to face him completely. Silence settled between them and she continued to just stare.

"I bought this place right before you moved out," he went on when she still said nothing. "I had plans for you and I coming here to renovate, but then you left and I had the changes made with you in mind."

Delilah took one step, then another. With her eyes locked onto his, she slowly closed the distance between them.

"You own all of this?" she asked. "And you're just now telling me?"

"I was going to surprise you, but then you packed and left," he defended. "So at that point I didn't want to say I did this and have you think I only did it to get you back. I had plans in motion before you ever moved out. But then as time went on, I knew I wanted to surprise you after everything was complete. I was seriously hoping you didn't see this property listed in the original divorce agreement."

She continued to stare in disbelief. The gentle ocean breeze lifted strands of her dark hair and slid them across her face. Camden reached out and smoothed the wayward pieces behind her ears and framed her face.

"All I could think was how happy you were on our

honeymoon," he went on, gliding his thumb over her bottom lip. "You looked so beautiful each night with the flower in your hair. You would smell it each time before you put it in."

"That's why there's been hibiscus here," she murmured. "How did you get all of this done, though?"

Camden shrugged. "I placed a few phone calls."

"What would you have done had I not shown up at your hangar?"

Cam laughed. "I would have enjoyed a massage and all the food I had stocked, I guess."

She looped her arms around his neck and smiled. "I can't believe you bought an island for us."

"I had to do something," he replied. "I was losing you... I *lost* you."

Delilah blinked and bit down on her bottom lip for a second before she let out a sigh and leaned her forehead against his.

"Part of me thinks there's no way we can get past the fact your parents never accepted me, and I don't want to be the person who keeps you guys in turmoil," she told him. "I still worry that your job will come before me and that you won't see me as an equal in this. I can take care of myself, but I need you by my side, not three steps in front of me trying to pave the way."

Camden tipped her head back and leaned in even more, his mouth hovering just above hers. "And what about the other part of you?"

Her lids lowered as she feathered her lips across his.

"The other part wants to be selfish and naive and pretend this marriage isn't in trouble." She trailed her lips down and across his jawline. "I want to live in this fantasy world you've created for me."

Camden covered her mouth, coaxing her lips apart.

She gripped the back of his neck and pulled him in even closer as she aligned their bodies from hip to chest. They always fit so flawlessly. How the hell were they not meant to be when everything seemed so right?

Okay, maybe not everything was perfect, but nothing in this world was. Delilah was *his* perfect.

Delilah pulled back and cocked her head with a saucy grin. Damn it, that woman knew exactly what to do to get his blood pressure up in the very best way. She hooked her thumbs in the waistband of her little shorts and slid them down her shapely legs, then kicked them aside. She slowly pulled the crop tank up and over her head, also discarding it without a care.

"Make love to me," she commanded. "Out here, with the sunset in the background. I want to stay in this fantasy for as long as possible."

Camden rid himself of his clothes in record time and had the distance closed between them in one stride. He gripped Dee by her backside and lifted her against his body, then carried her over to one of the plush sectional sofas. He eased her down right in the corner and immediately dropped to his knees.

"I can never get enough of you," he told her. "You're it for me."

He slid his hands over the outside of her calves and on up to her knees, moving over her smooth skin to her inner thighs as he spread her farther apart. Delilah leaned back and inched down toward him, silently pleading for him to touch her. That familiar look in her eyes had his own arousal pumping. She could give him a look that would make him do anything she asked.

His thumbs grazed over her core and she gasped, tilting her hips. Looking up her body was his absolute favorite view, but having her here in this home he'd bought for them to work on rebuilding their future was a whole other level of much-needed bliss.

"Wait." Delilah moved back and edged around him to come to her feet.

"Stand up," she commanded. "I think you need to be properly thanked."

His entire body stirred as he came to his feet and kept his eyes on hers. She smiled and reached out, trailing her fingertips over his bare chest and farther down. Then she dropped to her knees, her mouth closing around him. Camden slid his fingers through her hair and groaned as she pleasured him with her mouth. He ground his teeth to keep some sort of control, but he had never been able to hold himself back with Delilah.

He selfishly enjoyed the moment, but then stepped back and lifted her up. He was about to lay her on the sofa when she pressed her hands flat against his chest and pushed him down. With a smile on her face, she straddled his lap and arched her back, silently offering up her breasts.

Another aspect he could never deny. She was absolute perfection, especially with the kiss of the sun on her skin.

Delilah joined their bodies as he cupped her breasts in his hands. She groaned as she rocked against him. Her hands rested on his shoulders and the slight sting into his skin from her fingertips had his body climbing higher. And from the way she was breathing and biting her bottom lip, she was damn close to her own release.

Camden gripped her face and pulled her mouth down to his. She opened freely for him as he swept his tongue into her mouth. She jerked her hips harder, faster, and let go.

Her entire body tightened around him, but he held her

in place, not wanting to break that kiss until he had to. Camden's body tightened as he let himself go, too. Delilah shifted her lips over his and lightened the kiss as the tension from her body relaxed.

Once his own climax had waned, he nipped at her lips, feathering his mouth across hers.

"I think this balcony is my new favorite spot on the island," he told her.

Delilah stared down at him, her dark hair falling down around them. "I'm still partial to the cabana."

Camden slid his hands to her backside and carefully came to his feet. She wrapped her legs around his waist and rested her head on his shoulder.

"Where are we going?" she asked.

"I thought we could go lie in the bed and finish watching this sunset." He stepped into the bedroom and made his way to the bed. "Then we can go back out and I can see how your skin looks under a starry sky."

He laid her on the bed and his heart flipped when she stared up at him. Her midnight hair spread all around her on the stark white bedding. Her skin was still all flushed from the intimacy.

"I wouldn't mind seeing the stars with you," she told him with a wide smile. "We should rest, though. I might want to take a longer look at the stars than we did the sunset."

She was going to be the death of him. Her words…her actions. She knew exactly what to say and do to make him completely powerless where she was concerned.

He lay down next to her and wrapped his arms around her. A sense of peace settled over him. Right at this moment, nothing was wrong in his life. He chose to embrace this exact time with his wife in his arms, a gorgeous sunset in the distance, and the hope that something promising was coming from their time together.

Delilah stared out the window as the plane lifted from the runway. He knew she wasn't ready to say goodbye to this remote little island, but they both had treasured memories locked deep inside. No matter the outcome between them, nothing could erase the magic they'd shared over the past four days.

If four days with no outside interruptions could heal so much, what would happen if they tried this marriage again and focused more on each other and carving out that private time? While they hadn't broached those subjects, he had to believe they would, and because of what they'd experienced in the last few days, there was a new hope that once they had real talks, there might be a chance. He wanted to believe that, but he still had to be cautious.

Cam rested his hand on her thigh and Delilah turned to face him. From the look on her face, she definitely wasn't ready to leave. There was something so special about the memories that had taken place on this island—memories that would last a lifetime.

"We'll come back," he vowed.

"That implies there's a future for us."

He slid his thumb beneath her chin and tipped her head up slightly, then closed his lips over hers. The brief kiss only served one point and that was to show her, to make her feel, that he wanted to be with her and make this work.

"There can be a future for us," he told her.

She closed her eyes and dropped her forehead against his. He knew thoughts were racing through her head and he had no doubt she was already starting to think of all the obstacles in their way.

"These past few days make me want to believe that," she muttered. "There are just so many things, major things, that we didn't discuss before we married and we've glossed over since."

Camden had to do something to alleviate her worry, to prove to her that they could start taking steps toward the life she wanted...the life they both deserved.

"I know the timing of this topic might not be the best, but I need you to know something." He pulled back and took both of her hands between his as the plane leveled out. "If we stay together and decide to start our own family, I never want you to worry about where my loyalties would lie. I would love nothing more than to have a child with you, but mostly because I think we'd be kick-ass parents and we both have so much to offer."

"Children aren't really on my radar, especially right now," she replied. "I'm so busy with my job and with the animosity surrounding us from your parents, added with how busy you always stay with work...it wouldn't be fair to any child to bring them into this mess."

Camden nodded. "I agree with everything you said, that's why I need you to know—that chapter in our lives would be completely different. So if we have a family someday, fine. If we don't, that's fine, too. What matters is working on us."

Delilah eased her head down onto his shoulder and blew out a sigh. Silence filled the cabin and he wasn't about to push. This getaway had gone even better than he'd ever imagined, so he couldn't expect her to move right back in and pick up where they left off.

No. That's not where they needed to be. They had to start in a better spot than they left off.

Delilah didn't say anything else and after a while, he noticed her breathing had softened, her body had gone lax against his.

Carefully, so as to not wake her, Cam eased his arm around her back and cradled her against his side. He scooted slightly down, taking her with him so she wasn't so upright.

The fact she'd fallen asleep on him took him back to when they very briefly dated. He'd taken her to a concert and on the ride back home, he'd taken her hand and they'd sat in silence while he drove and she ultimately fell asleep. He didn't recall a time that she'd gotten that relaxed since.

Delilah was always go, go, go, and he thought that's what made them so perfect for each other. But now Cam was starting to see that she had been going nonstop with her work and start-up for Angel's Share all while trying to keep their marriage afloat. He'd been so damn oblivious, he'd thought everything was fine.

Well, other than his parents never approving and still trying to be part of his life but not Delilah's. After spending all of this time with her, his future was still quite questionable, but his goals had completely shifted. There was still so much left to explore in their relationship and giving up wasn't an option. He'd said that before, but his eyes and his mindset had been opened up and he had a clearer vision now.

Everything was at stake…and not just failing. There was so much more to this marriage than winning or losing. And the real possibility of having Dee walk out on him forever scared the hell out of him.

Camden closed his eyes and rested his head against the back of the couch as his own thoughts swirled around inside his head. He was already calculating what clients he could shift to his colleagues and what upcoming trips he could postpone or also hand off. He owned the damn firm. It's about time he acted like it and trusted his staff to handle more cases instead of overseeing every single thing.

As far as his parents, he was going to have to have yet another discussion with them. There was going to be an ultimatum declared and if they didn't like it, well…he'd have to deal with that when and if that happened.

Eleven

"Come back home."

Delilah stilled as Camden's bold command came out of nowhere. They'd landed safely and Camden had brought her luggage over and loaded it into the trunk of her car. She'd had every intention of talking about their future while on the plane, but she'd finally run out of energy.

Their precious, stolen time had come to an end and she was still so confused. Of course she wanted everything to be perfect and dreamlike the way it had been on their island. But she was realistic and that's just not how life worked.

Were they strong enough now? Was this reconciliation even a possibility?

"I'm not asking for an answer about our future," he added, reaching out to slide his hand into hers. "I'm asking you to give me another day because I'm not ready to spend another night without you."

Neither was she.

Delilah pulled in a deep breath and nodded. "I'll come over. Let me run back to my house first and change out my bag. I'll grab a few extra things and we'll see how one night goes."

Camden's smile widened. "Grabbing extra things sounds promising."

"I'm not promising anything yet."

He grazed his lips across hers. "But you didn't tell me goodbye."

Then he stepped back and moved his sunglasses from the top of his head to cover his eyes. "See you in a bit. At home."

At home.

This whole situation seemed too perfect, like they were moving fast again.

Just like they did the first time.

But Cam had said he wasn't looking for a solid, definite answer. No, he wanted one more night...and honestly, so did she.

Delilah got into her car and pulled out of the lot. She wasn't going to analyze this moment. She didn't have to be at work until tomorrow morning so she was going to enjoy the rest of her time off.

Then she'd have to go to her sisters and beg them to help her figure out what the hell she was going to do.

Elise and Sara were probably the worst ones to ask, though. Elise was still in that happy stage where hearts were dancing all around her head and Sara was like a walking happily-ever-after movie. The woman believed in love and she believed there was one person for everyone.

Added to that, both of her sisters loved Camden and

had tried to give her advice over the years. Now, though, she was more confused than ever.

Delilah made it to her rental and back to Camden's within an hour. She was surprised he didn't come out to greet her, but she grabbed her bag and her purse and headed up toward the front door.

She stood there for a half second trying to figure out if she should knock or just walk right in...which was ridiculous. This was still her house and if she wanted to start moving forward with Cam, she needed to show how she felt.

Dee opened the door and stepped into the two-story foyer. Old habits had her immediately turning to punch in the alarm code. She shifted back around and took in the place she'd called home for five years.

The ambience was exactly the same. The only thing that was different was the vase that used to be on the accent table by the door. That vase had been a gift from Milly for their wedding, but now it was secured in Bubble Wrap packed away in some box, probably still in the spare bedroom. For the past seven months she'd been meaning to get the rest of her things, but she'd gotten busy with work and one excuse after another had gotten in the way.

Delilah glanced toward the wide staircase leading toward the second floor and wondered if Camden was up there. A smile spread across her face as she sat her purse on top of her suitcase. Most likely he'd already started some sort of surprise for her, knowing him. She kept telling him she didn't like surprises, but he'd been so right in calling her out. She just didn't like that lack of control.

But he'd done a stellar job so far, so maybe she could learn to let go more.

Camden had been trying so hard to make her happy, which she appreciated. But at the same time, she didn't want him to feel like he had to do these things in order to keep her. Just being present was a huge improvement and she wished she could see into the future to see if he would keep that promise. She wished she could trust her gut and trust Cam to see his promises through.

Delilah started toward the staircase, but the light in the den down the hall caught her attention. She moved toward the room where Camden usually did late-night work. Odd that he would be in there now when he knew she was coming over.

As she stepped into the doorway, there he was standing at his desk, holding several papers in his hands. He still had on his shorts and T-shirt from this afternoon when they'd left the island. Clearly, whatever he was staring at was troublesome since he hadn't even noticed she was here.

Worry niggled at her and she could practically feel the invisible walls of reality closing in on them once again.

"Is everything okay?" she asked, remaining in the doorway.

He jerked his head up. "Dee. I didn't hear you come in."

Obviously. Concerned, she stepped into the room and stopped at the leather sofa. She eased her hip onto the arm and tried to see what he was holding, but he wasn't offering any insight. She tried to remain calm, but this wasn't the same Cam who she'd spent the last four days with and this wasn't the same man she'd just left at the airport who had asked her to stay.

"You seem a million miles away."

"They came," he said, holding up the documents for her to see.

He didn't have to tell her what "they" were. Her heart clenched; her breath caught in her throat.

The divorce papers. The first set had been wrong and had to be completely redone and now they were back. All she and Cam had to do was sign.

If this wasn't a slap of reality to the face after such a beautiful getaway…

Delilah clasped her hands in her lap and chewed on the inside of her cheek. She wasn't even sure what to say, what to do, and clearly Cam was in the same boat considering the room was dead silent.

It was that silence that spoke volumes. They were at a fork in the road and neither of them wanted to take the next step for fear of making the wrong decision.

"I… I wasn't expecting to come home to this," he finally stated. "I was just hoping for junk mail."

He turned and tossed the papers onto his desk before shifting his attention back to her. Cam rested his hands on his narrow hips and met her gaze, clearly waiting on something from her. She'd never seen him look defeated, but if there was ever a time, this would be it. His shoulders weren't so square now, his jawline lax, and his dark eyes were shielded by heavy lids. A punch of guilt and remorse hit her. She never wanted anyone to go through pain, not her or him. But she also had to think of long-term ramifications, and if staying would only hurt them more in the long run…

At this point, she wasn't so sure.

"I'm not sure what to do here," she told him. "I mean, a week ago I would have been ready to sign just to have a clean cut and move on. I would have signed to set us both free of this heartache."

He remained in place, as did his intense gaze. "And now?"

"That's the proverbial elephant in the room, isn't it?" She came to her feet, unable to sit still any longer. "If we sign, that's it. Our marriage is over. If we don't, then we're both saying there's a chance for something more, a fresh start."

She paced across the room to the desk and stared down at the papers. Their names in bold print stared back up, but it was the photo on the desk that caught her attention. It was a photo she'd seen there so many times and never thought much about it…until now.

She and Cam were kissing under a waterfall on their honeymoon in Kauai. That day had been amazing. They'd hiked for hours and then found the waterfall and dived right into the refreshing water. They'd been on a tour and hadn't known the guide had taken the picture until they were ready to check out of their resort.

Once they'd gotten home, Delilah had put the picture in a frame and Cam had immediately claimed it as his own. There were times she forgot about the photo until she had a reason to come in here, but for the past five years, that photo had been there where he wanted it, maybe where he needed it to be. Perhaps he looked at it and remembered the best time of their lives. While she didn't have the image to look at all the time, she did have the memories that she often pulled back up on rough days.

Delilah's eyes went from the photo to the papers and back to the photo. So much had happened from one event to the next.

"Say something."

Delilah turned her attention to Camden, who stood with his hands still on his hips, looking just as frustrated as she felt. But he kept his gaze locked on her. And, honestly, she wasn't sure if he was frustrated or terrified of what would come out of her mouth.

The chime from the front doorbell echoed through the foyer and down the hallway. When he didn't make a move, Delilah came around the desk.

"Are you expecting someone?" she asked.

"No, and nothing is more important than this."

She started to pass him, but he slid his arm around her waist before she could.

"Ignore it," he said.

His concentrated look left her no choice but to remain still. They did need to talk about the future, whether together or separate. While the getaway had been perfect, they were back to reality and all that came with it. Decisions would have to be made. She just didn't think she'd have this much trouble.

But when love was the center of everything, that made leaving so damn hard. If she didn't love him so much, this would've been an easy break. But perhaps their love had been misplaced. Maybe they loved the idea of the marriage, of being a dynamic team. Love had to flow between them, building a bridge that would keep them forged together forever.

The doorbell chimed once again and Camden jerked away, muttering a curse as he headed out of the room. Delilah blew out a sigh at the intensity of the moment and she didn't know if she cursed the unwanted guest or wanted to thank them for giving her a moment to think.

Moments later, Dee heard familiar voices and she stepped out into the hallway. Nothing good was going to come from this because if she thought the last few minutes had been trying, the next few were going to put that to the test.

Cam stood in the entryway with his parents and all eyes turned to her. Great, just what she needed to top off seeing her divorce papers…one of the main reminders of why they were in this situation to begin with.

Twelve

Camden wished more than anything he had not answered the door.

No, he wished he and Delilah had stayed on their own private island and said to hell with the rest of the world.

"We've been calling and texting for days," his mother fussed. "We were worried sick, Camden. We've been coming by, but then we saw her car and knew you were here."

Camden glanced over his shoulder as Delilah started down the hallway toward them. He wanted to shield her from any hurtful words that were no doubt about to be said, but he also knew she had her pride and wanted to stand on her own. There was such a fine line here.

"I forgot to give his phone back," Dee stated as she moved toward her bag in the foyer. "It's been off for a few days."

His mother rolled her eyes. "Of course you've had it. No wonder I couldn't get hold of my son."

"I texted you both and said I'd be out of town," Cam told them. "Is there an emergency?"

His mother's eyes went to Delilah, then back to Camden. "Not an emergency, but if you had listened to your messages or had she given them to you, you would know we are planning a trip to Tahoe. We actually wondered if you'd like to join us and get away to decompress. You've been dealing with so much."

Camden raked a hand over the back of his neck trying to ease the tension.

"We actually just got back from a trip, so I'll pass."

Both of his parents glanced at Delilah, who had come to stand beside him now. She handed over his phone and he pocketed it.

"So she's controlling you now?" his mother asked. "Money wasn't enough for her?"

"Listen—"

"I don't want, nor have I ever needed Cam's money," Delilah stated, cutting him off. "I don't know why you always say that or imply that I cannot take care of myself. I am part owner in a lucrative business and this marriage was never based on anything other than love. And I'm tired of defending myself to you. I'm tired of the way you're always meddling and making Camden feel like he's being torn in two and has to decide between his parents and his wife. You should be ashamed of yourselves."

Camden had to bite the inside of his cheek to keep from smiling. He also had to keep his applause inside his head, too. Delilah had never talked to his parents in such a way. In all honesty, she typically avoided them since they'd let it be known from the start that they didn't approve of her middle-class upbringing.

Damn, she delivered a verbal punch that had been a long time coming. Yes, they were his parents and he loved them, but Dee had put up with more than enough over the years.

"Nobody talks to me that way," his mother sneered.

Delilah reached down and grabbed her bag and purse. "I just did."

Camden gripped her elbow. "Don't go."

"You three need to talk without me and I need to get back to reality. Unfortunately, this is it."

Camden watched as she walked out of his house— their house. How the hell had he gone from bliss this afternoon to heartache tonight?

Dee was right. This was their reality for right now and something had to change. He had to change.

"I cannot believe you went on a trip with her." His mother crossed her arms over her chest. "What happened to the divorce?"

"What Delilah and I are doing or not doing is none of your concern," Camden informed her. "I've let this go on for far too long, thinking you two would come around to seeing what an amazing woman she is."

"Son, we just don't think she's the one for you," his father stated in that softer tone of his that grated on Cam's nerves.

"It doesn't matter what the two of you think because I'm the one married to her."

"For now," his mother quickly added.

No. That wasn't right at all. None of this was ever meant to be temporary and the marriage never should have been about winning or losing. He loved Delilah, more than he'd ever admitted—maybe even to himself. He needed her, more than he needed to succeed.

"Forever, if she'll stay," Cam chimed in. "Though I can't blame her for wanting out. She says it's to set me free, but the truth is, she's been stuck here trying to hold a marriage together that you two condemned every chance you got. But I have to take some of the blame as well. My work schedule is too much and I didn't realize that."

"She's trying to control you," his mother fired back. "You are too successful to back down."

"I'll still be just as successful, but I'd at least have a happy marriage. I hope."

Cam waited for one of them to say something else. The tension in the foyer had gotten out of control. He wanted Delilah back here; he wanted to carry on with the night they had planned. He wondered what she was thinking now. Was her mind on those damn papers in his den? Was she wishing she'd never come here tonight?

He hoped like hell she realized he had her back. He would always have her back, from here on out, no matter what.

So in a sense, he was deciding between his wife and his parents and he didn't know why it took him so long to realize.

"You both have put me in a position that I feel like I do have to choose one family or the other."

His mother blinked and jerked as if he'd slapped her.

"She is the one making you choose," she defended. "Not us."

"Actually, she's the one who walked away to try to save my relationship with you two." His heart ached just thinking about what she'd sacrificed. "So don't throw down your noble card just yet."

"Camden—"

"No." Cam held up his hand, cutting off his father. "I'm working on my marriage. You guys can either support that or not, that will be your decision. But know that if you force my hand in choosing, you won't like the outcome."

His mother's gasp echoed in the foyer. Frustration and fatigue hit Cam and he just wanted to be done here. He'd said what he needed to say and all he cared about at this moment was Delilah. She'd been through too much and he'd let it go, hoping everyone would eventually come around.

No matter his parents' initial thoughts on Dee, couldn't they see that she was a genuine person? That she loved and was loyal and stood on her own? If anything, he needed her. Not the other way around.

Camden stepped around his parents and went to the door. He opened it and turned to them.

"We're done here," he told them. "Enjoy your trip to Tahoe."

The silence and intensity went on for longer than he was comfortable with, but they ultimately left and Cam closed the door, reset the alarm system and raked a hand down his face. This whole day had done a complete one-eighty and he had no clue what to do next.

Did Delilah want space? Did she want him to come to her?

How the hell could he be so in control of his firm, his career, and lose hold of his family? His priorities were shifting and part of him worried what would happen if he eased up on work. His entire life he'd been molded to be a successful attorney, working for the next promotion, the next milestone. Once he'd gotten his own firm and started employing the best lawyers, he'd grown to that next level. His name was well-known among the most elite clientele.

No doubt he'd made his parents proud, which was what he'd wanted when he'd been younger. As an only child, who wouldn't want the accolades?

But then he'd met Delilah and suddenly he wasn't their

perfect son doing everything they wished. Slowly, so damn slowly, he'd started seeing that he'd been like clay to his parents. They'd shaped him into precisely the man they'd wanted him to become. Prestigious and wealthy.

Had he lost himself along the way? Is that why finding and marrying Delilah had been so appealing? She'd breathed new life into his world…she still did. He was going to fight for her, for them, to prove to her that she did come in first place in his life from here on out.

Cam wasn't sure if Delilah needed the space tonight or not, but he was going to give it to her because he needed to clear his own head. There were going to be some major changes coming up and he wasn't sure how everything would turn out. He could be putting everything on the line for a marriage that was still doomed to failure, but he wasn't going to just let the best thing in his life slip away.

Now, more than ever, he was determined to make this right.

"You look like hell."

Delilah glanced up from her computer and spotted Elise in the doorway to her office. She sank back in her leather chair and sighed.

"You're always so forthcoming with those sweet compliments," Delilah replied.

"I mean that in the best way." Elise stepped into the room and closed the door behind her. "It's my way of asking what's wrong? Because I thought I'd come in this morning and you'd be all chipper and ready to go after taking a sabbatical."

Yeah, well, she probably would have been if she hadn't been up all night worrying, pacing, playing out every scenario in her head of different paths in her life…wondering why Cam hadn't texted, called or come by.

What had happened between him and his parents when she left? Did anything get resolved? Did he tell them they were working on the marriage? Did they try to talk him out of moving forward with her? No doubt they reminded him over and over of how successful he was and how career and finances came above all else. Delilah doubted those two even knew what love was and she highly doubted they even loved each other.

"Where did you go, anyway?"

"To Georgia with Cam."

There was no reason to lie or evade the question. Her sisters were her very best friends, and now more than ever, she needed them. She really wished she had Milly for some sound advice, but Elise and Sara would be just as solid. They were all raised by the same astounding woman, and Delilah knew she'd get through this.

Silence settled between them as Elise sat with eyes wide open. Finally, she pulled out her cell, her fingers rushing over the screen.

"What—"

"Don't say anything else," Elise commanded. "Sara is on her way. We need details."

"We have jobs to do," Delilah reminded her.

"Tours are covered, every employee showed up today, no meetings or VIP clients are scheduled. We have the time."

Of course they'd make her rehash this right now. Delilah had hoped she'd come into work and get caught up before getting into everything. But better to just get it over with.

Sara burst into the office, immediately blowing her hair out of her face and closing the door behind her.

"I ran up here and I just know that tour starting thought I had a raging case of diarrhea."

Delilah couldn't help but laugh. "I'm sure they didn't think that."

"You spent the last four days with Camden?" Sara asked, taking a seat next to Elise across from Dee's desk.

"I'm laying it all out now and I'll take questions at the end," she informed them. "Cam asked me to give him four days to work on our marriage. So I met him at the airport, and we flew to a private island off the Georgia coast, which I found out he bought for us, by the way. The house was amazing and secluded with our own beach and cabana. We flew home, our new divorce papers had arrived and then his parents showed up and wasted no time in declaring their disdain for me once again. That pretty much sums up my last four days. Questions?"

Her statement was met with shocked stares and silence. There had been quite the whirlwind of emotions and events that Delilah was still trying to process herself, so no doubt her sisters were rolling over everything she'd just dropped on them.

"Does this mean you guys are getting back together?" Sara finally asked.

"That's the million-dollar question," Delilah replied. "We know what we want, but at the same time, I have to be realistic. I don't know what happened after I left last night. Cam and his parents likely had a heated discussion."

"Are they so stuck in their high-society ways that they still can't let you in?" Elise asked in disbelief. "I mean, they do see that we have a very successful business, right?"

"It's my background, I'm sure," Dee explained. "We all had humble beginnings, no real parents, and Milly was a simple schoolteacher. Nothing too exciting or brag-worthy in their world."

Elise rolled her eyes. "Those two aren't anything to brag about, either. I don't care what job or rank someone has. Treating people equally and respectfully is more important than anything."

Delilah nodded in agreement. "They didn't get that memo in grammar school."

"Have you talked to Camden since last night?" Sara asked.

"I haven't. No text or anything. I'm sure he's over-whelmed. That's just one of the reasons I'm trying to set him free."

"Oh, would you just stop with that nonsense?" Elise scolded. "Marriage takes two people and it's so obvious you two love each other."

"Love isn't the only thing that keeps people together," Delilah replied.

"No, you're right, but Antonio and I overcame obsta-cles and we're going to make it work." Elise leaned for-ward in her seat and held Dee's gaze. "Listen, I'm not judging you or saying you guys didn't work, but I think you both were working at the wrong things. Now that you know what the enemy is, you can better tackle it."

Delilah sighed. "There's just so much, and I know I definitely take part blame for not speaking up and stand-ing up before now, but I just thought things would get better, you know? But his work always comes first, his parents are against us, and what about if we ever start a family? I don't even know if that's something I'm ready for. Is that terrible?"

"Just because you're married doesn't mean you have to have children," Sara told her. "There's no rule book as to what you have to do with your life. What you and Cam need to do is get back to why you fell in love to begin with, before all this other stuff got in your way."

"That's why he wanted us to have that getaway," Delilah murmured. "He just wanted us without all the outside noise."

"Can we focus on the fact he bought you an island?" Sara laughed. "Because that is the most romantic thing I've ever heard."

Delilah couldn't help but smile. "It was pretty damn cool," she agreed. "He bought it before I asked for the divorce. He was going to surprise me. But once I left, he said he had the house remodeled to mimic various parts of our honeymoon."

"Okay, now *that* is the most romantic thing I've ever heard," Sara corrected.

"The house and island were pretty remarkable."

Too remarkable. Too perfect. And he'd done all of that for her not even knowing if she'd ever be there. He had that hope, so surely she could, too. Right?

"So what are you going to do?" Elise asked.

Delilah sat forward in her seat and rested her arms on her desk. She'd analyzed this situation from every single angle and still didn't have a solid answer.

"My biggest fear is that I go back and we end up here in six months or a year. If nothing changes, I've gotten my hopes up again and I'm in for even more heartache."

"But what if you go back and everything is absolutely beautiful?" Sara asked.

Delilah's cell vibrated on her desk and she glanced down to see Cam's name. She tapped the screen to pull up his message.

We need to talk

Yes, they did, but what would this conversation be about?

"What is it?" Sara asked.

Delilah glanced at her sisters. "Cam wants to talk."

"Then go," Elise stated, waving her hands. "Get out of here and go talk."

Delilah shook her head. "No. I'm working today and so is he. I'll tell him we can meet up tonight. I still need to think a little more before I see him."

When her sisters just continued to stare, Delilah tipped her head and smiled.

"I'll figure this out, so stop looking so worried."

"We can't help it," Sara told her. "But since you're thinking on Cam and we're up to speed, can I ask an opinion?"

"Of course." Delilah was so ready to change topics. "What's up?"

Sara pulled her cell from her pocket and typed in a few things before turning it around. "This is some information I found out about my father. I think his name was James, but I don't know anything else."

"Oh my word, Sara," Elise exclaimed. "You have a name. That's incredible. Your investigator works fast."

"I paid her enough to do so," Sara replied, then turned her cell back and scrolled more. "It might be a long shot, but my investigator said the timing is right for a guy named James who actually worked as a counselor at one of the facilities supposedly our mother had worked on during one time when she was clean."

Delilah was pretty impressed with the fact they had a name for Sara's father. Even though they all had different fathers, they were in this situation together and had to support each other no matter their decisions.

"What if she finds out more?" Sara asked. "I mean,

what if I get his information and he's alive? What if he still lives around here? Does he know I exist?"

"Those are all the same questions we've asked ourselves," Elise replied. "I'm still fine with not knowing. I love Antonio and the life we're going to have together. I just want to look forward to that. But I'm here for both of you, no matter what you decide."

"Agreed," Delilah said with a nod. "I want to, but it's just all the rest of the chaos in my life that's not letting me focus on my biological father."

Elise came to her feet and glanced down at Delilah. She offered that soft smile that oftentimes looked like Sara's…that trait had to have been from their mother.

"Tackle one major life issue at a time," Elise stated. "And whenever you all are ready, we'll get rolling on this wedding of mine."

Sara clasped her hands. "Girl, I got you. I've condensed the spreadsheet just for you."

Delilah snorted. "I'm ready whenever you are. It will be refreshing to focus on something solid and positive. Besides, working today on packages for events and weddings is the top of my list…ironically so."

Elise wrinkled her nose. "Do you want me to take that over?"

"Absolutely not." Delilah stood and shook her head. "I love my job and I want to do something creative. So, this and your wedding planning will be perfect."

Sara also stood and slid her cell back into the pocket of her maxi dress. "If anything gets overwhelming, for either of you, come to me. I've got no social life right now, so I'm available. Just living with the anxiety over what my investigator will find out."

Delilah came around her desk and opened her arms.

"Bring it in, girls. We haven't done a group hug forever and I think we all need one."

Her sisters gathered in and their foreheads touched as they huddled together. This might do more for Delilah's spirits than anything else. No matter what, she knew these women would have her back. They'd support her and comfort her no matter what and she'd do the same for them.

"Do we have to go back to work?" Sara asked. "I'm interviewing for a new gift shop manager. I hate doing interviews. I think I get more nervous than the applicants."

"I'll do it," Elise said. "It gives me a break from sales reports."

Delilah shifted in her chair and clasped her hands together. "That's settled then. You two get back to work and let me get caught up. We'll talk later."

"You'll let us know if there's any developments with Camden?" Elise asked as she headed toward the door.

"Of course, but you guys don't have to run up here if I text. Just go about business as usual."

Sara snorted. "Nothing about our lives right now is business as usual. We're all up in the air in one manner or another and Milly's house is still not—"

"Don't do it," Elise groaned. "Don't say there's more to clean out. I can't handle anything else right now. That house isn't going anywhere, but my sanity is."

"Fine." Sara crossed to the door and stood by Elise. "We'll wait to discuss, but you better keep us updated about Cam."

Delilah nodded and waited until her sisters were out of her office before she reached for her phone on her desk and fired back a text.

Meet me at my house after work

She didn't want to go back to the house they shared. If they wanted to talk and be alone, her new place was best. His parents didn't even know where that house was, so they wouldn't be interrupted.

Delilah had no clue where they stood, but talking about those papers and his parents had to come above all else. Definitely not the alone time she wanted with her husband.

Thirteen

Camden didn't want to go to her rental. That's not how he wanted to progress in their journey to reunite. He wanted to bring her home, where she belonged.

When she'd texted and told him to meet at her place, he'd waited a bit and mulled it over. Talking things over at her rental didn't sit well with him and it really shouldn't to her, either. He thought he'd get some backlash from her when he texted back saying he preferred their house. After several long minutes she'd agreed to meet him at his house. She kept referring to it as his, but he wasn't going to have any part of that.

They shared this place. Her stamp was all over it, from the wall art she'd chosen to hang in their bedroom, to the flowers she'd planted herself around their porch, to the sofa she'd fallen in love with and ordered even though he'd told her it was hideous. Every room had memories of Delilah, but he wanted the real deal.

He'd just poured her a glass of wine when the front door alarm echoed through the foyer. Camden sat the glass on the wet bar and moved through the living room to greet her. As he stepped through the wide arched doorway to the foyer, Delilah turned after resetting the alarm. She smoothed the moisture from the rain away from her face and sat her purse on the accent table. She didn't have a bag, which meant she hadn't planned on staying. That silent act spoke volumes for how this night would go.

"Hey," she greeted with a smile.

She'd left her dark hair down around her shoulders and had changed from her office clothes. Her black leggings hugged her long legs and she'd put on an oversize tee that hung off one slender shoulder. He didn't care if she dressed up or dressed down—or didn't dress at all—she was still the most remarkable woman he'd ever known.

Water droplets clung to her silky hair and her face glistened with dampness. With her dark skin and hair and that shoulder playing peekaboo, she looked like a seductress.

But there was something vulnerable beneath that sultry exterior. She looked terrified or worried or perhaps both. The last time they'd stood here had been so intense that he still hadn't recovered, and he had no idea where she was in her headspace.

"I have a glass of pinot in here for you," he offered, gesturing to the living room.

A smile spread across her face as her shoulders softened. "That sounds perfect. I've barely been able to catch my breath after work today."

"It's always a bit overwhelming that first day back after taking time off," he agreed.

Delilah took a seat on the chaise portion of the sofa while Camden went to get her drink. When he turned back around, she'd toed her shoes off and had already propped her feet up. The way she stared back at him already had his desires stirring, but they seriously had to talk.

He handed her the wine and stood over her, resting his hands on his hips.

"Are you hungry? I can go find you something."

Delilah took a sip and then shook her head. "No. Elise brought me a late lunch."

"You're not staying the night."

He didn't ask, but he wanted that put out there. He wanted to dive right into this conversation and work through any confusion or misconception. Because he'd assumed she'd want to spend the night…he'd hoped she did.

"I'm not," she agreed, licking the wine from her lips. "We need to talk and sometimes sex gets in the way of us staying on track and focusing."

Oh, he was damn well focused on his wife. He'd been unable to focus on anything else.

"Just because you're not spending the night, doesn't mean we won't have sex," he countered.

A hint of a smile danced around her lips. "True, but I'm trying to avoid temptation as much as possible."

"You're saying I'm too tempting?"

She shrugged and took another sip without answering.

Camden eased down to the foot of the chaise, next to her legs. He rested his hand on her thigh and stared back into her dark gaze. He'd gone over and over what he would say to her once they were alone again, but words failed him. He wasn't going to beg—he'd never be that person. Delilah either wanted to stay or she didn't.

His purpose was to show her exactly why she should. This marriage was worth fighting for.

"I want you to stay," he told her.

"I'm aware." She swirled the contents of her glass and glanced down. "There's just so much to process and I don't know what happened with your parents after I left. I never heard anything."

She brought her attention back to him, clearly waiting on a reply.

"I gave them the ultimatum that should have been done before now," he explained. "If I have to choose between two families, then that's what I'll have to do. It sucks, it's unfair to everyone, but I won't keep putting you through this."

"And that's exactly what I didn't want to happen. I don't want to be the reason you guys have a falling-out that you might never recover from."

He squeezed her leg. "You aren't the reason for their narrow minds."

"No, but I am the reason for the rift."

Camden took her glass of wine and sat it on the side table. Turning back, he rested his hands on either side of her hips and closed in.

"I won't live like this anymore," he told her. "We won't live like this."

"I want to believe it," she whispered, her eyes darting to her lap. "I want to think you and I will always put each other first."

Her expressive midnight gaze slid back up just as a crack of thunder shook the windows. Of course a storm surrounded them…that seemed to be the theme as of late.

"What happens when you slide back into working and traveling so much? Maybe I'm selfish and maybe I'm a hypocrite for wanting you to spend more time with me when I work so much, too."

Cam nodded in agreement. "Trying to get a new business off the ground requires work. We both had a tendency to assume the other would just be there."

Delilah reached her hand up and slid her palm over his jawline. Cam reached up and covered her hand with his own.

"When you left, nothing else mattered," he admitted. "Nothing. I had to drag myself into work to keep occupied and make sure my clients' needs were met, but all of my thoughts were on you and us and how the hell I let things get so out of control."

Delilah closed her eyes and sighed. "I'm tired. So tired of thinking this is a failure, tired of not being able to hold on to what I want and tired of the fear that if I open my heart wide again and it gets broken, I'll never be able to recover."

Hearing her so vulnerable and honest had his own heart cracking. He slid their joined hands down to her lap and held tight. Her lids fluttered open and there was no hiding her emotions. She looked at him as if seeking an answer she'd been needing—as if wanting him to tell her that their lives would be fine and she had nothing to worry about.

As much as he wanted his wife back, he also couldn't lie to her.

"I can't guarantee things will be perfect," he admitted. "All I can say is my priorities have shifted and I realize what is important."

"I swear, I never want to be that clingy, needy wife," she explained. "I just want to be a vital part of your life. I would never want you to feel like I love my job or anything else above you."

"The fact that you married me after knowing me such a short time speaks volumes," he told her with a smile. "You think about everything. You have all these detailed plans and are determined to check off every box. Once I realized that about you, I was shocked you agreed to marry me after only a few months of dating."

Delilah laughed. "I surprised myself, too, not to mention Milly and my sisters. They thought I was joking."

Camden shifted between her legs, maneuvering so he sat on the chaise and she straddled his lap. This was definitely one area of his life he didn't mind relinquishing control. He pulled her in tighter until she hovered just above him and her hair curtained their faces.

"We have something that has lasted five years," he explained. "Maybe they weren't the best five years, but I'm not ready to just give up and I won't let you, either. If I thought you truly wanted out, I'd step away, but I know you don't."

She rested her forehead against his. "No, I don't. I only wanted out to save both of us any more heartache."

Camden slid his hands down her back and to the hem of her shirt. Gathering the material in his hands, he eased back to keep all of his focus on her.

"You don't have to do anything anymore," he assured her. "You've fought for this marriage long enough and now I'm taking over."

He pulled the shirt up and over her head, tossing it aside. The lightning flashed once more as the thunder continued to boom.

"From here on out, I've got you," he vowed.

She opened her mouth to say something, but he wasn't in the mood to talk. That's why she'd come here, but seeing her again after that ordeal with his parents and knowing just how much she had sacrificed over the years only made her that much more precious to him.

His Delilah had stepped away so that he could repair a damaged relationship, but living without her wasn't an option. No matter what he had to do, he'd find a way to push on, even if he had to carry her the entire way.

Delilah's hands were up his shirt, her fingertips trailing along his bare skin. She started tugging and he pulled away just enough to rid himself of the tee. Then she came alive in his arms. Still straddling his lap, her hands went to work on his pants.

In a flurry of motions, they stood and completely stripped down to absolutely nothing. Camden went to the wall and dimmed the lights. He wanted nothing but that raging storm for the setting. The flashes of lightning lit up Delilah's bare skin as she lay back on the chaise and reached for him.

Damn it. This is where she belonged. There wasn't a doubt that she knew that.

She lifted her knees and eased her legs apart, silently pleading for him. He wasted no time in settling in right where they both wanted him to be. Flattening his hands on either side of her head, Camden leaned down to nip at her lips. His chest brushed against hers just as a groan escaped her. He reached down between them, feathering his fingertips over her core.

"Don't make me wait," she pleaded against his mouth.

Camden slid into her. He'd thought he would take things slow, but damn it, he couldn't. This moment didn't call for sweet and tender, but intense and powerful.

Delilah moved perfectly against him in a rhythm that matched his own. Clearly she was in a hurry as well. The lightning flashes came closer together as the rain pelted against the windows. Camden gripped the back of the sofa for leverage as he grew closer to his climax. Delilah cried out, wrapping her arms and legs tight around his body as she clung to him during her release.

Cam let go and followed, shutting his eyes as if he

could lock this moment in time. He never wanted her to leave, didn't want their intimate moments to end.

But once his body calmed and Dee had gone lax beneath him, he shifted to lie at her side. He still had one leg thrown over hers as he trailed his fingertips up and down her heated torso. Her body trembled beneath his touch and he hoped like hell she never got tired of him wanting her.

"I know I asked you to stay tonight, but I want you to stay forever."

She didn't reply. Silence filled the room while the storm continued its wrath outside. He wished she'd tell him what she was thinking, but maybe that was too much for her right now. He'd learned over the past seven months that she needed space. Hell, maybe they both did, because having her gone only proved to him how much he needed her and wanted her by his side.

Delilah reached up and stroked his beard. She sometimes did that before she fell asleep and it was a habit he'd missed. He cradled her tighter, knowing full well he'd slay any demons that threatened her happiness... even if that included his family.

"I was thinking about having the ceremony here."

Elise spread her arms wide at the outdoor garden area separating the main part of the castle and the old stone buildings they had turned into the rick houses that held all of their aging barrels.

The white blooms and all the lush greenery combined with the stone paths would be a gorgeous setting for an outdoor wedding.

"Is that okay with you?" Elise turned to Antonio, who was glancing around the open space.

"If this is what you want," he replied. "Do you have a backup area in case of bad weather?"

Elise smiled up at him and Delilah glanced at Sara, who was jotting down notes in her planner. Antonio and Elise had finally decided to get married in just a few weeks. The wedding planning would be rushed, but the couple wanted to be wed and at the end of the day, that's all that mattered.

Delilah made her own notes in her phone to remember to add various details and suggestions to the packages she was working on.

"I think the entryway into the castle would be perfect for any weddings held indoors," Sara chimed in without looking up from her notepad. "Especially if we go all dramatic and leave the drawbridge down."

"Yes, especially with all of those windows along the back wall," Delilah added. "It would be breathtaking and different."

Elise nodded. "I love it."

"We can also give other brides the option of using the ballroom," Delilah said, thinking out loud. "If they have the reception there, it's certainly big enough that we could use the stage at the front for the ceremony, set up chairs on the floor and run the aisle runner, but then keep all of the reception tables toward the back. There would still be room for the dance floor if the couple chooses that, too."

"Brilliant." Sara beamed. "This is going to take us next level. We are going to be booked solid once your photos get out and after the governor's daughter has her wedding here."

"I'm not sure I want a big wedding," Elise said, then turned to Antonio. "We discussed we really just want family and something intimate."

"That's even better," Sara stated. "We can advertise

that no matter the size of your wedding party or guest list, we can accommodate."

"Do you want to have any draped tents with chandeliers, or what's the feel you two are going for?" Delilah asked.

"I'm just here to choose the spirits for the reception," Antonio said, laughing. "Elise can do anything she wants."

Elise pursed her lips and surveyed the area once again. "I think just open. I don't want to block any beautiful views, and we'll be going in for the reception. I really want to embrace the beauty of this property. I think once we start adding more elements out here, it takes away from the grounds and wouldn't seem as intimate."

"I agree with that," Antonio stated, then pulled his cell from his pocket and stared at the screen for a second. "Excuse me. I need to take this."

As he stepped away to answer his call, Elise's smile widened as she clasped her hands.

"This is really happening," she exclaimed. "I never thought I'd get married, let alone in a gorgeous place like this. Can you guys believe this?"

"Oh, I believe it." Dee laughed. "You two are perfect for each other and this is going to be a stunning wedding."

"I think so, too. His parents will be flying in from Spain the week before to help with anything we need." Elise slid her hands into the pockets of her dress pants and sighed. "They are seriously the nicest people and I can't wait to get to know them more. I mean, they raised an amazing man, so I feel I lucked out with this family."

"I can attest to that," Delilah said, nodding. "See what you're marrying into. It's going to be key in the long run."

Sara tipped her head and opened her mouth, but Elise stepped forward and put a hand on Delilah's arm.

"Are you sure this isn't too much?" she asked.

Delilah shook her head. "I promise, it's fine. I'm so happy for you guys and thrilled to be part of something so special."

Sara took a step forward. "Can I ask how things are with you and Cam? We haven't heard anything since yesterday in your office."

"I spent the night at the house," she confessed. "I hadn't planned on it. I went there to talk, but then…"

"Good for you guys," Elise cheered. "I know you think physical isn't everything, and it's not, but it also helps that connection and bond stay strong. So, what about those divorce papers?"

"That subject wasn't even brought up. I had to wake early to get back to my place and get ready."

Elise dropped her hand and crossed her arms. "Honey, why don't you just move your things back in?"

Delilah bit her lip and shrugged. "I'm thinking about it. He asked me if I'd stay tonight and I thought about showing up with a couple of bags. The only way to really try this again, to move forward, is to jump back in. But I'm terrified."

"Okay, what did I miss?"

Antonio came back and stood next to Elise, but glanced at all the sisters, then took a step back.

"Maldito."

Delilah had noticed when Antonio cursed, he always did so in Spanish. He had a thick accent, but they were all actually learning quite a bit from him, which Delilah loved. Broadening her scope of understanding other cultures would only be beneficial and respectful as their business continued to grow.

"Apparently we've moved on from the wedding," he stated. "I have more calls to make if you need more privacy."

Elise reached back and patted his arm. "That would be great. Why don't we meet you in the ballroom in a few minutes?"

Antonio leaned down and kissed Elise's cheek before he walked away.

"The way he looks at you is pretty intense," Dee told her sister.

Sara snorted. "Cam looks at you the exact same way."

Did he? She had no idea, but looking in from the outside was completely different than being in the situation. Camden had never made his feelings for her a secret, which was just one of the other reasons she loved him.

Maybe it was planning this wedding or perhaps it was the fact they had rekindled on a whole new level, but Delilah had high hopes for their future.

Fourteen

Delilah parked her car in front of the garage. Just pulling into her old spot had her smiling. Maybe coming home could be this easy. Maybe she'd been making this more difficult than it needed to be. If she and Cam could get on, and stay on, the same page, they could tackle anything together…she hoped.

It was that faith that had her back with two suitcases. She would stay through the weekend and see how they adjusted back to married life. Staying last night had opened her eyes to how much she had missed since moving out. Being in her own place had been lonely and odd. She'd only been renting because she wasn't sure where to go, so none of the things in the house were really hers. She had a few personal belongings, but for the most part, she'd left furniture and major items for Camden.

When she'd left, she was certain she had to start fresh, make a clean break…but that was just naive thinking.

There was no easy way out or a quick path to heal heart-ache and erase five years.

She never wanted to erase them. She wanted to use that time and learn from it so they could move forward and have the marriage they deserved.

Delilah popped the trunk of her car and went to get her luggage. She was a little surprised that Cam's car wasn't in the garage, but he should be home anytime. He'd be so surprised when he saw her bringing some things. Maybe she should hang some of her clothes back in her walk-in closet and add a few toiletries to her vanity in the en suite.

He would be so happy she was here and, honestly, she was quite giddy herself. The whole idea of them starting fresh and really holding on to those important aspects of this marriage is what would make them successful. Neither of them wanted to be a failure at anything. And some marriages weren't meant to last—that didn't make them failures. But Delilah knew this marriage was meant to be and if she left now, that would be failing. She and Camden could be stronger than ever now that they had the weapons to fight the negativity that had plagued them for years. They had a knowledge they'd never had before.

Delilah hoisted her luggage up the steps and then wheeled the bags into the bedroom. She wasted no time in unpacking and placing her things just like she used to have them. When she took a step back from her vanity and glanced into the mirror, she knew this was right. This *felt* right.

But her appearance was all wrong. If she was going to be back and ready for this new beginning, she had to look like she hadn't spent all day at work charming their VIP clients, as well as figuring out her newly created position of events coordinator.

Delilah glanced at the time and wondered where Camden was. He hadn't texted to tell her he'd be late or some-thing had come up with work, which was odd. Shouldn't he have been here by now?

This was the perfect time for her to freshen up and maybe see if she could get some dinner started. A nice glass of wine on the porch swing later would really top off their first night back in the home together.

Nearly an hour, a change of clothes and one casserole later, Delilah's cell chimed.

She sat the hot dish on the stovetop and removed her oven mitts before moving to the oversize kitchen island to check her cell.

I've been swamped today, babe. I won't be at the house tonight. Something has come up and I'm at the airport. Shouldn't be gone long and I'll text when I can.

Delilah stared at the words and read them over...three times.

He knew she was coming. Hell, he'd asked her to come back and stay. She told him she'd meet him here after work, but she hadn't confirmed that she'd be spending the night—she had wanted that to be a surprise.

The aroma of chicken and rice filled the kitchen, mocking her at her attempt to make this new start. She glanced down at the fitted tank dress she'd put on and fig-ured the touch-up on makeup and hair were all for naught.

She didn't even reply. What was there to say? Night one back in the house and he already had a business trip. She'd worried he'd fall back into old patterns, but had no idea he'd choose to do them right now.

Delilah sat her cell back down and turned to the cas-serole. She wasn't in the mood for food anymore, but wine always seemed like the perfect idea. She chose a bottle from the wine fridge in the kitchen and gave herself a hearty pour.

Sitting on the front porch swing alone wasn't appealing anymore, so she took her glass to the bedroom. Might as well strip down and soak in a tub, because she was too tired to pack up and go back to her rental. She'd learned early on in this split that self-care was a legit need. Wine and a bubble bath would be the perfect ending to this day.

No, the perfect ending would be her husband coming home, but since that wasn't happening, she'd just have to make the best of the situation.

She couldn't help but wonder if he was even sorry for not coming home. If he even realized that he'd already slipped back into workaholic Cam when he'd vowed to put her and their marriage above all else. Did he even think of her feelings or how this would impact her at all?

The first sting of tears pricked her eyes and she blinked them away. She wasn't going to wallow in self-pity. She would relax in this bath and think about all the ways she could formulate the packages for the new brides who would want to book at the castle.

Just because her marriage was a disaster didn't mean others would be, and her clients deserved the best. She would make the most appealing package deals possible and sell their new venue offering like a champ. Delilah could and would focus on the positive—work plus Elise's wedding to Antonio would help her.

As for Camden…she didn't even know what to think anymore.

Cam's plane had just landed when his cell went off. He'd been gone two days, a day longer than expected. He'd texted and called Delilah, but she hadn't returned any of his messages. Clearly she was pissed, and rightfully so. No doubt she thought he'd deserted her, but he had a damn good explanation. He had every intention of making this up to her.

He pulled his ringing cell phone from his pocket, wondering if it was Dee finally getting back to him. But his father's name popped up and Camden sighed. Not the person he wanted to chat with right now, but he slid his finger across the screen to answer anyway.

"Dad."

"Son. Is this a bad time?"

The plane continued to taxi and Camden crossed his ankle over his knee and leaned back against the sofa.

"Just landed," he replied. "What's going on?"

"I was planning to tell you in person, but I didn't think I'd be welcome back in your home again."

Camden rubbed his hand over his forehead and thought about how he should reply to that statement.

"That would all depend on what you're wanting to say," Cam finally said. "If you and Mom plan on attacking my wife, then no, you wouldn't be welcome."

His father's heavy sigh came through the phone and there was no mistaking the frustration and, Cam thought, a little defeat. Silence filled the line and Cam leaned forward, suddenly concerned, because it wasn't like his father to hem and haw around.

"What's wrong, Dad?"

"There's no easy way to say this. Your mother and I have decided to get a divorce."

The plane came to a stop near his private hangar and Cam watched out the window on the opposite side as his SUV came into view. He'd been waiting to get home, to get back to Delilah and tell her everything that had happened.

But his world just exploded in a way he'd never, not in a million years, would have expected.

"Say something," his father demanded.

"I don't know what to say," Cam replied honestly. "Are you two serious? Or is this some tactic to get my sympathy?"

His dad didn't say anything for a moment and Camden wasn't sure how to take this, but his question was definitely justified. He wouldn't put it past his parents to stage something ridiculous for his benefit so he would push Delilah aside and focus on them. While his father had typically been a passive participant, his mother had been the louder voice in all of this. So, if anyone was going to call with some scheme, it would likely be her.

"Quite serious, Camden," his dad finally replied. "I understand why you would think this was a lie, but I assure you, we are parting ways. We've been miserable for a long time, but trying to keep up appearances for our friends and you. The longer our rift went on, the more your mother lashed out and felt she was losing you and me. I see how you are with Delilah. I understand why you've fought for what you want, and I want to say... Hell, son. I need to say I'm sorry."

Cam's pilot came from the cockpit, but Camden waved him off. This phone call was too damn important and he didn't want to miss a word of it.

The pilot opened the door and extended the steps, letting himself out. Cam would talk to him in a bit.

"You and Mom have been married for years." Cam realized he was stating the obvious, but still. This was crazy and totally unexpected. "Did you both come to this conclusion?"

"She's not happy about it, but she can't say she's surprised," his dad explained. "This has been years coming.

I just realized the other night when we were at your house that you and Delilah have something real. And maybe at one time your mom and I did, too, but I don't know that we were ever happy like you two. I lost sight of everything and worried about appearances. I have to take responsibility for my actions and I'd like to apologize to Delilah, too, if you think she will let me."

Camden gripped his cell and came to his feet. "She would love that, Dad. She's only wanted to be accepted, that's all. She never asked for more."

"You've got a strong woman, Camden. She's worth fighting for."

Camden's throat clogged with emotions as he simply nodded. He knew damn well how special Delilah was. It just took her leaving for him to wake up to how he'd taken her for granted. He never meant to be that type of husband. It never even occurred to him that his grueling self-imposed schedule would conflict with his personal life. Having it all had always come second nature to him, but nothing was worth losing her. Absolutely nothing.

"If your firm would handle our case, we'd appreciate that," his father went on. "If you see that as too much of a conflict, I understand."

"No. We'll do it," Camden promised. "I'm just still processing everything."

"It's a blow, I'm fully aware. Take the time you need," his dad told him. "I'm moving into our town house in Lexington, so let me know what you need from me and how to get this going. I have no idea what the process is. Never thought I'd need a divorce attorney."

Yeah, that made two of them.

"I'll make sure the firm handles this so everything is fair for both of you," he told him. "Call me if you need me."

"I appreciate that, son. And let me know when I can come in person and apologize to Delilah."

"I will."

Camden ended the call and slid his cell back into his pocket. Raking a hand over the back of his neck, he was still rolling all this information through his head. Not only his parent's life-changing bombshell, but also these past two days. He had so much to talk to Delilah about regarding their future and he hoped she wasn't too upset that he just took off on a whim, but sometimes circumstances couldn't be helped.

As he stepped off the plane, he headed toward the hangar to find his pilot. He needed to schedule another trip, possibly two, and wanted Rob to be on standby for what might be a moment's notice.

Big things were going to happen and Camden was already anxious and excited for the rest of his life with Delilah.

Fifteen

Delilah stared at her computer and the beautiful layout she'd created for Sara to start advertising the new wedding packages on social media. But, something was missing. She couldn't quite put her finger on it, but she'd let her sisters take a peek and see what they thought.

Of course, everything could be perfectly fine and she was just in a crap mood after being alone in her house for two days. Oh, she could have returned Cam's calls or texts, or even gone back to her rental house, but she was stubborn. She was allowed that right. She would call him today if he didn't come home.

What the hell was he doing? He'd gone out of town before for work, but she always knew what was going on. He seemed so cryptic right now and the fact that he left before saying anything was irritating.

Dee sighed and reached for her coffee cup. Maybe she should have added a shot of bourbon to brighten her day, but she didn't think even Angel's Share Ten Year would perk her up at this point.

Her office door opened and closed, but she took another sip of coffee and continued to analyze the mockup on her screen.

"I have something I need you guys to look at," she stated, assuming one of her sisters had just come in.

"I have something for you, too."

Delilah nearly spilled her coffee into her lap as she spun around at the sound of Cam's voice.

He stood right across from her desk with a folder. His hair stood on end, and T-shirt and jeans weren't typical workday attire for him. Something was off.

"Nice of you to show up," she told him, setting her mug back on her warmer. "Are you still working on those priorities?"

Maybe that was harsh. Maybe she was being bitchy, but she liked to call it cautious.

Camden offered her a smile, one that never failed to curl her toes and make her want him. Damn man always had a power over her she couldn't deny. No matter how angry or hurt she got, she clearly couldn't turn him away.

"You've been my priority since you left seven months ago," he informed her. "So, first things first."

Delilah watched as he set the folder on her desk, opened it and pulled out their divorce papers. Then he reached over to her organizer and fingered through until he found what he wanted.

He clicked the pen and Delilah's heart lurched into her throat as she continued to stare. But he made a large X over each sheet of the agreement. He slid the pen back into the holder and picked up one paper and tore it in half. Then he did the same with the next, and the next, until there was a pile of half sheets of paper.

"We're not divorcing," he told her.

"Apparently not." She leaned back in her seat, wondering what else was in that folder. "Are you ready to talk?"

"More than ready." He tapped the folder, but his dark eyes held hers. "I want you to know that no matter what you decide, I'm here."

Delilah's heart kicked up and she gripped the arms of her chair. "You're worrying me, Cam."

"There's nothing to be worried about," he assured her. "But this folder does hold some life-altering documents. When I left town, it was fast, I was hurried and there wasn't time to explain. I didn't want to say too much in case nothing came of it, but I have information for you."

Delilah eased forward, glancing at the documents beneath his hands. "About what?"

"Your father."

"What?" she whispered.

Slowly, she came to her feet, her focus going from Camden to the folder. She'd had no idea he was even looking into anything like this. He'd never said a word about it. She assumed he'd gone out of town for his own work, but he had gone for her.

"Right after you told me what you all found at Milly's house, I called my investigator." Cam flipped the top of the folder open again and pulled out a printed email. "This was his initial finding."

He handed the sheet to Delilah and she scanned it quickly, trying to take in the information all at once. Then she went back to the top and went slower. In this first look into her mother's past and her own, there was a good bit of information as to where her mother had been at that time.

In line with Sara's findings, their mother was working at a treatment facility as she was trying to get and stay clean. Then she left for about a month and came back. She wasn't back long before discovering her pregnancy. So wherever she had gone in that time, that had to have been where she met Delilah's father.

Dee pointed toward the folder. "What else?" she asked.

"You can have all of this information, but I'll give you the shortened version." Camden slid the folder across her desk. "Your mother went to Charlotte for reasons that are still unclear. Speculation is that she met someone and followed him there, but regardless, that's where your father is now. He's been there all these years. I'm not sure if he knows anything about you, but I can tell you that he's a widower and he has no children...except you."

Delilah sank back into her chair once again as she flipped through the papers. Did he want to know her? Did he want to have children? Or did he love his life the way it was?

Part of her felt a little pang of disappointment that she didn't have other siblings, but the other part knew she was blessed with the two sisters she did have.

"I saw him."

Delilah jerked her attention back to Cam. "You met him?"

"Sort of. I wanted to lay my own eyes on him." Camden shrugged and perched on the corner of her desk. "Maybe I wanted to see if you resembled him or perhaps I wanted to see how he lived his life. I just knew I couldn't come back here without telling you that I saw him."

Delilah's throat clogged with emotions and she blinked away the moisture in her eyes. "What did he look like?" she whispered.

Camden reached over and slid a photo out of the back of the folder. Delilah glanced down at a man she'd never seen in her life, but it was like looking in a mirror. The wide eyes, gentle smile and square jawline were all from her father. She'd always wondered who she looked like... now she knew.

Emotions became too much. Delilah bit down on her lip so she wouldn't start the ugly cry, but one tear fell, then another, and she couldn't stop. Camden got up and went into her adjoining bathroom, then came back out with tissues.

"Here." He handed them over and then sat on the edge of her desk beside her. "I wasn't sure how you'd take this news. I know it's a great deal to process and I didn't want you upset."

Delilah shook her head and wiped at her nose. "That's not it," she sniffed. "All of my life I've wanted to look like someone. You know? I mean, I always just said Elise and Sara were my sisters, but now we know they are. That didn't help, though, because we all are so different physically. But now I see this picture... I feel a connection to someone for the first time in my life."

She dabbed at her eyes and continued to stare at the photograph of this man.

"What's his name?" she asked.

"Luis Diaz. He's of African American, German and Puerto Rican descent. He's the owner of a coffee shop and bookstore in Charlotte."

Delilah smiled. "A business owner. Another commonality we have."

She set the picture aside and started searching through the other documents. Mostly there were printed emails and a basic background check, along with a list of Luis's parents and his siblings. There was so much material here and all of it pertained to her and her past. She'd never wanted to think too much about her past before because she didn't think it started before Milly.

Never did she think any of this would come about or that Camden would go to this trouble to obtain all of these details for her.

"I'm not sure if you want to meet him or if you just wanted to have this information," Camden stated. "No matter what you decide, I'm right there with you."

Delilah shifted all the papers back into the folder and closed it, but she kept the picture out on her desk. When she glanced back up to Camden, he stared down at her with such love and care, she wasn't even sure what to say. He'd done something so amazing—he'd given her a piece of herself that she never had before.

"Honestly, I don't know what I want to do right now," she told him. "Definitely take all of this in, but I'm going to really have to think about everything. I don't want to disrupt someone's life, but at the same time I feel he deserves to know he has a child."

"You could play this from both sides all day long," Camden agreed. "You're going to have to do what's best for you and be confident in your decision."

Delilah smoothed her hair over one shoulder as she bounced around the facts she'd just been handed.

"Now I feel guilty for not returning your calls or texts." She wadded her tissues up and tossed them in the trash beneath her desk, then looked up at Camden. "I'm sorry. I assumed you went away for work and I got cranky…and apparently petty."

Cam leaned forward, turned her chair slightly so he could place his hands on the arm and cage her in. "You weren't being petty. How could you know what I was doing? Even if you'd called, I wouldn't have told you. I needed to tell you in person and I didn't want to say anything until I was positive I had all of the facts."

"I can't believe you did this," she muttered, still shocked.

"There's nothing I wouldn't do for you," he insisted. "You're above everything for me, Dee. I know I can still have a successful career, but I can also put you and us first. And you're my family now. Since marrying you, I should have started that chapter anew, but I didn't. From here on out, you are my family, and kids can be a discussion for another time. Or maybe we can just get a dog… or maybe a cat since they aren't as much maintenance. Whatever you want."

Her heart flipped as she reached up and slid her hand over his cheek. "I moved a few of my things back in."

"Is that right?" Camden took her hand and kissed her palm. "When can we go get the rest?"

"My lease is up in a few months."

"We're going to be breaking that lease," he told her. "And tell your Realtor that our house isn't for sale."

"Gladly."

He leaned down and nipped at her lips. "Is it too early for you to leave?" he murmured against her mouth.

"You can't possibly be asking me to skip work," she mocked. "Of all people, I certainly expected better from you."

Camden laughed and eased back. "Oh, that's exactly what I'm suggesting."

She looked at the computer screen with the work she'd been doing before her entire life turned upside down. She could send this to her sisters and tell them she was taking the rest of the day off with Cam. They would understand, but even more, they would encourage this time off.

"I think I can spare the rest of the day for you," she replied.

"What about the rest of your life?"

Delilah came to her feet and stood between his legs. Looping her arms around his neck, she teased her lips against his.

"I think I can spare that, too."

Epilogue

"I don't know why I'm so nervous."

Camden leaned over and kissed her on the cheek.

"Nothing to be nervous about," he assured her. "All you have to do is be yourself."

In the week since Delilah had discovered her own father's identity, she'd been mulling over meeting him. She still hadn't decided what to do there, but today was for repairing torn relationships with Cam's family…or rather, his father.

The doorbell rang and Camden started to head toward the foyer. Delilah placed a hand on his arm.

"Let me," she told him. "He's taking a big step in coming here, so I will meet him in the middle."

Cam smiled and nodded, gesturing for her to go ahead.

Delilah took in a deep breath and went to the front door. She tucked her hair behind her ears and flicked the lock.

Cam's father stood there with flowers in hand.

"Delilah," he greeted, extending the enormous bouquet. "These are for you."

"Oh, wow. Um…thanks."

She took the flowers and turned to see Camden standing there with a smile on his face. Just that simple gesture eased her nerves.

"Come on in," she told him as she stepped aside.

The moment he was in and the door was closed, Cam's dad shook his head and spread his hands wide.

"I have no clue where to start," he began. "'I'm sorry' seems inadequate."

"'I'm sorry' is the perfect place to start," she assured him. "Just the fact you acknowledge this is a big move in the right direction."

"I told my son how lucky he was to have someone like you by his side."

Delilah couldn't help but smile. "I'd say we're both lucky. I am sorry about the divorce, though. I never wished for anyone to have heartache or be ripped apart."

"My divorce isn't your fault," he told her. "We've had problems for years, but it took seeing my son fully in love for me to realize that true love does exist. And I'm not eager to get out there and find it, but I am ready to start building my life the way I want it and putting myself first."

"I'm really happy for you, Dad."

Camden came up and gave his father a hug. Their masculine pats on each other's backs had Dee tearing up once again. This whole family comradery was seriously getting to her lately. She'd never been an emotional wreck before, but something about all of the ups and downs, losing Milly and then discovering her father had her thankful and she couldn't control her emotions.

When Camden eased back, he moved next to her and wrapped his arm around her waist.

"Are you able to stay for dinner?" Delilah asked. "We can grill something and enjoy the evening on the patio."

"I'd love to," he told her. "I feel like this is a new beginning for all of us."

Camden looked down at her and kissed her forehead.

"It definitely is," he agreed.

Delilah couldn't wait for all the possibilities to come to life. She was making amends with her father-in-law and was fairly certain she'd be reaching out to her own father. For a girl who thought she'd come from nothing, she had everything she never knew she needed right here.

* * * * *

BLACK SHEEP BARGAIN

NAIMA SIMONE

One

Whoever said "revenge is a dish best served cold" clearly possessed a lack of imagination.

When not administered immediately, the other person might forget they had it coming. Or they might have one of those "come to Jesus" moments where they're not the same bastard who deserved their comeuppance.

Or worse.

The person might die.

Oh no. Revenge was definitely a dish served piping hot and shoved down the throat.

Nico Morgan stood on the sidewalk outside the Brighton bakery on Washington Street, traffic a cacophony of horns and squeals. Pedestrians flowed around him, separating like the tide, caught up in heading to work, classes or the local coffee shops.

But none of the other bakeries in this neighborhood

could compare to the baked goods tucked in the glass cases of Evans Bakery.

The name was as simple as the food and family inside. Well…most of the family.

Giving the brick building with the pristine white, green and yellow awning one last glance, he strode forward and opened the wide door. There was a painting of an elegant white cake and chocolate chip cookies on the sparkling glass. If his memory was correct—and his memory was always correct, since he never forgot a medication dose, a profit or loss, or a slight—Glory Evans ensured her staff cleaned this glass every morning without fail. And a couple times through the day if needed. The older woman's motto had been, Dirty Windows, Dirty Ovens. His private investigator's report had noted Glory's death earlier this year, after she never fully recovered from her stroke a few years ago. And her granddaughter had now assumed responsibility of day-to-day operations.

As he stepped inside, the scents of sugar, vanilla, baked bread and freshly brewed coffee greeted him. Most people would find it odd that the sweet and nutty aromas had lust pumping through his veins. But then most people wouldn't take one look at the woman pushing through the swinging kitchen door and associate those scents with her.

Athena Evans.

Nico clenched his jaw, narrowing his eyes on the slender yet sensually curved manager of the bakery as she warmly greeted customers, holding conversations even though her slim arms bore the burden of a wide silver tray loaded with pastries. He tracked her slow but steady progress through the crowded space, tracing the familiar lines of her face, the delicate set of her shoulders, the seductive yet somehow innocent sway of her hips, the stride of those long, toned legs.

There wasn't a damn thing innocent about Athena Evans.

He had personal and intimate knowledge of that.

Athena called out to the shorter woman behind the counter—her sister. Returning his scrutiny to her face, he caught the subtle uptick of warmth in her smile—hell, in her entire expression. That's because Athena didn't just smile with her mouth. Never had. It began there with a shockingly sexual curve, but it also softened the sharpness of her cheekbones, brightened her hazel eyes so they appeared more green than golden brown. It loosened her shoulders, relaxed the straight line of her spine.

It'd been one of the most beautiful things about her.

It'd also come to be one of the things he resented most about her.

Today, her sister was the recipient of that show of affection as Athena rounded the corner of the bakery case, tray held high, arms not showing the slightest sign of strain. His breath stuttered in his chest at that negligent display of strength. Desire pulsed in his veins as he studied the flex of sleek muscle revealed by the sleeveless yellow sundress that emphasized the beauty of her dark brown skin. With an ease that would've shamed an award-winning body builder, she set the tray on top of the case, not appearing winded or tired. Years toiling in the family bakery would build up that kind of stamina.

Besides, even if Athena were bone weary, she would never let on. That's not what the perfect daughter, granddaughter or sister did.

And Nico counted on that futile pursuit of perfection to aid him in his own endgame.

It was the only reason he stood in his ex-lover's place

of employment three years after she ended their relationship, willing to face her "fuck you, now get the hell out."

Oh, the things one was willing to do to for revenge.

Anything.

Anticipation swirled in his chest. Yes, because all the plans he'd worked on, *existed for* were slowly coming to fruition. But also because he stood in *this* shop, within feet of *this* woman. Electric currents raced over his skin. Waiting for her to notice him. To look at him so he could glimpse the shock, the hate, the… He was a succubus, greedy for any emotion, any reaction.

Three years.

Three years he'd gone without allowing himself even the sight of her. But now, with an unforeseen twist of fate, he needed her. No one else but Athena Evans would do. And he could indulge himself in her.

Until their business was done.

Then *he* would be the one to end it. To walk away.

Because three years ago, Athena had reminded him of a very important lesson. Never become attached.

Only trust the one person who will never let you down—yourself.

Athena removed the eclairs and doughnuts from the tray, talking to her sister and the customers at the counter. As she finished up, she scanned the lobby, and he braced himself. Objectively, he should've been wary of the trickle of eagerness that invaded him. But he ignored it, chalking it up to excitement over the imminent commencement of his plans. Not to the moment when she…

Her eyes locked with his. They widened.

Filled with shock, horror—and fury.

He smiled.

Without removing her gaze from his, she leaned down and said something in her sister's ear. Whatever it was had Geneva Evans's head jerking his way with a glare. His smile didn't falter. Satisfaction burned so fucking bright inside him, it rivaled the iconic streetlamps outside his Beacon Hill home. Geneva nodded, and Athena emerged from behind the bakery cases and forged a straight path to him. This time, she didn't pause to hold pleasant conversations with customers. No, she marched toward him, that affable smile nowhere in sight.

And when she stopped in front of him, smelling of sugar, butter and freshly baked bread, the cold glitter in her hazel eyes didn't stop him from hungering to sink his teeth into that place where throat and shoulder met... and take a bite.

"What the hell are you doing here?" Then before he could answer, she gave her head a shake. "You know what? Don't answer that. Because I don't give a damn. Just leave."

He arched an eyebrow. "You don't want me to do that."

"Oh, I assure you, I really do."

"I need to speak with you, Athena. Five minutes. What's five minutes compared to three years?" he asked, pausing as her lips twisted down at the corners. Anger slashed through his chest, but he smothered it. Maybe at one time he'd given a fuck that she'd walked out on him, but not now. He'd have to care about her to feel anything about it. "Trust me. You want to hear what I have to say."

"Trust you." She crossed her arms over her chest. "Those are words you might not want to lead with," she muttered.

"Sticks and stones, and all that, Athena," he murmured. "Or should I say, pot meet kettle?" He cocked his head. "We can stand here and trade compliments or you can follow me outside so we can talk, and then you can get back to your duties in the kitchen."

He smiled, and it didn't feel pretty. Probably because it wasn't. When they'd been together, she'd enjoyed playing the role of Cinderella for her family, so he'd call it like he saw it.

"Still an asshole, I see."

She returned his smile. It differed so much from the one she'd given her sister that he would've laughed if he didn't know that would antagonize her further. Her earlier smile had contained love, warmth. This one was nothing more than a baring of teeth. Good. He didn't need her affection for this. Preferred her animosity. At least then he knew where they stood.

At least then there was a little bit of honesty between them.

"Still choosing a life of martyrdom and blind devotion, I see," he said smoothly, with only a tiny hint of bite. After all, it was her sense of sacrifice that would work in his favor. For once. He sighed, glancing down at his antique gold Omega Speedmaster Moonwatch. "Five minutes, and then I'm leaving. And, Athena…" He leaned down so their faces were inches apart. So he could pick out the golden striations in her green and brown eyes. "You'll regret it if I do."

Anger flared in her gaze, but so did uncertainty. Most likely because during the year and a half they'd been together, she'd never known him to exaggerate or threaten. He didn't need to.

No, he promised. Then followed through.

"Five minutes." She jerked her chin toward the back of the store. "In my office, not outside."

Not permitting him a moment to disagree, she pivoted on her wedge heel and strode across the store. At a more measured pace, he followed, aware of the curious stares shadowing them. But all of his attention was focused on the woman in front of him. On the gorgeous halo of dark brown curls that grazed her tense shoulders. On the slender back that flared into rounded hips and the ass that deserved its own religion.

He jerked his gaze away. She—and her ass—no longer had the power to influence him. Yes, Athena was a gorgeous woman; he would be a liar to deny that. But he'd allowed that beauty to lead him around by his dick one time before. Never again.

Athena pushed through the wide, swinging door that led into the kitchen and veered to the left, toward a brightly lit hallway. Framed photos decorated the walls here, as they did in the bakery's main room. Black-and-white pictures of the shop from the 1960s when it first opened as well as color images of the present day. Pictures of the family over decades, showcasing a shift in fashion and generations. The display proudly declared a heritage, a legacy along with a family business.

And he knew from their many conversations, Athena was determined to carry that tradition forward into the future. At any cost.

Pausing before a closed door, she slipped a key ring out of her dress pocket. She unlocked the office and entered, leaving the door open in silent invitation. Accepting it, he moved inside the small room that contained her scent and her stamp. Potted plants in the windowsills. More framed pictures of family on the desk. Cookbooks and tin boxes that looked familiar because they used to take up space on his bookshelves.

Opting to stand instead of taking a chance with the folding chair in front of her desk, he crossed his arms and met her steady gaze. She, too, stood behind the ancient, scratched desk.

"I'm sure you didn't travel all the way over to Brighton to stare at me since you could've done that anytime in the last three years. So what is this mysterious important topic you need to see me about?" she asked with no small amount of sarcasm.

"Barron died."

Her low gasp echoed in the room, and for just a second, sympathy softened her features, thawed the chips of ice in her eyes. Anger flickered in him like a struck flame, dancing to an unseen wind. She could keep her pity. He had no need of it.

And Barron sure as hell didn't deserve it.

"I'm sorry, Nico," she murmured.

A shiver stumbled down his spine, and only by sheer will did he not reveal his reaction to his name wrapped around her tongue. That same tongue might as well have been hugging his dick, that's how eroticly the sound had struck him.

And it seemed sacrilegious that the first time she'd spoken his name in three years was to apologize for the death of the man who'd donated sperm to his mother over thirty years ago.

Fuck her compassion.

"I'm not," he stated, blunt, hard.

She stared at him, and he met her gaze without flinching.

"How long?"

"Almost nine months."

"Really?" She frowned. "I hadn't heard. Not that I follow news from the corporate business world but…" She shook her head. "Still that's big. Are you…okay?"

"Am I okay?" He smiled. "Oh, Athena, I'm ecstatic. The bastard is roasting in hell. It doesn't get much better than that."

If only his mother had lived to see it—that would've made Barron Farrell's death sweeter.

After all the years of pain and suffering Rhoda Morgan had been through after he'd abandoned her with an infant, she should've stood by that graveside. It'd been her right, her due.

"Is that what you came here to tell me?" she asked, confusion coloring her voice. "That Barron Farrell is gone? Because while I hate to sound insensi—"

He waved a hand through the air in front of him. "No, I wouldn't walk across a room to talk about Barron's death, much less drive the twenty minutes from downtown to deliver the news. And while a part of me finds a great deal of satisfaction in him attaining his great reward, I'm also upset about it."

"That's understandable." She nodded, and a gentle note threaded through her voice. "Your feelings toward him must be…complicated. There must have been things you wanted to say to him before he—"

Nico's harsh bark of laughter interrupted her. "Complicated? My feelings for Barron Farrell were the simplest of all human emotions. Hate. Utter contempt. But you're right. There were things I wanted to tell him before he died. Like what a heartless bastard he was. Like that he didn't deserve to be called a 'man,' much less a father. And that one day he would know how it felt to have his world stripped of everything he loved. And I would be there to witness it. I would be the one to watch it all crumble around him."

"But he stole that from you. By dying."

Anger, scalding hot and brutal, slammed into him. "Yes," he snapped. "He robbed me of my right to pay him back for every tear my mother cried, every dime she scraped together, every prematurely gray hair she grew."

Fuck.

This wasn't how he'd planned this discussion. Shoving his hands into his front pants pockets, he paced across the office, attempting to expend the agitation crawling through him. But the tiny room didn't offer enough space, and he pivoted, retracing his steps until he stared at a battered gray file cabinet and a potted plant with overflowing leaves. Another framed photo sat on top. This one of Athena and Glory Evans outside the bakery.

Family.

How she clung to them like a buoy in a wind-tossed lake.

With his mother gone, he didn't have those moorings.

She'd been gone a year now, and God, did he miss her. In the worst of those moments—like early Sunday mornings when he didn't have her apartment to visit for breakfast before their weekly visits to Faneuil Hall Marketplace and SoWa Vintage Market—he convinced himself he was better off without those ties. No ties meant no waiting for them to be cut. No depending on people who could walk without a moment's notice or explanation.

No dying and leaving you broken and alone.

No using those same ties like a web to tangle and trap.

As he intended to do with Athena.

Guilt flickered in his chest but he smothered it. That didn't belong here. Not with her. And not when it came to Barron. Neither one of them had looked back when they'd left him. He hadn't been enough for either of them. So no, he didn't harbor any regret or shame for his course of action.

This was for him.

And for his mother.

"He's gone, Nico. You can't exact revenge on a dead man," she said in that same soft tone. The tone that reminded him of a time when he'd shared parts of himself with her that he'd hidden from everyone else except his mother. Reminded him of a time when he'd believed... in her. In them.

When he'd believed in a lie.

"That's where you're wrong."

He turned from his contemplation of the picture and faced her again. Maybe she sensed something in his voice, his demeanor. Or maybe, even after three years, she still knew him. A fine tension entered her frame, stiffening her shoulders.

"What're you talking about?"

"It means, he might be dead but his legacy is very much alive. Farrell International still continues to operate, and under his sons, thrive. If he's beyond my reach, I'll go after the only thing he's ever cared about—that company."

"Wait, wait." She held up her hands. "Sons? I thought you said he only had one son, aside from you."

"No, apparently Barron made a habit of fathering children, then abandoning them and their mothers," he said. "The news hit all the business papers and gossip sites. At the reading of Barron Farrell's will, Cain Farrell discovered not only that he had two, unknown younger brothers, but that he also had to share his inheritance with them. Farrell International. Barron had a stipulation that they all must work together at the company for one year or else Farrell would be dismantled and sold. They chose to stay, and in the last nine months, the business has done very well. Possibly better than it did under Barron's control."

She shook her head, frowning and winding a finger in the air. "Back it up a minute. You said Cain Farrell discovered he had *two* brothers. That's wrong. Unless you're one of the two?" Then she waved her hands, frowning.

"No, that can't be right," she said, answering her own question. "Because you're not working for Farrell International."

"It's not wrong. Barron included the illegitimate sons he meant to acknowledge in his will. And continued to deny the existence of the one he'd been denying for over thirty years," he drawled.

Her full mouth flattened into a grim line, and her hazel eyes narrowed with a gleam of anger.

Shock ricocheted through him. She was angry. On his behalf. Rarely did anything surprise him. But she'd just accomplished the impossible.

"I hate to speak badly of the dead but… What. An. Asshole."

The corner of his mouth twitched, but he smothered the spurt of humor. Finding Athena Evans adorable heralded a slippery slope to destruction. And since he needed her, remembering the wreckage she could leave behind— *had* left behind—was imperative. If she agreed to this— and he had no doubt she would—he'd never be so foolish as to allow her close again.

"Not that I'm unsympathetic, but I still don't understand what this has to do with me."

He approached the desk, cocked his head and studied her for a long moment. "Because you're going to help me get what I desire most, Athena. Justice."

For his mother. For himself.

She blinked. "I'm going to…help you," she slowly repeated. "I don't understand."

"I meant what I said about dismantling Barron's legacy. Stock by stock. Right now Cain and Achilles Farrell and Kenan Rhodes own the majority of shares with the remaining numbers distributed among Farrell International shareholders. Or so they believe. I've been working for years, trading and buying stocks, and I almost own just as many shares as they do. In another few weeks, I'll own more, and I'll have controlling interest in Barron's company."

"And what do you plan to do with the control, if you get it?" she asked, her gaze roaming his face as if she could find answers there.

"*When* I get it. I plan on being Barron Farrell's son." His lips lifted in a small smile.

She could take that however she wanted.

"I don't trust that purposefully enigmatic statement at all." She scoffed, crossing her arms. "But it doesn't matter because I want no part of—" she flicked her fingers "—whatever this is."

"Oh but you're not just 'a part,' Athena, you're going to be my partner."

Her chin snapped back, shock flaring in her eyes. Slowly, her arms dropped to her sides and she stared at him. Tension crackled in the room, popping over his skin, even through his suit jacket and shirt. Exhilaration. It sang in his veins.

How could he have forgotten that she'd never had a problem challenging him, going head-to-head with him? Where others showed him deference and even fear, she'd dared him with her gaze, her words...her body. No, Athena Evans had never kneeled before him.

Unless she desired to be there.

"And why the hell would I do that when being your partner the first time was so overrated?" Her mouth twisted into something not quite a sneer. "No, I think I'll pass. But hey, thanks for stopping by. Don't let another three years go by. Or I don't know...do."

"Do you know what your brother has been up to, Athena?" he asked, flattening his palms on the desktop and leaning forward. "While you've been chained to this bakery, undoubtedly running yourself ragged to keep the lights on and the employees paid, do you have any idea what your brother has been doing behind your back?"

If he hadn't been scrutinizing her so closely, he might've missed the glimmer of anxiety in her gaze. But he did spot it. He also noted that nothing else about her expression or demeanor changed.

Still the Evans family gatekeeper. The fierce protector.

He counted on that fierce loyalty.

And yet an ember of anger sparked to life deep in his chest. That same blind devotion to people who, yes, loved her, but who had never appreciated her or offered her the same consideration she showed them—that's what had broken her and Nico. She'd walked away, never looking back.

Today, she had no choice but to look back. He'd made sure of that.

He reached inside his jacket and removed three folded sheets of paper. Without breaking their visual connection, he set the thin sheaf on the desk and slid it across to her. After a long moment, she lowered her gaze and stared at the paper as if scared to touch it.

Smart.

Because she knew Randall Evans. Knew what he was capable of.

Nico could call Athena a number of things, and in those days after she left him, he had, but none of those names had included *coward.* And she reinforced that opinion when her jaw firmed and she picked up the stack, unfolded it and read the top paper. She wouldn't need to read the rest. The first page with Promissory Note boldly printed across the top would declare its purpose.

Straightening, he waited while she scanned the note,

already knowing what she read. A three-hundred-thousand-dollar loan Randall Evans took out with a local bank, putting up the bakery as collateral. Which he could do since, as the oldest child, the shop had gone to him when Glory Evans had died earlier that year.

Correction.

Oldest *biological* child.

Technically Athena was the oldest child, but she was also adopted. And apparently not good enough to inherit the Evans's precious bakery.

And yet even after that slight, Athena still stayed.

That ember inside him flared into a flame.

"This can't be..." she whispered.

"True? Real?" He arched an eyebrow. "Why? Because he's above this? Because he wouldn't do this without talking to you first? Because he wouldn't put your business in debt when you're already struggling to pay bills, to make payroll, to stay afloat?"

She glanced away from him and that's all the answer he needed.

She looked down at the note again, her fingers fisting the paper. "It states here that the maturity date isn't for another two years. Why are you showing me this now?"

"The loan would be due in two years if your brother were making the monthly payments. As of today, he's six months behind, and the bank is about to proceed with calling the loan. If that happens... No, *when* that happens—the entire balance will be due, and if your brother cannot pay it, they will take their collateral."

Her eyes closed, her lips moving on a silent curse. The note in her hand shook before she deliberately set it on the desktop. Spinning on her heel, she thrust her fingers through her hair, striding away from the paper as if being anywhere in its vicinity offended her—threatened her.

Yes, that was more accurate. Because that had been real fear Nico had glimpsed in her eyes before she'd shut them. His fingers and palm tingled with the need to... What? Tear that loan from the desk and shred it to pieces? Wouldn't change the fact that her brother had screwed her and the family by being the same selfish, self-absorbed ass he'd always been.

To cup her shoulders, turn her around and press her to his chest? To hold her?

No, that was no longer his right. And even if she'd allow it, he wouldn't. One touch to silken skin, one inhalation of her warm, sweet scent and he'd trick himself into believing maybe he could trust her. That she'd stick.

Only one person in his life had ever stuck. And she was gone.

All he had was himself.

And the certainty that Athena was devoted to an ungrateful, spoiled family.

Athena stopped in front of the small window that offered an uninspiring view of the back lot. The silence in the office stretched, but Nico didn't break it. Unlike most people, especially in the social circles he now swam in, he didn't mind the quiet. When a person grew up in Roxbury, where peace and silence were rare commodities, one valued the moments void of noise and confusion.

But nothing about the quiet in this office was peaceful or calm. He didn't need to see her face to feel the turmoil that emanated from her. The bend of her head, exposing the vulnerable nape of her neck, the slight slump of her shoulders and the flutter of her lashes against her striking cheekbones all relayed a story.

Weariness.

Worry.

Defeat.

Something ugly slashed through him. He'd caused that. She should never wear that. It didn't fit.

Fuck.

He took an involuntary step toward her—

"What is making that disappear going to cost me?" She pivoted, facing him again.

That unruffled, cool mask firmly back in place. Relief cascaded through him. *Good.* He didn't want a crushed Athena. He needed the warrior she was named after. And this woman, staring at him with contempt in her eyes, didn't tempt him to do something as foolish as reconsider his path. Or her part in it.

"That's why you're here, right?" she continued. "That's the offer I would regret not hearing? You need me to—how did you put it?—be your partner, or what? You allow the bank to call the loan?"

"Yes." Her sharp inhalation blew on the flame of anger still dancing in his chest. "That's your and your parents' job, to clean up after your brother's messes, not mine. You agree to the terms of my bargain and I'll pay off the loan. Evans Bakery will be debt free and safe. Until the next time. And we both know there will be a next time."

"What are these terms?" she ground out.

He slid his hands in his pockets again. So he would resist touching her, trying to shake some sense into her about the futility of covering for a nearly thirty-year-old man who persisted in behaving like a boy. Nico could see why her parents did. But her? No, he'd never get it.

"You pretend to be my fiancée for the next three months. That includes attending social and business events, dinners, parties or wherever I deem your presence necessary. Your job as my fiancée is to convince everyone, especially Cain and Achilles Farrell and Kenan Rhodes, as well as their significant others, that we are in love, devoted to one another and a solid couple. In other words, Athena, your sole purpose is to make me look like a good guy."

"I am not a goddamn genie," she snapped. "Because that's what you need to pull that off." Loosing a disbelieving laugh, she dropped her head back and pinched the bridge of her nose. "What the hell?" she muttered softly before raising her head and spearing him with a narrowed glare. "Do you hear how crazy this sounds? I mean, seriously. Play it back in your head and give it a minute. Maybe the absurdity of it hasn't had time to sink in." She shook her head. "Of all the things I expected you to say when you popped up in here this morning, Nico, that didn't even climb into the top twenty."

"And yet, you're going to agree. Because if you do, you'll keep this bakery. If you don't, you'll lose it. Those are your choices."

"Why?" she asked, the question bursting from her. Her desperation unmistakable. "Why me? And what is this…charade supposed to gain you?" Once more, she tunneled her fingers through her hair, dragging the thick curls away from her face and offering him a clear, unrestricted view of the frustration etched on her features. "Why are you doing this?" she finally whispered.

"Why you?" he arched an eyebrow. "Expediency and practicality. I don't have the time or patience to find a woman who will play the role of a woman who knows me when I already have one who does. And so well." He paused, letting his gaze roam over those jeweled eyes, the perfect slash of cheekbones, the decadent curve of her mouth and drop down to her slender body with its wicked, lush curves. "Besides, another woman might get ideas. This is an arrangement. Nothing more. When the three months are up, I don't want to go through the trouble of breaking off something that was never real to begin with. You, I have no worries, will have no problem leaving."

She'd already shown him she was so damn good at it.

"And with you by my side, I'll gain entry into Barron's sons' tight little circle without suspicion. Who would look wrong at a happily engaged man? And by the time we show up at just about every social event where they and their wives do, I'll accomplish that goal. As for why I'm doing this?" He stepped forward, his voice lowering with the bitterness he'd hoarded for decades. "Because I can. Because that bastard will rage all the way from hell, knowing I own his beloved company. Because I can't exist in a world where the name Farrell is praised and revered when it doesn't even deserve to be spit on. It deserves to be forgotten."

She inhaled a deep breath, then slowly shook her head. "No. I won't do it. I can't do it. You're making me an accomplice to a plan to destroy lives. And if you think none of that will blow back on you, hurt you…" She held up her hands, palms out. "I can't."

"So you're saying no out of worry for my soul?" He released a harsh bark of laughter that had her flinching. The movement was infinitesimal, but he caught it. "Save your false concern. Just to be clear, you're choosing to let me leave through that door, knowing your bakery is only weeks from closing. Because if I do, I'm not coming back, Athena."

Her gaze flicked toward the note on her desk, her chest lifting and falling on another deep breath. When her eyes returned to his, the resolve there telegraphed her answer. "Yes, we're clear."

Shock rippled through him, followed by a twisted stab of emotions he hadn't experienced in three years. Fear. Doubt.

But damn if he'd let her witness them.

Dipping his head, he said, "If that's your decision," then turned and left the office without glancing back.

In the past, she had stolen his heart. Broken it. And walked out on him. Since knowing her, she'd surprised him at every turn. Why should now be any different?

Because Athena Evans had never done the expected—even when he needed her to.

Two

Athena parked her sixteen-year-old Nissan Altima in front of her parents' Dorchester Victorian-style two-family home. As she switched the ignition off, something under the hood rattled in protest. She closed her eyes and squeezed her hands around the steering wheel.

Nico had tried to buy her a new car when they'd been together, viewing the used car as a hand-me-down from her older brother. True, it had been, but that didn't mean she valued it any less. Or needed it any less. And when her and Nico's relationship ended, she'd never been so glad she'd resisted. This was the car she'd driven away in.

"Dammit," she whispered, shaking her head. As if that could jerk loose thoughts of her ex. Of their past together. Of *them* together.

He'd reappeared after a three-year absence, hauling open the door she'd bolted shut with heavy-duty locks.

Now she couldn't shove him back in. And she'd tried. God knows she'd tried.

But one look at him standing in the bakery, and it had all rushed in like a swollen flood crashing through a flimsy dam. The dizzying exhilaration. The thrilling excitement. The blinding pain. The scalding anger.

The consuming lust.

She shivered.

Only Nico Morgan had ever elicited such a torrent of emotion from her. A woman could hate a man for that.

Fine. She was said woman.

Groaning, she exited the car and rounded the hood, pausing at the curb. The light blue, three-story home with its two porches, rounded rooms, wide picture windows and towerlike turret had always been home, even after she'd moved out six years earlier. Her parents, her brother, Randall, and his wife, Gina, and their two children still lived there. As had Mama when she'd been alive.

Pain, agonizing, scored her chest, and she lifted a fist, rubbing it over her sternum. Eight months. It'd been eight months since Mama had passed, and the grief, the ache had eased some. But it still took her aback at times. More often when she visited here, where the essence of her grandmother still lingered like the scent of the lilac powder she'd used every day after her bath. That scent, the memories—they laid into Athena every time she crossed the threshold. And today, she had to enter her childhood home from a place of strength. Especially considering the news she had to deliver.

Dragging in a breath, she held it, then slowly, deliberately let it go. And moved up the walkway toward the front porch. As if she'd been looking out the window—which was definitely a possibility since Winnie Evans loved to catch the goings-on in the neighborhood—her mother opened the door and waited for her, smiling as Athena climbed the top step.

"Hey, Mom." Athena walked across the porch and straight into her mother's outstretched arms. Hugging her tight, she closed her eyes, worry creeping through her. Was she thinner in the few days since she'd last seen her? Mama's death had hit them all hard, but her mother had barely left her bed for nearly a month afterward. "How're you feeling?"

"I'm fine, I'm fine. Stop fussing." Her mother squeezed Athena, then stepped back, cupping her upper arms. "Don't you look pretty today in your yellow? Your grandmother always loved that color on you." Patting her arm, she shifted backward, making room for Athena to enter. "Come on inside. I was surprised to get your call, but happy, too."

Guilt curdled in her belly like old milk.

If only she was just dropping by to visit and gossip. If only Nico hadn't come by the shop with his stupid bargain.

If only Randall hadn't gone behind her back and taken out *a three-hundred-thousand-dollar* loan on her bakery.

No, not her bakery. Randall's. All Randall's. And he had the documents that said so. As he'd told her many times.

Didn't matter that she rose at four every morning to make sure there were freshly baked muffins, doughnuts, cupcakes and an assortment of other pastries for their customers. Didn't matter that Randall had only showed up at the shop eleven times in the three years since Mama's stroke, not at all since she'd died—and yes, she'd kept count. Didn't matter that the staff, vendors and customers viewed her as their employer because she handled all of the managerial responsibilities.

None of it mattered because she might be the oldest child, but she wasn't blood.

An old ache bloomed behind her sternum, and she turned up the wattage on the smile for her mother to cover the hurt, to conceal the throb of rejection.

She'd become an expert at both.

"How about I fix you a cup of tea?" She looped an arm through her mother's and guided her out of the foyer. "Have you had one today?"

"Not since this morning. A cup sounds perfect, though."

They passed the gleaming oak staircase that led up to the second level and walked into the large living room with its high ceilings, round alcove and trio of floor-to-ceiling windows. The room opened off to a dining room and down another hall to the main hub of both sides of the house—Winnie's kitchen. Athena left her mother on the couch in front of the coffee table before peeling off toward the kitchen. Years had taught Athena exactly how her mother preferred her tea, and she prepared a cup, bringing it with her back into the living room ten minutes later.

"Here you go, Mom." She set it down on the coffee table, then took a seat on the couch beside her. "Are you sure everything's okay? You seem kind of…tired. Are you resting well? Eating?"

"Yes, yes and yes." Her mother softly laughed, patting her hand. "Stop worrying so much, honey. I'm fine. Now, tell me what's so important that you actually left the bakery early to come over and see me."

Right. Because she'd never leave Evans before it closed at six in the evening. Everyone in the family knew that. Randall definitely did. Just another reason he didn't bother showing up because Athena always stood in the gap to do it.

They call necessity the mother of invention for a reason. Your brother has never had to figure out how to make his own way because you and your family have always paved it for him.

Nico's voice, his admonishment from years ago, echoed in her head.

God, she needed him out of her head. Out of her life.

Why had he chosen to reenter it when she'd just started to erase him from her mind? And by *erase*, she meant go a consecutive two weeks without thoughts of him invading her sleep. Okay, a week, a week without waking up wet, trembling and aching…

Right. No dwelling on dreams of her ex while sitting next to her mother. Bad manners. And just plain awkward.

"Let me just put out there that you alone are important enough for me to leave the bakery early. You're important, period."

"Oh wow, this must be big," her mother murmured, picking up her tea and peering at Athena over the cup's rim before taking a sip.

"Mom, I mean it," Athena insisted, but then she sighed, splaying her fingers wide on her thighs. Fine, she was stalling. This was one of those Band-Aid moments—better to just rip it off and get it over with. But first… "Where's Dad? He should probably hear this, too."

"This is Tuesday so he's down at the barbershop. It'll be at another couple of hours before he's back home." Her mother frowned, setting her cup back on the table. "It's that serious? Do you want me to call him to come home? Is it one of you kids? Gina? Mya or Randall Jr.?" she pressed, naming Randal's wife and her grandchildren.

"No, Mom." Athena reached out, covering Winnie's hand and shaking her head for added emphasis. "We're all fine that I know of. This is…something else. I can tell Dad later. I just thought telling you both together would be easier." Inhaling, she straightened. *So much for ripping that bandage off.* She mentally grimaced. "I had a surprise visitor today at the bakery. Nico Morgan."

"Your ex-boyfriend?" Confusion clouded her mother's dark brown gaze and she tilted her head to the side. A second later, confusion slid into a moue of disdain. "Why did he show up? Like a bad penny. And after how long? Four years? What could he possibly want?"

"Three years," Athena corrected. But who was counting?

Winnie hadn't particularly cared for Nico. She'd believed he'd wanted to separate Athena from her family. Nico had his faults—emotionally unavailable, guarded, stubborn to a fault and too damn hot for his own good—but that one sin she couldn't lay at his feet. He hadn't sought to isolate her from her family. Set boundaries? Yes. But as someone who dearly loved his mother, he would've never demanded she cut her own from her life.

But he had put his foot down at Winnie calling at three o'clock in the morning to make sure Athena would open the bakery because her brother wasn't feeling well. Translation—he'd tied one on while hanging out with his friends the night before and was too hung over to open the store.

No, Winnie hadn't appreciated Nico sharing his thoughts on how her brother was a lazy son of a bitch who wouldn't know responsibility if it kicked him in the nuts. A direct quote.

Oh no. Winnie did not particularly care for Nico Morgan.

"Four, three," her mother said, waving a dismissive hand, "whatever. What does he want? Nothing good, I bet."

"You'd win that bet." God, how did she tell her mother this? "Mom, he showed me a banknote for a three-hundred-thousand-dollar loan that Randall took out. He used the bakery as collateral." Her mother's eyes widened, and Athena pushed ahead with the rest of it. "And he hasn't made any payments for the last six months so the bank is about to call the loan. If Randall doesn't come up with the full balance, we'll lose the bakery."

"You didn't know anything about this?"

The question shouldn't have slapped out at her. But it did. Because of the vein of accusation running through it. As if Athena were responsible for this deceitful action that could destroy the business Winnie's mother and father had defied the societal, racial and economic odds to build.

Because it was never Randall's fault.

Stop it. There's no time for this. And she didn't mean it like that. She never does.

Athena repeated the refrain to herself. Shoving the traces of bitterness down, she met her mother's gaze.

"No, I had no clue about any of it until Nico showed me a copy of the promissory note." And because she couldn't root out all the petty inside her, she added, "When you and Dad signed over control of the bakery to Randall without any kind of checks and balances, he didn't require any additional signatures or permission to apply for a loan. As a matter of fact, we don't know if this is the only one out there."

The horror slowly dawned on her. How that thought just occurred to her, she had no idea. What else had Randall been up to? And how could she find out? Could Nico—

No. Absolutely not. No way in hell she'd go to him for help.

"No, your brother wouldn't do that! Not without telling us…"

Athena stared at her mother. Only respect for the woman who had chosen to raise and love her kept the *"Are you kidding me right now?"* from exiting her mouth. But her face? Well, she couldn't control that. And Winnie was an excellent expression translator.

She threw her hands up, releasing a sound that was somewhere between a sigh and a tsk. "We don't even know if this is true. Just because it comes from Nico Morgan, who you haven't heard from in years, we're supposed to accept it as fact? I don't believe your bro—"

"I saw the documents myself, Mom," Athena quietly, firmly interrupted. "They're real. And it's Randall's signature."

"Dear God," her mother whispered, and for the first time since Athena dropped the news, it seemed as if the gravity of her brother's actions sank in. Pressing a palm to her mouth, Winnie stared at Athena. "Three hundred thousand? Athena, what're we going to do?"

A better question would be why did Randall get the loan in the first place and what did he do with the money? He still lived with their parents. And yes, he'd recently bought new cars for him and his wife, and he always dressed to the nines, but other than that? What did he have to show for all that money?

But history had taught her that trying to nail Randall down for answers would be like attempting to nail ambrosia salad to the wall. Impossible.

"I don't know," she answered. "First thing, we need to talk to Randall. See if he has any of the money left. And if not, what were his plans to pay it back." Obviously, he didn't have any plans or he would've been making the monthly loan payments, but she left that unsaid.

"Wait, wait." Winnie held up her hands, palms out.

"Wait for what, Mom?" Athena asked, confused. "We don't have time. *Six months*. If the bank hasn't already sent out letters demanding the balance of the loan, they soon will. We might have *weeks*, not months, before we lose the bakery."

Anger spiked inside her, but she inhaled, held the breath in her lungs. This wasn't her fault, but *damn*. They had to make decisions. And the main person who needed to be here—the one responsible—was absent, leaving them holding the bag. As usual.

"I know this, Athena," her mother snapped, then stretched out a hand, circling Athena's wrist. "I'm sorry, honey. I didn't mean to yell at you. This is…a mess. If this is true—"

"It is," Athena ground out.

"Then it's a mess and we need to take a minute and figure out how to address it."

"As a family." Athena stared at her mother, who glanced down at her lap. "Mom," she said, voice hardening. "As. A. Family."

"Why did Nico come by and tell you about this? What's his interest in it?" Winnie demanded.

"Mom—"

"Athena, please," her mother said, tone soft but brooking no argument. "Why did Nico tell you this? Why is this his business?"

She sighed, carefully choosing her words. "He proposed a…bargain. If I do a favor for him, he offered to pay off the debt."

Winnie jerked straight, a gasp tumbling from her lips. Hope flared in her eyes. "What?" She surged forward, clasping both of Athena's hands in her own. "You're kidding me? Why would he do that? Did you say yes?"

"What? No, I didn't say yes." Athena lurched to her feet, snatching free of her mother's desperate grip. Rubbing her hands together, she tried to rid her skin of that grasping sensation.

Or is that disgust you're trying to scrub clean?

As soon as the disloyal question popped into her head, she forced her arms to her sides, pacing away from the couch. From her mother.

"Athena," Winnie murmured.

"No, Mom." She pumped her hands in the air as if warding off whatever was bound to come out of her mother's mouth. Because instinct warned her she wouldn't like it.

"What does he want you to do? Is it illegal?"

"No, of course not," Athena said, tone sharp, but she immediately softened it. "Morally questionable, maybe, but not criminal." She glanced at her mother, frowning. "Forget it, Mom. I already told him I wouldn't do it."

"You won't tell me what it is?" Winnie quietly asked.

"No." Athena crossed her arms over her chest, uncertain why she felt...protective of Nico.

That proposal was so ridiculous, so filled with bitterness, that she wanted no part of it. There's no way she could get involved with something like that and not come away tainted. But his story didn't belong to her, so it wasn't hers to tell. She'd never even shared the truth about his parentage with her family. Nico Morgan might've broken her heart but she'd kept his secrets. And she had no plans to betray them now.

"It doesn't matter," she continued. "Now we have to—"

"How can you say that?" Her mother pushed to her

NAIMA SIMONE   37

feet, her fingers twisting in front of her. "How does it *not* matter? This is our lifeline, our way out. You know as well as I do your brother doesn't have that kind of money. If he did, he wouldn't have taken out that loan in the first place. Your father and I certainly don't. And we cannot lose Mama's bakery. It was her pride and joy, her everything. She loved…" She broke off. "We can't lose Evans," she finished on a cracked whisper.

"I can't, Mom," Athena whispered back. Desperation and…grief yawning deep inside. "What about Randall? Aren't you even going to ask him to step up, to take responsibility for this? He's threatened Evans, but once again…"

She didn't finish the sentence. Couldn't. A snarled ball of anger, sorrow and frustration lodged in her throat and she couldn't speak around it. She studied her mother's face, hoping she'd spy something there to belly her words.

But she found nothing. Nothing except what she expected.

"We're family, Athena. This is what family does. We have each other's back."

"Right," she whispered. Except, why couldn't she remember the last time they'd had *her* back?

Essentially disinherited.

Depended on to shoulder the responsibility of the family business.

Expected to give and give and give without complaint.

And she did it all.

She was so fucking tired of being the perfect, hungry-for-love daughter.

Turning away from her mother's dark, pleading gaze, Athena crossed the room to the dormant fireplace. Framed photos crowded the mantel. Black-and-white, cracked with age. Color and obviously more recent.

But all family. And in almost all of them, Mama. Glory
Evans, the matriarch of the Evans family. The linchpin
that had held them all together.

Winnie and Marcel Evans had adopted one-year-old
Athena, and though she didn't share their DNA, she'd
never viewed them as anything other than her parents.
Other adopted children experienced that need to search
for their biological parents, but she never had. Winnie
and Marcel had been it for her—all she'd ever needed.
And Mama… Well, Mama had been even more. No, she
might not be an Evans by blood, but the bond she'd shared
with her grandmother had run deeper than with any of
her other grandchildren. Even deeper than with her own
daughter.

Baking.

Athena had stood at her grandmother's knee with her
toy bowls and spoons, pretending to mix ingredients,
watching Mama until she'd been old enough to exchange
the pretend eggs, flour and sugar for the real things. Their
love for creating in the kitchen had resulted in not just
new recipes but a relationship cemented by respect, acceptance and adoration.

God, she missed her.

Reaching out, Athena stroked a finger down one of
the last pictures of Mama. Last year, on her birthday,
with all of them surrounding her. Mom, Dad, Randall
and his family. Athena and Kira, her younger sister. All
of them grinned huge, celebrating another year of life
for the woman they all loved and revered. Little had they
known she would be gone in three short months.

Athena's gaze switched to a black-and-white photo.
Glory and her husband, Thomas, standing in front of
the newly opened Evans Bakery in 1962. They'd with-
stood lean times, threats for committing the sin of being

a Black-owned business. They'd enjoyed success and survived the death of an owner, Thomas, long before Athena joined the Evans family. And through it all, Glory persevered, never closing Evans Bakery's doors.

And Athena couldn't allow them to close either.

Or allow anyone else to shut them.

Closing her eyes, she dropped her arm to her side.

She was going to do it. She was going to accept Nico's proposal.

But not for Randall. Not even for her mother.

She would do it for her grandmother.

Turning back to Winnie, she said, "Fine. I'll do it."

"Oh, Athena." Relief washed over her expression. "That's wonderful. Thank—"

"No, Mom." Athena shook her head. "I'm sorry. I don't mean to disrespect you. But please, don't thank me. I don't think I can handle that right now. Because I need to be clear, and you need to be clear as well. You're refusing to go to your son, the one who placed the bakery in jeopardy and demand he be accountable for his actions. That's it. And you won't do it. You'd rather ask—*beg*—me to take responsibility for him. Again. Even knowing it's placing me in an uncomfortable position. Involving me with a person who, by your own admission, you don't even care for. But the alternative—allowing Randall to face consequences—is abhorrent to you."

Never had she felt more expendable than she did in this moment.

"Honey, I love you," her mother whispered, extending a trembling hand. "You're so strong, and you know how your brother is…"

Athena took a step back and held her hand up. "One thing you need to understand, whether you tell Randall or not. I'm not doing this for him. And as much as I love you, Mom, I'm not going to Nico for you either. I'm doing this for Mama and her legacy, for Evans." Hiking her chin, she added, "And you'll need to do something to get Randall into the bakery. Because I can't save his behind *and* show up every morning at the store and work all day. It's your decision to spin whatever story you want, but he's going to need to step up."

Winnie nodded. "I'll do it."

Athena glanced away, mouth twisting. Her mother probably meant that. Literally. She wouldn't be surprised to find out Winnie showed up at the bakery tomorrow instead of Randall. Exhaling, Athena stared down at the floor, suddenly tired.

"I'll be in touch," she murmured and headed toward the front door.

"Athena, I—"

"Mom, I'll be in touch," she repeated.

Without risking a look at her mother, not when a whirl-wind of emotions whipped at her, she exited her child-hood home.

And for the first time since she'd entered it as a girl, she was unsure when she would be comfortable return-ing to it.

Because for the first time, it didn't feel like home.

Three

Why had Athena believed it would be simple to waltz into a downtown Boston office building and request to see a billionaire? On the twenty-minute drive here, the ten-minute search for an available spot in the parking deck and the seven-minute walk to the high-rise where Brightstar Holdings LLC occupied one of the top floors, she'd convinced herself it would be easy.

It seemed knowing how said billionaire sounded when he came deep inside you wasn't enough to gain access to him.

Not that she'd tried to explain that to the security guard currently staring at her as if she had mayhem on her mind.

"I'm sorry, ma'am," the dark-haired guard said for the third time. "But unless you have an appointment with Mr. Morgan—and according to his assistant, you do not—it's not possible for you to go up and see him today. I would suggest calling his office, scheduling an appointment, then returning at a later date."

The *"As for today, you're not getting past me,"* went left unsaid but she heard it loud and clear.

Sighing, she jerked open her purse and removed her cell. It'd been three years, but he probably hadn't changed his phone number. Nico hadn't been a fan of change. She doubted *that* had changed either. Not delving into why she hadn't erased his number from her contacts list, she pulled up his information and pressed Call. One ring. Two rings. As the fourth ring started, disappointment slicked through her. But just before she lowered the phone, a deep, smooth voice echoed in her ear.

"Athena?"

It appeared she wasn't the only one who hadn't removed old contacts.

"Yes," she said, glancing away from the security guard. "I'm downstairs in your office building at the security desk. Sorry for showing up without an appointment, but I need to speak with you about...about yesterday."

A beat of silence. Then, "Give the guard your phone."

She complied, extending the cell toward the other man. "It's for you."

Eyeing her, he accepted it. "Yes?" From one second to the next, his expression shifted from suspicious to stunned to contrite edged in panic. "Yes, sir. Right away. Thank you, sir." The guard passed the phone back to her. "He'd like to talk to you."

She pressed it to her ear. "Hello?"

"He's going to escort you upstairs." A pause. "And Athena?"

"Yes."

"I'm assuming the reason you're here isn't to give a repeat performance of yesterday's conversation."

She ground her teeth together, needing to unclench her jaw before saying, "No."

"Follow him. I'll see you in a few minutes."

The call ended, and she tried—and failed—to suppress a shiver at the ominous silence in her ear. Whether that shiver originated from trepidation or excitement? Well, she'd think about that later. When she wasn't headed up to the lion's den.

"Goodbye to you, too," she muttered, tucking the phone back in her purse. Turning to the guard, she smiled. "I've been ordered to follow you."

A gleam of humor lit his eyes as he slid the log-in book toward her. "If you'll sign in first, I'll take you upstairs to the Brightstar executive offices."

"Thank you."

Moments later, she stepped into the elevator with the guard, and as the doors soundlessly closed, she couldn't help but compare her surroundings to those of three years ago. When she'd dated Nico, his offices had been housed in a beautiful brick building in the Back Bay area. He'd been a millionaire then, the holding company he'd founded at twenty-four considered one of the fastest growing and wealthiest of the decade. An online search had provided a ton of information on him—and nothing personal.

Nico Morgan, Boston native, graduate of both MIT and Stanford University with multiple degrees in business management. With the assistance of investors, he'd founded Brightstar Holdings LLC at twenty-four years old and earned his first million at twenty-six. By twenty-nine, the business had expanded from not only holding the controlling stock in other companies under the parent entity, but Brightstar owned real estate, patents, trademarks and other assets. And other than a few on-dits and photos about who he'd been seen with, emerging from this restaurant or that gallery opening, that'd been it. Nothing else.

All the information about his past—his love and respect for his mother, the identity of his father—had come directly from him. Even now, as she rode up this pillar of glass and steel to his high-rise offices, awe shimmered inside her that Nico, a man who guarded his privacy tighter than the Hope Diamond's security detail, had shared parts of himself with her. Of course, that had been when she'd been so in love he could do no wrong. That had been her excuse. What'd been his? Momentary lapse in judgment triggered by bone-liquefying sex?

Yes. Putting the kibosh on thoughts of sex when about to meet said man who'd redefined the meaning of it seemed like a fabulous idea.

Swallowing a sigh, she instead focused on what she'd say to him. And just how much crow she could digest, since not twenty-four hours earlier she'd basically kicked him and his proposal out of her bakery.

God, this was going to be painful. Especially since crow tasted nothing like red velvet cupcakes.

The elevator slid to a stop and the door opened to a well-appointed lobby. A light wood—with serene blues and dark greens encompassed the decor's theme and lent the space a calming effect. Couches, tables and beautiful art of sweeping landscapes occupied half the room, and a wide, circular desk of the same wood claimed one corner. The effect exuded wealth and exclusivity while also inspiring confidence in the abilities of the personnel behind those closed doors to the left of the desk.

Oh yes, though her time of researching him online had

passed, the new address, the atmosphere that reeked of money—it all telegraphed just how well Nico had done in the last few years.

"This way, Ms. Evans." The guard guided her toward the young man rising from his seat behind the desk. "Mr. Morgan asked me to bring up his guest, a Ms. Athena Evans. He's expecting her."

"Yes." The young man, whose nameplate identified him as Paul Landon, said, "I can take Ms. Evans back. Thank you." Turning to Athena, he nodded. "If you'll come with me."

She moved toward the closed double doors but paused to offer the security guard a smile, and a warm one this time. "Thank you for your help."

"You're welcome." Dipping his chin, he headed for the elevators, and she…

Well, she headed for her fate.

Paul led her through the doors and she stepped into an open, surprisingly bright area. Desks and small sitting nooks dotted either side of the hall. She passed a wall of windows and a large conference room with black leather chairs and small computer monitors mounted on the table like soldiers in front of them. Offices, some with open doors and others with closed, claimed the rest of the space, and at the far end, Paul paused in front of a closed one.

With a quick knock, he opened the door and stepped inside.

"Mr. Morgan, Ms. Evans to see you."

"Thank you, Paul. Please shut the door behind you." Nico rose from behind his desk, and her gaze zeroed in on him.

She didn't see or hear Paul leave behind her. Nico commandeered every sense, creating a vacuum in the room so everything centered on him. Yesterday had been like falling into a vortex of *him*, and today was no different.

How many times had she lost herself in that onyx gaze? How eyes so dark could blaze so hot had been an enigma she'd never solved. She'd just enjoyed the burn. Even now, as he rounded his desk and stalked across the cavernous office, that black stare roamed over her face, dipping to her mint green sleeveless blouse and high-waisted, emerald, wide-legged pants. Her exposed skin tingled, as if sunburned, and it required every ounce of restraint she possessed not to skim her fingertips over the affected area. She refused to acknowledge—even to herself—that he affected her.

Affected her. Hah. Such a poor word to describe the... the gravitational pull that seemed to wrench her in his direction.

She wanted to pounce on the excuse of a three-year absence intensifying his magnetism, but that would be a lie. This *thing* between them had always been powerful, electric. From the first time they'd met at a restaurant opening to the last time she'd walked out of his penthouse...

And he let her go.

Her birth parents. Nico. And even, in some ways, her adopted parents.

Why was it so easy for people to let her go?

What was it about her that...?

No, she'd traveled that road, pitted with doubts and insecurities, so many times. None of the sharp curves and ditches remained a mystery. She had filled those potholes with enough tears to flood them out. And for what? Nothing changed. So she did what she always did.

Kept moving forward.

Kept...fixing.

Which was what brought her here today. Fixing a mess.

"Thank you for seeing me, Nico," she said, surprised and grateful her voice held steady when her thoughts ping-ponged all over the place, taking her emotions with them.

"Call it curiosity."

He cocked his head, sliding his hands in the front pockets of his pants, the move spreading his dark gray suit jacket open. A light gray and black tie bisected the white shirt stretching over his wide chest, and she jerked her gaze back to his face. Heat poured into her throat and cheeks. *Please, God, don't let him have noticed. Or at the very least, let him pretend he didn't notice.*

But this was Nico. Nothing got by him. And the arch of that dark eyebrow informed her he'd caught the slip.

Deny, deny, deny. Or ignore, ignore, ignore.

"Curious?" she parroted.

"About what could have possibly torn you from that bakery and caused you to come down here. To me."

...Come down here. To me.

That shouldn't have sounded like an erotic invitation. But from the syrupy lust pouring through her veins and the liquid heat gathering between her thighs, her body heard it as one.

There'd been a time when she hadn't needed permission to tunnel her fingers through the thick, black waves that framed his face. A time when those deep-set, obsidian eyes had glittered with pleasure as her lips mapped the fierce features of his face. Either a loving, meticulous sculptor or a mad, frantic artist could be blamed for the broad brow, slashing cheekbones, arrogant blade of nose and the indecently lush mouth. The angles, slants and curves formed a work of art so harsh, so brutal, so sensual, a person vacillated between worshipping it or scurrying away.

With that tall, lean, powerful body, he reminded her of a wolf. Lethal, untamed, gorgeous and hungry. Always hungry for more, whether it was success, contracts, companies, revenge…her.

She shivered.

God, how he'd once been ravenous for her.

Her gaze dipped to his mouth, and a buzz like downing a fast shot of whiskey sizzled inside her. Glancing away, she focused on the sitting area with the couch, chairs and tables with a stunning view of the city and Boston Harbor as a backdrop.

"I need to speak with you about your…proposal from yesterday," she said.

"Look at me."

She jerked her attention back to him, the blunt demand brooking nothing less than obedience. And dammit, she gave it to him.

"I don't feel like having this conversation with the back of your head," he continued, his tone smooth, with a hint of steel. "Don't get shy now, Athena. Look me in the eyes and confess why you're here."

Shy.

Right. They both knew what he really meant. *Don't be a coward. Say the words.* Because he wanted them. He would feast on this pound of flesh.

Anger flashed inside her, so bright and hot she should be a pile of ash in front of him.

"You're enjoying this, aren't you?" she ground out.

"Yes." He inclined his head. "Now tell me why you're here."

She bared her teeth in a facsimile of a smile, spreading her arms wide. "Why, I'm here to whore myself."

Oh yes, she was being facetious, but in a way, the words struck too close to home. Bile churned in her belly. She was selling herself for her family.

God…

"Get out."

The cold order snatched her from her own head, and she blinked, staring at him. Noting the *furious* lines of his face, the gleam in his black eyes and the flattening of his full lips. She nearly stumbled back. Only pride kept her rooted, and that might very well be her downfall. But it couldn't prevent a tingle of foreboding from tripping over the nape of her neck.

"What?" she asked, shaking her head.

"Get out," he repeated. "If this is your play, I'm not interested. Because I'm not your family. They're in the victimization business, not me. They make a fucking profession of playing the victims and expecting you to be their savior. I'm not going there with you. I offered you a bargain. Accept the terms or don't. Those are your choices. But this sacrificial lamb bullshit? Do it with them, not me."

His words—no, his accusation—pummeled the breath from her lungs. She stood there, bruised and shaken by the ugly truth in them. She'd wanted the choice to be taken from her, to be a victim so she could have no blame in this situation. When in truth, she had as much account-ability as her mother, as the rest of her family. Because she could've said no. She could've tracked her brother down in whatever bed, bar or hole he'd hidden in and or-dered him to straighten out what he'd fucked up.

But she hadn't. She done what she always did.

Raced to the rescue. Or trudged, in this case, but the result was the same.

Trouble, that one. And if you're not careful, he'll take

*you down in the mud while he comes out smelling like
a rose.*

That hadn't been Nico's warning about Randall, but
Mama's. And as much as Athena longed to yell at Randall for screwing up and being so damn selfish again,
and at Nico for, well…everything past and present, she
couldn't. Wouldn't. Because in the end, this wasn't about
either one of them.

This was about her grandmother and the legacy she'd
worked over fifty years to ensure succeeded. If Athena
had to save her brother's ass from the fire one more time
and enter a devil's bargain to do it, then it was a small
sacrifice.

It was the least she could do for the woman who'd
loved her unconditionally and never made her feel any
less of an Evans.

"You're right," she murmured, catching the flare of
surprise in Nico's dark eyes.

But in the next moment, his gaze became hooded,
suspicious.

"I'm right," he drawled, arching an eyebrow. "Forgive
me if I'm stunned—and skeptical—of this sudden agreement. Especially since your very presence here contra-
dicts the words coming out of your mouth." He cocked his
head, that intense stare probing, cutting. "If you're here
to assume the role of the walking wounded, there's the
door. On the other hand, if you're going to own your decision, then tell me what that is and let's move forward."

"I get it, Nico," she quietly said.

"Do you?" He softly snorted. "That would be a first."

"I offended you, and I'm sorry."

He studied her for several long moments. And those
black eyes revealed nothing of his thoughts. She'd always
resented—and admired—that talent.

"Why are you here?" he finally asked.

Sand seemed to coat her tongue, but she swallowed, barreling past the suffocating sensation. "To ask you if the offer to cover my brother's loan is still open. If it is, I've changed my mind, and I'd like to accept it."

"Not offer, Athena. Bargain. Proposal. Because I want something from you for that three hundred thousand dollars, plus interest. Are you willing to meet those terms?"

She parted her lips but before she could answer, he stepped forward, his hands sliding out of his pockets. His big body glided with a grace and power that sent a frisson of excitement skittering through her. Of their own volition, her thighs squeezed as if remembering embracing those lean hips as he moved over her, thrusting deep inside, claiming her...

"Should I spell out those terms for you?" he asked, crossing the office and not stopping until only inches separated them. He didn't touch her, but that achingly familiar scent of sandalwood and soap wrapped around her, teasing her senses and bombarding her with memories better locked away. Was breathing really necessary? "I'll pay off your brother's debt, saving your precious bakery. And in return, you're going to pretend to be my fiancée. My lover, Athena. In front of Cain and Achilles Farrell and Kenan Rhodes and their significant others, we will be two people hopelessly in love, who look seconds from finding the nearest corner to fuck in. I don't give a damn if you begrudge every breath I take, when we're in front of them—in public, period—for the next three months, you will make everyone believe there's no other man you want." His head lowered until their breath nearly mingled, mated. "No other cock you need inside you."

She should be disgusted at his language, at the infiltration of her personal space when they'd ceased being *that* to one another long ago. Should... Instead lust shimmered between them, thick and heavy. She *inhaled* it. But just under that desire pulsed the resentment he mentioned.

That, too, should've disappeared after three years. But it beat within her, making its presence known. And with each throb in her veins and ache between her thighs, that anger grew.

"You couldn't even say that word aloud when we were together," she whispered, trying and failing to keep the bitterness out of her voice. Not so with her. She'd been the first, and the last, to say "I love you," in their relationship.

"Fuck?" His gaze flicked to her mouth, then returned to her eyes. "Not true. I used it quite frequently and creatively if memory serves."

"I'm glad I amuse you." Because she couldn't draw in one more sandalwood and fresh soap-infused breath, she stepped back and to the side, not caring if he interpreted it as a retreat. She needed space. "And no worries, Nico," she said, curving her mouth into a tight smile. "I have three hundred thousand reasons to bring my best performance."

"And I intend to get my money's worth," he murmured, and damn if that didn't sound like a threat...or a promise. "Out of curiosity—" he stalked back to his desk and hiked a hip on the corner "—who begged you to come to me? Your parents? Your brother? Or do they even know you're here?"

"I have terms of my own," she said, avoiding his question. "My family is off-limits. We don't talk about them. We don't involve them. From here on out, this is just between you and me."

"Still the fierce protector." The corner of his mouth quirked high, but it contained more than a hint of derision. "A shame they've never thought to return the favor."

"Off. Limits." she ground out. "Second, before I begin…anything, I want a contract spelling out that you will clear Randall's debt regardless of whether your plans come to fruition or not."

"One would think you didn't trust me." He scoffed, shrugging a shoulder. "Done. You're not the only one with trust issues, baby girl. The contract will be in your in-box this evening. With an NDA. Which will pertain to your family as well. Because I don't want them in my business any more than you do."

Shit. She rubbed her fingertips over her forehead. "That's a problem. I already told my mother about the loan and your offer to pay it off. I didn't go into the details of the arrangement you proposed, but she is aware of your involvement."

"Well, that answers my question, doesn't it?" His eyes narrowed on her. "Your mother offered you up like a lamb to the lion." He chuckled and the dark sound held no trace of humor. "Do you ever get tired, Athena? Martyrdom must be so exhausting."

"You're already violating my first stipulation," she warned, even as her mind railed, *Yes, dammit, it is.*

He waved a hand. "Right. My apologies." He dipped his head, although nothing about his flinty gaze or grim smile relayed regret. "I'll send your mother a nondisclosure agreement as well."

Athena flinched. "Are you serious? You're sending an *NDA* to my *mother*?"

"You're damn right. I trust her even less than I trust you. She possesses a blind spot the size of Longfellow Bridge when it comes to your brother."

She wished she could argue.

"Anything else?" he asked. "Any more provisions you wish to add?"

"Yes." She met his gaze, even though a small voice whispered that she was pushing it. "About this plan of yours…"

He didn't move from his perch on the desk and yet his body seemed to loom closer. The space that separated them suddenly didn't feel adequate. But she stood her ground.

"Yes?"

She didn't fool herself. That almost gentle "yes" did not invite further inquiry.

"I don't want to be involved in anything that will hurt someone," she said. "I'm not going to let you make me a party to that."

Now he did move. Slowly, his big frame unfolded, and her breath caught in her throat at his carnal grace. He was sex in motion. She couldn't do anything but watch him. Take him in.

"After Brightstar had been in business for three years, Barron came to my office. Smiling. Proud. Bragging that he was my father. He acted as if he was responsible for my hard work, my success. Even told me I got my killer instinct from him."

Athena's fingers fluttered to her throat, circling the column as if she could capture the gasp there. Nico had never mentioned meeting his father. Why hadn't he…?

"Nico," she breathed.

"I told him I knew exactly who he was and to go fuck himself. That went over well." A faint smile, void of humor, ghosted across his mouth. "His response was to try and ruin my company. But I'd expected that and had been prepared. When he couldn't destroy my business or reputation, Barron made it personal. My mother worked for a department store at the time—Bromberg's. Farrell International owned the chain, and he had her fired. Not that she needed the money, but Mom enjoyed her job.

None of that mattered to Barron. He made sure she was escorted out by security and humiliated, just to get back at me for not needing him."

"I'm so sorry." She shook her head in disgust. "Rhoda was such a proud woman. I can't even imagine how…" She gave her head another shake. "I'm sorry," she repeated, softer this time.

"Barron wielded that fucking company like his personal weapon. It was his everything. His lover. His power. His legacy. The only thing he cared about. Even more than his family—his sons. And just like he came after what—who—I loved most in this world, I'm going after what he cared about. Even if he's not here to see it. He would've sacrificed the happiness, the welfare and peace of anyone who got in his way if it meant protecting his reputation or Farrell International. By the time I'm done, neither will remain." His chest rose and fell on his deep breaths. On his anger. "That's *my* legacy."

"And your brothers?" she whispered. "What about them? I looked them up. Except for Cain, none of them knew Barron or grew up with him. And Achilles appears to have a similar background as yours. You might have more in common with them than you think. Have you met them? Have you even considered that you might be punishing them in this plan?"

"This isn't about them, nor is this a family reunion. Just as they have no idea I even exist, I have no affection or loyalty toward them. They're men who have the misfortune of sharing the same DNA as me. That's it." He slashed his hand through the air. "The fact is they were blackmailed into overseeing that company. A company that is a monument to a man who didn't give a fuck about people in life and gave even less about them in death. No, Athena, I'm not walking away. Not until Farrell International lies in rubble. And you have a choice. Stay, knowing what's ahead. Or leave. But if you leave this time, there's no second chance."

She could go. And her grandmother's bakery would go with her. He wasn't the only one who had a legacy on the line.

"I'm staying," she said. "But you should know that I'm not going to stop trying to convince you that there's a better path than the one you've set yourself on.   Revenge, Nico…" She spread her hands wide, palms up. "You can't possibly believe you'll escape the fallout. And I know you can't—or won't—believe this, but I don't want to see you hurt. And this has pain written all over it."

Something flickered in his eyes, and if possible his face hardened even more. The curve of his lips did nothing to soften it.

"You're right. I don't believe it." He angled his head, and an edge sharpened his silken tone. "Let's be clear, Athena, we're pretending to be an engaged couple who cares for one another. It's a pretense that doesn't spill over into reality. There's no need for method acting. Unless…"

His hooded gaze dropped once more to her mouth. *Dammit*, she nearly sank her teeth into her bottom lip. She managed to prevent that telltale action but could do nothing about the catch of breath in her lungs. God, if he heard that… His glittering eyes shifted back to hers. *Oh yes*. He'd most definitely *heard*.

"I don't want to hear one damn lie from your mouth, but if you want to rehearse other aspects of our performance, I believe in perfection."

The low rumble of his voice stroked over her exposed skin, caressed her breasts, leaving her nipples beaded. Her belly pulled so tight, she swallowed a whimper, attempting to ignore the throbbing ache deep in her sex. And failing.

She hated his effect on her. Hated how…empty she felt.

Hated how she needed him to fill her.

Only him.

"Next stipulation," she whispered. "We save all public displays of affection for the public."

"And you save your pretty lies for yourself."

They stared at one another, only the jagged rasp of her breath punctuating the silence.

You left me first!

The scream ricocheted off her skull. Despair threatened to sweep her feet out from under her, because she'd believed she'd moved past this. *This.* This right here was why she didn't—couldn't—allow the door to her past with Nico to creak open. It jeopardized all her hard-won control and contentment.

He'd *devastated* her.

In *his* narrative, he was the injured party. She'd constantly chosen her family over him. She'd walked out on him. But he'd abandoned *them* long before she'd left his penthouse that day. At some point, she'd convinced herself it was okay that he'd never love her, even though she'd given him her heart. But in the end, investing all of herself into a relationship, into a man who refused to do the same, had drained her. She couldn't do it any longer. But Nico had only seen her returning home as once more allowing her family to manipulate her.

And he'd let her go.

He hadn't come after her. Because his feelings for her had limits.

He wasn't so different from everyone else in her life, after all.

"Three months," she whispered.

"Three months," he said. "Then we go back to business as usual. Where I don't exist in your perfect world and you're no longer a part of mine. But until then," he moved forward, blocking out everything in the room but *him*, "you are mine and I'm yours. Better learn how to act like it."

"And you?" she demanded, hiking up her chin. "Can you *act like it*?"

What the hell are you doing?

He didn't answer her.

Then again, yes, he did.

Nico shifter closer, until the lapels of his suit jacket grazed the ruffles on the front of her blouse. And then closer still. Until the unyielding granite of his chest pressed against her breasts. This time, the whimper in her throat clawed free. Mortified, she closed her eyes. But when that only amplified the lust crackling in her veins, she quickly opened them again.

Damn. It'd been *so long*.

So long since she'd been touched.

So long since a man's body had aligned with hers, thighs bracketing hers, dick—*oh God*—dick nudging her stomach.

No, no. Not any man. *This man*. Nico.

The backs of his fingers trailed down her cheek, and a whisper of air shuddered from between her lips. Nico leaned back, staring down into her face. He rubbed a thumb over her bottom lip, seeming not to care about messing up her lipstick or that it would stain his skin. The caress wasn't gentle. He pressed the tender flesh against her teeth, and she fucking loved it. Loved the messiness of it, the eroticism of it.

Just loved that he touched her.

"Can I act like I want you? Like my hands itch to tangle in these beautiful curls? Or that my cock gets hard just from me touching this rude as fuck mouth and remembering how well you use it? Or that my body is on the verge of taking you down to this floor and covering you like the animal you think I am?"

He slipped the tip of his thumb between her lips. Her tongue barely dabbed the skin before he withdrew.

Nico stepped back. Taking his heat. The carnal pall he'd dropped over them. She shivered in the sudden loss of temperature. Blinked against the abrupt return to reality.

Oh shit.

She met his narrowed, assessing gaze and humiliation crept into her face.

"I think I have it covered," he said, arching a dark eyebrow.

He'd played her. Of course he'd noticed her physical reaction to him—the man missed nothing—and he'd played her.

Well, screw him.

"Yes, I kind of got the notice." She deliberately lowered her gaze to the still-hard erection ruining the pleat of his suit pants.

"Touché." Without trying to cover the evidence of his arousal, he crossed his arms over his chest. "Are we in agreement, Athena? No more terms to discuss?"

"Yes." She inhaled—then exhaled. And sealed her fate. "And no."

"Good." He nodded. His voice lowered. "Do you want to shake on it?"

She didn't, and he didn't expect her to; it's why he offered.

And it's why she crossed the space between them,

hand extended. Surprise flared in his eyes, and maybe a glimmer of admiration. She didn't give a damn about his admiration. But the satisfaction that careened inside her at the surprise? That was sweet.

Still…she braced herself. Because pride might be driving her forward but it didn't fool her.

When her palm slid across his, those long fingers wrapping tightly around hers, she couldn't prepare for the punch of lust that barreled into her like a runaway freight train. Hell, this was ridiculous. She'd just had his cock on her stomach, for God's sakes. But his hand surrounding hers had her sex clenching hard.

Damned if he'd know it, though.

Schooling her expression, she met his gaze, even gave his hand a firm squeeze before letting go. And ordered herself not to scrub away the tingle in her palm.

"The contract will be in your in-box this afternoon, Athena. As soon as you sign and return it, we begin. Don't even think of walking away."

Again. He didn't say it, but it echoed between them loud and clear.

"I wouldn't dream of it."

She turned and left. But she would be back.

Three hundred thousand dollars and her grandmother's dream ensured that.

Four

Nico stepped from the back of the town car, absently buttoning his tuxedo jacket, his gaze focused on the three-story apartment building in front of him. The Cambridge condominium was new; Athena had lived in a duplex near her family's Dorchester home when they'd first started dating. He glanced around the quiet street, noting the designs of the other buildings that differed enough to prevent a cookie-cutter view. A bicycle rack outside one downstairs balcony. A small garden in front of another. A waterfall of hanging plants and colorful flowers decorating yet another. The neighborhood seemed nice, peaceful.

What the hell was Athena doing here?

Moving onto the curb, he again checked the discreet black iron number on the building, then climbed the covered stairs to the second level. Verifying he had the right apartment, he knocked on the green door with the gold three in the center.

Impatience flickered inside him, and he ruthlessly smothered it. He couldn't afford to be anything but clear-headed. Especially tonight. Tonight would be the commencement of years of planning. Tonight he would make his first overt move into Barron's inner circle—the one he'd created after his death. Nico couldn't make mistakes, not with the men who were his half brothers.

Half brothers.

His mouth twisted. As did something buried deep in his chest.

Nico had followed Cain and Achilles Farrell and Kenan Rhodes over the last nine months. The three men who'd once been strangers seemed close and supportive of one another. They definitely worked well together. Farrell International had thrived under their joint ownership, even in just these few months. With Cain's experience with the company, Achilles's technology knowledge and recent acquisition of a gaming software design company, and Kenan's marketing expertise and recent revitalization of the Bromberg's department store, they'd exceeded the board's and shareholders' expectations.

Had Barron foreseen that? Or had he wanted his offspring to crash and burn without him at the helm? Hard to tell with that bastard. Probably the latter. But Barron hadn't counted on them bonding like real brothers.

I have no affection or loyalty toward them. They're men who have the misfortune of sharing the same DNA as me.

The words he'd hurled at Athena a week earlier in his office paraded through his head. For a moment, he'd frozen, fearing she'd caught a trace of bitterness in his voice. For all his life, it'd been just him and his mother, until she'd died. No father to call on for advice. No brothers to lean on. He hadn't cared.

Until Athena asked him about his half brothers.

That had always been her superpower and his kryptonite. She'd made him *fucking* feel. It'd terrified him even as it'd brought him to his knees. Only for her.

And what had she done while he'd been there? Torn his figurative throat out.

She'd taught him a valuable lesson that no college professor, cunning businessman or even his so-called father had.

Vulnerability and trust were risks not worth the high cost.

Only a fool repeated the same mistake when the losses damn near wiped him out.

He wasn't a fool.

So being alone—didn't bother him.

Not when the alternative meant letting another person tear a hole open in him.

Again.

The condominium door opened, and his resolve took a direct hit.

Fuck.

It required every ounce of the icy control he was known for not to crowd her back into her apartment and peel that cocktease of a dress from her body.

Not push deep into that tight, wet warmth he remembered.

"What's wrong?" She frowned, glancing down and skimming her palms over sweetly rounded hips and slender thighs. "You can't complain. This is one of the dresses you sent over. Which, by the way, I'm sure you didn't mean to imply that I'm not capable of choosing clothes for myself."

"I'm not an idiot." For choosing this dress? Yes, he was. "I wouldn't dare to presume that. Or tell you if I did." He nodded toward the entryway. "Are you going to allow me in?"

She hesitated, and he didn't know whether to be offended or amused. Before he could decide, she shrugged a bare shoulder and shifted to the side.

He didn't try to quell the curiosity that swept through him as he entered. When he'd known her years ago, her tastes had ranged from bohemian chic to eclectic—a nicer term for damn near weird. Athena would conscript him into going on shopping jaunts to the Cambridge Antique Market to hunt down what she called "treasures." Sometimes, her grandmother would join them, and the two of them could go for hours, while Nico trailed behind, their glorified caddy. They had been some of the happiest times he'd shared with her.

But the atrocities and oddities that had ended up in her little Dorchester apartment? Those he could've gone his whole life without seeing.

Stepping inside this new place, he surveyed the open living area that flowed from one room to another, the only partition an exposed brick wall separating the kitchen from the rest of the home. A hall branched off from the entrance of the sunken living room, leading to, he assumed, bedrooms and bathrooms. As he moved farther into the condo, he spotted the glass French doors leading to a balcony.

But these details didn't catch his attention. The total lack of personality—*her* personality—did. He scanned the area once more, certain he'd missed…something. Anything that betrayed the vibrant person with so much vitality that it emanated from her, even into her kooky decor.

Yet *she* was missing.

What happened?

The question weighed on his tongue like a massive boulder. A band constricted around his chest. His palms tingled, the muscles in his arms tensed, preparing to... what? Grab her? Drag her close, fold around her and hold her tight? Rub up and down that ramrod straight spine and demand to know what the fuck happened to strip her of joy? Because he sensed with a certainty that had earned him his first million that's what had happened. The uninhibited glee with which she used to decorate her place had been her safe, happy space.

What—or who—had stolen that from her? And what did Nico need to tear down, to raze to the ground to return it to her?

"Nico?"

The sound of his name wrapped in her sultry voice yanked him back. The three years she'd been out of his life were her business, not his. And opening that door only invited a trouble he had no desire to entertain.

Three months.

Three months, with rules. And then she would be gone, disappearing like smoke once more. Only this time, he would be the one extinguishing the "relationship."

"You look lovely," he said, unable to contain the edge of a growl that roughened his voice.

"This old thing?" she drawled, but again, she rubbed her hands down the emerald lace gown, the nervous gesture belying her snarky tone.

He could've told her to stop fidgeting, that she had zero to worry about. That she was a goddamn vision. He could go into detail about how the wide off-the-shoulder straps emphasized the beauty of her breasts, lifting them and throwing him back into memories of when he had permission to cup their soft, firm weight.

Could tell her how the lace conformed to each perfect

curve like a lover. Could express how that thigh-high slit offered him a seductive peek at her long, toned leg.

Could finish with how her crown of curls was the very picture of elegance. But it also had him battling the urge to remove each and every pin until those wild, gorgeous spirals filled his hands, tangled around his fingers.

Yes, he could inform her of all of that.

Instead, he glanced away from the temptation of her. "Are you ready to go?"

He felt her considering gaze on him rather than saw it. That's because he refused to meet it, like a coward. But if she glimpsed what he suspected he did a damn poor job of concealing... No, until he got his shit together, he'd avoid that too-perceptive scrutiny.

"I am. Let me just get my wrap."

When she strode over to the couch, he deemed it safe to turn around. He watched the subtle, sensual sway of her hips and ass.

It was going to be a long night.

She picked up a length of matching satin material off the back of the sofa, then headed back in his direction.

"Here, let me." He took the wrap and settled it around her shoulders because manners dictated he had to, not just so he could inhale her sugar, vanilla and warm skin scent.

"I'll admit, the stylist chose well. Thank you for arranging all of this," she murmured. "I didn't mean to sound ungrateful."

Stylist. Right. Here's where he could've admitted that he'd personally chosen all the gowns sent over, including this one because it'd made him think of the green in her hazel eyes, but he trapped that confession behind a clenched jaw.

"You're welcome."

He stepped back.

Touching her would be a part of the pretense, and if his reaction to her now was anything to go by, this night would be far more difficult than he'd first believed.

Mentally, he chuckled at himself and it held no trace of humor. Hubris. He'd been accused of possessing more than his fair share a time or two. Not until this moment did he believe it. Because he'd thought being in Athena's presence, casually caressing her, hell, even looking at her, wouldn't affect him. Not after she'd betrayed him, abandoned him—abandoned *them*.

But he'd been laughably wrong.

If he was going to maintain any semblance of control over this situation, then he had to pace himself. Which meant only touching her if he needed to.

Resolve hardening inside him, he headed toward her front door and stepped outside into the hot August night, waiting until she followed behind him and locked up her apartment. Nico waved away his driver, who'd exited the town car, and opened the rear door for Athena himself. Once she moved inside, he folded in after her.

Her warm, sweet scent permeated the interior, and he ground his teeth. When this was over, first thing he'd do was detail the car. Damned if every time he rode in his own vehicle her scent would haunt him like a ghost that refused to be exorcised.

Like his memories.

He silently growled at that unwanted reminder. And untrue. He hadn't spent the last three years mired in the past.

Can I act like I want you? Like my hands itch to tangle in these beautiful curls? Or that my cock gets hard just from me touching this rude as fuck mouth and remembering how well you use it? Or that my body is on

the verge of taking you down to this floor and covering
you like the animal you think I am?

Shit. That had been a monumental Freudian slip. But
it didn't mean...fuck it.

"So, details about tonight," she said, her fingers going
at each other on her lap, twisting and tangling. "What
is this again? And what's our story? We didn't even nail
down any backstory about how we met or our engagement? Every couple has a proposal story," she muttered,
babbling.

Without permission from his brain—and in direct defiance of the edict he'd just issued about no unnecessary
touching—he covered her hands with one of his, still-
ing the agitated motion. Beside him, she stiffened, but
he didn't remove his hand, even though a part of him
yelled to do just that. They weren't *this*. He didn't give
a fuck about soothing her. All he needed from her was
to be convincing as his fiancée and make him appear
nonthreatening to Cain and Achilles Farrell and Kenan
Rhodes. Make him appear...human.

And yet...he still didn't remove his hand.

And she didn't slide hers out from under his.

"We're attending a party celebrating the renovation
of the Bromberg's department store."

"I'd heard about the possible closing of the store,"
she said, frowning. "We all shopped there when I was
younger. Not so much now, but it's definitely a part of
my childhood and has been an institution in Boston for
decades."

"Under Kenan Rhodes, it's being rebranded and mod-
ernized to not only appeal to its established customer
base, but also invite a younger clientele. He proposed
a fusion of classic and contemporary that makes sense.
Which is why I voted to approve going forward with the

project and invested in it." A small sound came from her direction and he turned, meeting her steady gaze. "What?"

"Nothing," she said.

He arched an eyebrow. "Which means something. I might regret asking this, but, Athena, what are you thinking?"

"Now I really want to tell you." She scowled, but neither the expression nor her tone contained much heat. Angling her head, she studied him, the passing shadows not hiding the contemplation in her eyes. "If I'm not mistaken, I heard admiration in your voice for your brother. And I might not know much about the corporate side of business, but you're a shareholder of Farrell International. You could vote to approve the project without investing in it. You must believe in it."

Don't you look away from her. Don't fucking do it.

If he did, it would only encourage Athena and cement, in her mind, that her ideas were true. And they were the furthest from reality.

Irritation flickered in his chest, a flare that would only take a soft gust to blow into flame.

"I admire any businessman who can yield a return," he said, ice crackling from each word. "Nothing more, nothing less. To me, Kenan Rhodes is one of the owners of the company I plan to take over. Not a brother, not anything, in spite of your persistence in seeing what doesn't exist." He shook his head, letting loose a soft scoff. "I'm surprised, Athena. You, of all people, should've stopped believing in family reunions and happily-ever-afters long ago. Real life doesn't work like that."

"I should've stopped believing in family reunions because I'm adopted and my birth parents never came looking for me?" she murmured.

Damn. Oh *damn*. "No, Athena," he softly objected. "I didn't—"

"Or I should've stopped believing in happily-ever-afters because the relationship I had crashed and burned so badly that three years later I still bear the scorch marks?"

He went rigid, that flame leaping into a full-out fire. Tension punched into the car's interior, so dense, he could choke on it. Slowly, he withdrew his hand from hers, but he didn't remove his gaze from the emotions stealing over her expression. Fury. Defiance. Sorrow... Pain.

Those last two only stoked the heat razing a path across his sternum. She had no right to show him grief or hurt. None. *She'd* broken them. *She'd* thrown them away.

She'd deemed him unworthy of a place in her world.

Like his father.

Horror pierced through the anger, and he scuttled away from that last thought as if it had spindly legs and venom.

He didn't need her. Didn't need the vulnerability she exposed in him.

"Yes," he finally said, convincing himself that her flinch didn't cause him pain. "Exactly." Then, because he couldn't let the first part of her assumption go, he flatly added, "I don't know why your birth parents put you up for adoption. It could be as simple as not wanting the responsibility of a newborn or as complicated as desiring to give a child they loved a better life. Or anything in between. What I do know is that the fact they haven't tried to reach out to you or find you has nothing to do with your worth as a person. You are the best thing those people ever created together, and as much as I don't see eye to eye with your adopted parents, that's one sentiment we probably agree on."

She stared at him, lips parted, surprise gleaming in her hazel eyes.

The same surprise echoed in him. He hadn't meant to say that, but he also refused to rescind it.

Ducking her head, her long chandelier earrings grazing the tops of her bared shoulders, she whispered, "Thank you."

He didn't reply. Several moments passed, the tension in the car no less thick but not as kinetic with emotion.

"So," she cleared her throat, "as for how we met? What are we going with?"

"The truth. We met three years ago but lost touch. Then we saw each other again when I came into the bakery. We reconnected. We'll just adjust the timeline. Instead of a week ago, we'll say four months. Everyone loves a whirlwind, second chance romance." He smiled, and it barely lifted the corner of his mouth. "If we stick as close to the truth as possible, there's less chance of messing up and we appear more believable."

"Have a lot of experience in deception, do we?" she mocked. Before he could reply, she flipped a hand over, holding it up. "Makes sense. But I think I'll leave out the 'pretend fiancée or lose your sixty-year business' part. Kind of takes the romantic shine off things."

He snorted. "Probably a good idea."

"What about our proposal?"

A throb set up in his temple. The memory that wavered across his mind should've dimmed with age and distance. Instead it popped up in front of his mind's eye, too clear, too vivid. Almost immediately, he ejected it. But not quickly enough. The footprint of it remained, and he briefly closed his eyes, dragging in a deep breath.

"Nico?" Athena asked.

"You decide. Doesn't matter to me."

The words emerged rough, terse, and he switched his gaze to the side window. *Dammit*. He clenched his jaw. If he didn't stop allowing the past to creep into the present, he wouldn't have to worry about Athena not holding up her end of this bargain. He'd wreck it. And he'd watched his mother struggle too long to fuck up now.

The rest of the ride passed in silence, and only when they stopped at the last light before Bromberg's did he reach inside his tuxedo jacket and remove a small, black box.

Passing it to her, he said, "Here. You're going to need this."

She stared down at the box, not immediately taking it from his palm. Just as he was about to utter her name, she blinked and he caught the slight tremble in her fingers as she picked it up and opened the lid.

The princess cut, five-carat diamond ring sat on a bed of black velvet and winked under the light that slanted into the car from the streetlamp. The jewelry exuded beauty, elegance and wealth.

And it was impersonal as hell.

He glanced at her, and an emotion he had no trouble identifying flickered over her face before she cleared it. Dismay. Panic.

Athena wanted that ring on her finger about as much as he desired to slide it on there.

How fucked-up was it that her obvious aversion had him ready to snatch the damn thing from the box, shove it on her finger and demand she wear it and like it?

Very.

"It's just a ring, Athena," he said, voice flat. "It's nothing but a necessary prop and means nothing."

Unlike another one for an aborted proposal a long time ago. But as it turned out, that had meant nothing, too.

"I know. I—" She stopped talking, her mouth thinning into a firm line. After another moment of peering at the jewelry as if it contained poison, she finally removed it from the box and slid it on with abrupt, economical movements. "You're right. Can't have a fiancée without a ring. Amateur mistake."

She turned and gazed out the window, and as if drawn by a relentless force, his scrutiny dropped to her lap where her hand rested. The diamond covered the width of her ring finger, staking an unmistakable claim that was false. Of all the deceptions he was ready to commit on behalf of meting out justice to a dead man, this one sat like ash in his mouth.

Jerking his attention from the lie of a ring, he stared straight ahead. In moments, they would arrive at Bromberg's, and the latest step in his plan—the most important besides quietly purchasing shares through shell companies and obtaining the majority—would commence. Focus was key. And not on the woman beside him.

"We're here," he announced as the town car slowed, entering the line of vehicles waiting to approach the front of the department store. "Are you ready, Athena?"

"To aid and abet you in duping your brothers and their women into trusting you so they're looking the other way as you blindside them with a hostile takeover?" She turned away from the window and flashed him a tight, humorless smile. "Sure. I'm ready, Nico."

Guilt flashed inside him. Guilt and shame. But as quickly as they flared, he snuffed them out. And drew up the memory of his mother's face as she'd looked just before she'd passed.

Pale. Waxen. Exhausted from the constant coughing and wheezing. Swollen from fluid buildup. Undiagnosed congenital heart failure had exacted a toll on her physically and emotionally. With regular doctor visits, proper medication and changes to her lifestyle, she could've managed the disease and enjoyed a longer life. But with mostly menial or low-paying jobs that offered no insurance for doctor appointments or prescriptions and being too busy working sometimes two jobs, she had been more concerned with providing shelter and food for him rather than focusing on herself. By the time Nico could afford to take care of her and convince her to go see about her health, it'd been too late. The disease had progressed.

A simple check to ease his mother's burden all those years could've made a drastic difference. But Barron, angry that she'd refused to abort Nico, had punished her. And Rhoda Morgan had been too proud to beg him to be in their lives. Not that it would've changed anything. By the time Nico was born, Barron had already become engaged to another woman. His replacement family had been in the works, and Barron had no need of Rhoda or his son. So he'd abandoned them, resigning them to a life of backbreaking work, struggle and poverty.

So yes. Fuck guilt and shame.

He'd lost the person he loved most in this world. His rock. It was only fitting that he'd take the same from Barron since it'd been his negligence, arrogance and lack of humanity that set them on this path. Death didn't mean a damn thing. Nico's brand of hate exceeded the grave.

"Good," he finally replied to her as the town car pulled up in front of the department store's entrance. "Your brother and the bakery are depending on it."

Not waiting for his driver to open his door, Nico

pushed it open and stepped out. Resolve and purpose settled on his shoulders, and he turned back toward the car, extending a hand toward her. She slipped her palm across his, and his fingers closed around hers, the large diamond pressing into flesh. As soon as she exited the vehicle, she didn't move forward but remained standing between him and the open car door. Tilting her head back, a smile curved her mouth, probably for the press that congregated on the sidewalk and the cameras that flashed and popped in their direction.

A consummate actress.

Oh, he knew just how good.

"Don't you dare threaten me," she snapped through a lovely smile and gritted teeth.

"Not a threat, baby girl," he murmured. To the observers outside the department store and to the reporters, it would appear as if he bent his head to whisper something sweet or flirtatious in her ear. "Just a reminder. Or motivation. Take it any way you want."

Lifting his head and stepping back, he held his arm out to her, and she settled her hand on the crook of his elbow. The small touch, though obligatory, burned through his tuxedo jacket and arrowed straight to his cock.

The jolt of lust grounded him, driving home the need to concentrate on the evening ahead and the ultimate goal. If he allowed the grinding arousal she stirred to distract him, he could lose everything.

She'd damn near eviscerated him once before.

Never again. This time, he was in control. Of the narrative, of his response to her and of their "relationship." And most importantly, when it ended.

Because when these three months were over, so were they. He would return to his life of the past three years—

one where he depended only on himself. One that might be solitary but was also free of pain and betrayal. Free of her.

Just the way he preferred it.

Five

For the year and a half she'd been with Nico, Athena had moved in the more rarified circles of Boston society. The numerous fundraiser galas, dinner parties, gallery openings, business functions… They'd introduced her to a glittering, moneyed and privileged world she'd previously only read about in the gossip columns or come across online.

She hadn't missed it.

And now, temporarily back in the realm Nico navigated with a grace that belied his humbler upbringings, she wished to be anywhere else. Bromberg's department store had been closed to the public for tonight. The lower level and food court were transformed into a space worthy of a reception at the Met. Long gold and cream curtains hid the various food kiosks. Tiny gold lights wrapped around the columns soaring up to the fourth level, flowers intermingled with them, gifting the usually overbright area with an ethereal decor. High round tables draped in champagne-colored cloths dotted the floor, while chairs upholstered in the same soft color offered places to sit. A full bar had been erected on one side of the food court and a tuxedoed band currently played classical renditions of current Top 50 hits.

Among it all mingled the rich and connected of Boston's elite.

And then there was her.

"Can't make a silk purse out of a sow's ear, big sister. Isn't that what Mama always says?"

Her brother's voice sidled into her head, and for a second, she almost glanced around to see if he'd somehow sneaked his way into this gathering. Ridiculous. She gave her head a small shake, then stared down into her glass of champagne before finishing it off. That smug gem had come from Randall just after she and Nico had broken up. Her older brother's idea of consoling her had been to remind Athena she'd had no place in Nico's world in the first place. Not the first time he'd hinted at that during her relationship with Nico, but that last time had seared her soul.

Because when she'd walked out after he'd issued that final ultimatum—*if you move out of here to return to your parents' house, don't bother coming back*—Nico hadn't attempted to contact her. To try and save what they had. She'd been disposable and easily forgotten. And Randall's thoughtless words had only cemented what she'd already believed.

She didn't belong here. And maybe Nico never thought she did either.

Yet he was the one who'd dragged her back in. *For his reasons, his plans, not because he missed or needed you.*

Best she remember and keep that uppermost in her

mind. Last time, it'd taken over a year to obtain any sense of her old self. If she dared to forget, she might find the road to recovery longer…or endless.

"Oh I don't know what caused that look on your face, but more champagne definitely cannot hurt the situation."

Before Athena could register that another person had not only joined her but had directed that pitying statement toward her, the empty glass she held disappeared. In seconds, a full glass replaced it. Glancing up from the golden, bubbly wine, Athena met a pair of dark brown eyes that reflected the smile curving her full mouth. The gorgeous, petite and curvy woman with natural dark curls that grazed her shoulders sipped from her own nearly full glass and eyed Athena over the rim.

"Sorry," the woman said, lifting a bare shoulder. "But you reminded me of *me* so much that I had to come over and introduce myself."

Athena made a show of scanning the crowd before returning her attention to the woman in front of her. "Black?"

The woman snickered. "Yes, that, too. I hate to say it, but it's true that when we spot the few Black people in the room, we gravitate toward them like they're long-lost family." She arched an eyebrow. "And pray they're not assholes."

Athena nodded but said nothing. Experience from years ago had taught her that people who approached and seemed friendly often did so with their own agenda on their minds, not a budding friendship. But her reticence didn't seem to discourage the woman in front of her.

"Smart." She lifted her glass in a small toast. "You don't know me. I could be coming over here, talking smack just to lure you into a false sense of security and then carry tales about how you trashed people in the room." She arched an eyebrow. "You might look like you'd rather be anywhere but here, but you've obviously been in these circles long enough. I'm still learning that pretty faces can sometimes hide the bitchiest of souls. And that is not gender specific."

Against her better judgment, Athena snorted. Because, *truth.* But the wealthy did not corner the market on trashy people. That trait transcended tax brackets.

"Eve Burke." The woman extended her hand toward Athena. "It's a pleasure to meet you...?"

"Athena Evans." She shook Eve's hand, her mind whirling.

Eve Burke. Kenan Rhodes's fiancée. And apparently the owner of Intimate Curves, the exclusive lingerie boutique that the guests in attendance would glimpse for the first time this evening. The unveiling of the brick-and-mortar version of what had previously been exclusively an online business—and a hugely successful one, at that—was the main reason for the party tonight. Nico had explained all of this after they'd initially arrived and had drinks and appetizers in hand.

Shit.

What had Eve said? Athena looked like she didn't want to be there. She was already messing up her one job. Heart thumping against her rib cage, Athena flipped through things to say to Nico's half brother's fiancée. Apologize? Offer an excuse? Or worse, another lie about how she was delighted to be here at Bromberg's?

No. Dammit, just...no. She couldn't add one more lie on top of the others. The biggest deception being the one weighing down her ring finger.

Yeah, not thinking about that right now.

What had Nico said? Better to stick as close to the truth as possible?

"To be honest," Athena said, silently ordering herself not to flinch, "I'm not at all comfortable in these settings." Leaning closer, she lowered her voice a shade and admitted, "I never know what to talk about. Somehow I doubt most of the people here care about how long you have to refrigerate crème brûlée before serving." She shrugged a shoulder. "So I end up standing there and smiling like an idiot. An idiot with a sore face at the end of the night."

"Oh my God, I think I might be crushing on you right now," Eve whispered, eyes gleaming with humor. "That's the most fascinating thing I've heard all night."

Athena laughed, and Eve grinned back at her.

"So you bake? Are you a chef? A caterer?" Eve asked, propping an elbow on the table next to them. "Real talk? I know nothing about cooking, especially baking. But I love to eat. As all these pretty curves attest to." She waved a hand down her divine, hourglass figure displayed to perfection in a floor-length, blush-colored bandage dress.

"My family owns Evans Bakery in Brighton."

"Did I hear Evans Bakery?" A woman with beautiful, long caramel hair and bright green eyes joined them. Clad in a royal blue, mermaid-style dress that highlighted her lush curves as well as her small baby bump, she reminded Athena of a Mother Earth pinup model. If such a thing existed. "When I first moved to Boston, I used to haunt that place. It had the most delicious snickerdoodles."

Pleasure flooded Athena for the first time since arriving. "My grandmother made those fresh every morning. They were her own recipe and she insisted on baking them herself. She wouldn't trust anyone outside the family with the recipe."

The other woman laughed. "I don't blame her. They

were fabulous. I remember your grandmother. Petite woman, but a deep voice that carried over the whole bakery? Gray hair and brown eyes? And she wore an embroidered, dark red apron every time I went there."

Athena nodded, a bit of her pleasure snuffed out by an unexpected pinch of sorrow. "That was her. My grandfather gave her that apron, and she never worked without it."

"Was her," the woman softly repeated. Surprise ricocheted through Athena when the woman reached out, gripped her hand and squeezed. "I'm sorry. She treated me with kindness and never like a stranger. That meant the world to a young woman new to the city and without friends."

"Thank you," Athena rasped.

Oh God. Don't let her start tearing up in the middle of this event.

"Eve, who did you loose Devon on now? You know her sensitivity superpowers have only increased with pregnancy. Now she's about to have this poor woman weeping in her glass. And that's a perfectly good waste of champagne. That's the true crime here."

Devon Cole, well, Farrell now—Cain's wife. So the new woman who joined their group must be Mycah Farrell, and the big, brooding giant behind her wearing the impeccable black suit and long-suffering expression had to be Achilles. Nico's brother.

Curiosity swept through Athena at her first glimpse of one of his younger half siblings. Although as tall as Nico, that's where the similarities between the men ended. Achilles's long, thick black hair tied back into a bun and his warm brown skin declared a biracial heritage, and he carried more bulk than Nico. Then there were the startling blue-gray eyes that scanned over the group, and Athena quelled the urge to glance away when his gaze landed on her.

There.

There lay the resemblance. That incisive, intense gaze and the sharp intelligence behind it. She bet this man missed nothing, just like his unknown older brother.

"No, the true crime is I can't have the champagne," Devon muttered, but her soft smile and the hand that curved around her stomach contradicted the petulance in her statement. "If I can't have it, then everyone will drink a river of salty tears." Then she emitted a wicked cackle.

A bark of laughter broke free from Athena without her permission, and she covered her lips with a hand, but none of the others seemed to find her outburst inappropriate. No, they joined in. Even Achilles smiled.

"Since I now don't remember what it feels like *not* to be pregnant, I have zero sympathy. The taste of anything alcoholic is nothing but a distant memory to me." Mycah released an exaggerated, heavy sigh. With her large baby bump, the woman did appear to be on the verge of going into labor at any second. Yet, even with her lamentations about wine deprivation, happiness and…contentment sparkled in her dark eyes. Especially when she tilted her head back and pinned her husband with a look. "Your turn next time."

"Duly noted," Achilles said, solemnly nodding. Then he turned that aquamarine gaze on Athena. "And you are?"

Mycah swatted his arm, and he slid her a look that on another person would've clearly said, "What'd I say?" But on Achilles Farrell, it was the visual equivalent of a shrug.

"Please excuse him," Mycah said to Athena, then offered her a slim hand. "I'm Mycah Farrell and this bastion of manners and decorum is my husband, Achilles."

"It's a pleasure to meet you both." She accepted Mycah's hand and shook it, giving Achilles a nod. "I'm Athena Evans. I'm here with my fiancé, Nico Morgan." She'd managed to say *fiancé* without tripping over it. Go her.

Achilles's eyebrows drew down in a slight frown, but before she had time to wonder—okay, panic—over that, all three women turned in the direction where she'd left Nico. And stared.

"Wow," Devon whispered.

"That man has always been—*whew*," Mycah muttered. Then she patted Achilles's hand. "Not you 'whew,' though."

"Thanks," came his dry reply.

"I remember meeting him a couple of months ago at the board meeting to approve the Bromberg's renovation. He's one intense man." Eve tapped her bottom lip. "Intense is sexy."

"I'm sure she's talking about you," a new, masculine voice drawled.

Athena glanced over her shoulder to find two men, both tall and wide shouldered, but one white with dark, short hair and the other with light brown skin, close cut hair and clean-shaven. Both shared the same stunning eyes as Achilles, and it declared their identity to Athena.

Cain Farrell and Kenan Rhodes.

Without even trying, she'd found herself surrounded by Nico's family. The family he refused to acknowledge and didn't want anything to do with. Sadness sank inside her like a leaden ball. He was alone; with Rhoda's passing he had no one. And here stood six people who could be family for him, but Nico wouldn't allow it. It seemed he almost preferred a solitary existence marked only by business associations and shallow social attachments.

She gave her head a mental shake. Three years he'd been out of her life. She was the last one to presume anything about him.

Yet… The ache refused to subside.

Kenan waved his brother off. "Of course, she's talking about me. Who else would she describe as intense, sexy and gorgeous?"

"I must've blacked out for a moment, because I don't remember Eve saying *gorgeous*," Cain said, voice dry.

"I've been telling Devon to get that checked out. All the stress of impending fatherhood has probably affected your faculties. Because she definitely said *gorgeous*."

"Oh my God," Achilles growled.

A chuckle bubbled up Athena's throat, and maybe she didn't contain her amusement as well as she believed, because she drew the attention of all three men.

"Athena, these are my brothers Cain Farrell and Kenan Rhodes." Achilles introduced her. "Cain, Kenan, this is Athena Evans, Nico Morgan's fiancée."

"It's wonderful to meet you, Athena," Cain said, briefly but warmly clasping her hand in his. Kenan followed suit, smiling down at her. "And congratulations. I have to make sure and congratulate Nico as well."

"Now is as good a time as any," Nico said, materializing beside her and wrapping a strong arm around her waist.

An electric charge rippled through her, and she stiffened in reaction. It wasn't lost on her that the first time they'd truly touched after a three-year absence was an act for the benefit of an audience. It played with her head. While her brain screamed "This isn't right!" her sex cheered, "More, more, more!" It was laughable how much of a cliché she'd become.

As quick as she'd gone rigid, in the next moment, she deliberately relaxed against him, curving into his side. As she used to do. Her whole body…sighed. As if in relief or contentment. Because how many times had she dreamed of being held by him? Of having carte blanche to touch him? Even if it was under these circumstances…

But what if these were the perfect circumstances? What if she could indulge in touching him, and being touched by him, if just for these stolen moments? It would be harmless, a performance. It would be safe. And Nico would never know that she privately craved each caress, each embrace, each soft and hungry look and word.

It would be her little secret.

Cain shook Nico's hand, slapping him on the shoulder. "Congratulations, Nico." He grinned. "I need to take lessons from you on how to keep a relationship out of the press. I bet it's much less stressful that way."

Nico dipped his head and his hand stroked the curve of Athena's hip, leaving waves of heat behind. Swallowing a whimper, she took a sip from her glass, but the champagne did nothing to quench the fire.

"I don't think there's anything 'less stressful' about being with me," Nico said, voice heavy with self-deprecation. "And yet, Athena's stayed anyway."

"I told him, I'm adding my halo to our wedding gift registry," she drawled.

As Cain and Kenan laughed, she absorbed the small jolt that shivered through Nico. Surprise? Probably. Up until this moment, he had cause to be concerned about her acting skills. She hadn't been pulling her weight. But being weighed down with worries about not fucking up and lust for her costar kind of disrupted her focus.

"If that's the case, request a few more. We're in arrears with ours." Kenan grinned as Eve curled against him, wrapping her arms around his waist.

"You're right about that. I'm a saint and it's about time you recognize it." Eve smiled at Nico. "It's nice to see you again, Mr. Morgan. And thank you for coming out tonight and bringing Athena with you. I think it's only fair you should know that we're officially in a custody battle for her."

Nico arched an eyebrow, glancing down at Athena then at Eve. "Please, it's Nico. And I'll give you visitation but I'm going to have to insist on primary physical custody."

"Fine," she grumbled, eyes gleaming with humor.

"Cain, Athena runs Evans Bakery." Devon looped her arm through her husband's. "Remember I told you about the bakery I found after moving to Boston? And how it was one of the places that made me feel at home for the first time? That was Evans Bakery."

"That's a small world," Cain murmured, and when he looked at Athena again, she resisted the urge to lift her fingers to her face and check for any droplets of champagne. Did all the Farrell men own those scalpel-sharp stares? "So you own Evans?"

"My family does," she corrected, and though she didn't glance at Nico, displeasure damn near emanated from him. Anger flickered in her chest. *Yes, dammit. I know how you feel about my family. You've expressed it. Ad nauseum.* But because they were supposed to be a happy couple, she bit back the scorching retort. "You can usually find me there most days, though."

"How did you two meet?" Mycah asked. "The billionaire and the baker sounds like a really cute Hallmark movie or the start to a bad joke."

Athena snorted, and the corner of Nico's mouth quirked. "I think we're a little bit of both."

"And to answer your question, he squashed my buns." Six pairs of eyes landed on her, and she shrugged. "It's true."

"Okay, that's a story," Kenan said. "Gimmee." Then he arched an eyebrow and shook his head. "Nico, I feel like you should prepare to lose cool points. No worries. We won't judge you...too much."

"My grandmother had a longtime customer, and every birthday she'd make hot cross buns just for her. This year, Mrs. Lemmons had fallen ill and hadn't been to the bakery in weeks. Even though my grandmother passed, I still baked the hot cross buns for her and was going to deliver them. I'd just found a rare open parking spot in her Back Bay neighborhood and was heading toward her building when someone—" she tipped her head back and gave that "someone" a narrow-eyed mock glare "—came barreling out of nowhere and slammed right into me, crushing my buns between us."

"In my defense..." Nico began amid all the hoots of laughter. He held up a hand, palm out. "I was late for a lunch meeting for a charity function. This, by the way, did not impress Athena. I think 'rich boy,' 'eyes in your ass' and 'jacked up my buns' were tossed around, and she might've given me the finger."

"I did not!" Athena objected, tapping him on his tight abdomen.

Even caught up in the memory and onetime happiness of their real first meeting—albeit an altered version as she'd been on a delivery errand for her grandmother and he'd been on his way to a lunch date with his mother—she couldn't erase the feel of those firm muscles and warm skin from her hand. The feel of him was branded into her fingers. She barely resisted the urge to scrub her fingers down the side of her thigh.

"She did."

"So love at first sight, then?" Eve asked, grinning.

"For me?" Nico lifted a shoulder. "Yes. But her? Not so much. I had to track her down, apologize profusely, carry more buns to Mrs. Lemmons, drink the most godawful tea in the world with her and then buy my weight in baked goods for the office. All that before she even agreed to let me take her on our first date."

"She was worth it, though," Achilles rumbled.

Nico leaned down and brushed his lips over her forehead, and God help her, she closed her eyes, savoring the sweetness of it. The artificial sweetness.

"Every hot cross bun and swallow of tea that tasted like minty dirt," he murmured.

Achilles snorted, and a bark of laughter escaped her. The others' joined in, and Athena met Nico's dark gaze.

What a phenomenal actor.

Because for a moment, she almost believed the glimmer of affection in his eyes and the warmth in his deep voice were real. But she knew better.

And all the pretending in the world wouldn't change reality.

Turning back to his family surrounding them, she resumed the performance.

"I think that went well," Athena said into the silence that filled the back of Nico's town car.

That silence carried weight, had density. And it sat on her chest like a suffocating winter blanket. She longed to kick it off, free herself. Even if it was with inane conversation.

"It did. Better than I expected." He drummed his fingers on his thigh, staring out the side window.

More silence. More…heaviness.

"I liked them." His shoulders stiffened, but he didn't remove his gaze from the window or acknowledge her statement. "Your brothers and their wives and fiancée," she expounded. "They were very nice and not at all what I anticipated."

More silence.

"Your brothers… They seemed to like you. Definitely respect you." She studied his strong, chiseled profile and didn't miss the tensing of his jaw. "Are you sure—"

"Did you notice their eyes?" he murmured, his tone almost casual. "Farrell eyes. It's a family trait. Barron had them and he passed them down to his sons." He finally turned to look at her, and in the deep shadows, his dark eyes appeared more shadowed. "All of his sons except me."

Her breath stuttered, then stalled in her lungs, a looming sense of unease yawning wide in her belly. A part of her almost told him to stop, that she'd mind her business and leave the topic alone. But the other, bigger part hunkered down, hungry to discover anything else about him. The pieces of him that he'd hoarded when they'd been together. Yes, he'd shared with her more than he'd shared with anyone else outside his mother, but still, he'd held back, guarding himself.

From her.

It'd only deepened her craving for him, and not just physically, but emotionally. Back then, Nico had showered her with jewelry, clothes, fancy dinners, even a car. But she would've given up every last gift just to have his heart. And that hadn't been an option.

So now, three years later, here she was, still aching for…pieces.

"Where most men would be proud over the birth of their first child, his first words to my mom were, 'He doesn't have the Farrell eyes. This boy isn't mine.' And he followed those up with a paternity test. Do you know when Mom told me that story, she seemed embarrassed, ashamed? As if it were her fault he rejected me instead of his arrogance. She blamed herself for giving me her eyes." His mouth twisted in a corrupted semblance of a smile. "That one and only meeting with Barron I told you about? He bragged about that paternity test, and said though I didn't inherit his eyes, I did get his killer instinct when it came to business. Those fucking Farrell eyes. As a kid, I would've traded my soul for them. But as I grew older, I was thankful for my own. And not just because I didn't want to look in the mirror and see him. But now, not having the same color eyes as Barron's sons has allowed me to have business dealings with them without suspicion or questions regarding my identity. Irony, right?"

Fury mingled with a soul-deep grief. Fury at a dead man and grief for the damage he'd inflicted and left behind. What kind of man purposefully hurt others for his own sport? Especially his sons? No wonder Nico hated Barron Farrell. Yet…

Yet at what cost?

He'd already cut off a part of himself from the world, from other people. From her when they'd been together.

What price would this plan of his demand? Worry spiked inside her, and though an ocean of pain and anger lay between them, she still feared for him.

Feared he traveled the road to becoming a replica of his father.

"I'm sorry, Nico," she whispered.

"For what?" He shifted in his seat, more fully facing her. "For having a mother who was both parents to me? For discovering my biological father wasn't just an absentee sperm donor but a bastard? For allowing his neglect and spite to strengthen me?" He cocked his head. "Or for pressing an issue I told you to let go?"

"Yes…and no," she said, not flinching from his hooded stare. "Yes, I'm sorry for all of that, but mostly because no child should be rejected by the person who is supposed to love them unconditionally. We tell ourselves that doesn't leave a scar, but we're deceiving ourselves. And no matter how successful, wealthy, strong or powerful we become, it doesn't rewrite history or erase the pain. I'm sorry you have to know that."

"*We* tell ourselves? You know it, too, don't you, Athena?"

An old, familiar ache pulsed just under her rib cage. "Yes."

Leave it. Don't say anything else. Let. It. Go.

But her lips parted, and as if an invisible force drew the words out, they unraveled between them. "I've never sought out my biological parents. Do you know why?" She didn't give him time to answer because the words tumbled out. "Fear. And not just because I'm afraid of discovering the truth behind why they gave me up. But also, I'm terrified if Mom and Dad found out I wanted to search out my birth parents, they would be hurt and angry—and throw me away. How pathetic is that? Thirty years old and scared of being abandoned by her adoptive parents because I've already lost the ones I don't remember. The ones who rejected me when they gave me away."

"Athena, you don't—"

"I don't know their reasons. Yes, I get that here." She

tapped her temple. "But here—" she splayed her fingers over her chest, her heart "—here, sometimes I just wonder what about me made it okay for them to hand me over to strangers." She let loose a raw chuckle and clasped her fingers in front of her, dropping her hands to her lap. Staring down at them, she shook her head. "God, that sounds incredibly self-pitying and ungrateful. Those strangers ended up being absolutely wonderful parents. I shouldn't complain—"

"You're entitled to your feelings, baby girl. And you should never apologize for them."

His "baby girl" slid through her like thick molasses on a Sunday morning. Warmth filled her, offering her something sweet and sinful. It wasn't the first time he'd said the sexy endearment. With barely a tug on her imagination, memories of other times he'd uttered it wavered in her head. Whispering it against her lips before he took her in a searing kiss. Groaning it into her ear as he pushed deep, so damn deep inside her. Breathing it against her damp neck as his big body shuddered above her.

"And you?" she asked.

"What about me?"

Caution. The warning snapped like a red flag in a winter wind. But she couldn't heed it. Not when the dimness of the car's interior and the privacy glass encased them in their own private world. Not when recklessness bubbled inside her. So she pushed, even knowing he could very well lash out.

"You were hurt. *Barron* hurt you. And that's the purpose behind this plan, isn't it? To hurt him back?"

He didn't move, but she *felt* his emotional withdrawal.

"The performance ended as soon as we left the department store. Don't try and pretend to know me, Athena."

Oh she should've remembered that when he did lash

out, it wasn't hot and quick. Nico turned cold, his cuts like freezer burn.

"I wouldn't dare claim to know you," she said, voice low, but by some minor miracle, steady. "Even after moving in with you, sharing your bed and loving you, I still wouldn't say it."

"Loving me?" The corner of his mouth curved, and he softly chuckled, the sound ugly, dark. "Is that what you called it? Did you love me when you walked out and didn't look back? If that's love—" he sneered the word as if it left a filthy taste in his mouth "—then I want no part of it. Love is fickle, faithless and will betray you as soon as look at you."

"Yes," she admitted. "I loved you even when I left. I loved you so much that it was a matter of survival. Stay in a relationship knowing you were only willing to give me pieces of you while I gave you all of me. Or leave, choosing more for myself."

"You never offered me the chance to give you more. You never asked."

"Every time I said 'I love you,' I asked," she murmured.

His head jerked back as if she'd clipped him in the chin. An emotion passed over his face, there and gone before she could decipher it in the shadows.

"Don't twist this around," he ground out, slashing a hand through the air. "You left because your family called and you came running like you always did. And nothing's changed. Before you take my inventory, you need to start taking account of your own. If it makes you feel better to blame me, go ahead, but we both know I, or any man, will never be able to compete with the only loyalty and love you have."

"You wanted me to cut them off," she hotly objected,

slamming a hand up, palm out. "You're right. I won't do that."

"No, Athena." He leaned back, his expression shuddered, eyes opaque. "That's what you never understood. I didn't want you to cut them off. I just needed you to make room for me, too."

I just needed you to make room for me, too.

The statement rebounded off her skull but resonated in her heart.

That's not true!

The objection surged up her throat, hovering on her tongue. Her family had needed—still needed—her in a way he hadn't. Toward the end of their relationship, she'd been a silent roommate and lover. He'd spoken of irony.

No, the greatest irony was he needed her now, to infiltrate his half brothers' inner circle, in a way he never had needed her when they'd been together.

So if it'd seemed like she put her family first, maybe it'd been because they'd done the same with her.

Did they, though? Or did they take advantage of your willingness to always be there?

She shook her head as if it could dislodge that disloyal thought.

But Nico continued in the same flat tone, "But that was then, and we're not back there. We'll never go back there." The car pulled to a stop in front of her condo, and he pushed open the door, stepping outside. He turned to her, extending his hand. By rote, she slid her palm across his and allowed him to guide her out of the vehicle. As soon as she cleared it, he dropped her hand and shifted backward. It was a small movement, but huge. Loud. "We made our choices. That's the past, and from now on, let's focus on the present. Keep your end of the bargain, and I'll keep mine. Then we can part ways—again."

He didn't add "for good," but it echoed on the warm night air.

Silly her for trying to breach those carefully constructed, barbed wire fences that guarded his feelings, his heart. She should've remembered the consequences of trying to scale those walls. Last time, she'd survived with a shattered heart. If she dared to forget, the damage would be much worse a second time.

But she wouldn't forget again.

No, he'd reminded her clearly of the lesson she'd learned three years ago.

Nico Morgan broke things and didn't stick around to piece them back together.

Six

"Hey, big sister. You're looking awfully comfortable there behind my desk."

Gritting her teeth, Athena looked up from the payroll system to see her brother leaning a shoulder against the bakery office door, grinning.

That grin contained charm and humor. But his emphasis on "my desk" kind of peeled away some of that charisma. Randall seemed to enjoy getting in subtle digs and reminding her that he owned the bakery, and she was no more than an employee.

Usually, she ignored his immature need to assert his dominance. Today, though, she wasn't in the mood.

She'd asked—no, demanded—one thing of her mother before she agreed to the bargain with Nico. Get Randall into the bakery to take over the managerial duties she'd assumed in his absence. In the last three weeks, she'd attended more social events than she had in the last three years. Nearly every night, she accompanied Nico to dinners and parties in his bid to appear more approachable and—how had he put it?—*human* to his half brothers. And nearly every night, she'd returned home stressed, emotionally drained and so turned on. Touching herself to thoughts of him had become a nightly routine, like brushing her teeth.

Shower. Floss. Orgasm. Repeat.

Needless to say, early four o'clock mornings at the bakery were a thing of the recent past. And yes, she could've gone into the store later in the morning or afternoon. But she'd refused, granting Randall the chance to step up and prove himself a responsible leader. And son and brother.

The call she'd received last night from one of the employees disabused her of that idea.

Payroll had been missed last week. They'd asked Kira about their wages, and her sister had promised to let Randall know, but he hadn't shown up to the bakery, and the bakery's employees had gone without a paycheck. Why Kira hadn't called her...

God, Athena had to stop deluding herself. She knew perfectly well why her sister hadn't reached out to her. Their mother had probably forbidden it. Because then Athena would know Randall had been...being Randall.

Frustration coalesced inside her. Frustration threaded with resentment.

Frustration because her mother would rather not pay their loyal, hardworking employees than order her son to *do. His. Fucking. Job.*

Resentment because her parents, fully aware their son was an overgrown boy who hadn't shown the slightest interest in the bakery while Mama was alive, had still turned the reins over to him. Because he had a penis.

No, because he was a *real* Evans.

Yet they expected the oldest, passed over child with the unknown bloodline to helm the ship. To smile, accept the dismissal of her tireless hours and faithful commitment and carry on as usual.

A live coal burned in her belly, and it had bitterness branded into it. When had she become so cynical, so unsatisfied, so…angry? Staring at her brother as he straightened, stretched and sauntered into the tiny office, a king surveying his land, that piece of coal burned red.

Handsome, with tawny skin and dark brown eyes, Randall had always been popular. Whether it'd been school, sports or just in the neighborhood, he was known for his playful, outgoing, always-up-for-a-good-time demeanor. And he hadn't been required to grow up. Randall Evans, the Peter Pan of Dorchester.

Even now, he ambled in wearing clothes wrinkled to hell and back, giving her the impression he was just rolling in from a long night out.

Wow.

"I will move and let you finish up payroll. Just say the word," Athena said, smiling and holding up her hands. "Is that why you're here today? To take care of it?"

His grin didn't waver, but his eyes narrowed. Right. Because they both knew that was not the reason he'd decided to show up. The true reason remained unclear, but she'd bet her brother hadn't suddenly appeared to work.

"No." Randall waved a hand at her, and she ground her teeth at the entitled gesture. "You got it. Besides, that's what you do. I trust you to handle it."

Handle it? She'd been *handling it* since Mama's stroke almost three years ago. *Her.* Their parents hadn't been involved in the business in years, and when their grandmother became ill, Athena had stepped up. So yes, *handling it* was her forte.

"Well, I hope you remember the training we received on the system. Because I'm going to be unavailable to do this again for the next few months. The only reason I'm in today is because our employees have gone a week without pay."

"*My* employees should've called me instead of you if there was an issue."

She snorted, and Randall lost his grin.

"You have something to say?" he asked, voice low.

"Yes." She tilted her head, studied him. The faintly red eyes, the sullen curve of his mouth. All signs of spoiled behavior. "If Kira could've called you, she would have. If the employees knew you or your number in the first place, they might have contacted you. But should've-could've doesn't pay the bills or their wages."

"I'm the owner of this bakery, big sister. Mom and Dad decided I should take it over, not you. That means you work for me, and if I need you to take care of the payroll, then you'll do it without all the lip."

"Wrong." Fury vibrated through her, and she rose from her chair. "I don't work for you. You don't pay me a salary. I've taken over this bakery because you've been an absentee boss. I've done this family a favor by stepping into the hole you've left. But don't ever get it twisted, Randall. You didn't hire me, and you can't give me orders. You never have and don't think you can start today."

He smirked. "And yet, here you are. Taking care of business. Keeping the place running."

"Not for you."

"Same difference." He shrugged. "But whatever. If you don't want to do it anymore, show Kira. She can take over payroll. I don't know what the hell crawled up your ass."

Ten. Nine. Eight. Seven... She counted down, dragging in breaths.

You can't put hands on him. One, he's your brother. And two, you won't do well in jail.

"What're you doing here?" she finally asked.

"Do I need a reason?" he scoffed. When he hadn't been here in years? Why yes, he did need a reason. "But Mom called and asked me to come over and check on things."

Athena bit the inside of her cheek, swallowing down a flaming retort. More likely, Mom told him to meet Athena here, claiming she had something to tell Randall. In other words, let Athena take care of the dirty work.

"Kira cannot take over the payroll since she doesn't know the system. If you don't remember, the number to the company representative is in the email contacts. She'll come out and give everyone a refresher training course. You'll need to do this ASAP since I won't be available for the next pay period." Leaning down, she tapped several keys and closed out of the program. "Last week is taken care of, and since you're here, you can cover the rest of the shift."

Athena pulled open the bottom drawer, removed her purse and then rounded the desk. Pausing in front of her brother, she tipped her head back and met his defiant dark gaze.

"So you're just abandoning the bakery? Leaving us high and dry?" he sneered. "Kira mentioned something about Nico Morgan showing up here a few weeks ago. That would explain this sudden switch in attitude. When you were with him years ago, before he dropped you like a bad habit, you acted all brand-new then, too."

She recoiled from his verbal attack, blinking up at him. "Are you serious right now?" she rasped. "You would say that to me when I've done nothing but show up every day for this place, for this family? For three years, since Mama had her stroke, since she died, where have you been? Even before that? The only thing you've done for this bakery, for this family is put us in more debt," she snapped. His chin jerked back toward his neck, and she nodded, emitting a harsh chuckle. "Oh yeah, Randall, I know about the three-hundred-thousand-dollar loan. And so does Mom, even though she won't say anything to you. So don't you dare come at me about what I'm doing for the bakery. We're not even on the same playing field."

"Y-you know about that? Mom does?" he stammered, swallowed. His eyes jumped over the office, as if their mother would suddenly appear from one of the corners. "How did you find out about that?"

"Does it matter?" She hiked the strap of her purse over her shoulder. "What does matter is you didn't say anything about it to Mom or Dad and you haven't made a payment in months. When would any of us have found out? The day the authorities came to put chains on the bakery's doors?" She shook her head, not bothering to hide her disgust. "No, Randall, don't you come at me about abandoning Evans. You did when you put it up as collateral for a loan with no concern for the employment of anyone who worked here. And for what? What do you have to show for it? Maybe you can give our mother those answers."

"What did Mom say?" He shifted forward, grasping her upper arm. Panic laced his voice, and his eyes widened. "What're we going to do?"

The terms of her deal with Nico prevented her from divulging the truth to Randall. Of how she'd agreed to be Nico's fake girlfriend in order to cover his debt. But even if he hadn't issued that stipulation, Athena wouldn't have told Randall. He deserved to sweat over this dangerous decision that placed their business, their livelihood in jeopardy.

"We?" She arched an eyebrow. "We didn't take out that loan. You did. I don't know what your plans were to repay it at the time, but you should probably get on that."

His grip on her tightened, and he gave her arm a small shake. "What about your boy? You can't ask Nico Morgan for a small loan? Hell, he's a millionaire. A few hundred thousand is a drop in a bucket to him. He'll—"

"No." Her answer, flat, final, resonated in the room. "I will *not* ask him that. It's not his responsibility either. I don't care how many millions he has to spare."

Yes, Nico was prepared to pay the debt if she successfully held up her end of the bargain, but she hadn't *asked* for his help or his money. And she wouldn't sink that low, to use him for what she hadn't earned.

Randall's face twisted into a mask of rage. "You're such a holy roller." His hold on her hardened, and no doubt bruises would mar her skin. "Well, Athena, you're not. And when that asshole drops you again, you'll find out you're no better than the rest of us."

Yanking her arm free of his grasp and ignoring the throb, she shifted backward, out of his reach.

"Don't turn this on me," she said, pain at his ugly words an open wound inside her. She hitched up her chin. "Like I told Mom, this is your mess to clean up. And you can start by taking responsibility for *your* bakery. By showing up every day. By managing it." By showing he freaking cared.

"And where are you going to be? Too busy playing house with your millionaire boyfriend to help your family out?"

That stung. But his ungrateful, self-entitled attitude stung even more.

Giving him one last long look, she didn't bother dignifying his question with an answer. Instead, she moved past him and out the door, well aware she wasn't just leaving her brother in the office. She left the bakery in his hands. And that scared her.

All she could do was pray that by the time Nico paid off the bank loan, there would be a bakery left to save.

Seven

Nico knocked on Athena's apartment door, impatience whispering through him. He didn't need to pull his phone from his pocket to glimpse the time and see they had about forty minutes before the fundraiser ball benefiting pediatric medical research. Of all the social events they'd attended in the last few weeks, this one could be termed the social event of the season. With ticket prices ranging from fifteen to sixty thousand, a silent auction and games with prizes such as seats at New York Fashion Week or a walk-on role on a major motion picture, most of Boston's social and business elite attended. It was not only an opportunity to further his agenda with the Farrells, but the ball also presented other advantageous networking opportunities.

Now if only Athena would open the door.

He knocked again, unease joining the impatience. Earlier, when he'd called to make sure she would be ready, Athena had sounded a little…off. Not distant as had been the case since their confrontation in the back of his town car after the Bromberg's reception. But definitely subdued.

His disquiet increased, and just as he raised his hand to rap on the door once more, it opened. Athena stood in the doorway.

Like every time he saw her, she struck him momentarily deaf and mute. Her beauty. Her innate sensuality that she wore more perfectly than the gorgeous lilac gown that molded to every curve of her tall, slender, deliciously curved body.

He deserved a fucking medal for keeping his hands to himself.

But he had, and not just because losing his focus would prove detrimental. The full, humiliating reason lay in him. He feared losing himself in her. Touching her, tasting her, becoming reacquainted with the wet, tight clasp of her body would be the slippery slope into a dangerous pit he might not be able to claw his way free of.

He'd slipped that night at the Bromberg's reception. Wrapping his arm around her waist, caressing her hip, inhaling her sweet scent, teasing her, laughing with her… For a moment, he'd forgotten it all was an act. For a moment, he'd allowed himself to sink into the fantasy. And when they'd left the reception, reality had been waiting. It'd doused him in a frigid wave.

Forgetting the pretense wasn't an option. Not if he wanted to emerge from this unscathed.

And he intended to do just that.

Skimming his gaze up her silk-clad body, he asked, "Are you—what's wrong?"

Not your damn business, he growled to himself. But as

he narrowed his eyes on her, he didn't rescind the question. Question, hell. Demand.

Because there *was* something wrong. That disquiet that had curdled in his gut earlier returned. On the surface, Athena appeared as beautiful and composed as ever. But a closer inspection revealed the shadows that dimmed the vibrant green in her hazel eyes, the rigidness that invaded her usually graceful frame. The tightness around her lush mouth.

Small details that most people wouldn't notice. But he wasn't most people. He'd spent a year and half learning every inch of her face, body and demeanor. And three years remembering…everything.

"Athena," he said, stepping into her apartment. "What's wrong? And don't tell me nothing."

She snapped her lips shut and frowned up at him. For his high-handedness or moving into her home, he didn't know. Probably both, but she turned and walked inside, leaving Nico to close the front door behind him.

"Just give me a few minutes to grab my purse and put on my shoes, and I'll be ready," she said, avoiding his question.

As if it would be that easy.

"Athena." He called her name again, softer but no less firm. "We're not going anywhere until you answer my question."

She huffed out a breath, then halted midstride, whirling around to face him. With her mouth in a grim line, she glared at him. But as he prepared to dig in for an argument, her expression gentled—no, unraveled. She seemed to wilt before his eyes. Pinching the bridge of her nose, she closed her eyes.

"I'd rather not do this, Nico. Take my word for it, you

don't want to have this conversation. So let me just finish getting ready so we can head out."

"No." Even as every instinct he possessed screamed to maintain his distance, he crossed the space separating them and circled her wrist, tugging her arm away from her face. "Look at me, Athena." He waited. And several seconds later, she complied, her thick fringe of lashes lifting. Those stunning hazel eyes met his, and a spiral of heat corkscrewed in his gut. "Talk to me, baby girl. What's wrong?"

"This is about my family. My brother. You still want to talk?"

She threw the information down like a gauntlet. And he smothered the flare of anger at the mention of Randall Evans. This wasn't about her brother, about the dysfunction that existed within her family.

This was about her.

Correction. If he couldn't get her to talk about what bothered her, then that would affect the performance he required of her. He needed her to be at her best, her sharpest. It benefited him to hear her out.

It wasn't personal.

Fuck, he could spin bullshit when needed.

"Yes, I want to talk."

She stared at him, as if weighing the veracity of his words. Her teeth sank into her bottom lip, one of her tells, and he curled his fingers into his palm, preventing himself from smoothing his thumb across that lip. From following the caress with one from his tongue.

Dragging his gaze from her mouth, he met her eyes again. And didn't miss the flash of heat there. That blaze stirred an answering one in him, tossing kindling on already simmering flames.

Blinking, she glanced away. "I'm sorry. It's been a… trying day. Seriously, though. I'm good—"

"Athena."

She sighed. "Fine. You're incredibly stubborn," she muttered. "I received a call from one of the bakery's employees last night. She, along with the others, hadn't been paid. My mother had agreed to get my brother more involved with the store, to cover me because I couldn't—wouldn't—work *and* pay his debt. Needless to say, that didn't happen. And our employees are paying for it—or are *not* getting paid for it." She heaved another sigh and smoothed her hands over the curls brushed into a bun at the nape of her neck. "I couldn't allow another day to go by without them getting a check, so I went into the bakery and Randall showed up. We got into it, and I told him I knew about the loan, although not about our—" she waved a hand back and forth between them "—arrangement. I left him sweating it out and not long after I left the bakery, my mom called me."

Damn. He didn't need the gift of clairvoyance to see where this was headed.

On bare feet, she strode toward her kitchen. Within moments, she returned with a bottle of wine and two glasses. She didn't ask if he wanted to partake but poured him some anyway. Sliding one of the elegant flutes toward him across the breakfast bar, she picked up the other and sipped. Only then did she continue.

Staring down into the deep red depths, she said, "Mom was not happy." She flicked a look at him. "She hasn't been happy with you since that NDA, but she's abided by it. Still, it's stuck in her craw, and since she can't take it out on you, I've been the lucky candidate." The corner of her mouth quirked, then she took another sip. "Randall had phoned her, of course, complaining. He doesn't want to be at the bakery because he has more important things to do, and why can't I just run it like I have been? And he'd only acquired the loan to invest the money so he could make improvements to the bakery. I called bullshit. Because if that were true, then why is this the first time we're hearing about it? But Mom bought it, hook, line and my-baby-wouldn't-lie-to-me. And now, because Randall is *so* busy—still don't know with what—she wants me to cover his loan *and* come back and run the bakery for him. All because he called and whined. As usual. Still no consequences for his actions."

"What did you tell her?" he asked, attempting to remain neutral.

She slowly lowered her glass to the breakfast bar and lifted her gaze to his. The shadows that swirled in her gaze couldn't conceal the turmoil and hurt there. And his grip on the glass tightened.

"I told her no," she quietly said. "Just because she's flipped the script and changed her mind doesn't mean I will. And she's furious." Her tremulous whisper belied the smile that ghosted across her lips. "She called me selfish. *Selfish.* I think she could've called me a bitch and it would've been less offensive, less hurtful. She told me to call her back when I've decided to put family ahead of my own petty grievances." Athena leaned her head back and laughed, the sound jagged…wounded. When she quieted, she looked at him, reaching for her glass of wine. "Go ahead, say it. Because as much as Mom never cared for you, the feeling was more than mutual. Here's your chance to say, 'I told you so.'"

Several blistering comments leaped to his tongue. About her lazy, manipulative brother. About how her family wouldn't know a boundary if it flashed its neon red tits. About how they didn't appreciate her, took advantage of her kindness…of her almost desperate need for their approval.

Oh yes, there was plenty he could say.

Instead, he went with, "What would you like for dinner?"

Athena froze, the glass midway between the bar and her mouth. Blinking, she peered at him. "I'm sorry?"

"Dinner. I'll have it delivered. You have a taste for something in particular?"

She frowned, once more setting the wine down. "I'm confused. What about the ball? We're not going?"

"No."

Shock melted into confusion and then into understanding. Well, at least that made one of them. Even though he'd said the words, part of him still couldn't believe it. Not twenty minutes ago, he'd been impatient to leave for the social event of the season, and now he was blowing it off.

"But why? I thought tonight was important," she murmured.

Because you're in no state to attend a gala.

Because you're hurting.

Because someone needs to put you first today.

"One ball is the same as another." He shrugged a shoulder. "Unless," he arched an eyebrow, "you're just dying to attend?"

She smiled, and it was only a curve at the corner of her mouth, but it contained genuine warmth. "Somehow I think I'll carry on if I miss this one."

"Good." He looked away from her, from the eyes that were a shade freer of shadows. "About dinner… I'm feeling Italian or Chinese. Is that good with you?"

"Either sounds perfect. And Nico?"

He looked up from pulling up a browser on his phone.

"Yes?"

"Thank you."

"You're welcome." He cocked his head. "Now, lasagna or shrimp egg foo yong?"

"I'm not discussing this with you anymore."

"Hah!" Athena stabbed her tiramisu-stained fork in his direction, a triumphant grin stretched across her face. "That's the refrain of a loser."

"No, it's the statement of someone who refuses to argue with an illogical person," Nico shot back.

Athena chuckled, the sound wicked. "Illogical? When you start tossing insults, it's another sign you've been thoroughly beaten. Just admit it. You're wrong."

"I'm not."

"You *so* are."

Nico ground his teeth together. "We're going to have to agree to disagree. Although you're wrong as hell."

"Say it," she sang. "Just say it. Gandalf is a better wizard than Dumbledore."

"I don't know what's in that tiramisu," he said, jabbing a finger at the half-eaten dessert, "but no doubt it's one hundred proof."

Snickering, she scooped more of the sweet into her mouth and hummed in pleasure. He swallowed down a curse as his cock jerked behind the zipper of his tuxedo pants. His heart squeezed at the humor in her eyes, no traces of her earlier pain in evidence.

"You're still a sore loser, Nico."

"That would imply that you're the winner of this argument. And that would be a fallacy, Athena."

More chuckling, and Nico fought back a smile. Rising from the couch, he said, "I'm a little afraid to offer you more wine, but can I get you another glass?"

She grabbed hers off the coffee table and held it up with a wide grin. "Yes, please."

Shaking his head, he headed for the kitchen for refills of the Moscato. As he returned to the living room with the two glasses, he surveyed the open floor space of her condo, as he often did when he arrived to pick her up. The ordinariness of it struck him again. There was nothing wrong with the matching canisters in the kitchen or the landscape painting on the wall of the living room or the royal blue throw rug in the hallway. All perfectly fine—for an apartment staged by a real estate agent preparing for a showing.

Athena was missing.

"Why're you looking around like that?" Athena asked as he stepped down into the living room.

"Like what?" Nico handed her a glass and sank down onto the couch.

She tapped a finger against the bowl of her glass. "Like you're trying to figure out a puzzle."

"That's pretty accurate," he said, weighing whether he should go forward with the conversation.

They'd enjoyed a rare, good evening. One where the thorny past hadn't intruded. Even now, she sat, curled up on the sofa, dressed in a loose-fitting, off-the-shoulder T-shirt and black leggings. He'd shed his jacket and bow tie and had rolled his sleeves back. Since they'd reentered each other's lives, it was the most relaxed they'd been together. Almost as if they'd silently agreed to lower their guard. At least for tonight.

And he loathed fucking up that temporary truce.

"Let me guess what you're thinking right now," she murmured, leaning forward and cradling her wine. "We're having a great evening where no verbal swords have been crossed or blood shed, and you don't want to ruin it with a possible argument. Let me make you a promise." She held up a hand, palm out. "I hereby do solemnly swear not to be offended at whatever comes out of your mouth. Or not to show it."

He huffed out a soft laugh, and after a moment, nodded. Scanning her living room once more, he frowned.

"I'm assuming you moved to Cambridge to be closer to your grandmother, but what happened here? In this apartment," he clarified. "I remember your old place, and how you put your stamp on mine. Kitschy shit, refurbished pieces from flea markets, framed photographs or art from local artists. This—" he took another visual tour of the apartment, gestured toward the perfectly bland wooden-fruit-in-a-bowl centerpiece on the coffee table "—is almost sanitized. It's not you."

She didn't immediately answer but scanned the room as if seeing it for the first time. And maybe, in a sense, she was. Through his eyes.

"You're right. I did move here after Mama went into assisted living a couple of years ago. If I wasn't at the bakery, I spent my time there, only coming here to sleep and shower. And since she's passed, I just…" She again shrugged a shoulder. "I guess I just haven't viewed this place as anything more than a way station. It's hard to transition from that thinking to something else."

He frowned, tipping his head to the side. "Why were you so worried about your grandmother? Wasn't that part of the reason behind her moving to the facility? To ease your concern about her care? Cambridge Grounds is one of the best assisted living residences in the state."

"Yes, they were wonderful. That wasn't the problem— Wait. How do you know what facility she was at? I didn't mention the name, and we broke up before she went to Cambridge Grounds."

Shit.

He slowly leaned backward until the arm of the couch pressed into his spine. For two years, he'd kept his promise, maintained his silence. Not that it'd been hard. Though he had no use for most of her family, he'd always respected Glory Evans. Respected and liked her. It'd been Glory he'd visited and asked for her blessing before proposing to Athena, not her father. So, yes, he held the woman in high esteem and had intended on guarding their secret past her death. But then, he hadn't expected to become involved with Athena again either.

Just…*shit.*

"Nico?" Her gaze roamed his face as if seeking answers. And maybe she found them in his eyes or in his silence. Or more logically, her quick brain worked it out. She flattened her hands on either side of her hips, bracing herself. Against the truth? Maybe. "You. It was you," she breathed, a quick emotion spasming across her face. "Mama said a grant or some social service aid came through that paid for Cambridge Grounds. We didn't want her to leave home, but she insisted on going, especially since all the expenses were covered. At the time, I didn't question the story. Not even when I visited the facility. She had her own private room, the staff was professional and attentive, the building and grounds were immaculate. I was just happy she would be somewhere safe, clean and comfortable. Somewhere she seemed content. And she was. Right until…"

Athena trailed off, blinked. When she lifted her hazel eyes back to him, they contained bruised shadows, pain. Everything primal within him howled to haul her across his lap. To curl his body around hers and protect her from that hurt. But even if that was his right—which it wasn't—she didn't want that from him.

"Tell me the truth." Though softly spoken, she didn't issue the words as a request. No, it was pure, velvet demand. Yet, underneath, he caught the plea. The need.

He couldn't resist that need. To be honest, he never could.

"Yes, I paid for your grandmother's assisted living care."

Her low inhale echoed sharply in the room, and she stared at him, the scrutiny bordering on invasive. But he didn't glance away.

"Why?" she rasped. "Why did you do it? We weren't together. We…"

"Because your grandmother asked me to."

Her head snapped back as if his blunt statement tapped her in the chin. "What? No, you're lying. Why would she do that? She knew about—"

"Yes, she knew how you felt about me. But she loved you. Worried about you. And that trumped your feelings over her reaching out to me." He worked his jaw, uneasy with betraying a confidence, even though Glory Evans was gone. But knowing the kind of woman she'd been, Nico didn't think she would mind so much now. Especially if it meant releasing Athena from whatever guilt held her captive. "Glory hated that you moved back into your parents' home after her stroke."

Athena's gasp broke on the air between them, and this time, he had no problem deciphering the emotion twisting her lovely features. Hurt. Sorrow.

He swore low and long under his breath. "Athena," he murmured, breaking his personal vow and extending his hand toward her.

But she recoiled, pressing back against the corner of the couch, shaking her head. "That's not true," she whispered. "I moved back to take care of her. Because I loved her. That's just not true."

Dammit.

He couldn't stand it. Fuck what had come between them before now. That agony in her voice. The hint of the lost, insecure girl so uncertain of love...

He stood, and in two short strides he curled his hands underneath her arms and lifted Athena from the couch. In the next moment, he claimed her place and settled Athena on his thighs, wrapping his arms around her. Though he held her, a part of him braced for her rejection. They weren't in front of an audience; he had no legitimate reason to touch her. Other than every protective instinct when it came to this woman roaring that he do just that. So he waited for her to wiggle out of his embrace and demand to know what the hell he was doing.

But she didn't.

Instead she hid her face in his neck, her warm breath bathing the base of his throat. Her arms encircled his chest, and she curled against him, as if seeking his heat... his protection. That thought shouldn't cause a growl of satisfaction to rumble in his chest. Shouldn't have pleasure careening through him or his head bending to brush a kiss over the top of her head.

"She loved you," he said, his lips moving against her thick curls. "She loved all of her grandchildren, but she found a kindred spirit in you. And she wanted only the best for you—your happiness, your peace...your freedom. Which is why it saddened her when you moved back home. Because she hated being a burden on you."

"She could never be a burden." She fisted the back of his shirt. "Why would she think that? We're family. I would've done anything for her."

"She knew that, too. She also knew..." He hesitated,

her family being a touchy subject between them. "She knew your family would place most of the responsibility for her care on your shoulders, and you would accept it because of your love for her. Glory couldn't do anything about it that first year, but as soon as she had some of her mobility and speech back, she contacted me. Your grandmother—" he shook his head, and a smile played about his mouth in remembrance of the strong, feisty woman "—she was proud. I was aware of her story, of how her and her husband had built their business from the ground up. It couldn't have been easy to come to me, a man she believed hurt her granddaughter. But she did. For you, she would've sacrificed anything. And understand this, Athena." He leaned back, lifting his hands between them to cup her face and tilt it back so she had no choice but to meet his eyes. Glimpse the truth there.

"Coming to me? Asking that I cover the assisted living expenses? Moving from the only home she'd known for decades? It was all for you. Because Glory knew if she didn't leave, you wouldn't either. And more than anything, she wanted you to have your independence, your freedom back."

A breath shuddered from between Athena's lips and her thick fringe of lashes fluttered down. But that didn't prevent a tear from tracking down her cheek.

Even though his brain blared a high-pitched warning, he bowed his head and rubbed the moisture away... with his lips. The saltiness hit his tongue, and he shifted to the other side, claiming another tear. Behind him, her hands balled his shirt tighter, harder, stretching the material across his back.

Lust left him intoxicated, off-balance. Burning up. Before he teetered over the edge and committed a sin they would both pay for, he raised his head, staring down into her flushed face. He shouldn't have touched her. Or kissed away her tears. No, he shouldn't have cradled her, hugged her, buried his nose in her hair, inhaled her sugar-and-vanilla scent. He'd crossed a line, and now he struggled to drag his ass back across it.

Because he'd done a lot of things in his life—some he was proud of, some not so much. But he couldn't take advantage of her vulnerability. That he refused to do.

Dropping his hands from her face, he murmured, "Athena."

She released his shirt and cuffed his wrists, holding on to him.

"She always liked you. Trusted you," she whispered. "In hindsight, I'm not surprised she went to you. I'm…" She swept her mouth over the heel of his palm, and electrical currents pulsed up his arm, down his spine. He ground his teeth against the charge, battled the need to take that delectable mouth with his own while spreading her legs and rocking his dick over her pretty sex. He ordered his body to stand down and focused on her soft admission. "I'm grateful she had you to turn to. Thank you for taking care of my grandmother, Nico."

He locked down the groan that barreled up his throat as she delivered another caress to his hand. Until that moment, the lines in his palm had just been that—creases. But now they'd transformed into erotic hot spots that connected straight to his cock. And it required every ounce of his control not to shake his hands free, burrow his fingers through her hair and drag her head back so he could suck the elegant column of her throat. Mark it. Bruise it, so when she looked in the mirror the next morning, she would feel him, never forget him.

Fuck, he needed space before he did something stupid that neither of them could take back.

Gently but firmly, he released his wrists and cradled her head. Once more, he tipped her head back, ensuring she looked at him.

"You know who I am, Athena. What I am," he said, unable to keep the growl from his voice. "And right now, all I'm thinking about is if you'll open up wide and let me fuck this pretty mouth. Or if you'll make me work for it, starting with soft kisses, gentle bites."

He tipped her head back farther, lowering his until their breath mingled, mated. "But I'm not in the habit of taking advantage of women when they're in a vulnerable place. Next time you're on my lap, though, ass against my cock and lips against my skin, I won't hold back. Not until your nails are digging in my back and your voice is hoarse from screaming my name." He bent his head closer, eliminating all but a mere inch of space between them. "Not until this tight, gorgeous little body is shaking from pleasure."

He abruptly dropped his hands away from her, straightening and dragging in a breath. Not that it did him any good. Her scent still filled his nose, coated his tongue. Athena stared at him, hazel eyes hooded, her full lips parted, as if silently begging him for the corruption he'd described. And God help him, he almost gave in.

"Baby girl," he growled. "Move."

His guttural order seemed to shake her loose, because her eyes widened the tiniest bit. With a small, jerky nod, she scrambled off his thighs, launching across the room in several long strides. She halted at the window, wrapping her arms around herself, and the protective gesture wasn't lost on him. But just who did she seek to guard herself from? Him…or her?

Maybe both.

If she were prudent, both.

He rose to his feet, studying her. The same urgency, the same need that had propelled him across the couch to hold her, insisted he cross the room and take her in his arms again. But this time, he resisted that urge. Because he was the burden.

"Are you okay?" he asked.

She nodded. "I'm fine." She lowered her arms to her sides, palms up. "I'm sorry," she murmured. "I crossed a line tonight. It won't happen again."

He dipped his chin in acknowledgment. "There's nothing to apologize for. We'll chalk tonight up to emotion and let it go." Ignoring the almost tangible pull toward her, he strode in the opposite direction, grabbing his discarded tuxedo jacket from the back of a dining room chair. "I'll text you with next week's schedule."

"Okay." A pause. "Nico."

He turned to face her, his hand on the doorknob. She remained standing by the window, sorrow and weariness on her face.

"Yes?"

"Thank you. For everything. I'll never forget that."

He nodded, then opened her front door and…paused. Dammit, he needed to get out of this apartment. Get away from her before he ended up with more than the taste of her tears on his tongue. Yet, he stood there, unable to move, words he should've said months ago a weight on his heart for the woman who'd shown him kindness and trust when no one else but his mother had.

"I'm sorry about your grandmother. She was a good woman. One of the finest people I've met, and when someone like that dies, they leave a hole in this world. One that can't be filled. Maybe shouldn't be filled. She was that special. I'm glad you had her in your life, Athena. And I know she's thankful she had you."

Not glancing back over his shoulder or giving her a chance to respond, he exited, pulling the door closed behind him with a soft *snick*. For a long moment, he stood on the other side, his hand still curled around the doorknob. He closed his eyes, his grip tightening.

I'll never forget that.

Her statement shivered through him like a warning, a threat.

Because he needed her to forget, to not treat him any differently than the uneasy, wary partners they'd become. Partners who didn't trust each other and would separate, returning to their own lives at the end of this.

Anything different, and he would start to forget himself.

And that, he couldn't allow.

Eight

The desk phone intercom buzzed, interrupting Nico's concentration. Dragging his gaze from the Farrell International report on the Bromberg's renovation. So far, the project was surpassing expectations, especially with the opening of the Intimate Curves flagship store. The spark of happiness in his chest for Kenan and Eve had taken him by surprise. Nico had been there when Kenan proposed the project and praised Eve's company, holding her up as the jewel of the rebranded Bromberg's. Kenan hadn't been wrong; the investment had been sound.

That still didn't explain the "spark." Or why it suspiciously felt like pride as well as happiness.

Frowning, Nico rubbed his knuckles over the offending spot as he pressed the button on his desk phone with the other hand.

"Yes, Paul?"

"Sorry to disturb you, Mr. Morgan, but the security

desk downstairs called. There's a Mr. Randall Evans here to see you, even though he doesn't have an appointment." There was no mistaking the disapproval in his executive assistant's tone. "Should I have this Mr. Evans schedule an appointment?"

Nico fell back in his office chair, staring at his closed office door. Anger simmered in his chest. His fingers curled into his palms, his blunt nails biting into his flesh.

What the fuck was Randall doing here? There was absolutely no love lost between them. Of all Athena's family members, Nico had the least use for her brother.

Especially since the last time he'd seen Randall, he'd threatened to ruin Nico's planned proposal unless Nico handed over money for his latest get-rich-quick scheme.

Threatened, hell. It'd been a promise. One he'd followed through on.

Athena was responsible for her own choices, and she'd chosen to blow them up. But her brother had lit the match.

So what the hell was he doing here? According to Athena, she hadn't told Randall about their arrangement.

Firming his mouth, he punched the intercom button again. Only one way to find out.

"Tell security to bring him upstairs."

"Yes, sir."

Nico rose from his chair, fastening the button on his suit jacket, the flame of impending battle alight in his veins. Maybe he didn't know Randall's purpose, but he harbored zero doubts it had something to do with money or an asinine scheme. Three years had passed since they'd last had contact, but the man hadn't changed that much. As proven by his taking a loan out behind his family's back.

No, Randall Evans hadn't changed at all.

Within minutes, a knock sounded on Nico's office

door and he rounded his desk just as Paul opened the door and stepped inside, Randall behind him.

"Mr. Morgan, Mr. Evans is here to see you," his assistant said, stepping to the side and allowing Randall entrance. "Do you need coffee, tea or water?"

Randall smiled and parted his lips to answer, but Nico shook his head.

"No, thank you. Mr. Evans won't be here that long."

The other man's expression darkened, whether from embarrassment or anger, Nico didn't know. And frankly, didn't give a damn.

"Thank you, Paul."

His executive assistant nodded and exited the office.

"What do you want, Randall?" Fuck the pleasantries.

Nico wouldn't call Randall's baring of teeth a smile. Maybe if fury didn't glitter in his dark eyes, he could've achieved it.

"It's nice to see you again, too, Nico." Randall's laugh held a tight quality that belied his claim. "I was surprised to find out you and my sister were back together. We're a very close family, as you know, so imagine my shock when my mother mentioned it." Randall cocked his head and rocked back on his heels. "I can't lie, though. I have my concerns about the renewal of this relationship. And I expressed those concerns to Athena. But as her brother, I'm supportive…to a point."

"How about you get to that point?" Nico asked, injecting a note of boredom in his voice even as his anger crackled. To anyone else, Randall Evans might pass as the "supportive" brother he called himself. But Nico knew him for the grasping, greedy and self-entitled asshole he truly was. "You dropped by my office without an appointment. And I only agreed to see you out of curiosity, not loyalty to your sister. Because let's be honest, since it's just us—you have no loyalty to her. Or anyone else, for that matter. So how about you get to the reason you're here. I have work to do."

Once more, irritation ghosted over the other man's features before he seemed to catch himself. Apparently, Randall believed he would stroll into this office and control the conversation. The man possessed a nearly sociopathic narcissism to believe people didn't see past his bullshit. Just two nights ago, he'd left his sister emotionally bruised because of his emotional manipulations.

The sad part?

His family would let him continue on, business as usual.

Even after his bargain with Athena ended and Nico paid off Randall's loan, Athena would continue to run the bakery in his stead, and his mother would keep enabling him. And Randall would face no consequences, wouldn't even be uncomfortable because of his careless decisions. Who would bail them out the next time Randall placed the business in danger? Because as sure as Barron Farrell had been a bastard, there would be a next time.

"Fine. I came here for two reasons. To ensure my sister was in good hands—" Nico snorted, and Randall's hands fisted in his pockets "—and to bring a business venture to you," he finished through clenched teeth.

"There it is," Nico murmured, crossing his arms.

His first inclination was to deliver an automatic no, and kick Randall out of his office. But again, that damn curiosity. Not that he had any intention of investing in whatever scheme Randall proposed or handing money over to him. But this ought to be good.

"You're a smart businessman and can appreciate a good deal when you hear it," Randall said, his smile returning as he dropped compliments. As if they would make any difference with Nico. "I have the opportunity to get into a new chain of barbershops on the ground floor. These are going to be special. Each shop staffed with only the top barbers, stylists and manicurists. They will offer not just cuts but grooming services and hair-care products. These will be the premier places to go for self-care and pampering."

The enthusiasm coloring his voice glittered in his eyes. And if it'd been anyone else but Randall, Nico's interest might've been piqued. But it *was* Randall. And Nico didn't trust the other man.

"And?" Nico pressed, certain there was more to it.

"And I need one hundred thousand to invest in the project. When the shops are up and running, you'll receive your money back. This is a can't-fail investment!"

"Oh really?" Nico arched an eyebrow. "Anytime someone says the words *can't-fail investment* I get suspicious because no such thing exists. What makes your barbershops different from other full-service establishments? What demographic are you targeting? Where is the business plan?" Nico extended his hand, palm up. "You can't just come in here asking me for one hundred thousand dollars on the basis of your smile and sister's connection."

Randall's face darkened. "It's a sound business project. I've examined it from every angle and we already have several investors. This is personal."

Nico snorted again. "You're damn right it is. You didn't come here in a professional capacity. If you did, you would've scheduled an appointment and had a proposal with projections for me to analyze. This whole thing—" he flicked a hand back and forth between them "—is personal. In addition, you're not asking me to be an investor. You're the investor and you're expecting me to front you the money."

"So you want me to sign something? Fine." He gestured in the direction of Nico's desk. "Draw up something and I'll sign it, promising to pay you back."

The corner of Nico's mouth curled. "Somehow I doubt a piece of paper would hold you to your word about repayment if this fell through."

Case in point, the copy of the banknote with Randall's signature in his desk drawer.

"You weren't even trying to hear my idea, were you?" Randall sneered. "What's one hundred thousand dollars to you? A drop in the bucket? Still the same selfish bastard you were three years ago."

Nico dipped his chin in acknowledgment. "Game recognizes game," he praised. "Now that my curiosity's been satisfied, you can go. I have a meeting in ten minutes."

He turned to head back to his desk but Randall's sly voice stopped him.

"You're so cocky, think your shit can't be touched. But remember what happened last time. I called all the shots. You had plans that involved my sister. A proposal, if my memory serves me right. And how did that turn out when you didn't give me what I asked for? I wrecked that shit. So you can look down on me all you want, but I hold all the power here. I can fuck you up again if you don't hand over what I want. And we both know who Athena really listens to. If you don't want a repeat of last time, I need a check for a hundred thousand by the end of the week."

Nico slowly pivoted, facing Randall again, studying his smug smile and gleaming dark brown eyes as if from the distance of a long tunnel.

In that tunnel, images from that evening came at him in Technicolor with full sound, drilling into his head and eyes, blinding and deafening him.

Randall, arriving at his penthouse and asking for a

loan for another get-rich-quick business venture much like today, and Nico denying him.

Randall, spotting the small, dark blue velvet box with the ring Nico had bought for Athena.

Randall, threatening him, that if Nico didn't give him the money, he would get Athena to leave Nico.

Athena, walking out a week later.

A heat born of hurt, resentment and grief swirled through him, ripping through the memories like flames through paper. Leaving blackened edges and ash behind.

Only one thing prevented the fire from blazing out of control, from consuming both him and Randall.

Randall couldn't influence Athena into abandoning him this time. Not when the bakery and Randall's ass were on the line. She wouldn't leave Nico before the three months were up. Not before he accomplished his goal.

Then he would let her go. He would be the one to walk.

Caustic laughter scratched at his throat. Oh the irony. Randall's thirst for money and power prevented Athena from leaving Nico now, when three years ago, it'd been his weapon to influence her to go.

"You're so confident of your sway over your sister, Randall," Nico murmured. "A little overconfident, I think." He tipped his chin up, allowing a hard, cruel smile to curl his mouth. "Give it your best shot. Because you're not getting one dime from me. Now—" he made a show of flipping his wrist over and glancing at his watch "—I really do have to end this meeting, as…entertaining as it's been. You know the way out."

Turning again, Nico didn't bother looking back as he strode across the room to his desk. Only once he was seated did he spare the other man a glance, and that was to see him disappear through the office door.

Nico propped his elbows on the arms of his chair and

templed his fingers underneath his chin. He wasn't fool enough to believe this was the last he'd see or hear from Randall Evans.

Not by a long shot.

Nine

"Whoa," Athena breathed.

Oh how she wished something a little more sophisticated had passed through her lips, but she couldn't manage more. The historic Beacon Hill mansion of white stone had large bay windows, sconces and honest-to-God turrets.

"It's something, isn't it?" Nico drawled from beside her, his hand cupping her elbow.

She tore her gaze away from the monument to excess and glanced up at Nico. His face rivaled the stone before them.

"*Something* is a good word for it." She tilted her head. "Is this your first time visiting your father's home?"

Nico blinked, dragging his hooded stare from the mansion and dropping it to her.

"Yes."

His abrupt answer didn't invite discussion, but she'd

warned him she'd do everything in her power to convince him this path of revenge was destructive.

So, she pushed.

"Are you okay with going in there?" she asked. "Up until now, you've been little more than a business acquaintance. Kenan and Eve would understand if you left an apology about not being able to make it."

"Why should I have a problem entering into Barron's, now Cain's, house?" His mouth curved. "Because my father has never allowed me to enter its hallowed halls before? Tell me, Athena," he murmured, lowering his head, the scent of whiskey and the red licorice he used to eat ghosting over her lips. "Are you concerned my feelings will be hurt?"

"You'd have to possess feelings first," she muttered. He snorted, and she shook her elbow free, looping her arm under his and gently clasping his hand. "Doesn't matter if you want to admit it or not. I'm here with you tonight. We'll get through this together."

This being facing the past, the childhood years that he and his mother could've enjoyed had Barron been a man of integrity, or just owned a soul. Undoubtedly, Nico didn't want her support—or believed he didn't need it—but he had no choice. He'd provided for her grandmother until the day she left this earth; Athena would pay that debt. But not by assisting him in stealing his father's, now his brothers', company.

No, Glory Evans cherished family, and if she could repay Nico for his generosity, it would be with that gift. So Athena would do it in her grandmother's stead. Nico believed he needed revenge to be whole; she'd return to him what Barron had truly stolen from him—his brothers.

"So we're a team, now?" he asked, his cynicism so thick it was a wonder he didn't choke on it.

"I realize that suspicion must serve you well in business, but it must be hell on real-life relationships."

Case in point, theirs. If only he'd opened his heart to her, they might've had a shot at something real, something lasting. But water under the bridge now. *Everything doesn't only happen for a reason, but for a purpose and a plan*, Mama used to say. And as painful as the ending of Athena's relationship with Nico had been, she'd saved herself from the devastating pain of falling deeper in love with him, if she'd stayed longer.

Nico Morgan wasn't a man to be trusted with a woman's heart—not if she didn't want it returned in jagged pieces.

"You're lucky I have a naturally optimistic personality," she continued. "Because you could drive a saint to a drunk and disorderly charge."

"Well good thing you're not a saint, isn't it?"

Heat sizzled up her bare arms and down her spine, which was completely exposed by her red lace, sleeveless, floor-length gown. She tried to drag her gaze away from his, but that dark, knowing stare might as well as have been a hard grip. She *couldn't* avoid it. Neither could she avoid the images bombarding her. Just days ago, she'd perched on his lap, holding his hand to her mouth. Kissing that hand. Tasting that sandalwood and earthy musk that belonged only to him.

Pushing him.

So it'd been for the best that he'd pumped the brakes. Best for both of them. The last thing either of them needed was this bargain muddied by sex.

But that clear, cold logic didn't halt the march of lust. If a shattered heart and three years' absence didn't do the impossible, hell, most likely nothing would. She just had to accept that. Didn't mean she had to act on this clawing, relentless hunger, though.

No matter how bad it ached—

The peal of her phone pierced the night air, and she flinched at the jarring sound even as she breathed a sigh of relief. Fingers fumbling, she popped open her clutch and removed her cell. One glance at the screen squelched the relief, replacing it with annoyance and dread.

What. Now?

Grimacing, she glanced up at Nico. "I'm sorry, I need to take this. It'll be quick." If possible, Nico's obsidian eyes darkened even more, but he gave her a terse nod. Ducking her head, she swept her thumb over the screen and lifted the phone to her ear—convincing herself that the twisting in her stomach was not due to her feeling as if she'd disappointed him. "Yes, Randall?"

"Good evening to you, too, sis."

Closing her eyes, she pinched the bridge of her nose. They hadn't spoken since that morning at the bakery, so what could he want with her? Especially at eight o'clock at night.

"I'm in the middle of something, Randall, so if you could just tell me what you need?"

His abrupt chuckle echoed in her ear. "Let me guess. Out on the date with your millionaire?" She didn't need to see her brother's face to hear the sneer in his voice. "So that means no time for your family?"

God, not this. Again.

"I'm answering my phone, right? What do you need?" she asked, not masking her impatience. Damn, how could an almost thirty-year-old man still behave like a spoiled toddler?

And frankly, she was being a little unfair to the toddler.

"Since you asked so nicely," he mocked. "Listen, Mom is going through Mama's things tonight, and we need you to come home and be with her."

Hurt and grief seized her chest, squeezing and squeezing until she had to, by force of will, smother her pained gasp. She lifted a fist to her chest, as if she could massage her breaking heart. In the months since her grandmother had passed, none of them had been strong enough to go through her clothes, knickknacks, jewelry and other belongings.

For Mom to do it now... What happened? What changed? Was she okay—

A large hand cupped the nape of her neck, and the warm, solid weight of it grounded her. Yes, she might regret it later, but here, in this moment, she leaned back into that strength, depended on it. Borrowing just a little of it.

Opening her eyes, she stared ahead at the Beacon Hill mansion, but in her head, she saw the cheery, cozy room where her grandmother would sit by the window, playing solitaire the old-fashioned way—with actual cards—or organizing her coin collection.

God, Athena missed her. And she needed her, more than ever.

"Athena? Did you hear me? We need you to come home."

Drawing in a trembling breath, she shook her head, even though Randall couldn't see it. "I can't right now. I'll go by to see her tomorrow, though. Make sure she's okay."

"What?" Randall barked, his fury nearly pulsating down the connection. "I said Mom needs you. Fuck who you're out with. This is our mother. Get here. Now."

Anger poured through her like gasoline, his words

and tone a match tossed on it. Who the hell did he think he was talking to?

"Excuse me?" she said, her grip on her phone tightening until the edges bit into her fingers. "I think you forgot it's me, your sister, you're talking to, not your wife, not your daughter. As I said, I cannot cancel my plans tonight, especially on such short notice. And as hard as going through Mama's belongings are, Mom isn't alone. She has you, Kira and Dad there with her."

"It's not the same," he snapped. "And besides, I'm not home at the moment—"

"Oh really?" She stiffened, that fury snapping hard inside her. "Well, let me give you the same advice you offered me. Get home *now*. Your family needs you. Good night, Randall."

Ending the call, she turned the ringer off. It immediately lit up again with a call from her brother, but she dropped the cell in her purse and snapped it shut.

"Sorry about that," she said, forcing her lips to curve into a smile. "It won't hap—"

"Are you okay?" Nico's hold on her didn't shift, didn't ease up.

"I'm—" The *fine* stalled on her tongue, halted by the sharp gaze studying her features. "Pissed. So damn pissed. And hurting for my mother at the thought of her going through my grandmother's things by herself. But I'll be okay. I'm committed to being here and not bailing, if that's your worry."

"I'm not worried about that." He flicked the hand not cradling her neck. "I am concerned about you. Your brother can be…" His eyebrows jacked down into a vee, his full lips flattening as if trapping that description of Randall behind them.

She snickered, surprised at the burst of humor.

"Look at you, trying to be diplomatic." She smirked, then sighed. "Yes, Randall can be an insufferable asshole and he was at his best just now. But I can't..." Her lips twisted. "I can't keep standing in the gap and making it okay for him to dodge his responsibility. He wants me to come home and help Mom go through our grandmother's belongings, but not once did it occur to him that he should be there. Not once did it occur to him that maybe I'm not able to do it. But Randall never considers the cost to others, just to himself."

She heaved a sigh, tipping her head back and staring up at the cloudy yet star-studded sky. Nico shifted his hand, sliding it from her neck to the small of her back. Immediately, she missed the possessiveness of his hold. But she didn't have time to dwell on the curious pull in her chest, because his palm connected with the skin bared by her backless dress. Sizzling electricity emanated from that point of contact and spasmed straight to her core. Her thighs shivered, and only pride kept her from cupping her suddenly full, sensitive breasts.

"We should probably head in," she murmured, desperate to be in front of people. An audience would prevent her betraying her resolve. Hopefully. "It's probably bad manners to show up fashionably late to an engagement party."

He dipped his chin in acknowledgment, and led her toward the mansion's gated entrance and front steps. The building impressed her even more up close. Impressed her in the way the Louvre or the Met did. As something to appreciate for its beauty and architectural features, but not as a place to live, to make a home. It lacked...warmth.

"Four generations of Farrells have lived here," Nico said, the flame from a sconce next to the door casting shadows over his profile. "I lied before. I've never been inside, but I've been here. I used to drive by as a teenager, trying to catch a glimpse of my father and his family. I don't know what I expected to happen when I finally did," he murmured, his gaze steady on the door as if even now, he was seeing the father who'd abandoned him emerge, along with the wife and the son he'd kept. "A sense of vindication? Of satisfaction? Of joy, maybe, because I'd seen him? I felt like shit. Worse than shit. That was the last time I came here."

"Until tonight." She stepped forward so his hand slipped from the base of her spine, and she reached behind her, once more tangling her fingers with his.

His scrutiny shifted down to their clasped hands, then lifted, meeting her eyes.

"Until tonight." He squeezed her fingers and didn't let go.

The front door opened, and an older man, short, with an almost regal bearing, a military straight posture and a forthright gaze, stood in the entryway.

"Good evening," he greeted with a nod of his white-haired head. "Name, please."

"Nico Morgan and Athena Evans," Nico supplied.

The man must've had a guest list in his head, because he stepped back and permitted them entrance.

"Welcome to Mr. Rhodes and Ms. Burke's engagement party." The older man closed the door and moved farther into the huge foyer.

Athena's heels clicked over a pristine marble floor. Above them, light from a crystal chandelier rivaled the sun. Artwork in ornate frames hung from the walls and, contrary to the cold, intimidating appearance of the building outside, the area was inviting. Lovely, comfortable-looking armchairs and chaise lounges dotted the area, welcoming guests to sit a moment while surrendering their coats or mingling.

"If you'll follow me, I'll show you to the other guests," the man said, turning and heading down the hall that passed a stunning marble staircase.

"Thank you," Nico said.

They followed, clasped hands between them, her knuckles brushing his powerful thigh. A small caress, but it pulsed through her. Tempted her to straighten her fingers, turn her hand around and feel that strong, flexing muscle against her skin.

She might have a thing for his long, toned legs.

In moments, the older gentleman paused at the entrance to a large room that could've been a ballroom. About sixty tuxedoed and gowned guests were gathered, their chatter and laughter filling the air. A spirit of gaiety filled the space, and it didn't strike her as forced or fake. The people here, smiling and drinking champagne, seemed to actually delight in being here, celebrating Kenan and Eve and their impending marriage.

From her time in Nico's world, this…genuine happiness for someone else was rare.

And inspiring.

She scanned the crowd for the engaged couple, and soon located them at the other end of the room. A smile that started deep in her chest spread across her face. Though they were surrounded by well-wishers, Kenan's arm circled Eve's shoulders, cradling her into his side. And she leaned into him, her trust and love evident. If the room had plunged into darkness, they would beam bright like a beacon.

The thrust of envy between the ribs caught Athena by surprise. There'd been a time when she'd worn love like that. When she'd been sure anyone glancing at her would see adoration in her eyes, on her very skin, like sun reflecting off glass.

Oh God, if she'd stayed longer, Nico could've owned her heart and soul.

She'd wanted him to.

She would've gladly given him all of her if he would've just given all of himself in return.

That was a lie.

If Nico would've offered even a sliver of himself, she wouldn't have left. Maybe they would be celebrating their engagement now. Or even a marriage.

The hell, Athena. Get it together.

Giving her head a hard mental shake, she jerked her enraptured gaze from Kenan and Eve. She couldn't afford to drop her guard and slide down the slippery slope of the past.

She didn't trust herself.

"Look at you!" The excited feminine voice tore her from her morose thoughts. Athena almost moaned in relief when Devon approached her, arms outstretched, beautiful in an emerald green, empire waist, halter top gown. Devon cupped Athena's arms and beamed up at her. "You're gorgeous. This dress is amazing."

Athena fought not to glide her palms down the red silk and lace gown that fit like it had been stitched onto her. With a deep neckline in the front and a nonexistent back, the dress was more revealing than anything she'd worn before. But the flare of lust in Nico's eyes when he'd first seen her had eased all her concerns about showing too much skin.

"Thanks," Athena said, smiling. "You, too. I love your dress, and you look hot."

Devon grinned. "Aw, go on you flatterer, you. Cain

certainly thought so." She wiggled her eyebrows, and Athena snickered.

"I'm going to get a drink. Athena, would you like one?" Nico interrupted.

Athena shot him a glance. "Sounding a little desperate there, buddy."

His expression remained stoic but she didn't miss the faint quirk of his lips. "Not at all. I just can't have my fiancée dying of thirst."

She released a bark of laughter, not caring if it was considered gauche. "Right. But I'll grant you a reprieve. I'd like a glass of Moscato, please."

He nodded. "Mrs. Farrell?"

"Oh please, Devon." She shook her head, holding up a nearly full glass and grinned at him. "Sparkling cider. Thank you, though. And I apologize for traumatizing you."

"No worries. Whiskey will help me forget," he said, tone smooth.

Devon cackled. "Good thing we serve only the good stuff."

"I'll be right back."

He turned and disappeared into the crowd, and Athena stared after his tall, powerful figure. A tender pang resonated in her chest, and she tightened her grip on her purse—either that or rub the spot and admit that it might be there because she missed him by her side. Missed the intimate pressure of his hand wrapped around hers. She curled her fingers into her palm.

Was this the beginning of her downfall? Of her plunge into another heartbreak that would do just that—break her?

Fear streaked through her, jagged and lightning bright.

"Oh, hon." A small, delicate hand patted hers. Devon

tsked. "I recognize that look. You're not going to be able to wait until he gets back with your wine. And you need something stronger. Let's go find it. Then you can tell me what has you terrified. Although I can guess. I fell in love with Cain Farrell, after all." The other woman looped her arm through Athena's and gently tugged her in the opposite direction of where Nico had headed. "We've just started to get to know one another these last few weeks, but you're not alone in this."

That's where Devon was wrong.

Athena was alone.

When it came to Nico Morgan, she always had been. Always would be.

"Thanks, Mark." Nico shook hands with the distinguished older gentleman. "I'll have my executive assistant call your office next week to schedule an appointment to nail down the details."

"Sounds good." Mark Hanson clapped Nico on the shoulder, smiling broadly. "I look forward to hearing from you. Good doing business with you, Nico."

"Same here."

With a nod, Nico continued on the path toward the bar that had been interrupted by the businessman. Not that the disruption hadn't been welcome. He'd been trying to close a deal with Mark Hanson for over a month. And now it seemed the deal was steps from being closed. The other man had been eyeing a telecommunications company Nico's corporation owned. Nico had only been willing to part with it at the right price, and those seven figures included five of Mark's Farrell International shares. It'd required some negotiating, but just now, they'd come to an agreement.

Which meant, only six more shares stood between him and control of his father's company.

Fierce satisfaction should fill him. Or at the very least, anticipation. But as he wound through the crowds of people, nodding at those he knew, only a grim, hollow resolve yawned wide in his gut. This was what he had to do, the road to justice, but the pleasure he'd expected... He gave his head a small, hard shake.

Where the fuck was it?

He deserved it.

Unbidden, he glanced across the room toward Kenan and Eve. At the very obvious love that damn near emanated from them. Nico's private investigator had been very thorough, so he knew their complete story. And *they* deserved *that*. For however long it lasted. Because in his experience, it wouldn't survive the test of time and hardship. But for their sake, he almost hoped it would...

"They're disgustingly happy, right?"

Nico jerked his attention from the engaged couple to meet Cain's blue-gray eyes. As in every occasion when he'd come in contact with his half brothers, Nico's heart thundered against his rib cage. Cain, especially. Because he had been the boy Nico had once watched from afar. The one he'd envied for so long. The chosen one, while Nico had been the castoff.

Part of him wanted to study Cain, discover what made him so lovable and worthy that Barron kept him and raised him. So Nico could do...what? Emulate those qualities? It was too late, but still... That insatiably curious boy in him refused to let it go. And that same little, *lonely* boy who'd desired a brother couldn't stop being nervous around this man. So Nico hid those feelings behind reserve. While he'd warmed up a little with Kenan and even Achilles, who made Nico look like a Chatty

Cathy, Cain dragged him back to that vulnerable, *hurt* boy, and it scared him.

And now here Nico stood, unable to avoid Cain or that piercing Farrell stare.

Desperate for that whiskey, Nico stepped up to the full-service bar.

"Whiskey. Neat. A glass of Moscato." Then, arching a brow at Cain, he drawled, "This said from the man whose wife drove me to drinking with comments of just how hot you find her."

Cain smirked. "She's not wrong."

"Jesus," Nico muttered, reaching for his tumbler filled with the amber alcohol. "I should've ordered a double."

Laughing, Cain clapped him on the shoulder. "Sorry."

"Somehow, I don't get 'sorry' off you," Nico said, eyes narrowed.

Cain shrugged, an unrepentant smile curving his mouth. "I tried." He paused as Nico took Athena's glass of wine. "Thank you for coming to the party. We've been business associates for a while, but Eve has really come to like Athena. So has Devon and Mycah. I'm sure it means a lot to her that you two are here for their engagement party."

"You're welcome. It's our pleasure."

Cain fell silent and his bright scrutiny moved over Nico. By sheer will, he didn't frown or demand to know what the fuck he was looking at? Yeah, he might be a little defensive. Finally, Cain shook his head, a rueful smile touching his lips.

"I'm sorry, that was rude, and I promised Devon I'd work on that. It's just that you look familiar to me. You always have, and I just can't put my finger on it…"

Panic and, dammit, just a little excitement, clawed at him. Who did Cain glimpse when he looked at Nico?

Himself? Their father? What if he figured out their connection? No, Nico didn't want that. Not yet.

Right?

Damn, *no*. No, *he didn't*.

"Thank you, Cain. Thank you very much," Achilles growled, approaching them, his giant frame parting people like a biblical miracle.

With amusement that he hid behind a sip of whiskey, Nico watched as guests regarded the large, scowling man with wariness, despite his flawlessly tailored suit.

"What did I do?" Cain lifted his hands. "I've just been standing here. Nico is my witness. Tell him." He dipped his head toward Achilles.

Nico shrugged, taking another sip from his tumbler. "Depends. What're you offering for my cooperation?"

"Wow. Really?" Cain scowled, but the gleam of amusement in his eyes belied the frown.

"No, you're guilty because your wife is guilty." Achilles jabbed a finger at Cain. "You know how much I hate these things and Mycah is my lifeline. And Devon comes along and shanghais her for some 'girl time,' whatever the fuck that means. Her, my wife and your fiancée—" he jerked his chin up at Nico "—have disappeared, probably to talk all kinds of shit about us. Which means all three of us will no doubt be paying for old and new tonight. This is a fucking engagement party, Cain. *Engage* your wife."

Nico blinked, caught between laughter and shock. That was the most he'd heard Achilles speak in one breath since he'd met his younger half brother.

Cain lifted a hand again, palm up. "I'd go find her but I'm on parent watch."

Achilles's expression cleared, his broad shoulders drawing back with tension. "Right. How's that going?" He shifted to the other side of Nico and plucked the wineglass from his hand. "I'm guessing this is for Athena? She won't be needing it." Achilles sipped it, grimaced, then took another sip. "Nothing beats a good Guinness."

"So far, so good," Cain answered Achilles's question. He shot a glance at Nico. "Sorry, I'm being rude again. Kenan's parents are here tonight."

"They're not happy about the marriage?" Surprise winged through Nico. Not only at this news—Eve was wonderful—but that Cain and Achilles so openly shared it with him.

"It's complicated," Achilles muttered. "But the mom's okay. It's his father who's just not…happy. So we're on interference duty. Like—*fuck*. Now."

"Well damn," Cain muttered, striding across the room.

Achilles charged after him, and for some inexplicable reason, Nico followed.

In moments, they reached Kenan and Eve just as an older couple and a handsome younger Black man did. Kenan still wore the smile he'd been wearing all evening, but it seemed strained and his blue-gray eyes had dimmed, losing that gleam of happiness. Eve turned to the couple Nico assumed were Kenan's parents and smiled, sliding her arm around Kenan's waist.

"Hi, Nathan and Dana. I'm so glad you could make it tonight. The occasion wouldn't have been complete without all of our family here to celebrate with us." She turned to the younger man with them and her smile warmed. "And of course, you, too, Gavin. Thank you for being here."

"Of course," Gavin said. "Do I get to kiss my soon-to-be sister-in-law?" He glanced at Kenan, grinning. "What do you say, Kenan? Or am I risking a broken face?"

Kenan squinted. "Possibly. But I'm feeling magnanimous."

"Uh, hello." Eve waved. "Agency here." She laughed.

Stepping forward, she hugged the other man and kissed him on the cheek. "It's good to see you."

"Mom," Kenan said and held his arms open.

Nico caught the flash of relief that flickered across the lovely older woman's face before she moved into her son's embrace. They hugged, and Nico almost turned away from the emotion that crossed Kenan's mother's face. Regret, sorrow and a deep love.

In that moment, his own arms ached with emptiness. Times like this, he missed his mother with a strength that threatened to drag him to his knees. He'd never get to hold her again, inhale her scent or hear her voice. And it struck him like a punch to the gut. He stiffened his spine and breathed deep, deliberate.

A shoulder nudged his and stayed there, not moving. As if propping him up. Nico glanced to his left and Achilles stood next to him, not looking at him but was…there.

Right.

If anyone would understand the loss of a mother, it would be him.

He should move; he didn't need this support. Especially from a stranger. Their father's DNA might connect them, but Achilles didn't know that.

But Nico didn't move away.

And in this moment, he chose not to analyze why.

"Hey, Dad." Kenan turned to his father and extended a hand. "Thanks for coming."

His father accepted it, then quickly let go. "Thank you for inviting us. I was pleasantly surprised to be included, since I wasn't sure we were still considered a part of your family." He flicked pointed looks at Cain and Achilles, his lips curling in disdain.

Well…damn.

That'd been rude as hell.

"Nathan," Kenan's mother murmured, pink tingeing her high cheekbones.

"Come on, Dad," Gavin admonished with a frown. "Not tonight."

But Nathan's expression hardened, and his family's appeals had the effect of pebbles bouncing off a brick wall. One glance at the anger and pain flashing in Kenan's eyes and Eve clutching his arm, and Nico jumped in.

"If I'm not mistaken, you're Nathan and Dana Rhodes of Rhodes Realty?" Nico stepped forward, his hand outstretched toward Kenan's mother first, who shook it, and then his father, who, still frowning, repeated the gesture. "I apologize for the interruption, but I'm Nico Morgan. I own Brightstar Holdings, LLC. Perhaps you've heard of it?"

Nathan's frown disappeared and he nodded, his entire demeanor changing from combative to amiable.

"Of course. It's a pleasure to meet you, Mr. Morgan."

"Nico, please. I've admired your company's work and reputation for a long time now. I realize it's your son's engagement party, but I also believe in serendipity—or taking advantage of an opportunity." Nico smiled. "Would you mind if I stole you away? Kenan? Are you okay if I borrow your dad? Just for a few moments."

"Uh, no," Kenan said with a shake of his head. The corner of his mouth lifted and he slid an arm around Eve's shoulders. "I don't mind. You fine with that, Eve?"

"Our family using any occasion for business? Shocker." She beamed, and if Nico wasn't mistaken, gratitude shone from her eyes. "No, it's okay. You two go. But don't forget us."

Nico nodded and stepped toward Nathan, sweeping an arm. "Nathan, how about a drink? I hear they're free," he said, earning the chuckle he'd been after.

As he and Kenan's father walked away from the group and Nico launched into a business pitch, his pulse hammered. Eve hadn't meant him when she'd mentioned "family." But in that instant, it'd felt like it. And the glide of warmth that had slid through his veins unsettled him.

Because in that same instant, he'd craved being a member of that family.

Ten

Athena stared ahead at the privacy divide separating the front of the limousine from the rear, where she and Nico sat.

A very quiet Nico.

She peeked at him from the corner of her eye. He'd been lost inside himself since she'd emerged from the study with Devon and Mycah, where she'd enjoyed a brandy and the other two had sipped on glasses of sparkling cider. The impromptu girls' session where they'd regaled her with stories about their relationships and gently probed her about her own "romance" had been fun. And though Athena had kept up the charade and suffered guilt at her lying, she'd rejoined the party more in love than ever with Devon and Mycah.

But her delight had been dimmed by Nico's reserve. It wasn't obvious. No, to everyone else, he appeared as charming and polite as always. But she noticed the difference. Noted the stiffness. As if one touch would shatter him like glass.

What the hell happened?

The question burned on her tongue like a live coal. But the last time she broached a subject about his family, he'd shut her down. And it'd hurt.

Risking another peek, she studied him. The taut pull of skin over his chiseled cheekbones. The hooded, forward-focused stare. The rigid set of his frame. The almost too relaxed spread of his fingers along his thighs.

Pain. It reverberated through him. Self-preservation screamed leave it and him alone. But her foolish, suicidal heart...

Hell.

"Nico?"

"Yes?"

She waited several seconds.

"Look at me, please."

His chin jerked and he turned his head, his onyx gaze fixing on her.

"You wanted my attention, baby girl. Now you have it."

"Don't do that," she murmured. "Don't shut me out."

"Is that what I'm doing?"

"You know you are." She shook her head. "But it won't work. Not this time." Risking rejection, she laid her hand on his leg. "Talk to me."

His jaw worked as if it struggling with the words. He lowered his gaze to her hand, studying it. And when he finally met her eyes again, the impact nearly shoved her back against the seat. So much anger, sorrow, grief, fear...need.

They all blazed in those eyes.

If she possessed the sense God gave a gnat, she'd let it go.

But apparently, when it came to this man, she had zero wisdom.

"Please let me in," she whispered.

How many times had she said that same thing to herself when they'd been together? So many, it'd become her personal mantra. And each time, she'd never believed he would. And if she were honest, she didn't believe he would now either.

Letting loose a soft sigh, she slid her hand off his thigh—

His hand covered hers, holding it in place, pressing it to the thick muscle underneath.

She froze, her fingers curling into him out of reflex or…need.

Oh God, what was she doing? Again?

"You want in," he said, his voice a low rumble that stroked over her skin, leaving pebbled flesh behind. "Are you sure about that? Because it's not a place of sunshine and roses. It's ugly. It's scary. Half the time, I don't want to be there either. You still 'want in,' Athena?"

"Yes," she said, without hesitation.

His jaw worked again, his eyes glittered brighter under the passing streetlamps. But he shifted, leaned forward, still keeping her hand prisoner under his.

"I'm filled with hate," he growled. "For Barron for fucking my mother and me over. For my mother for dying. For you for leaving. For my brothers for…for…" His mouth snapped shut, his eyebrows arrowing down above his nose.

"For having what you've always wanted," she whispered. "For making you feel."

"Yes," he agreed, the answer blunt, unadorned. "Tonight, seeing them together, celebrating one of their own, having each other's backs, with their wives... It reminded me of everything I could've had. Everything that, at one time, I longed for. Things that were within my grasp but slipped through my fingers." He lifted up his other hand and stared at his spread fingers, as if seeing ghostly images sifting through them. "Them." He looked at her again, and she swallowed a whimper at the pain that spasmed across his face. "They were those things. Brothers. Someone to be in the fire with you. Someone who unconditionally supported and loved you. Someone who saw you, the real you with all your flaws and bullshit, and accepted you anyway. Someone who offered a place to belong." His heavy breathing filled the interior. "They could've been that for me. I saw that tonight. I *felt* that tonight. It also hit me that if not for a will and the spite of one old man, I could've had it."

"Nico," she breathed.

But he didn't hear her. So caught up in his head, in the past, in his pain.

"What did I do, besides *be fucking born*, that made my own father hate me so much? What did he see? What did he know that he deemed me unworthy of even acknowledging after death? Of giving me brothers, family? I want to go down to that cemetery, dig that old bastard up and ask him, because I need to know. Goddammit, I need—"

"Stop it." She yanked her hand out from under his and cupped his face between her palms. "Stop. It. I won't let you use Barron Farrell as the yardstick you measure yourself by. Just hearing you call him a father turns my stomach, so I refuse to allow you to go down this road where his warped opinion matters."

Nico gently cuffed her wrists and tugged her hands away from his face. A face that had hardened into an aloof mask but whose eyes, swirling with shadows, belied that coldness.

"Thank you, Athena," he murmured. "I appr—"

"No." In moments, she wiggled and hiked her skirt to around her thighs and straddled his lap. His big hands gripping her hips—to move her, to hold her, she didn't know—and she squeezed her legs around him. "No," she repeated.

"Dammit, Athena," he rumbled. "What the hell are you doing?"

"Not letting you dismiss me."

She lowered her face to his, the heat from his anger licking her skin. But that didn't stop her from trailing her fingertips over the sharp arch of his cheekbone, the arrogant slope of his nose, the lean planes of his cheeks. She drew short of touching the bottom curve of his mouth. But her fingers tingled in objection.

Cradling his face once more, she tipped his head back. "Barron abandoning you and Rhoda had nothing to do with you or your mother. Some men have the paternal instincts of a quokka. Barron is one of them. Has it occurred to you that maybe Barron rejected you because he was jealous? You are everything he could never be. You earned your success by your own hard work, sweat and perseverance, not because of your name and someone handing it down to you. Present bargain notwithstanding, you're honest. You have integrity and are respected. With all his money and power, Barron had none of that and couldn't buy it. And it probably ate at him to no end that he had nothing to do with you ending up to be the man you are. So instead of being proud of his son, Barron tried to destroy everything in you that he could never have. A good reputation. The company you built. Your mother's security. And in the end, a family."

05

She brushed her thumbs over his skin, her breath hitching at the silken feel of it. She marveled over his wild, almost cruel beauty.

He *was* beauty.

"Tried, Nico. He tried to destroy. But he didn't accomplish it. Including stealing your chance for family. Your brothers are there for you. All you have to do is reach out to them. I believe they'll accept you—love you."

"Like you?" If he'd snapped it or even added an arched eyebrow, she might have returned to her side of the back seat. But the question emerged on a ruined tone. And it damn near broke her. "You knew me, slept beside me, fucked me for a year and half. And yet you still walked away. Outside of business, they've known me for what, a few weeks? If you didn't find anything good enough to keep you with me, why would they take me in?"

"Nico." She shook her head, shattered and struck speechless.

"No answer? It's okay, Athena. I already—"

She crushed her mouth to his.

Taking advantage of his parted lips, she thrust her tongue deep, moaning. The smoky bite of whiskey and ever-present red licorice greeted her, but so did *Nico*. God, she'd never forget the unique, musky, addictive taste of *him*. It'd been so long, and she'd been so damn hungry. But not just for anyone. For him. For Nico.

His grip on her hips tightened, almost bruising, and she feared he would lift her off him. But he didn't. Bright joy ricocheted inside her as he balled up her gown, dragging it higher. The cool air kissed her bare legs, the damp skin of her inner thighs…the soaking wet flesh between. He tugged her forward, and her breasts pressed to his chest, her sex ground against the rigid length of his cock.

Pleasure, wild and raw, raced through her, setting off

long-dormant nerve endings. She awakened with a brutal snap of fire, and cried out with it. She'd missed this consuming, nearly overwhelming hunger. Out of necessity, she'd buried this side of herself, but with one kiss, one glide of his beautiful cock over her core, he'd resurrected her.

Nico swallowed her cry, trading it for a low, rumbling groan. It rolled into her mouth, vibrated against her breasts, drawing her nipples into taut, aching peaks.

"Give me more," she begged, but the plea had barely left her lips before she took his mouth again.

Or tried to.

Nico cupped her chin in a careful, unyielding grip. That hold—possessive, dominant—had need twisting in her lower belly. She tried to shake her head, to clear it of the haze of lust clouding it, but she couldn't. He wouldn't allow it.

And damn if that didn't have her squirming in his lap.

"More of what? Be specific, baby girl," he ordered, onyx eyes glittering. "More of this?"

He nipped her bottom lip, then plunged into her mouth, his tongue dueling with hers in an erotic battle. When he lifted his head, she tried to chase him, but his hold prevented it. She glared at him, frustration a beast within her. He chuckled, the sound wicked, dirty.

"Or more of this?"

His hand on her hip firmed, pressed her down as he stroked up. His dick made a mockery of her thong, rendering it irrelevant as he ground against her folds and the tiny bundle of nerves cresting her sex.

"Oh God," she breathed, her head falling back on her shoulders. Heat engulfed her, fanning from between her thighs, speeding up her spine, into her breasts, her belly before sizzling down to the very soles of her feet.

Was she so primed for pleasure, for his touch, that one nudge to her clit would send her over the edge into release?

Yes. If the way her body lit up like a damn torch was any indication, then yes, she was.

"Which one, baby girl?" He grazed a kiss over her lips, her chin. Rolled his hips. "Do I fuck this mouth or do I let you get the front of my pants even wetter?"

Oh damn. That dirty mouth should be outlawed. Or knighted for heroic deeds.

"Why can't I have both?" She tunneled her fingers through his thick, black waves, tugging them away from his face, glorying in the silken glide over her fingers. This, she'd missed, too. "Give me both."

She couldn't be sure, but delight flashed in his eyes. The smile that curved his mouth was all hunger...and promise.

"Greedy," he murmured, his fingers caressing her jaw. "One of the things I enjoyed about you most."

Enjoyed. Not loved.

The prick of pain sliced true, but she firmly smothered it. Nothing in this moment had to do with love. They'd had their chance at that and lost it. Right now, as he molded his mouth to hers, licking it, sucking and owning it, while guiding her to ride him, the pursuit of satisfaction reigned.

Soon, prickles tingled at the back of her neck, danced down her spine and gathered at the base. Hips stuttering, a choked cry escaped her, but she didn't need words, didn't need to explain.

"Take it, Athena," Nico encouraged. "Take the edge off." Even as he spoke, he lowered his other hand between them and slipped underneath the band of her panties, unerringly locating the sensitive, stiff button. "But the next time is mine. You come around me." He firmly circled, giving her just the right amount of pressure.

In seconds, she exploded.

She cried out, arching into his fingers, riding the ridge of his dick. The tight, cresting pleasure was good, so good, but not enough.

Not nearly enough.

As soon as the shudders eased from her body, Nico slid his fingers into his mouth, licking her from his skin. His lashes fluttered down, and that quick hunger flashed inside her as if she hadn't just orgasmed moments earlier.

"That dress have a zipper?" he growled.

Instead of answering, she moved her hands to the hidden clasp and zipper at her side. Lowering it, she slid the straps down her arms, baring herself to him. Maybe modesty should've filled her as his gaze roamed over her breasts. Maybe she should've at least attempted to cover herself.

But it didn't, and she didn't.

She wanted Nico to see her, to want her. She exulted in witnessing those full, beautiful lips flatten in lust, and twin flags of color slash across his cheekbones. Watching his eyes become hooded. His need had haunted her dreams, and seeing it again in real life...

Oh no. She wanted to see it.

His mouth captured a nipple, his tongue and lips drawing on one while his fingers teased and tweaked the other.

She buried her face in his waves, whimpering, her body undulating and arching against the ecstasy he pulled from her. She'd say he worshipped her, but that would be profane. There was nothing reverent about how his tongue lapped and sucked, how his teeth raked and nipped. Nothing deferential about how his fingers molded, squeezed and twisted.

He possessed.

He corrupted.

And she loved every damn bit of it.

Lifting his head, Nico pinned her with his gaze. He cupped the nape of her neck, pressed his mouth to hers, and she greedily opened for him, accepted his kiss.

"What more do you want?" he asked. "I'll make you come again and end this. Or I'll give you my cock and make both of us burn. Your choice."

"Make us burn," she whispered against his lips.

He tilted his head back, stared at her. Then, whatever he saw, whatever he'd sought in the first place, must've confirmed something for him, because he nodded and dropped his hands to his pants.

"Let me." She brushed his fingers aside but didn't start on the band of his tuxedo slacks.

Instead, she tugged at his bow tie, casting it aside. Next, the buttons of his shirt received her attention. When she slid that last button through its hole, she sighed, sliding her hands up his broad, hard chest. Let her fingertips sweep over the flat male nipples. Delight in their tightening. But she didn't linger there. Not when a throbbing and persistent emptiness beat inside her, insisting she fill it.

She opened the tab of his pants, jerked the zipper down, her fingers grazing his skin. His abdomen went concave, and a sharp hiss sounded above her. His thighs shifted beneath her, and his restless, hungry movements only ratcheted the need in her. Dipping her hands inside his black boxer briefs, she cupped him.

Their twin groans saturated the limousine's interior.

The hot, thick weight of him pulsed in her hands, and she couldn't resist squeezing him. Couldn't hold back from pumping him.

How could she have gone three years without touching him, having him, inhaling his scent? Even now his heavy musk teased her nose, made her mouth water for a taste. Already she could feel the heft of him on her tongue, sliding toward the back of her throat…

"No, baby girl." His hands clutched her arms, and only then did she realize she'd been on the verge of sinking to the floor between his thighs to fulfill the vision in her head. "Not this time. I want you too bad. Need to be here—" he cupped her wet, swollen sex "—too bad." Tangling his other hand in her hair again, he drew her head down until their breaths mingled, mated. "Are you sure?"

"Yes." Again, no hesitation. She had zero doubts. About this. About needing him inside her, taking away the ache.

Now about other things… God, yes. But this? No.

It was a long time coming.

Giving her that nod again, he reached into his jacket pocket and removed his wallet.

"No." She shook her head. Nico went still, his gaze on her face. "I'm on the pill. And I've been tested. You don't have a reason to believe me but I—"

"I believe you," he interrupted. And dropped the wallet to the seat beside them. Without removing a condom. "I've been tested, too." A beat of charged silence. "And I haven't been with anyone since you."

Wait. *What?*

"That's…" she started, disbelief spiraling through her like a shrieking whirlwind.

"Three years. Yes."

Why? How? Why?

The questions bombarded her, but his tongue curled around them. And by the time he lifted his head, she didn't care about the answer. For now.

"Athena," he rumbled, one of his hands brushing both

of hers aside to fist the base of his cock and hold himself. "Take me inside."

He didn't have to tell her twice. Reaching down, she looped her fingers in the band of her thong and—

Nico fisted the band and ripped it. Gripped the other side and shredded it, too.

Well, okay. That was one way to handle them.

Lifting her gaze to his, she straddled him again, her chest rising and falling, her breath whistling from between her lips. Slowly, she lowered her body until the head of him brushed her folds, her entrance.

And then he pushed inside her.

Then he was inside her.

The moan rolled out of her, pained and ecstatic. The pressure. The stretching. The *taking*. With one hand clasping the nape of her neck, pressing her forehead to his, and the other a vise grip at her hip, holding her steady as he pulsed his hips, claiming her. Conquering her. Until he left no inch of her untouched.

God, he touched her *everywhere*.

And it was beautiful.

It was everything.

Only once he was fully seated inside her, his cock an undeniable, pounding presence, did he pause, allowing her to become reaccustomed to him.

As if she could ever become used to this…to this body-and-soul event.

She wrapped her arms around his neck, brushed her lips over his ear.

"I was afraid."

His head jerked back and that onyx gaze burned into her like fire.

"Afraid of what, Athe—"

She pressed her hand to his mouth, and his jagged, hot

breath bathed her palm. The fire in his eyes blazed hotter, but she closed her own and sank her teeth into her bottom lip, choking back a whimper. That only served to emphasize the sensation of him filling her to damn near overflowing, reclaiming her, rebranding her.

"That's why I left you. I was scared of falling so deep in love with you that I'd disappear. That there would be nothing left of me. I was terrified of loving you more than myself. Of what I'd do because of it."

Like stay with a man whose heart was so hardened, he couldn't love her back.

Shivering, she rose off his cock, pleasure rippling through her as his thick, hard flesh dragged over her slick, sensitive core. When only the tip of him nudged her entrance, she plunged back down, driving the air from her lungs and a small scream from her throat. Panting, she kissed his ear, the rim of it, the lobe.

"Not a day hasn't gone by that I didn't second-guess my decision," she rasped, voice hoarse. "Because, no, you aren't perfect. But you're beautiful, protective, loyal. You're imperfect perfection, and I—"

He yanked her hand from his mouth and slammed his lips to hers, swallowing whatever else she would've confessed. Thank God. Because with her sex full of him and too many emotions shoving against her chest, she might have said something she couldn't have taken back. Something that would've left her more naked, spread open and exposed then she was right now in the back of this limousine.

"Ride me, dammit," he demanded in a ragged, hoarse voice.

And she obeyed.

She rode him with uninhibited abandon, rising and falling, grinding into him, fucking him. His growled

praise urged her to take him, and with every raw com-
pliment, each hoarse command, he shoved her closer and
closer to release. Electricity sizzled through her, and she
opened her arms to it, transforming into pleasure's willing conduit. And when he reached between them and
rubbed the nub of engorged flesh, she soared.

In the grip of her orgasm, he followed, thrusting and
pouring into her. She held him through it, relishing the
evidence of his desire for her. Of their cataclysmic desire for each other. With his raw shout still ringing in her
ears, she buried her face in his neck, clinging to him.

A quiet settled around them, and only then did she realize that the limo had stopped. Damn, how long had they
been sitting… Where? She lifted her head high enough
to glance at the smoked-out window and glimpsed the
front of her condominium's building.

Leaning forward, Nico pressed a button under the di-
vider.

"Please take us to my penthouse."

"Yes, sir," came his driver's clear, disembodied voice.

"That okay with you?" Nico asked, hitting the button again and glancing down at her. "I don't want to be
done tonight."

"Yes, it's okay."

He threaded his fingers through her hair, smoothing
the curls away from her face.

"Good," he murmured.

She should be at least a little embarrassed that the
driver must know they'd been fucking. But for the life
of her, curled up against Nico, breathing in his sandal-
wood-and-sex scent, still full and throbbing from the delicious burn of his fierce possession, she couldn't bring
herself to care.

And as the limousine pulled away from the curb and

headed toward his penthouse, she closed her eyes and brushed her lips against the base of his throat, savoring the beat of his pulse against her lips.

Tomorrow.

Tomorrow would be soon enough to worry about the actions and consequences of tonight. Because she didn't fool herself. There would be consequences. But...

Tomorrow.

Eleven

The scent of vanilla, sugar and sex greeted Nico before he opened his eyes, and he burrowed his face into the source of it. Immediately, images from the previous evening and early morning hours flooded him.

The best fucking limousine ride of his life.

He and Athena back at his high-rise penthouse, in his bedroom, losing themselves in each other time and time again. Him taking her like a man possessed.

Like a man unsure of when he'd touch her, taste her again.

Yeah, he'd been frenzied.

And now his bed and the tangled sheet were empty.

He didn't need to open his eyes or stretch out his hand to touch the cool sheet to verify that. An emptiness in the room and in his chest did it.

Sitting up, he scanned the room, confirming what he'd known. Athena had slipped out.

Disappointment burrowed deep within him. He tried to deny it, but shit, what was the point? He tossed a look at the digital clock on his nightstand. Six ten. How long had she been gone? Did she wait for the fucking sweat to dry—

"Hey, you're awake." She stood in the open bedroom door, his white dress shirt draped around her. And it had never looked that good on him. "Hi."

"Hey." More than that one word piled up in his throat, but none of them emerged. He could only stare at those gorgeous curls piled on top of her head, at those long, slender brown legs bared under his shirt's hem. At that lovely face wearing a shy yet beautiful smile. "What're you doing up?"

She arched an eyebrow, her gaze dipping to his dick that tented the sheet over his hips. Hell, she made him hard. Why deny that either? Especially when just last night he'd admitted to being celibate for three years.

"I planned on making breakfast for us and went to your kitchen to see what you had. Which, to answer that? Everything. I was thinking an omelet, bacon and French toast? Sounds good?"

"Sounds perfect. After I have you." He stretched out a hand toward her and watched with satisfaction as her chest quickly rose and fell and her hazel eyes brightened with lust. "Come here, baby girl."

She took a step toward him, then her cell phone rang; he recognized her ring tone from last night.

His arm dropped and dread curled in his gut as did a sense of déjà vu. He'd been here before with her. Three years ago.

Athena glanced toward the phone she'd left on the nightstand sometime last night, frowning.

"Go on." He hiked a chin in its direction. "Answer it."

They both knew she would, just as they both knew who it was on the other end of the call.

Indecision warred on her face, but Nico settled the battle by throwing back the sheet and swinging his legs over the end of the bed. He stood and crossed to the bathroom, closing the door behind him.

By the time he showered, brushed his teeth and emerged with a towel wrapped around his hips, Athena sat on the edge of the mattress, dressed in the red gown from the previous evening. A helpless anger burned inside him, and he strode to his walk-in closet, grabbing a pair of sweatpants and jerking them on. He used several more minutes to calm his temper before reentering his bedroom. But the helplessness clung to him like a burr he couldn't shake.

He hated it.

Resented her for its return.

"I take it this means breakfast is off," he said, crossing his arms over his chest.

"Nico, I'm sorry." She rose, spreading her hands in front of her, palms up. "That was Mom."

"Of course it was." He nodded. "Let me guess. She needs you at home. Or no, wait. There's a problem at the bakery."

Her wince supplied his answer.

"I'm sorry," she repeated, her arms falling to her sides. "Randall's a no-show at the bakery, Kira's sick and another employee called in. She's shorthanded. Plus, she hasn't worked in the store for a long time. She's not familiar with how it runs. She needs me, and I can't…" She shook her head, her shoulders lifting and falling in a shrug. "I can't just leave her hanging."

"Of course you can't."

Athena sighed, pinching the bridge of her nose. "Nico, don't do this. Not after... Please, just try and understand."

"Not after what? Not after last night?" The temper he'd tried to rein in snapped at its tethers. "What does last night have to do with this?" He waved a hand between them. "I'm having a wicked fucking case of déjà vu, Athena. But the difference between then and now? I refuse to beg you to stand up for yourself. To set boundaries for yourself, for us. Because there is no us. So no, I don't have to understand. This is you. This is who you insist on being. I can't fight to make you see different, to be different when you don't want that for yourself."

"What do you want me to do, dammit?" she snapped. "Throw my mother to the wolves? Tell her, 'Sorry you're in a tough spot, sucks to be you'? Yes, they can be annoying and trying as hell, but they're still family. I can't abandon them."

"Did I ever once ask you to do that, Athena?" he growled, advancing a step on her.

He drew to a halt, whipping around and stalking in the opposite direction. Thrusting his fingers through his hair, he fisted the strands, the bite of pain centering him before he faced her again.

"I never asked you to give up your family for me, Athena. I never tried to isolate you as they accused me of doing. I only asked that you make room for me, for us. Which meant setting boundaries, protecting our relationship. So if we were in the middle of lunch and your brother called, saying your mother needed you home to help cook for that evening's dinner, you didn't drop everything, including me, to go do their bidding. Or if your grandmother ordered you to leave the bakery so Randall

could man a shift and learn responsibility, you still chose
to stay 'just in case.' But that meant showing up an hour
late to our evening together. Or calling at all hours for
whatever reason even though it didn't just disturb you but
your man. If you didn't make our relationship a priority
or respect it, why would your family?" He dropped his
arms to his sides and twisted his mouth into a humorless smile. "You're an enabler, Athena. They will never
find out if they can manage their own lives or that bakery
because you won't step back, take your hands off and let
them. And you won't, because you're afraid they'll discover they don't need you."

"That's not true," she whispered, flinching.

Stop, a voice demanded. *Stop this now.*

But he couldn't. And he didn't.

"Yeah, it is. You're terrified they won't depend on
you, and then what would your place be in the Evans
family? Where would you belong? Would they love you
less? It scares the shit out of you to find out the answers
to those questions."

"Stop it." She threw her hands up, as if warding off
him and his words. *"Stop, Nico."*

The pain in her voice shut him up as effectively as a
hand being clapped over his mouth.

Their rough breaths punctuated the air, and his harsh
words seemed to echo in the room. That same voice that
urged him to stop also pushed him to apologize, but he
couldn't. The delivery might have sucked, but he'd spoken the truth.

Still… His palms itched to hold her, soothe her.

"I'm going to leave," she said, her hazel eyes dark,
haunted.

And he'd done that.

"I'll call my driver to take you home." He moved toward his phone, because as much as she wanted to leave, he also needed her to go.

This... It fucked with his head. Took him back to a place he'd vowed never to return. A place where he'd been vulnerable, weak, her puppet.

Love's victim.

"You don't need to do that. I can call—"

"Athena, my driver picked you up, he'll take you home," Nico ground out.

She shrugged. "Fine. I just... Fine."

Turning, she walked out of his bedroom.

And he didn't follow.

Déjà vu, indeed.

"Whew, either I'm getting old, or I completely forgot how busy this place can get. Probably a little of both." Winnie chuckled, dropping into the chair behind the desk in the office.

"And we still have the afternoon rush to go," Athena warned with a smile, sinking into the visitor's chair with a sigh. "All those hungry college students pouring in after evening classes and people needing a snack on their way home from work."

Winnie groaned, covering her eyes with her arm. "Well thank goodness for them," she said with another laugh. "They're how we keep the lights on." She dropped her arm, smiling, a wistful note in her voice. "I have no idea how your grandmother did it all those years and never seemed tired. Not one day. Like you. Honey, thank you for coming in today. As soon as you showed up, a calm settled over me. I didn't have to worry about a thing. And neither did the staff. Everything just flowed so smoothly. Thank you."

"You're welcome."

She should leave it there, with her mother's gratitude spreading through her like liquid sunshine. But she couldn't.

You're afraid they'll discover they're capable and don't need you... You're terrified they won't depend on you and then what would your place be in the Evans family? Would they love you less? It scares the shit out of you to find out the answers...

All morning and afternoon, Nico's words haunted her. No, that wasn't accurate. The truth in them haunted her.

He was right. Not just about how she hadn't placed boundaries with her family, but that she enabled them. And she did it for herself, not them. She did it out of fear, out of a need to belong. A need to be an Evans. But the time had come to stop hiding. From the truth, and from herself.

"Mom?"

"Yes, honey?"

"Why didn't you call Randall to come in and help you today?" She inhaled. *Do it. Just...do it.* "Actually, why isn't Randall here instead of you? Especially since his presence at the bakery was part of our deal."

Irritation crossed her mother's expression before she flattened her hands on the desk.

"Athena, not this again." Winnie shrugged a shoulder. "Your brother is involved in a new business deal. A new chain of barbershops. He had something come up so I volunteered to come in. It's no big deal."

"And the last time I had to step in and take care of payroll?" she countered. "Where was he then?"

"Athena," her mother snapped. "Stop this. I'm getting

tired of your constant criticisms of Randall. And don't think I don't know where this is coming from."

"Oh really? That's news to me. The constant criticisms and the source. Care to enlighten me?"

Blowing out a breath, her mother flicked a hand. "Please, Athena. Your brother told me how he called you to come over the other night but you were too busy with Nico. You're putting *that man* before family again. And you remember how that turned out last time."

"*That man* is helping us save the bakery, remember? The bakery Randall placed in jeopardy in the first place. Have you asked him about the loan, or did you just ignore that like you did asking him to take on his responsibility at the store?"

Anger flashed in her mother's brown eyes and she straightened in her chair.

"Excuse me? I don't know where this disrespect is coming from, but I'm still your mother, and you won't talk to me like that," she demanded. "I didn't realize it was such a hardship for you to help us out."

Athena jerked, her hands clutching the arms of her chair. A disbelieving laugh tumbled out of her.

"Are you seriously saying that to me? *Me?*" She pressed a hand between her breasts. "I sacrifice everything for this family. Right now, I'm repaying the loan for Randall. You didn't even expect him to do it. It became my responsibility, and I did it. Because I've always done everything I could for all of us, including cleaning up Randall's messes. Who has run this bakery every day since Mama's stroke? Me. Even when you and Dad turned the store over to Randall, I continued to come here every day and run this place because *he doesn't care*. He can't be bothered to be accountable because no one—not you, Dad or me—has demanded it of him."

"Is that what this is about?" Winnie tilted her head, studying Athena. "Your father and I signing the bakery over to Randall instead of you? I understand you worked here with Mama and were very close with her, but you have to know why we made that decision. He's the oldest. It's only right that he should—"

A blast of cold swept through her.

The import of her mother's words must've hit her seconds after she uttered the words. Winnie's face fell, her fingers fluttering to her parted lips. "Oh, honey, I didn't... You know what I meant..."

But Athena had already risen to her feet. She moved as if through a fog.

He's the oldest. It's only right... He's the oldest. It's only right...

The incriminating statement continued to hit her like punches to the chest. Each strike ripped back the curtain on her secret fear, confirming it. Yes, she believed her mother slipped, but that didn't make the sentiment any less true.

Her parents saw Randall as the oldest Evans child. Because he was blood.

And Athena...wasn't.

"Athena! Wait, don't go—"

But she walked out, closing the office door behind her. Somehow she made it through the bakery, answering those who called out to her, putting one foot in front of the other, pushing out the front door.

The warm late afternoon air couldn't breach the ice encasing her. By rote, she reached into the back pocket of her jeans and pulled her cell free. There was only one person she could call, and without conscious thought, she pulled up his contact and dialed.

And when his voice resounded in her ear, the first crack snaked across the numb shield she'd wrapped herself in.

"Nico," she rasped. "I need you."

Twelve

For the second time that day, Nico woke up to an empty bed.

But unlike earlier this morning, he didn't wonder about Athena's whereabouts.

The scents emanating from the kitchen and into his bedroom assured him he could find her there. Climbing off the bed, he stretched, his attention catching on the clock. Eight twenty-five. About six hours since he'd broken several traffic rules speeding over to Brighton after that phone call from Athena.

Nico, I need you.

If he dwelled too long on it, he could still taste the faint residue of terror on his tongue. That drive from his office to the bakery had been the shortest and longest of his life. He'd pulled up outside of the store, spotted her standing on the curb, arms wrapped tightly around herself. He'd started to calm—until she'd lifted her head and he'd glimpsed those haunted hazel eyes. The fierce, howling need to destroy whatever had placed the pain in those golden depths roared inside him like an animal.

She'd whispered, "You were right," and fell into his arms, sobbing as if someone had died—or broken her heart.

He'd guided her into his car and taken her home.

Not the downtown penthouse.

But his home. The one he'd bought a couple of years ago that she'd never been to. She'd seemed to barely notice the drive to Beacon Hill much less the classic, Greek revival home as he lifted her from the car, into the house and up the sweeping staircase to the second level. As soon as he'd laid her on the bed in the master suite, she'd passed out, either from the crying or exhaustion. Maybe both. After removing her shoes and stripping off his jacket, tie and shoes, he'd crawled behind her and curled his body around hers. And they'd slept.

But now, as he made his way down the stairs to the kitchen, he needed answers. First being, was she okay? Second, what had he been right about?

He moved into the kitchen and the sweet scents of caramel, sugar and cream greeted him. It didn't take him long to locate Athena at the wide marble island, a tiny frown of concentration creasing her brow as she slid cookies from a pan to a plate.

"Well, you've been busy," he said, leaning a hip against the counter and crossing his arms.

She didn't jump, but continued moving the cookies and waved toward the cake next to them.

"Snickerdoodle cookies and raspberry sponge cake with caramel crunch and crème brûlée topping." She briefly peeked up at him with a wary smile. "I hope you don't mind. I bake when I can't sleep."

"You could've woken me up."

She shook her head once. "This is a beautiful house. A gorgeous kitchen."

"Thank you." He pushed off the counter and stepped closer, stopping on the other side of the island. "Let's get it out of the way. Nine bedrooms, eight baths. I bought it two years ago with the thought of having a place to entertain, but I haven't yet. I have two formal dining rooms, one with a domed skylight, a living room, family room, library, a two-story balcony and a walled garden and patio. I'll give you the full tour later. For now, tell me what you meant by saying I was right. What happened to have you crying in my arms?"

She finished with the cookies and flattened her palms on the marble island top.

"Like I said, you were right. About my family. About me. I was scared of those answers. And for good reason. They were what I feared—all along."

"Baby," he murmured.

"No." She shot up a hand and stepped back. "You were right. All these years I've been working, sacrificing, giving everything to them and to the store. No complaining. Ever. Because that's what family does. But they never saw me as family. Or real family. Not where it counts. I'm not a real Evans. And all these years I've tried to earn their love, earn my place, when I can't. I'll never be enough for them. I'll never be an Evans."

"Athena." He rounded the island and took her into his arms. Her fists curled into the front of his shirt, and she buried her face in his chest. She didn't cry, but her frame shook against him. "Athena."

Gripping her hips, he lifted her onto the island. Moving in between her thighs, he pinched her chin and tipped her head up. The brown in her eyes nearly swallowed the green and gold, and he smoothed the pad of his thumb over her cheekbone.

"Do I have complaints about your family? Yes. But have I ever doubted their love for you? Never. That's evident in how they look at you, talk about you. Maybe they don't always treat you with fairness—and no, they don't—yet it's not out of maliciousness but ignorance. Baby girl, my questions were less about them and more about you. About you discovering who you were outside of them. You are more than Winnie Evans's daughter or Randall's big sister. You're even more than Glory Evans's granddaughter. What is your place in this world? If it's not the bakery, why are you not out there claiming it? You deserve so much more than what you're settling for. And you're settling out of fear of rejection. That's not fair to them and it's damn sure not fair to you. That's what I wanted you to think about."

"Who would I be without the bakery?" she said, the note of uncertainty in her voice reaching into his chest and fisting his heart. "For so long, it's been the center of my world. It's where I learned about baking and fell in love with it. It's where Mama became my best friend, not just my grandmother." She settled her palm on his chest, over his heart. "You've thought all this time that I agreed to your bargain to save Randall. That's not true. I did it because of my grandmother. She built Evans Bakery, her and my grandfather. She put everything of herself into it. I couldn't see it sold off as collateral because of Randall's selfishness and greed. Not her legacy. It was only for her."

He should've guessed. Hell, Athena had moved residences for Glory. The truth leaped to his tongue. If he had a soul, a conscience, he'd tell her right now that he'd paid off that loan weeks ago. But he didn't. Because if she knew, he couldn't be certain she'd stay the remaining two months. And he hadn't accomplished his goal yet.

Yes, keep telling yourself that's the reason you want her here.

He briefly closed his eyes. It *had* to be about the business deal, nothing else. He couldn't let it be about anything else. Because now or two months from now, Athena would walk. It was what she did.

"Athena, your grandmother never intended the bakery to become your burden. Her legacy is here—" he gently tapped her temple "—and here." He brushed his fingers over her breast, her heart. "It's the reason she called me and asked for help. She knew you wouldn't reach for your own freedom, so she sought to give it to you. That's how much she wanted you to be free, to be happy. To be fulfilled. Baby, *you* are Glory's legacy, not the building."

She closed her eyes and bowed her head. He didn't disturb her, and moments later, when she grazed her lips over his, he let her take whatever she needed from him.

"Thank you." She pressed a kiss to the corner of his mouth. "Thank you for that."

"You're welcome."

She tunneled her fingers through his hair and drew him down to her. He met her halfway, and as her tongue thrust between his lips, he met her there, too. He allowed her to take the lead, set the pace. But all those good intentions burned to ashes when she trailed a hand down his chest, abdomen and cupped his cock through his pants.

"Baby girl…" He growled a warning, covering her hand with his.

"I want to lose myself in you, Nico. Please let me."

Not lose herself in pleasure, but in him. No way in hell he could resist that plea.

He took control of the kiss, bending her head back as he unleashed his hunger on her. Cupping her jaw, he tilted her head and dived deep, taking, consuming, gorging on her. And Athena devoured him right back.

"Move that," he ordered, nodding to the desserts behind her.

She quickly obeyed, sliding the dishes to the side, and he balled up the hem of her shirt in his fists and jerked the top over her head. After tossing it to the floor, he stripped off her jeans and panties, leaving her naked on the island. The most delicious meal that would ever be eaten out of this kitchen.

And fuck, did he eat.

Bending, he hauled her legs over his shoulders and spread her wide for his gaze and his fingers. And his mouth. He touched, licked and sucked every part of her. He pumped his fingers into her fluttering entrance. Licked a greedy path up her folds. Sucked on the engorged bundle of nerves at the top of her beautiful sex, loving every shudder that denoted her climbing pleasure. She wanted to lose herself in him? No, he could lose himself in her. Right here.

Above him, her cries caressed his ears. Her hips writhed, twisted, and he crossed an arm low on her belly to hold her in place. He corkscrewed his wrist, finger fucking her and searching out that smooth patch of skin high inside her. Rubbing it, he suckled her clit, granting her no mercy, and from her demands not to stop, it didn't appear Athena wanted any.

In seconds, she stiffened under his mouth, her sex clamping down on his fingers. Her scream rebounded off the walls of the kitchen. And while his dick furiously pounded, he still thrust his fingers, giving her every measure of the orgasm rocking through her. Only when she slumped back on the island, did he lift his head. And attack his zipper.

Goddamn, he needed inside her. Now.

"Athena?" He placed a hot, open-mouthed kiss below her navel. "Yes or no?"

"Yes. Please, yes." She reached for him, her dark curls wild around her face and shoulders. Her eyes glazed with pleasure and mouth swollen from his. "Inside me."

Before she finished the demand, he seated his cock deep inside her. Her gasp bathed his chest, and he tangled a hand in her hair, pulling her head back so he could taste that gasp for himself. Tugging her to the very edge of the island, he withdrew from her, the drag of her tight, hot sex over his hard, thick flesh hauling a soul-deep groan from him. Mimicking the thrust of his tongue, he pushed back in.

Holy...

Nothing like it. Nothing in the world.

Her whimpers spilled into his mouth, and he took every one of them even as he pistoned into her, over and over. The slap of bodies and the sweet suction of her sex accepting and releasing him punctuated the room. She took him so perfectly, as if she was created just for him.

"Touch yourself, baby girl," he rumbled against her lips. "Take us both there."

Eagerly, she reached between their straining bodies and swirled her fingers over the top of her sex, circling, getting there, getting there...

With a loud cry, she went rigid and detonated in his arms.

That beautiful core seized him, milking him, demanding he follow her over the edge, and after three, four more thrusts into her spasming channel, he did.

And for once, he didn't worry about where he landed.

Thirteen

Nico glanced down at his watch, noting the time, then frowned toward his study door. He had a meeting at the office in an hour and a half. If he didn't, he would have done the unthinkable and called in today. Or at the very least, worked from home.

He'd left Athena sleeping in his bed. The corner of his mouth lifted. For once.

As soon as the thought passed through his head, he frowned at the jolt of warmth that thought brought. Oh shit. What was he doing?

He didn't fucking know anymore.

"Mr. Morgan." His housekeeper appeared in the doorway of his study. "There's a gentleman at the door to see you."

Surprised, Nico blinked. In the two years he'd been in this house, he'd never had a visitor. And who in the hell would arrive at seven thirty in the morning?

"Who is it?" he asked Phillip.

"He says his name is—"

"It's me, Achilles." Achilles Farrell filled the doorway behind Phillip, dwarfing the other man. "Sorry, patience has never been my strong suit. Neither have manners."

Nico should've been annoyed—hell, the man walked into his house without an invitation—but instead, he had to smother a snort. From what he'd come to know about Achilles, he wasn't lying.

"Phillip, it's fine. Thank you."

The housekeeper nodded, stepped aside so Achilles could enter and closed the door behind him.

"Well, I would be lying if I said this isn't a surprise," Nico said, rounding the desk and crossing the room, his arm outstretched. "What brings you by, Achilles?"

"Good news that I wanted to deliver in person." He clasped Nico's hand and squeezed it before reaching into the back pocket of his jeans and removing a thin cigar. As Nico accepted the gift, Achilles grinned, and holy shit. This was the first time Nico had ever seen him fully smile. Joy lit up his blue-gray eyes and handsome face like the sun. "I'm a dad."

Happiness for Achilles bloomed inside Nico's chest. The man's pride and his absolute love for his wife and child beamed from him. Underneath the happiness, though, threaded sadness and confusion. Sadness because he could only congratulate Achilles as a business associate and not as a brother. And confusion, because why was Achilles here, in Nico's home, at this early hour telling him news that should be shared with family?

"Congratulations, Achilles." Nico smiled, clapping him on the shoulder. "To you and Mycah. I'm happy for both of you."

"Thank you." Achilles nodded toward the cigar.

"Natia Michelle Farrell was born yesterday morning. Nine pounds, eight ounces. I just left the hospital this morning to go home and get some things for Mycah, to shower and change clothes. I pretty much hate all this fancy society bullshit, but I've always wanted to give out cigars if I ever had a kid. Since Cain and Kenan were already at the hospital, I gave them theirs. But I couldn't go without giving my last cigar to my other brother on my little girl's birth."

"Thank—" Shock rippled through Nico, an icy avalanche that smothered him. "I'm sorry—what?" he rasped.

Achilles nodded again, his Farrell eyes too piercing. "My brother. Yeah, I know. Your eyes may be different than Cain's, Kenan's and mine, but I don't think you realize how much you and Cain resemble each other. The resemblance plus you buying up Farrell stock under different names and companies. The damnedest things happen when they put the bored IT guy in the basement. He digs. And when you started being nice—" he growled the word as if it were a curse "—and bringing your fiancée around, well, that kicked off all my spidey senses. Didn't take long to dig up birth certificates and old history. Barron thought he was a slick motherfucker, but he wasn't. And he had a hidden file on you inches thick. Metaphorically speaking, anyway. He didn't like you very much. Which might put you in the running for my favorite brother."

Nico couldn't speak. Not when shock still gripped him. *He knew.* Achilles knew they were brothers. Relief, joy, fear and sorrow crashed into him, nearly knocking him to his ass. He locked his knees against the wave of emotions.

"The questions is," Achilles continued, eyes narrowing on Nico, "what are your plans now? I'll be the first to admit, I'm not a natural businessman. But I have common sense and I know enough to recognize a hostile takeover when I see one. You plan to take over Farrell International and from there, I can't guess. But I won't let you. Not because of the money or the power. Fuck that. I didn't have it months ago—I can provide for my family if all this shit goes away tomorrow. Hell—" a smile flickered over his mouth "—my wife could take care of us. But I won't let you for Cain and Kenan. I haven't told them about you yet, but I plan to. I just wanted to talk to you first and judge for myself that you're the man I believe you to be."

"Is that why you're here? To warn me?" Nico asked, his heart pounding.

He couldn't think. Or rather, too many thoughts whirled in his head. Part of him longed to grab his brother—now that he could call him that aloud—and sit down, talk with him, laugh with him…as brothers. As family. Something he yearned for, especially with his mother gone.

But the other part of him, the part that'd had every outstretched hand slapped away and every trust betrayed, couldn't believe in this. That part curled up on itself, afraid to…hope. That part would rather be suspicious and harbor no expectations that could be hurled to the ground.

"Is that what you heard from all of that? So like Cain," Achilles muttered. "I'm telling you the same thing our brother once told me. You're not alone. Not anymore. You're our brother, one of us. And we'll fight for you. Even if we have to fight against you while we're doing it. That's all right. What brothers don't brawl? But get that through your head. *We'll fight for you*. All you have to do is stop being so goddamn stubborn. Now, don't wait

too long. I'll show back up here, and I won't be alone."
Dipping his chin at the cigar. "Enjoy it."

Then Achilles strode out of the study, leaving emotional chaos in his wake.

"Did that just happen?"

He jerked his head up, and Athena appeared in the doorway. Once more, she wore one of his dress shirts, and she stared at him, hazel eyes wide, full lips parted.

"Did Achilles Farrell just out you?"

Hell.

Athena moved into the study, giving the cavernous room with its dark wood furniture, expensive rugs and floor-to-ceiling bookshelves a cursory scan. All of her focus remained on Nico, who stood in the center of the room like a statue. If it'd been anyone else, she might've called it shell shock. But it wasn't anyone else. And even as she watched, those obsidian eyes sharpened and Nico thrust his fingers through his hair, tugging the waves away from his face. Wheeling on his heel, he stalked across the room to the large bay window, staring out of it to the garden below.

"Nico?" She followed him, settling a hand on the center of his back. "I didn't mean to eavesdrop but when I heard voices…"

"You eavesdropped."

"I did." There wasn't any point in denying it. "But it sounded like Achilles wasn't mad. At all. Actually, that last part sounded like he wanted to welcome you as his brother. He believed Cain and Kenan would, too."

"So he said."

She frowned at the flat tone, and it took everything in her not to grab him by the arms and shake him. Get some kind of reaction.

"This is good, right?" She tried again, leaning forward to peer at his strong, chiseled profile. That's what he reminded her of now. A man fashioned from stone. "You can go to them, be honest. Be brothers. Be a family. Give up on this silly revenge plan."

"Silly revenge plan?" He finally turned, an eyebrow arched high. "Justice for the way that man threw my mother away, threw me away is silly? Justice for every menial job, every shitty apartment, every asshole boss and pitiful check just to put food on the table, clothes on my back and a roof over my head? That's silly? Justice for her dying too fucking early is silly?" he growled. "What does Achilles Farrell showing up here change about any of that?"

"Nothing can change the past. Not even God can do that. All we have is the present and hope we're writing our future. And you have the opportunity to do that, Nico. Write a beautiful future that is so different from your past. But you can't if you're determined to hang on to it."

He snorted, walking away from her to his desk.

"That sounds pretty, Athena. But that has nothing to do with real life. I made a promise to my mother, to myself, that I would make Barron Farrell pay, and I'm not going back on it. Not for anyone. Or anything."

"I was at Rhoda's funeral." His shoulders stiffened, but he didn't turn and look at her, didn't speak. Didn't react at all to the news that she'd attended his mother's homegoing service. "Even though we were no longer together, I had to pay my respects to the woman who welcomed me into your small family like a daughter. The woman I knew wouldn't have approved of this path you're going down. And not out of concern for Barron. But because she loved you so much. She would've known that revenge, spite, hate—they don't just leave their mark on the intended victim. They leave scars on you. And she would've hated that for you."

"You don't know what you're talking about," he snapped, spinning around, eyes flashing. And in that moment, as she glimpsed the anger, the pain, the hurt in that gaze, she knew... She *knew*.

She'd lost him.

"I do," she softly countered. "But you're so stuck in your hate that you can't see past it." She shook her head, spreading her hands, fingers splayed wide. "Remember when you told me how you were filled with hate? For everyone. Barron. Me. Your brothers. Even your mother. But you forgot someone on that list. You. You hate yourself. For not protecting your mother. For not keeping your father in your life. For not saving your mother in time. For not being worthy. For all manner of bullshit reasons. And make no mistake—they're bullshit reasons. But that doesn't make them any less real for you. And because you can't love yourself, you'll never be able to accept the love of anyone else. Not your brothers. Not me," she murmured.

Confessed.

Because she did love him. Had possibly never stopped.

And that made her an idiot. Especially since he still didn't return the affection.

She closed her eyes, drew in a deep, shaky breath that hurt.

"I'm out," she quietly said.

His eyes narrowed, and he slid his hands into the front pockets of his suit pants. But she didn't miss the tension that entered his body.

"You're out," he softly repeated. "We have a bargain."

"Yes. And I'm breaking it."

"You're running," he accused, his mouth twisting into

a grim smile. "You're running back to your family." He let loose a harsh laugh. "Your brother told me this would happen. Warned me he could follow through on his threat again. And he did, didn't he?"

"What're you talking about?"

"Ask him about three years ago when he showed up at my house, asking for money. And his threat when I turned him down. He warned me he could get you to walk away from me if I didn't give him what he wanted, even though he knew I intended to propose to you. And he did. Not a week later, you were gone. And last week, he paid me a visit and did the same thing. And here we are. You walking away. Again."

Propose?

Pain bloomed inside her chest, exploding like shattered glass.

"God, you're desperate." Fury at Randall and Nico replaced the hurt, stirring bright inside her. Her fists curled at her thighs, but then the flame extinguished, just leaving her exhausted. And broken. "I feel so sorry for you, Nico. You must be fucking terrified right now if you lobbed that bomb out there between us. Just so you know? I'm not running. If the bank calls the note, they call it. Randall will just have to face the consequences. I'm through cleaning up his mess. I'm also through watching you self-destruct."

She pivoted on her heel and strode across the room but paused at the doorway, holding herself steady by a hand on the jamb. No way in hell would she cry in front of him. She'd wait until she'd gathered her things and was behind her own apartment door for that. It wasn't a lot, but she had her pride.

"So you don't misunderstand what happened here or twist it around to suit your narrative. I didn't leave you.

You pushed me out this door. I love you. I love all of you—every brilliant, driven, generous, vulnerable, stubborn, arrogant, broken and beautiful bit of you. You're utterly perfect in my eyes. But I can't stay with someone who's scared of life. Scared to live. Scared to love. I won't remain in a prison with you. When you decide to be as free as you told me I should be, come find me."

Then she walked out.

Probably for good.

And she did it, knowing she would have to be okay with that possibility.

Fourteen

Nico knocked on the door of the mansion that had housed four generations of Farrells. At one time—as recently as a week ago—that thought had angered him. But now it didn't even evoke a flinch. Now he just didn't care.

And hadn't that been his problem for the last five days?

He didn't care.

Not about the meeting he'd scheduled with Mark Hanson that would've given him more Farrell International shares.

Not even about the meeting he headed into right now.

The emptiness that had dropped into his chest when Athena had announced she loved him, then left his home—his life—had only yawned wider, engulfing him.

Why he'd agreed to this particular meeting? Hell, he couldn't answer that himself. Nothing good could come from it. When Cain Farrell called and asked him to come to his Beacon Hill home instead of the offices at Farrell International, Nico had known something was different. If he'd been the smart businessman his reputation lauded him to be, he'd have shown up with a lawyer. But no, he'd arrived at Cain's to face God knew what and couldn't summon up a single fuck. He was fresh out.

The same butler from before opened the door, and in moments he stood in the doorway of the library. His brothers waited for him.

Cain stood in front of his desk, his hands in his pants pockets while Kenan perched on the desk. Achilles leaned against one of the floor-to-ceiling shelves, arms crossed over his chest. They all stared at him.

"Well, don't just stand there. Come on in here and let's get a look at you," Kenan called.

As if they'd never met. But then again, they never had—not as brothers.

Still suspicious of the almost jovial tone, Nico moved into the library. He stopped several feet in front of them, tension vibrating through him, braced for...anything.

Anything but the hard, fierce embrace that Cain yanked him into.

"He's getting so soft in his dotage," Nico heard Kenan stage-whisper.

Achilles snorted in reply.

But Nico dimly paid attention to this byplay. The man hugging him consumed all of his attention. That and the tight ball of emotion pressing against Nico's sternum. Slowly, Nico lifted his arms and wrapped them around Cain, returning the embrace.

After several moments, Cain pounded him on the back and released him, clearing his throat as he stepped back.

"We don't get some of that?" Kenan grinned, holding his arms wide and hopping off the desk.

Before Nico could agree or object, his younger brother pulled him into a hard, quick embrace, too. And that knot of emotion in Nico's chest expanded.

"I'm not hugging you." Achilles grunted. "I gave you a cigar."

Kenan snickered, and in spite of the shock swirling through him at this strange turn of events, Nico snorted.

"Now," Cain said, pinning him with his straightforward blue-gray stare. "Where the hell have you been? Why didn't you come to us instead of trying to conduct a hostile takeover?"

"Right, Morgan." Kenan tsk-tsked. "Bad form."

Nico waited for his usual defensiveness to rise up within him. Waited for that resentment to take over. But nothing. Nothing but the truth tumbled out of him. And he didn't hold back. He revealed everything about Barron abandoning him and his mother, from his rough childhood, to spying on Cain and his family, to Barron visiting him and then Barron trying to destroy his business. And finally to his mother's death and his decision to get revenge on their dead father by ruining his beloved company.

"I'm sorry about your mother," Cain said. "If anyone understands how much of a bastard Barron was, it's me." Pain spasmed across his face before it hardened. His head bowed for several seconds before he lifted it again with a stoic expression. "I'll tell you like I told Achilles and Kenan. I grew up with Barron, but I'm not the lucky one—you were. He was a bastard who used his fists to get a point across as much as his voice. So I don't blame you for wanting to go after his company. It was the only fucking thing he loved. It's what I would've done in your position."

"It was brilliant," Achilles said. "If I hadn't gone

looking for something on you, I wouldn't have caught it. But why didn't you come to us? Why the charade with Athena? Are you two even engaged?"

"Because I…" The pat answer of "I didn't trust you," died on his lips. It was past time for honesty. And hadn't that been what Athena had begged of him? To be open? To—how had she put it?—not be scared to live? To love? That included embracing the love of brothers. "Because I wanted this—" he waved a hand between them "—too badly, and I believed I could never have it. Barron didn't want me, why would you?"

"Because Barron was an asshole?" Kenan supplied.

"Yes, there's that." Nico huffed out a short laugh. "But I…couldn't accept it would be that easy."

"And Athena?" Achilles pressed.

"She's real," Nico said. "Well, almost," he amended, then quickly explained their bargain and how he'd fucked up their relationship.

"Oh yeah." Achilles grunted. "You're a Farrell. Fucking shit up with your woman. That's another trait."

Kenan winced. "Ouch. True. What're you going to do about that?"

Nico shook his head. "I don't know." He glanced at the men in front of him, and for the first time, he found himself with a support system. One that didn't judge him. One that, with time, might one day…love him. One he could love in return. That possibility alone whispered at him to take a chance. To risk it. "I love her," he murmured.

God, he loved her.

And he was tired of being scared.

Of running.

He'd accused her of running, but it'd been him all this time.

Kenan rolled his eyes. "Of course you do." He clapped his hands in glee. "Fortunately for you, I am the relationship whisperer in this crew. I single-handedly saved both of their asses."

"Revisionist history," Cain drawled.

"Anyway," Kenan said loudly, "we got your back."

"Hold on, Millionaire Matchmaker." Cain held up his hands and turned to Nico, his smirk falling from his lips. "Nico, I asked you here for one more thing. Kenan, Achilles and I talked this over. Barron might not have recognized you, but we do. You're the oldest, and if things had been fair, you would've been CEO of Farrell. Barron cost you your birthright, your name and tried to destroy your business. And in the end he was responsible for your mother's hard life, which led to her undiagnosed illness. Barron didn't do right by you, but we will. So I'll step aside as CEO for you. We've all agreed on it."

Nico blinked, shock punching through his system. He stared at these men, his brothers, lost for words. And humbled. They would sacrifice for him. They would declare to the world in no louder fashion that he not only belonged to Farrell, but to them.

He squeezed his eyes closed against the sudden sting.

"Oh shit. We broke him," Kenan whispered.

Yeah, they did.

They absolutely did.

Fifteen

"Well this is a little dramatic, isn't it?" Randall strode into the bakery office, grinning. "Hey, Mom."

Athena didn't answer her brother as he approached their mother, swooping her into an embrace and planting a kiss on her cheek. Usually, Winnie would glow under Randall's charm and attention—he had that effect on people, didn't matter age or sex—but today, she patted his shoulder and murmured a subdued greeting.

It'd been a week since their conversation in this office, and while Winnie had tried to call Athena, she hadn't been in the space to talk to her mother just yet.

Now she was there.

Now she could talk to her from a place of strength.

"Hey, sis." Randall came over to her, sliding an arm around her shoulders and squeezing. "Long time, no see." Dropping a kiss on the top of her head, he rounded the desk and plopped down into the chair. "You called me down here, so what's going on? I didn't know Mom was going to be here, too, though. So much mystery."

God, he was such a chatterbox. Why hadn't it annoyed her before? Oh wait. It had. She'd just sucked it up.

Not any longer.

"Thank you two for coming down here. I'm sorry if it seems a little melodramatic, but I didn't want to do this at home since Dad isn't aware of the situation with the loan." She picked up a folder off the edge of the desk. Opening it, she removed a copy of the note stamped Paid and laid it in front of Randall. "Here's the note for the three-hundred-thousand-dollar loan."

The original had shown up in her mail days ago, and she'd cried. Nico had saved her grandmother's bakery despite Athena not holding up her end of the bargain. Yes, he'd broken her heart, but he'd rescued it, too.

And now, here she stood in front of her brother, giving it away.

The smile evaporated from Randall's face and her mother's soft gasp echoed in the office.

"You did it, Athena," he breathed. "You paid it off. How— I can't believe it." He snatched the document up, gaping at it before lifting his gaze to her. "I don't care how you did it! Thank you!"

"That's the problem," she said, wistfulness creeping into her voice in spite of her best intentions. "You don't care how I did it. Which lets me know you'll jeopardize this bakery again. But it doesn't matter to me anymore. It's no longer my concern because I'm stepping away."

"Athena." Her mother shifted forward, settling a hand on her arm. "What're you talking about? Is this about what I said—"

"No—yes." Her mother needed to hear the truth. "It is

about what you said. And it's also about me. I'm choosing me. While I'm here at this bakery, I'm stuck. I've never given myself a chance to find out who I am outside of it. And I'm excited to find that out. And the fact is, Mom, you and Dad made the decision to give Evans to Randall. So you have to live with that. Good or bad. And so does he. So do you," she said, turning to him. "It's time for you to grow up, Randall. I'm no longer going to be your safety net."

"What're you talking about?" he snapped, rising to his feet, the note clutched in his hand. "You're just going to walk out on us? Leave? This isn't how you treat family!"

"No, what you've been doing for the last few years isn't how you treat family. Mom and Dad won't say it to you, but I will. You're a selfish, spoiled brat. You need to grow up because you have a wife and kids depending on you, and now employees depending on you, too. No one can afford for you to fuck around and find yourself. Oh—" she flattened her palms on the desk and leaned forward, pinning him with an unblinking stare "—if you go to Nico Morgan and try to extort money from him again, I'll disown you without batting an eyelash. And it won't hurt me."

She straightened. And smiled.

"Do better, little brother."

Turning to her mother, she pressed a kiss to her cheek.

"I love you. Please respect me and my decision and don't call me about this bakery or Randall." Athena hugged her, kissed her again. "I'll call you and keep you updated, okay?"

"Okay, honey," Winnie whispered.

Then, tears stinging her eyes, Athena walked out of the office and the bakery.

And it felt good.

It felt...freeing.

Sixteen

"This is the funniest-looking restaurant I've ever been to," Athena grumbled as she followed Eve through the front entrance of the downtown building that housed Farrell International.

"Hah." Eve smirked over her shoulder. "We're just picking up Devon. She's visiting Cain." She looped her arm through Athena's. "I can't wait to get to Mycah and Achilles's and talk about this new business adventure of yours. A catering company. It makes perfect sense! And I've already told Kenan that Farrell will be your first client."

Athena smiled even as she blinked against the sudden sting of moisture in her eyes at the unconditional show of support from her new friend.

"You didn't have to—"

Eve waved away her soft objection. "Please. That's

what we do. We support one another. And I have it on very good authority that you can cook your ass off."

"Devon," Athena said with a laugh. "Devon is your very good authority."

Eve grinned. "True. And speaking of Devon, where is she? I can't wait to get my hands on little Natia. She's gorgeous, Athena." Eve sighed.

Athena snorted. "You sigh like that again, I'm going to start thinking you're ready for one of your own."

"Bite your tongue, missy." Eve slapped Athena's arm, gasping. "I love babies and want one of my own with Kenan one day. But *one day*. Right now Intimate Curves is the only child I need."

Athena laughed. "And it might keep you up at night sometimes, but at least it doesn't shit in diapers."

"There's that."

Chuckling, Athena scanned the building's lobby. For the first time, she noticed a podium with mics set up at the far end and a throng of people gathered in front of it. An excited hum filled the air.

"I wonder what's going on," she said to Eve.

But Eve didn't answer, as she waved to Devon, who stepped out of the bank of elevators. The petite woman strode toward them, smiling.

"Hey," Devon greeted them. "Let's head over. It's about to start."

"What's about to start?" Athena asked, a seed of suspicion springing roots inside her. She glanced from one woman to the other. "Why do I have the feeling both of you know what's going on and are holding out?"

"Because you're smart as hell," Eve said. "Let's go."

They practically tugged her over to the people crowded in front of the podium, and before Athena could question them further, Cain, Achilles and Kenan appeared on the platform.

And a moment later, Nico followed.

Oh God.

She stared at him. It'd been over a week since she'd seen him, but it might as well as have been months, years. The punch of hunger, of yearning slammed into her and she sucked in a hard, sharp breath. Dark waves framed his lean, beautiful face, brushing his jaw. And when those onyx eyes swept the throng, she held her breath. Waited… Waited… There. It landed on her, and she lit on fire.

Stop, she wanted to yell at him. *You don't have the right to look at me like that. Like you want me. Like you...love me.*

So she looked away. She switched her gaze to Cain, who stepped up to the bank of mics, but Nico's eyes branded her, and she shivered.

"Thank you for attending this special press conference, especially on such short notice. I'll be brief and won't be accepting questions at this time. We'll set up a separate time for a question and answer session." He glanced behind him at his brothers. "As you know, a year ago, our father, Barron Farrell, died, leaving an unusual stipulation in his will. Achilles Farrell, Kenan Rhodes and myself, who until Barron's death hadn't been aware we were brothers, were directed to manage Farrell International together as siblings for a one-year period. At that time, we were strangers, but we have become true brothers. But our story hasn't ended with just the three of us. We have another brother. Nico Morgan, who many of you may recognize as the CEO of Brightstar Holdings. He is also the oldest son of Barron Farrell."

The lobby erupted in a cacophony of shouts, questions and camera flashes.

Athena's lips parted, and she jerked her attention away from Cain to Nico. Shock still rippled through her, but so did joy and hope. For him.

"This is the dawn of a new day. We might have started this journey as strangers, but we continue it as brothers. As family. We just adjourned a board meeting. I'm proud to announce that we are now no longer Farrell International. From this day forward, we are Brightstar Farrell Incorporated. We're united by blood and by business. Thank you."

Shouted questions bombarded Cain, but he stepped back from the podium and so did the rest of the Farrell men. Athena couldn't move. Even when Devon and Eve greeted their husband and fiancé, she remained rooted. Even when Nico came to stand before her.

She could only study him, searching for…

"I've missed you."

That.

"I love you."

And that.

"Please forgive me, Athena, for pushing you away. I'm not scared to live, to be. I'm not scared to love you or to be loved by you. Please, baby girl, love me."

And oh God, that.

"Nico," she breathed.

"Because of you, I have a family. But with you, I have a home. I *am* home." He lifted his hands toward her, but at the last second stopped, as if hesitant to touch her. "Let me come home, Athena," he whispered.

Something inside her cracked. Her last resistance. Because she wanted to hold nothing back from him. She decided to give him everything. To risk all of her. Trusting he would never let her fall. He would be there to catch her.

Circling his wrists, she lifted his hands to her cheeks and turned her face into his palm, kissing it.

"I love you," she said. "And I will always run to you. You're where I belong."

With a groan, he kissed her, and she melted into him, opening wide, taking him.

She would always take him. Always welcome him.

Always love him.

* * * * *

COMING SOON!

We really hope you enjoyed reading this book. If you're looking for more romance, be sure to head to the shops when new books are available on

Thursday 1st September

To see which titles are coming soon, please visit

millsandboon.co.uk/nextmonth

MILLS & BOON

THE HEART OF ROMANCE

A ROMANCE FOR EVERY READER

ODERN

Prepare to be swept off your feet by sophisticated, sexy and seductive heroes, in some of the world's most glamourous and romantic locations, where power and passion collide.

STORICAL

Escape with historical heroes from time gone by. Whether your passion is for wicked Regency Rakes, muscled Vikings or rugged Highlanders, awaken the romance of the past.

EDICAL

Set your pulse racing with dedicated, delectable doctors in the high-pressure world of medicine, where emotions run high and passion, comfort and love are the best medicine.

rue Love

Celebrate true love with tender stories of heartfelt romance, from the rush of falling in love to the joy a new baby can bring, and a focus on the emotional heart of a relationship.

Desire

Indulge in secrets and scandal, intense drama and plenty of sizzling hot action with powerful and passionate heroes who have it all: wealth, status, good looks…everything but the right woman.

EROES

Experience all the excitement of a gripping thriller, with an intense romance at its heart. Resourceful, true-to-life women and strong, fearless men face danger and desire - a killer combination!

To see which titles are coming soon, please visit

millsandboon.co.uk/nextmonth

LET'S TALK
Romance

For exclusive extracts, competitions
and special offers, find us online:

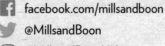 facebook.com/millsandboon

🐦 @MillsandBoon

📷 @MillsandBoonUK

Get in touch on 01413 063232